Secrets

Satisfy your desire for more.

Winner of the 1997 Under the Cover Readers Favorite Award

"An unabashed celebration of sex. Highly arousing! Highly recommended!"

—**Virginia Henley,** *New York Times* Best Selling Author

⁂

"*Secrets, Volume 3* leaves the reader breathless. Each of these tributes to exotic and erotic fiction offers a world of sensual pleasure and moral rewards. A delicious confection of sensuous treats awaits the reader on each turn of the page. Sexy, funny, thrilling, and luscious, Secrets entertains, enlightens, and fuels the fires of fantasy."

—**Kathee Card,** *Romancing the Web*

⁂

"*Secrets, Volume 3* is worth the wait… and is the best of the three. This is erotic romance reading at its best."

—**Lani Roberts,** *Affaire de Coeur*

⁂

"From the FBI to Police Detectives to Vampires to a Medieval Warlord home from the Crusade—*Secerts Vol. 3* is SIMPLY THE BEST!"

—**Susan Paul,** Award Winning Author

Reviews from Secrets Volume 1

"Four very romantic, very sexy novellas in very different styles and settings. ... The settings are quite diverse taking the reader from Regency England to a remote and mysterious fantasy land, to an Arabian nights type setting, and finally to a contemporary urban setting. All stories are explicit, and Hamre and Landon stories sizzle. ... If you like erotic romance you will love *Secrets*."

—*Romantic Readers* review

"Overall, for a fan of erotica, these are unlike anything you've encountered before. For those romance fans who turn down the pages of the "good parts" for later repeat consumption (and you know who you are) these books are a wonderful way to explore the better side of the erotica market. ... *Secrets* is a worthy exploration for the adventurous reader with the promise for better things yet to come."

—Liz Montgomery

Reviews from Secrets Volume 2
Winner of the
Fallot Literary Award for Fiction

"*Secrets, Volume 2*, a new anthology published by Red Sage Publishing, is hot! I mean *red hot!* ... The sensuality in each story will make you blush—from head to toe and everywhere else in-between. ... The true success behind *Secrets, Volume 2* is the combination of different tastes—both in subgenres of romance and levels of sensuality. *I highly recommend this book*."

—Dawn A. Long, *America Online* review

"I think it is a fine anthology and Red Sage should be applauded for providing an outlet for women who want to write sensual romance."

—Adrienne Benedicks,
Erotic Readers Association review

Reviews from Secrets Volume 3

Winner of the 1997 Under the Cover Readers Favorite Award

"An unabashed celebration of sex. Highly arousing! Highly recommended!"

—Virginia Henley, *New York Times* Best Selling Author

"*Secrets, Volume 3* leaves the reader breathless. Each of these tributes to exotic and erotic fiction offers a world of sensual pleasure and moral rewards. A delicious confection of sensuous treats awaits the reader on each turn of the page. Sexy, funny, thrilling, and luscious, Secrets entertains, enlightens, and fuels the fires of fantasy."

—Kathee Card, *Romancing the Web*

Reviews from Secrets Volume 4

"*Secrets, Volume 4,* has something to satisfy every erotic fantasy...simply sexsational!"

—Virginia Henley, *New York Times* Best Selling Author

"Provocative...seductive...a must read! ★★★★"

—*Romantic Times*

"These are the kind of stories that romance readers that 'want a little more' have been looking for all their lives without crossing over into the adult genre. Keep these stories coming, Red Sage, the world needs them!"

—Lani Roberts, *Affaire de Coeur*

"If you're interested in exploring erotica, or reading farther than the sexual passages of your favorite steamy reads, the *Secret* series is well worth checking out."

—*Writers Club Romance Group* on AOL

Reviews from Secrets Volume 5

"*Secrets, Volume 5*, is a collage of lucious sensuality. Any woman who reads *Secrets* is in for an awakening!"

—Virginia Henley, *New York Times* Best Selling Author

"Hot, hot, hot! Not for the faint-hearted!"

—*Romantic Times*

"As you make your way through the stories, you will find yourself becoming hotter and hotter. *Secrets* just keeps getting better and better."

—*Affaire de Coeur*

Reviews from Secrets Volume 6

"*Secrets, Volume 6* satisfies every female fantasy: the Bodyguard, the Tutor, the Werewolf, and the Vampire. I give it Six Stars!"

—Virginia Henley, *New York Times* Best Selling Author

"*Secrets, Volume 6* is the best of *Secrets* yet. ...four of the most erotic stories in one volume than this reader has yet to see anywhere else. ... These stories are full of erotica at its best and you'll definitely want to keep it handy for lots of re-reading!"

—*Affaire de Coeur*

Reviews from Secrets Volume 7

Winner of the Venus Book Club
Best Book of the Year

"...sensual, sexy, steamy fun. A perfect read!"

—Virginia Henley, *New York Times* Best Selling Author

"Intensely provocative and disarmingly romantic, Secrets Volume 7 is a romance reader's paradise that will take you beyond your wildest dreams!"

—*Ballston Book House* Review

"Erotic romance is at the sensual core of Red Sage's latest collection of short, red hot novels, *Secrets, Volume 7.*"

—*Writers Club Romance Group* on AOL

Reviews from Secrets Volume 8

Winner of the Venus Book Club
Best Book of the Year

"*Secrets Volume 8* is simply sensational!"

—Virginia Henley, *New York Times* Best Selling Author

"*Secrets Volume 8* is an amazing compilation of sexy stories discovering a wide range of subjects, all designed to titillate the senses."

—Lani Roberts, *Affaire de Coeur*

"All four tales are well written and fun to read because even the sexiest scenes are not written for shock value, but interwoven smoothly and realistically into the plots. This quartet contains strong storylines and solid lead characters, but then again what else would one expect from the no longer *Secrets* anthologies."

—Harriet Klausner

"Once again, Red Sage Publishing takes you on a journey of sexual delight, teasing and pleasing the reader with a bit of something to appeal to everyone."

—Michelle Houston, *Courtesy Sensual Romance*

"In this sizzling volume, four authors offer short stories in four different sub-genres: contemporary, paranormal, historical, and futuristic. These ladies' assignments are to dazzle, tantalize, amaze, and entice. Your assignment, as the reader, is to sit back and enjoy. Just have a fan and some ice water at your side."

—Amy Cunningham

Reviews from Secrets Volume 9

"Everyone should expect only the most erotic stories in a *Secrets* book. ...if you like your stories full of hot sexual scenes, then this is for you!"

—Donna Doyle, *Romance Reviews*

Satisfy Your Desire for More... with Secrets!

Jeanie Cesarini

Ann Jacobs

Angela Knight

B.J. McCall

Volume 3

Secrets

Satisfy your desire for more.

SECRETS Volume 3
This is an original publication of Red Sage Publishing and each individual story herein has never before appeared in print. These stories are a collection of fiction and any similarity to actual persons or events is purely coincidental.

Red Sage Publishing, Inc.
P.O. Box 4844
Seminole, FL 33775
727-391-3847
www.redsagepub.com

SECRETS Volume 3
A Red Sage Publishing book
All Rights Reserved/December 1997
Second Printing,2000; Third Printing, 2002; Fourth Printing, 2003; Fifth Printing, 2004
Copyright © 1996–2004 by Red Sage Publishing, Inc.

ISBN 0-9648942-2-X

Published by arrangement with the authors and copyright holders of the individual works as follows:
THE SPY WHO LOVED ME
Copyright © 1997 by Jeanie Cesarini
THE BARBARIAN
Copyright © 1997 by Ann Jacobs
BLOOD AND KISSES
Copyright © 1997 by Angela Knight
LOVE UNDERCOVER
Copyright © 1997 by B. J. McCall

Photographs: Copyright © 2000 by Greg P. Willis; email: GgnYbr@aol.com

Printed in the U.S.A.

Cover design, layout and book typesetting by:
Quill & Mouse Studios, Inc.
2165 Sunnydale Boulevard, Suite E
Clearwater, FL 33765
www.quillandmouse.com

Contents

Jeanie Cesarini

The Spy Who Loved Me

1

B. J. McCall

Love Undercover

103

Angela Knight

Blood and Kisses

175

Ann Jacobs

The Barbarian

259

The Spy Who Loved Me

by Jeanie Cesarini

To My Reader:

Wouldn't it be a wonderful world if all undercover work ended with a happily ever after?

Decisions. Decisions.

Special Agent Paige Ellison froze in the open doorway. Inside the cramped dressing room, a man came to his feet, his broad frame stealing the air. Her hand itched to grab a weapon that should have been within easy reach, her fingers burned to feel the comfortable weight of a gun in her hand. But Paige didn't need a weapon. This time. She recognized her unexpected guest.

Her pulse steadied its rapid-fire tempo. After two years of living undercover among scum, she should have been used to the clandestine meetings, the subterfuge, the backstabbing, the corruption that clung to these people like stale sweat.

But she wasn't used to them. Not yet. Not ever.

"What do you want?" She hoped he would interpret her terseness as annoyance when a nervous sweat was already beading her brow. This man was no ordinary thug—he was Lewis Goddard's right-hand man.

"The boss wants to see you. Now."

Paige didn't hesitate, just nodded her consent and followed him out the door.

Lewis Goddard wanted to see her. She wondered if this was the opportunity she had been waiting for. Waiting forever it seemed. Day after lonely day living among criminals and assuming an identity not her own. Something important must have happened, because if Goddard had made her cover, she'd be dead by now.

Smoothing the fringe of her hem as the elevator shot toward the penthouse, she wished there had been time to change her dance costume. The beaded fabric suddenly hung heavy on her shoulders, the plumage of her headpiece cumbersome and awkward even though it forced the bodyguard to keep his distance in the elevator.

Her heart accelerated as the doors hissed open and she was directed through a reception area furnished in a tasteful contemporary style that contrasted dramatically with the opulence of Goddard's casino.

But Paige had no time to admire the details of this inner sanctum before the bodyguard swept her through the office doors and left her facing one of the most wanted criminals of the nineties.

Lewis Goddard.

She had never been formally introduced. He spent most of his time on a private island in the Pacific or jet-setting around the world. She had only seen pictures of him in the FBI dossiers and glimpses through his crowded casino.

A striking man with jet black hair and fair skin, he was tall, leaner rather than muscular, but not without a raw-boned strength. Women found him attractive, but Paige couldn't get past the iciness emanating from him. The flat gleam in his eyes made her wonder if he had a soul.

Yet she was surprised. He seemed smaller, only man-sized compared to the monster proportions he had assumed in her mind. Goddard was just a man, she reminded herself. Even the most heinous mass murderers and serial killers throughout history had only been human.

He motioned her toward the desk. "Thank you for coming, Paige." Despite the words, his voice conveyed no appreciation.

Coming to his feet, he extended a hand across the desk, and Paige forced herself to respond calmly, even though it struck her as horribly incongruous they should be conducting business like two normal people when nothing about this situation was normal. She slid her palm into his, willing herself not to recoil from his granite-like grip. A grip that reminded her of touching a gravestone.

"What can I do for you, Mr. Goddard?"

His midnight gaze pierced the distance between them, assessing her appearance in a single glance, but Paige felt every inch of his perusal as though time moved in slow motion. The cool air shimmered along her bare neck, her breasts suddenly much too exposed above a costume that seemed to shrink beneath his gaze.

She felt the whisper of feathers against her skin as her shoulders rose and fell with each tight breath. The beaded fabric molded every curve of her body, and she read the appraisal in his gaze, as though he was calculating her worth to him.

He withdrew his hand. "I caught your show tonight and wanted to meet you personally."

"I hope you were pleased."

He didn't respond, just circled the desk in a few long strides and positioned himself half-sitting before her. She resisted the urge to step back and met his gaze instead.

"You've been working for me for almost two years now. Isn't that right, Paige?"

She nodded. Of course he would have done his homework. Goddard made it a point of knowing everything about his employees.

"You were hired in my LA club, dance rotations there and in the casino, too. Something not many of the girls get a chance to do. Why, do you think?"

"Luck, Mr. Goddard," she replied easily. "I was at the right place at the right time." Luck had definitely brought her here, and Paige was damned near positive all of it was bad.

"That's not what I heard." He flashed a thin smile, showing a row of straight white teeth. "Had to do with your dancing ability and willingness to help out, I believe."

Paige forced herself to return his smile. Every single gesture mattered. She wasn't sure what he was auditioning her for, but this was an audition if ever she saw one.

"Mr. Corvasce was short a dancer for the New Year's show and didn't have time to train someone here in Vegas." The humble approach was her best bet. Goddard was used to women coming on to him, but Paige knew conventional sex didn't interest him.

"I studied dance professionally for several years and learn the routines quickly."

"You were well-received, I understand."

"As I said, I've been lucky." Leaning back, Goddard studied her openly, his brow creased as if trying to read her mind. It took a Herculean effort not to flinch beneath that stare, especially when she was on the most humiliating form of display.

Despite all the glitter and plumage and make-up, Paige felt naked and hoped he mistook the goose flesh on her arms for anticipation and not the revulsion it was. "That's very kind of him to mention. But I don't have any ties to LA, no family or anything, so it's easy for me to fly to the casino at a moment's notice."

He braced his arms on the desk and leaned toward her until she couldn't draw a breath without the scent of Opium filling her nostrils. "I believe loyalty should be rewarded. Have you been rewarded for your loyalty, Paige?"

"Absolutely. Not only has Mr. Corvasce allowed me to work here and earn the casino's wages, he's given me the chance to headline the chorus show several times already."

Goddard didn't respond, and despite the air conditioned coolness, a trickle of sweat slipped between her shoulder blades. She held his gaze, hoping she hadn't blown it. Her entire demeanor was accommodating, as though she would never dream of displeasing him, yet she didn't want to come off like a wimp either.

But nothing flickered in those cold black eyes, no sense of encouragement, no emotion whatsoever. Just flat, dead eyes. This man was more dangerous than even his dossier had prepared her for. Warning bells rang inside her head, but Paige had no choice—she must get him to reveal himself, to trust her.

This was first contact, and it frustrated her to no end that while she knew everything about Lewis Goddard, knew his every sin intimately, she couldn't interpret his simplest expression. No FBI file could tell her what he was thinking.

"I've been quite pleased with the direction my career has taken since coming to work for Goddard Enterprises." She may as well toss out the hook and see if he bit. He had asked her up here for a reason, and she was tired of waiting. "I hope I can continue to prove myself as valuable."

Goddard pushed away from the desk and stood before her, so close she noticed the fine threading of his Italian jacket. "I gather it's not your ultimate career goal to be a chorus girl." Laughter softened the edge of his words, and Paige knew she was winning him over.

"I plan to become an entertainer." The lie rolled off her tongue with just the right blend of desperation and guile that it was spooky. She'd been living this lie for so long she was almost buying her own cover.

"Perhaps I can help you." He swept the turquoise feather from her cheek with a flick of his long finger. "Do you know I make movies, Paige?"

Movies? Her heart began to thump madly, and she struggled to keep her hands from fidgeting. "Yes," she answered simply. Now was not the time to get squeamish.

His finger trailed along her cheekbone, so softly she was certain she had imagined it until he cupped her chin and tipped her face upward. "What have you heard?" There was no mistaking the silken threat in the question.

"That you make… special movies." Special wasn't the ideal word to describe Goddard's porno flicks, but it was the only one she could think of when his hot breath fanned her face.

Besides, he didn't produce pornography in the conventional sense. Goddard's films were not for public distribution. He catered to a very wealthy, very depraved crowd.

"They are special, Paige. And I want you to star in one."

Her throat suddenly went dry, and she couldn't seem to draw a decent breath. "A… a movie?"

"I have a delightful screenplay. A collection of vignettes about sex through the centuries." He took her hand and let it rest gently within his. Such a gentle touch, a deceptive touch, because what he offered was death.

"Why me?" She inhaled deeply, a spark of fury making her fingers itch to gouge his skin.

"I'm not interested in teenagers. I want a woman for this role." His grip tightened ever-so-slightly. "I want you."

Her mind raced. She had known the case might ultimately lead to this, but had hoped, no, prayed she would find some other way to penetrate his "inner circle." She needed a moment to think, to control wayward emotions before she ruined everything.

Withdrawing her hand, she took a step back and fanned herself for effect. "I am completely overwhelmed by this opportunity, Mr. Goddard." She restrained the tremor in her voice. "I need a moment. Please, tell me about the movie."

Apparently satisfied with her response, he smiled and reached across the desk. "I have a copy of the script right here." He passed her a spiral bound sheath of papers. "I film on my island. I'm almost ready to start production."

This was the chance she had been waiting for. "Your island?" she repeated as casually as possible, flipping through the pages even though her palms were sweating and she couldn't dry them on the beaded costume.

"I have a studio there." He eyed the script as she let it flutter closed. "I understand you have some experience as an exotic dancer."

The FBI had provided her with a background that would fit in with Goddard and his ilk. She nodded. "I did a stint a few years back."

"But no nude film work?"

"I'm afraid not."

He dismissed the problem with a shrug. "Doesn't matter. We'll begin rehearsals immediately. You will leave for the island tonight." The statement was a command.

Tonight?

"I have an apartment. Some bills to pay. I'll have to make some arrangements, but it will only take—"

"I'll send someone to take care of everything." His hands cupped her bare shoulders, and he leaned down to meet her eye to eye. "If you accept my offer, you are to concern yourself with nothing but this script. I demand excellence from my actors." His voice swelled with pride. Paige felt sick.

"But before you agree," he continued, "I want you to understand what I mean by excellence. I have a very special method of rehearsing. You'll have an entire wing of my house where you can get to know your co-star intimately. You can absorb yourselves in your roles without all the distractions of the set. It's a technique I have found works brilliantly."

He sounded so logical, but her stomach clenched tight with dread. Rehearse? Sent to the west wing to perform sex with a stranger.

While Lewis Goddard watched.

The man was a voyeur, the rehearsals nothing more than a private peep show.

His unsuspecting actors didn't realize they were being watched or that they would be murdered in the final scene of the script. Goddard made snuff films. One actor died on screen. The other actor died as soon as the cameras stopped rolling. "Do you have any questions?" His dark eyes bored into her.

Panic made her voice lodge in her throat. She could not do this. Paige had thought she could handle this assignment, but she wouldn't perform for this monster. There had to be another way to gain access to his island.

There was no other way. It had taken almost two years to find this one. Time spent taking baby steps when she needed to be sprinting. Since she had gone undercover, Goddard had claimed two more lives. More names added to the FBI's list of victims.

But fear scattered their names like leaves in the wind, and Paige suddenly knew that going head to head with this sick bastard wouldn't make any difference. She would just end up dead like everyone else who got involved with him. She had to get a hold of her contact and get an exit code. Now.

"I believe you'll like your co-star. Quite an impressive gentleman," Goddard said, his scowl letting her know he was conscious of her indecision. "A bit older than you, but I believe you'll be exceptional together."

"Older?" she ground out.

Goddard laughed, such a blend of arrogance and lack of conscience that a chill raced through her. "I cater to a very exclusive clientele, Paige. I work with actors and actresses of all ages."

All ages.

Fear roiled inside her like brushfire—the very same fear Goddard's victims surely felt before they were murdered.

Suddenly images of those people imprinted on the backs of her eyelids. She had seen the aftermath of his work before. She remembered their names and her own horror and rage. One of his stars had been a beautiful fifteen-year-old girl, who was bright, full of life and potential.

Shelby.

As a volunteer for a community service program in college, Paige had been assigned to help Shelby through her first traumatic years in the state foster care system. But Paige's friendship and nurturing hadn't been enough to save the young girl from the lure of Goddard's venom, disguised as it was as a ladder to the stars.

Now Shelby was in Witness Protection while the FBI built a solid case against him. When she should have been making friends and going to proms like a normal teenager, she was running from city to city, scared to death of Goddard's vengeance because she had fled after her co-star had been murdered. Now Paige had a chance to give Shelby back her life. A chance to demand justice.

Could she walk away?

The answer tore through her like a gunshot. No. Her job would not be finished until this bastard stood before a jury.

If she had to play the porn star for his benefit, then so be it. Whatever it took to get on that island and retrieve a copy of Shelby's film and proof the other victims had been there—because even with eyewitness testimony, Paige had to have concrete evidence for a murder conviction. She would settle for nothing less.

"Are you having reservations?" Goddard asked. "If you don't think you're up to this, I have to know now. Once we begin filming—"

"This is a marvelous opportunity, Mr. Goddard. You are so well connected in the industry. All the exposure I'll get... I'm just a bit overwhelmed," she explained, determined to control her raging emotions, to lead this man into her trap.

"Good. Before we go, you can write your instructions down. Right now we need to discuss business. I want to see what I'm dealing with." He motioned to her costume with an impatient flick of his hand. "Undress."

Every fiber of her being cried out to lunge for him, to smash his skull with his own crystal paperweight and drop him where he stood. But she wouldn't. The need to put him behind bars tempered her hate and strengthened her resolve. She reached for the hook that held the costume secure.

The breath seemed to freeze in her lungs, and Paige could not suppress a shiver. The weight of the beaded fabric fell away as the zipper separated, the chilly air piercing her skin like pinpricks. Garters and shimmery hose slipped to her ankles, leaving her exposed. Vulnerable.

Goddard's black gaze raked over her. He had seen her on stage before, but appraised her with the practiced eyes of a professional. With the eyes of a man who thrived on power. On watching.

His mouth compressed into a straight line, and his nostrils flared. Raw carnality rolled off him in palpable waves, blasting her with the force of his hunger. The air grew thick, cloying, and she fixed her sight on the glittering skyline through the windows, refusing to give in to the revulsion pumping through her veins with each beat of her heart.

Burying every shred of emotion deep inside, Paige stood naked before him, head high. She would not let Lewis Goddard destroy her, too. She would bury her feelings deep inside, protect herself, so when this game was over, her heart wouldn't be a hollow cavern in her chest. She would win her case and then enjoy the peace of knowing justice had been done.

But tonight was only the beginning. Tomorrow she would have to submit to a stranger's touch.

Ace in the Hole

Special Agent Christopher Sharp unstrapped the chamois roll hanging around his hips and slid it from beneath his running shorts. Weighing the familiar heaviness in his palm, he outlined his "tools of the trade" through the soft leather. The weatherproof roll definitely wasn't much by way of bureau-issue gadgets, but it just might come in handy when the time came to escape the island.

Wedging his fingers in the crevice of the rockface, he grappled for purchase on the rugged slope and shifted a stone enough to create a hiding hole behind it. Shoving the roll inside, he set the stone back in place with a satisfied grunt. His ace in the hole. He never left home without one. Damn good thing, too, since he had been in Goddard's lair less than twenty-four hours and this case had already taken an unexpected turn.

Caught with his pants down.

The phrase played over and over in his head with irritating regularity. He had been caught   both literally and figuratively. After months of arranging the perfect legend and living his cover, Christopher had auditioned for the male lead in Goddard's upcoming snuff film and won the role.

His first surprise came when he hadn't been given a chance to pack a toothbrush before flying to this island fortress. Goddard had preached some crap about "taking care" of his actors, but Christopher recognized it for the security measure it was.

And should have anticipated it.

Lewis Goddard hadn't eluded the nation's top law enforcement agencies without being cautious. Miscalculations like this had gotten agents killed. He could only claim preoccupation. In his impatience to see Paige, he hadn't been using his head.

Sweat trickled down his brow, and he wiped it away while visually marking the twisted clump of tree roots in relation to the rock his tools lay under. He scrambled down the slope to the beach. Paige's contact could put him back in touch with his own. He would get harassed royally when he returned to Washington, but if that was the worst of it, he would consider himself lucky.

Resuming the pace of his run, Christopher breathed deeply of the sea air as the Pacific wind cooled the sun pounding on his bare shoulders. Goddard was expected any time now. Paige would be with him. He couldn't suppress his anticipation at the thought of seeing her again.

She had captured his heart when she was his student at Quantico. Strict regulations and personal honor had forbidden him from pursuing her then, but he couldn't forget her. She lurked in the darkest reaches of his mind, the memory of her full lips turning upward in an easy smile, a vision of her lithe dancer's body gleaming with perspiration as she scrambled over iron corrugated walls and rope bridges. After her training at the Academy, she had left sporting a gold badge. He had gone back into the field. And the game of cat and mouse had begun.

What a game it was. Every time he maneuvered them together—a stint in Washington or some quickie surveillance assignment or, hell, even a layover in some remote field office—Paige managed to slip through his fingers, leaving him a little more fascinated. A little more frustrated. She rebuffed him. Rejected him. Almost made him believe she didn't want anything to do with him.

Almost.

Even though she routinely denied that sparks flew between them, those beautiful sapphire eyes didn't lie. The way she had melted in his arms when he kissed her in Montana told another story. Paige wanted him as much as he wanted her.

Now the chase was over. They were stuck together on an island where she couldn't get away. He would finally discover why she fought the passion between them and learn to respect her resistance.

Or wear away her every last defense. But this time she wouldn't get away.

Christopher drew a deep breath and slowed his pace as the footpath gave way to craggy cliffs. Taking care with each step, he considered the role he played. The role Paige played. What they must do to stay alive in Goddard's world.

Sex.

Everything he had ever fantasized about was detailed in a script, and his heart raced just thinking about it.

True, the intimacy he had always imagined was not a part of this scenario. They would be performing for Goddard's benefit. And they would be murdered after filming.

That grisly thought dragged him back to reality.

Below, waves exploded against the cliffs in a violent dance, reminding Christopher of those who never made it beyond that churning current, their lives ended in a host of inventive, grotesque ways to pleasure a sick audience. Lewis Goddard was an animal and meeting the man hadn't changed Christopher's opinion.

He still marveled that Paige had actually taken this case. She had always fought so hard against the chauvinism that had haunted the FBI since the days of Hoover and his G-men. Yet this assignment forced her to face the worst of sexual crimes, to use every feminine wile created since the dawn of man. Totally against her "if he can do it, I can blow him away" mentality. She had barreled through the Academy with brains and physical prowess, yet here she was wielding her femininity like a sword to carve her way through Goddard's camp.

All to protect a witness? He wondered.

The cliffs beveled into a rolling grade as he approached the harbor. An increase in activity along the docks alerted him to the new arrivals. Christopher kept his pace as the marina came into view but couldn't slow the pounding of his heart when he saw Goddard's powerboat occupying a previously empty slip.

Paige had arrived.

He had barely dried the sweat from his face when one of the

marina attendants met him at the bottom of the cliff.

"I was just about to come looking for you," the attendant said with a gravity that suggested he was announcing the end of the Cold War. "Mr. Goddard is in. He wants to see you up at the house."

A twenty-five-thousand-square-foot showpiece designed to impress, Goddard's house served its function admirably. From its lofty perch on a cliff, the house eclipsed a sheltered harbor. White-stone walls glinted in the sunlight with a brilliance that drew the eye, a sprawling angel with wings spread in a protective embrace over the island. How deceptive appearances could be.

Composing himself as he wove through the halls toward the west wing, Christopher had no success at curbing the sudden rush of adrenaline that powered his footsteps into a barely dignified trot.

He found them in the library discussing the script."Good morning, Christopher." Lewis Goddard came to his feet behind the desk and motioned toward the woman who stood and turned toward him. "I want you to meet your lovely co-star, Paige. Isn't she everything I said she'd be?"

Christopher still recognized the idealistic young rookie in the exquisite woman before him. The lines of her body were long, fluid, beneath the casual silk pantsuit she wore. The delicate fabric revealed more than it concealed, emphasizing the fullness of her breasts, the slim curves of her waist and the incredible length of her legs. Images of those legs twined with his threaded through his imagination, and blood pounded through his body.

Her auburn hair fell in a riot around her shoulders, its length a silent tribute to the time that had passed between their meetings. God, just the sight of her was like gasping much needed air. How had he survived from one breath to the next?

The slight parting of her lips drew his gaze to her face, to the dimples that peeked at the corners of her mouth, to the smooth cheeks blushing in shades of peach and cream, to the thick fringe of lashes silhouetting eyes bright with sapphire lights.

Deep inside, he had hoped Paige would be pleased to see him, at the very least relieved her co-star was not a stranger. A lot to hope for, he knew, but hope sprang eternal. Yet in all his imaginings, Christopher had never expected to be greeted by the surprise that flashed across her face now.

She stared at him, eyes wide, posture rigid. She was not pleased to see him. But her shock was even more of a blow. The worst had happened—Paige had lost touch with her contact, too, or she would have known to expect him.

Renewed Acquaintances

What in hell was he doing here?

Paige could only stare. The breath had solidified in her throat, and she could scarcely swallow, let alone breathe. Why hadn't the bureau warned her? She would have insisted they find another agent. Any other agent!

Christopher faced her with a warning glint in his deep chocolate eyes. Years melted away, and she was instantly transported back to the role of student. Christopher Sharp was in charge, always in control of himself and everyone around him. The "iron spy" they had called him at Quantico, an appellation that summed up the man to a T.

He had forged himself an almost legendary reputation within the bureau as an internal spy—a man who specialized in undercover operations reminiscent of those immortalized by the CIA. He was called in to deal with heavy hitters like Cosa Nostra, industrial espionage and crime rings the caliber of Lewis Goddard's. Word had it that he was a chameleon with a knack for bringing the bad guys down. Paige knew better. The iron spy was a power junkie who liked playing the odds.

And now he was here.

Plastering a smile on her face, she extended her hand, and he caught it within his, gaze raking over her in one bold stroke.

"She is everything you said." He brought her hand to his mouth and pressed a kiss to the center of her palm, his lips rough velvet, his breath a warm puff against her skin.

A wave of desire that betrayed every shred of her reason spiraled straight to the pit of her stomach. Damn!

"A pleasure," she replied, her throat barely forming a whisper. She withdrew her hand, needing distance between them, needing to collect her thoughts before she blew this whole meeting and got them killed.

"I knew sparks would fly between you two," Goddard announced, sounding so pleased Paige wanted to kick him. She schooled her emotions and faced the one agent in all the world she did not want to see.

"This is Christopher," Goddard announced, obviously in the throes of some ego trip at the sight of them together. "You two will get to know each other very well in the next few weeks."

Paige swallowed hard. If that wasn't the understatement of the century.

Christopher smiled a roguish smile. "I believe the pleasure will be all mine."

No doubt!

Goddard laughed, and the sound grated along her nerve endings. "We've been going over the script, Christopher. Grab a chair. There are a few things I want you to keep in mind during rehearsals."

Goddard circled the desk while Christopher took the seat beside her. His nearness sent a shimmer along her spine and brought to mind all the lurid details of the script she had been discussing with such calm detachment.

Damn, but the man was gorgeous! The last time she had seen him, his deep golden hair had been cropped close in a style that emphasized the rugged line of his jaw, the strong shape of his head. Now it was long—longer than she had ever seen it. Rebellious waves escaped the clip at his nape, sculpturing his face like a tawny mane.

With his broad, high cheekbones and deep-set eyes, he reminded her of a lion. King of the jungle. King of wherever he was. There was a predatory air about him, about the erotic fullness of his mouth, about the plated muscles that shifted with sleek grace as he reached for the script, about his sheer size that made him overshadow everything in his presence. Including her.

How could she work this case with him? Just looking at him

bombarded her with that familiar melange of emotions she struggled with every time she saw him. Christopher Sharp the mentor. The slave-driver. The predator.

The man who wouldn't take no for an answer. Like the time he had kissed her in that Montana field station. She had melted in his arms then, confirming her denial of him meant nothing beneath the potency of his maleness.

God, how embarrassing—she still cringed at the memory.

And just when she thought her fascination with him was finally under control, he showed up again to prove her wrong.

Oh, so wrong.

Perhaps her hot/cold response to him wasn't so surprising. The male domination thing had been a issue her entire life. Her father had controlled her mother, had controlled her for far too long.

"Paige, you'll study dance because it's cultured... Paige, you will not go to the prom with that motorcycle-riding dope head, you will go with the boy in the Baccalaureate program... Paige, you'll go to med school, specialize in cardiology like me... Paige, you'll date this resident. He's a fine man with a promising future... ."

No. Paige wouldn't.

Paige was finished being controlled. She was becoming a federal agent—a career she found interesting. A career that allowed her to exercise some control of her own.

But with visions of G-men dancing in her head, Paige had found Christopher Sharp, instead. Exactly the type of man she needed to stay away from. A man with a need to control.

He had manipulated her completely during training, forced her to surrender to his tutelage so he could mold her into the perfect agent. A perfect "spy" like him. Through the years since Quantico, she had blessed him for it. And cursed him every time her convoluted sense of duty made her accept an assignment like this.

And this one was certainly proving to be a winner. She had just about convinced herself that performing sex with a stranger while Goddard watched would be worth it just to put the sick bastard away. Besides, after Goddard went before a judge, she would never see her co-star again.

But Christopher Sharp wouldn't disappear. She hadn't been able to get him out of her mind before. She'd never get rid of him now.

As if that wasn't bad enough, the heavy-lidded look in his eyes made her tingle, made her think about how his strong hands would feel on her body.

"This rehearsal is not about learning your lines," Goddard said, tapping a manicured nail on the desktop and dragging her back to attention. "It's about arousal and sex. I want tension between you. The script is a build up toward a climactic finish, and it won't work if you are indifferent to each other."

Climactic finish. Paige suppressed a shiver. Murder was more like it. Dread knifed through the edges of her calm. She wondered who was scripted to die, yet it didn't really matter. Whoever didn't die on film would die as soon as Goddard yelled, "Cut."

But unlike the other actors, Paige knew this was a snuff film. What she didn't know was how Goddard could sit there so coldly, so blatantly unaffected, while playing god with their lives.

Sick bastard.

"I'll answer any questions that come up, but I want your rehearsals to remain unstructured," he continued. "Stick loosely to the script, but remember that this time is for you to interact, to find out what turns you on. When we do start filming, I expect chemistry. I want your sex to be much more than an act." He formed the words carefully, as if savoring the idea of seeing them together.

Christopher stiffened beside her, so subtly she might not have noticed had she not known him. But she recognized the way his fingers flexed as if he was having trouble keeping his fists to himself.

The iron spy.

He was a miracle in self control. While she could barely suppress the urge to lock her hands around this pervert's throat, she marveled at Christopher's restraint when Goddard gave them a tour through the luxurious stage that was the west wing.

He had designed every room with a carnal purpose. Her gaze traveled over the lay-out, spacious and open, with no walls to obstruct the surveillance equipment concealed in the ornate wainscoting. The furniture provided a staged panorama so exact she could easily pinpoint the camera's positions.

They toured room after room—an enormous kitchen where she found five separate surfaces to make love on at first glance, a study with a huge fireplace and a real bearskin rug, an opulent indoor spa she could easily envision as a mystical spring—with Goddard playing both tour guide and director.

Christopher's jaw was set, his gaze fixed beneath burnished brows, as they listened to Goddard's lurid suggestions. She walked along at his side, acutely aware of his presence, but he only remarked upon the rooms, paying no particular attention to her, as though they were indeed the strangers they pretended to be.

"You can rehearse your striptease in this dance studio." Goddard rested a long-fingered hand on the bar that circled the room and cast her a penetrating glance as though her clothes would start melting off of their own volition. "I want classy, not slutty. Think Gypsy Rose Lee or Tempest Storm, not some strung-out thrash from the Mons."

Paige only nodded, eyes darting to the corners of the room. No cameras in here. The entire studio was walled in observation mirrors.

As if those mirrors reflected her vulnerability, Christopher placed a hand on her shoulder, his touch firm but gentle. She met his gaze, wondering how much her eyes revealed. Did he know that the very idea of dancing for him made excitement clench low in her belly?

A smile curved his full mouth and sparkled in his eyes. He knew all right. And with every step, her pulse increased in tempo until it slammed through her veins like a tidal wave. But the enormity of their situation didn't really strike home until she stepped into her suite and realized it was Christopher's, too.

His robe lay across the bed like he had discarded it carelessly before his morning run. Personal items sat askew on the dresser, a bottle of Calvin Klein's Escape, a sweat band from some work-out session that had been left to dry in a heap.

On the floor sat a pair of well-worn topsiders, slipped off and forgotten, but marking his presence in the room. His room. Her room. The room they would make love in. A knot formed in her throat. This was a scene from her worst nightmare. Her most secret fantasy. Her eyes kept darting back to the bed. She shivered.

"You've got all kinds of toys here." Goddard cracked open a night table drawer and revealed an assortment of sexual paraphernalia. Twisted silk ropes in a variety of sizes. A double-headed vibrator. A whip.

His excitement was almost tangible, transforming the room into a high-tech sexual chamber. His pale fingers trembled slightly when he held up a set of handcuffs. The sudden silence pulsed in her ears.

"I want much more than a performance."

Paige cast a surreptitious glance at Christopher and had no trouble at all envisioning his powerfully built body clad in leather and furs, his sensuality potent as he played the role of medieval chieftain.

Whatever had possessed her to accept this assignment?

"The days are for rehearsing, but the nights are yours," Goddard told them. He slid the drawer closed and stepped off the platform that made the bed the visual focus of the room. "Enjoy my hospitality. Let me know how you are progressing." He clasped Christopher's hand and then pressed a kiss to her cheek. "Make it good. You are part of my team now, and I only work with the best."

Paige watched him retreat, anxiety spiking each breath. She jumped when the door slammed shut behind him, leaving her alone with Christopher.

Before she had a chance to swallow a calming gulp of air, Christopher's hand clamped around her wrist and she was propelled into motion.

"Come on," he ordered, not bothering to glance back as he dragged her across the suite. "I need to shower, and you're coming with me."

Paige came to an abrupt halt that was less a show of resistance than surprise. Either way, she forced him to stop in mid-stride. "Excuse me?"

That chocolate gaze snared hers, and there was no mistaking the intensity of his mood. "I said let's go."

She recognized his tone from the Academy. Once she had obeyed him with no questions asked. Never again. "I have no intention of showering with you." She fixed him with a glare that would have caused anyone else to think twice. Anyone except Christopher.

He only exhaled sharply, a breathy burst that clearly conveyed his annoyance. Paige didn't care. Better he learn right here and now that her days of obeisance were over.

Before she could tell whether or not he got the point, his arms lashed around her and he hoisted her over his shoulder as easily as he shrugged on body armor. "I have no intention of starting rehearsals without a shower. Call it a quirk of mine, but I can't perform until I know we're both squeaky clean."

Of all the... Paige struck at him with her fists, but he only grunted and tightened his grip. Marching through the doorway leading into the bathroom's spacious outer area, he wedged her through another doorway toward the spa. She eyed her retreating reflection in the mirrors as dispassionately as the sterile surroundings. Her attempts to resist were futile. She stopped struggling when they emerged in a sort of a mini spa with a Jacuzzi tub and glass-enclosed shower. He kicked the door shut behind them.

Without a word, he let her slide to the floor, her breasts riding the length of his hard chest, her abdomen rounding the arch of a very noticeable bulge between his legs. The tightness in her belly twisted into a knot. He was excited by her? The iron spy couldn't possibly suffer from something as base as arousal. That would suggest a loss of control, and Christopher Sharp never lost control.

The very idea contradicted everything she knew about him, and Paige wasn't at all sure she wanted to deal with any more surprises today. Not when she was facing the most important case of her career. Not when Shelby's future—not to mention her own and Christopher's—rode on nailing Goddard with a charge that would stick.

She pulled away, and he released his grip so suddenly that she staggered back a full step. Turning his back to her, Christopher flicked on the light switch then turned the shower on full blast.

"Undress." He pulled the rumpled shirt over his head, and her gaze stuck on his broad chest with its thick muscles and tawny hair trailing down his stomach into a slim line at his navel.

He radiated sensuality, as though his bronzed body had been created for the sole purpose of pleasure. Her pulse throbbed in her temples as she took in every hollow and ridge of that muscular physique, so strong, powerful—not the raw-boned strength of a boy, but the solid, sun-hardened strength of a man.

Paige blinked once, twice. The skimpy running shorts only emphasized his size, making him appear more erotic than sheer nakedness would allow.

"I have no intention of..." the protest died in her throat as he pushed the shorts over his hips and kicked them away.

His thick sex sprang out from a thatch of lionine fur, and Paige could only stare. He was hard. And enormous. Blood pulsed through a network of veins toward a wide smooth head that pointedly accused her of being responsible for its current state.

"Everything meets with your approval, I hope." His throaty laughter resounded above the steady pulse of water, shocking her from her unwitting inspection.

Fire erupted in her cheeks, and she turned her back to him. Desire simply had no place in her thoughts right now. She should make another attempt to escape, but his sheer masculine presence rooted her to the spot. To reach the door she would have to face him, and she just couldn't do that. Not when her face would reveal how much he affected her.

"Don't get prissy on me now, Paige." His laughter echoed in her ears.

Before she could think up an adequate defense, his hands were on her. She whirled to resist and met his nakedness head on like a train. A dizzying current soared through her as he wrestled the thin blouse over her head, his size an advantage she simply couldn't overcome. Not when all rational thought fled. Not when her gaze seemed locked onto the sight of his broad hands sliding the silky pants over her hips and down her legs, leaving her standing before him in nothing more than a sheer bodysuit.

She heard his breath catch, and the sound snapped her out of her daze. "Christopher, stop!" she commanded, but her voice betrayed her, the words tumbling from her lips in a garbled rush.

He had no intention of listening anyway and pulled her hard against him, his touch hot, potent, as he peeled the bodysuit away.

Her reaction was instant.

Desire speared straight between her legs, and her imagination conjured all sorts of ways to indulge the sensation. Just an inch or two more, just the simplest of motions, and those hot fingers would stroke her, caress the tender skin that ached with the promise of his touch.

"God," he whispered as his hand skimmed her bare flesh and pushed the bodysuit down her legs.

She swallowed back a moan, exhilarated he was so similarly affected. Steam billowed from the shower stall in amorphous clouds, glossing her skin with hot silk and slicking their bodies together with moist suction. She wanted him to touch her. Desperately. The need was so sudden, she couldn't make sense of anything except his body pressed against her.

Christopher growled, a throaty male sound, and his mouth found hers, tasting, causing the most delicious deluge of pleasure to pour through her. A sigh slipped from her lips. Christopher caught the sound, sharing the strength of his attraction, making her realize just how much she wanted him.

With each greedy taste of his lips, with each demanding thrust of his tongue, he wrung the most heady responses from her. She had never reacted like this to a man.

But then Christopher Sharp was no ordinary man.

He had been her instructor, had held her future within his grasp. From the way she dressed to the way she handled a gun, she had tried to please him.

As always, he was unmerciful. He had driven her past all perceived boundaries until she had discovered that no limits existed between them. He would make her sample passion the same way. Unless she stopped him.

She would not get caught in this power struggle. Not after finally escaping a lifetime of dictates and commands. Not after she had grown accustomed to calling the shots. Christopher threatened her fiercely-won independence. Everything had to be his way. Always. Paige would fight.

But even as her mind made the vow, her will seemed to melt. Their flesh molded together as one, and she abandoned all pretense of resistance, wanting to touch him, to feel the play of muscles beneath her fingertips. Slipping her hands between them, she smoothed her palms over his chest, exploring the raspiness of hair cushioning the muscles below.

Christopher had won. Again.

The heavy languor of desire lapped through her veins like hot wine. And he knew. Oh, yes, he knew, just like he had always known her every strength, her every weakness, her every thought. And as always, he pressed his advantage to tip the scales into his favor.

She struggled to remain standing when his thigh found a welcoming niche between hers. No matter how hard she willed herself not to, she rode that length of hard muscle, the ache inside propelling her into motion along his flesh.

Her hand slid down the arc of his waist, over the trim line of his hip, drawn toward his tantalizing maleness. Her fingertips skimmed the ruff of hair at its base, her palm cupping him until a throaty groan echoed between them.

Ah, a flash of triumph. She savored the sound of his reaction, savored the sensation as that hot shaft jumped in her hand.

Christopher Sharp never could handle defeat, and Paige knew it. He tore his mouth from hers with a growl, a sound so raw, so primitive she almost took a step back. Her hand fell clumsily to her side.

Without a word he dragged her into the shower and stood beneath the spray, eyes closed, breaths coming in ragged gasps. The echo of his touch faded as she watched his struggle, knowing he fought his desire for her.

The iron spy had lost control.

So had she. Passion turned resolve to water, and she leaned against the wall, pushing hair out of her face, dignity dissolving in the sensuality of the moment. How could she have liquefied in his arms as if starved for his touch? Paige knew the answer even as the question formed in her mind.

She had spent her whole life seeking approval. First her father's and then Christopher's. Ice skated across her nerve endings despite the steamy heat of the shower.

"You're out of touch." He glared at her.

She brought her finger to her lips in a plea for silence, shocked by his lack of caution.

There's no surveillance in here." He dismissed her concern with a scowl. "I checked out the place last night. That's why we're in here."

"Are you sure?"

His tawny brows shot up upward. "Of course."

Well, she didn't take chances. He had taught her that. "I guess it's a good thing we have a place to talk. Now that you're here."

Christopher snorted. "Goddard apparently thinks we deserve some privacy in the bathroom. And inside the closets." He leaned into the spray to grab a bar of soap from a niche on the back wall.

"Cordial host, eh?" Paige tightened her arms across her chest. He would read the defensive gesture for what it was, she knew, but couldn't stop herself from reacting. She was defensive. Christopher might be back in control again, might be able to dismiss what had passed between them so easily, but she was standing within arm's reach, bare-assed, her body still trembling with the memory of his kiss.

"You're out of touch." A frown drew his brow together as he pinned her with a stare.

"How did you know?" she whispered.

He worked a lather over his chest. Water sluiced over him, and his muscles shifted and glowed beneath rivulets of soap. Bubbles cascaded down his body, playing along the trim lines of his waist, into the hair surrounding his sex, down the muscular hardness of his thighs. His body gleamed like bronze under the rush of water. She couldn't manage more than a blink when he said, "You'd have expected me otherwise."

She hadn't expected him. Not in a million years.

"You came here knowing you were out of touch with the bureau." His words were an accusation. "What in hell were you thinking?"

His nakedness may have made it difficult to think, but his indignation sparked her temper.

"That should be obvious." She erupted from her daze, ignoring the muscles that glinted beneath the bubbles. "I was unwilling to blow this chance just because Goddard threw me a curve."

"A curve?" Christopher shook his head, incredulous, sending water droplets spattering.

Paige hugged her arms around her as much to shield herself from the spray as to protect herself from his relentless stare. "I know it wasn't procedurally correct—"

"Procedurally correct," he repeated, his soapy fingers grasping her chin and jerking her face upward. "I don't give a damn about procedure. This man makes snuff films. Your life is at risk."

She wanted to point out that his life was also in danger, but something in his face, some emotion she didn't recognize, made her hold back.

Her voice dropped to a whisper, and she asked, sweetly, a concession to whatever sentiment the iron spy had let slip, "You'll put me back in touch with my contact, won't you?"

Christopher's hand fell away, leaving a bubbly trail in its wake. A scowl shadowed those warm eyes, gathering like cloud cover before a summer storm. Had Paige not known better, she would have thought he looked... well, sheepish.

Christopher surprised her by drawing a deep breath. "I'm out of touch, too."

She should have mercy on him, knowing as she did how difficult his admission must be, but even after all these years, there was still a rookie inside who demanded justice.

When the urge to laugh struck, it struck hard. She managed to swallow most of it back, but the sarcasm was there, biting, tangy. Whoever said revenge was sweet?

"Explain something to me, Christopher. Why are you here if you're out of touch?"

If he could have devoured her in one bite, he would have. "I assumed I could get back in touch through you."

"That'll teach you to assume."

Oops! The man had no humor whatsoever, she remembered too late when his hands locked onto her shoulders. He shook her. Hard. "Paige, this is serious. You know Goddard's dossier even better than I do. This mission is out of control."

She tried to shrug away, irritated when she couldn't shake off his wet grip. "What are you suggesting?"

"Abort." The command echoed through the shower stall with eerie finality.

"Abort?" she blurted out and immediately lowered her voice to a strained whisper. Even if there wasn't any surveillance equipment in the bathroom, Goddard's cronies could be lurking behind closed doors.

"I've worked for two years getting Goddard to invite me here."

Christopher ran impatient fingers through his long hair and pushed the dripping strands back from his face. "I cannot approve this, Paige. We're of no use to the bureau dead."

Could she possibly make him understand? One glance at the unyielding set of his jaw told her that any attempt to reason would be useless.

Paige did the next best thing—took the offense. Thumping him hard on the chest with an outstretched hand, she growled, "Listen, buddy, you may be the senior agent here, but this is my case. If you want to abort, that's your call. Swim back to the mainland for all I care." She snapped the shower door open with such force the glass rattled in its casing. "Just don't jeopardize my cover."

Paige left the bathroom without looking back.

Put Your Money
Where Your Mouth Is

Christopher reappeared in the suite dressed to watch a striptease. "Have you spent much time going over the script?" he asked, heading toward the dresser and running a comb through his damp hair.

He had apparently decided not to swim for shore, but his expression told Paige he wasn't thrilled about it.

Neither was she. His mention of the script and its explicit sexual scenarios reminded her of exactly what she was expected to do with him.

"Enough." More than enough.

She had spent the better part of her career dodging Christopher and his *chance* meetings. Avoiding the man and the emotions he aroused inside her. Refusing to give in to feelings that made her vulnerable.

His gaze caught hers in the mirror as if he knew her innermost secrets. Sensed her hesitation. "Are you ready to put your money where your mouth is?" She couldn't miss the challenge reflected in that deep gaze.

Ready? Now that was another question entirely. Christopher Sharp was here to have sex with her. Lewis Goddard would be watching. An icy fist hammered at whatever courage she had mistakenly thought she possessed. Paige was not ready.

She nodded anyway.

"You certainly dressed for a striptease." He cast a wry glance at the full leotard she wore.

Everything except her toes, heels and hands was covered, and she had thrown on a sheer skirt that fell to mid-calf for good measure. Not the easiest costume to strip out of, but one that kept her sufficiently clothed as she battled this overwhelming sense of vulnerability. "I was cold."

A smile twitched at the corners of his mouth, and she dug the crescents of her nails into her palms to resist the urge to slap him.

"You still want to start with the striptease?"

"Rehearsing the scenes sequentially seemed like a novel idea," she remarked dryly.

The striptease was the first vignette. She was expected to slither around a pole and have sex with Christopher—while Goddard watched from behind observation mirrors. She understood what she had to do, and this vignette had seemed tame compared to the submission and bondage in the rest of the script. Now she wasn't so sure.

"Shall we, then?" Christopher grabbed the script off the coffee table and offered his arm in a gentlemanly fashion.

She ignored him and sailed through the door.

Hogan's Alley hadn't prepared her for an eventuality like this one. Shoot outs—yes. Hostage negotiations—yes. But never had any courses or subsequent work experiences explained how to make sex with Christopher a casual experience.

Her throat constricted, and she padded down the carpeted hallway beside him in silence. He appeared much larger than life in the light cotton sweats that emphasized the muscular length of his legs, the loose-fitting tee that didn't quite cover his taut stomach.

She never dreamed he would take on a case like this one. Suddenly he no longer resembled her brusque instructor from the Academy. The man who had trained the next generation of "spies" for the FBI. This man was a stranger.

The dance studio was equipped with all the modern conveniences, including a stripper's pole. An image of herself hanging onto it, breasts jingling and hips undulating while Christopher watched, made her stomach flip-flop precariously. And all those mirrors. Goddard was back there somewhere waiting for the show to begin. Watching.

Christopher tossed the script on to a shelf above the sound system and began flipping through CDs. "Anything in particular? There's quite a selection here."

Paige shook her head, not trusting herself to speak. He chose a piece with a two-second beat, perfect for warming up, but she stood frozen in the doorway, unable to move, risking everything with an amateurish display of nerves.

God help her, she couldn't do this.

"Paige, are you ready?"

No! She wanted to cry out, but swallowed the protest on the edge of a strangled breath when she lifted her gaze and met chocolate eyes warm with understanding.

He strode purposefully toward her, and suddenly she wasn't alone. As he clasped her hand firmly and led her into the center of the room, fear eased its garrote.

"Come on, Gypsy. I'm looking forward to a show."

No doubt. Paige sank to the floor and closed her eyes, letting his nearness flow through her. He squeezed her hand in quiet reassurance.

Inhaling deeply, she focused on her body, on muscles tight with tension, trying to forget that somewhere behind those mirrors lurked a man who killed for a sexual thrill.

But Paige would do her job. She might have to rehearse, but this was the last rehearsal Lewis Goddard would watch.

Arching her back, she flexed to isolate specific muscles through her body and gradually built up a rhythm, letting the music soothe away her stiffness, working each muscle sequentially from her ankles to her toes, searching desperately for some corner of her heart where her emotions could hide.

But mingled with dread was an intense awareness of Christopher, of his breathing in deep even bursts, over-riding her own tempo. Her awareness of Goddard became overshadowed by the man physically beside her.

She opened her eyes. Christopher sat nearby, arm draped casually across his knees as he watched her with the very concentration she lacked. Paige redoubled her efforts. This entire charade wouldn't work unless she got a grip on herself. Christopher's appearance may have upset her plans, but she had to focus.

Much easier said than done.

She found her gaze drawn again and again to his reflection. Her every movement revealed a new glimpse of his body: the strong lines of his thighs, the supple curve of his hips, the rippled length of his torso, the bold sweep of his back.

Spellbound by the sight, she rose to dance a sequence in an effort to distract herself. Relevè, pliè, parallel, arabesque. Every motion became a study in unity, arms cascading in smooth glides, her body dipping and swaying in time with the music.

Panic melted beneath a warmth that suffused her entire body and made her muscles glow. She danced close to him, but never touched, only their reflections revealing how perfectly matched they were. His powerful body contrasted boldly with her lithe grace. The gleam of artificial light illuminated the golden highlights in his wavy hair, the bronze of his skin.

She was fire to his light, and Paige knew why Goddard had cast them together. If nothing else, the lecher had an eye for the aesthetic. A fleeting image formed in her mind of a lion chasing a gazelle across a sun-burned plain, and she recognized Christopher as the lion. He was the predator and she the prey. Always.

How she had avoided getting caught, instinctively knowing what her response to him would be. But now she was trapped. Desperation raged inside. She must finally face these feelings he aroused in her.

His gaze challenged her to take pleasure in the dance. In him. She wanted to resist, prove herself immune to his virility, but found herself kneeling beside him, reaching out to touch him instead.

Reality retreated to the fringes of her consciousness and filled her with sensation, the pulsing heat of his skin beneath her fingertips, the gravelly sound of his voice when he asked, "Do you hesitate because of me or the script?"

"You," she confessed.

His smile was warm, satisfied. "I don't care how I catch you, Paige. Just as long as I do."

"I know." And she did. That's why she had always run. He possessed the power to consume her. To reduce her to ashes with the heat of his flame. "You're too arrogant for your own good."

"Or for yours?" He reached up and stroked the curve of her cheek. And just like in the shower, her body sang in response to his touch.

"I've no doubt I'll suffer." She swayed against him, feeling his coiled strength, the desire in his smile as he stared into her face. Music surrounded her. Inhibitions melted beneath his touch, leaving behind only the thrill of the moment.

"This isn't suffering," he murmured against her ear. "Not by a long shot."

Paige had known it wouldn't be. Whether her hand was connecting with his cheek in anger or stroking that magnificent body in a lover's caress, touching Christopher meant losing herself in the blaze of his passion.

She shouldn't surrender so easily. Even though they were bound together by the unwritten laws of deep cover, she should simply do her job. Detach. Show him he wasn't affecting her.

But he was. Oh, how he was affecting her. Somehow the knowledge of Goddard's presence lurking behind their reflections only spurred her need to touch this living, breathing man.

Her fingers stroked the length of his forearm, eager to indulge this fascination she had denied herself for so long. And when she did, Paige realized she wasn't the only one on fire. The iron spy wanted her as much as she did him.

With her hand tightly in his, she dragged him to his feet. Swaying in time with the music, she parted her legs until her thighs straddled the strong muscles of his. She arched backward in a spine-melting curl, trusting the hand he clasped securely around hers, and glided suggestively against his thigh.

His eyes widened just enough to betray his surprise, and she was rewarded by his quick intake of breath.

Paige laughed, delighted by his response and feeling a rush of wicked excitement. "You like that."

Those warm brown eyes glowed. "Audience participation, is it?"

Paige only smiled. Balancing herself on the balls of her feet, she drew herself upright in a fluid motion, and brushed her hand lightly across his jaw.

Christopher shivered, and she was delighted by his response. She had been so busy avoiding him that she hadn't realized how much power his attraction gave her. Or given any thought to what she could do with that power.

But this was Christopher Sharp, and he would give as good as he got. With a quick maneuver, he circled her until her back came hard against his chest. Suddenly she faced the mirror with full view of the bold hand he traced along the curve of her breast. The length of his maleness swelled against her as if it had a life and voice all its own.

Tease me, will you?

His palm cupped her breast for the barest of instants, but long enough for her nipple to pucker through the spandex. His deep chuckle was a warm burst against her ear, making hairs flutter against her face and her stomach somersault with tension.

Glancing in the mirror, he said, "We look good together." The approval in his voice flowed through her like a drug. "I knew we would."

His eyes were heavy-lidded with promise, and though he held her pinned, his grip barely mattered because it was the sight of their reflection that held her transfixed.

Mirrors were said to capture the soul, and if that myth was born of truth, then the creature who stared back, mouth parted slightly and hips swaying in time with the music, must be her dark twin. Surely she couldn't be this aroused with Goddard so close. She could almost feel his dead black eyes upon her, caressing her just as surely as Christopher's hands traced the curve of her waist.

She should feel revulsion. Or outrage. Or fear. But there was something erotic about the sight of those strong hands on her body...

something compelling about the danger of Goddard's presence.

Blood pulsed through her veins. A feeling, not unlike the high she got during a bust, sparked a heat inside.

"I want you to dance for me." Christopher nibbled on her earlobe, sending little shivers of pleasure darting outward and surprising her with the intensity of the sensation.

His tawny head burrowed in the curve of her neck, and the sight made her realize just how thoroughly she was enjoying this game. The situation was so tantalizing.

Forbidden.

The iron spy looked literally wrought from metal as he watched her arch sideways in a deep stretching curve, the skirt parting like sheer wings to reveal her leotard-clad body. Tugging the bow at her waist, she let the skirt slither to the floor, then pushed it aside with a toe.

Christopher looked like he was about to pounce.

"Indulge yourself," his hungry expression seemed to say, "Indulge me."

The arousal in his face urged her on, sparked her appetite for control. Paige slipped away from him and covered the distance to the pole in one well-executed leap. Her hand met the solid metal with a resounding ring, and she pivoted, turning her back to him and catching his gaze in the mirror.

With an easy swaying motion, she shrugged the bodice off her shoulders, coaxing down the spandex sleeves. Baring one lacy bra strap then the other. One bare arm. Then the other. Until the leotard clung to her breasts precariously, and the promise of disaster was only a deep breath away.

Stretching back against the pole like a cat, she arched her body in a long motion. One shrug, and the spandex snapped over the swell of her breasts and rolled down her ribs. A flash of white lace caught her eye in the mirror, and she almost laughed at how virginal her choice of intimate apparel appeared given the twisted dynamics of the situation.

"Are you a white lace man?" she asked huskily and spun around, separating her thighs and straddling the pole.

The bulge in his pants was his only reply. His need would translate into skillful hands on her body, Paige knew, but she was not ready to relinquish this power she had over him. Some quirky inner voice urged her to push him beyond endurance. To test him, test his limits, define new boundaries just like he had done to her at the Academy.

As she lifted her hand to her head in a exaggerated motion, his gaze followed. She felt beautiful, daring, in the face of his desire, and his reaction to her dance acted like wildfire on her senses. Shaking her hair free, she let it tumble down her back, glad she had grown it long when Christopher's gaze grew hot and desperate and his magnificent body grew taut.

She laughed again, not only because he was chomping at the bit, but because Fate had played such an ironic little game. What she had expected to be a denigrating and mechanical sex act had become a fever singeing her blood. She had never known such desire. Her body vibrated with excitement, made her ache, electrified her with the thrill of danger.

Her movements took on new purpose as she arced and curled around the pole. Closing her eyes to the sight of them reflected in triplicate, she absorbed the music into her dance, reveled in the knowledge of Christopher's hunger. Her body burned, the lack of visual stimuli exaggerating other senses, making her aware of the men who watched her.

Fire ignited her imagination. Watched. Wanted. With one skillful twist, she released the clasp of her bra and rolled her body forward, knowing Christopher's gaze locked on her, not her reflection, as the bra straps danced a slow glide down her arms.

The bra slipped from her fingertips. Her nipples grew diamond hard as the air grazed her skin. Drawing up full length against the pole, she anchored herself against it, pressing her breasts together, unable to suppress a shiver as the cool metal caressed her hot skin, naked, brazen.

Paige opened her eyes to see the effect of her boldness on Christopher. What she saw made her insides melt.

He was on fire. Pressing the discarded bra to his lips, he caressed her with eyes glowing from passion. She ached to reach out and touch him, to give in to the sizzling attraction that arced through the air between them.

"Do you want to touch me?" Her words were a whisper above the silvery strains of music.

He shook his head, golden hair flying in halo around that rugged face, a wry smile touching his lips. "No, Paige." His voice was thick. "I want to flip you over that bar and take you."

She bet he would. Whoever said power was a drug hadn't been kidding. Christopher struggled visibly for control. Executing a series of hip spirals that brought her around the pole, Paige thrust her breasts proudly before him and was rewarded when a violent shudder rocked his powerful body.

He spanned the distance between them in a whipcord motion. In the space of a heartbeat, the balance of power shifted. His hands locked onto her hips, and when she pulled away, the solid length of the pole blocked her escape.

"Christopher, don't—"

"I'm participating," he gritted the words out between clenched teeth and hooked his fingers into the wad of fabric around her waist.

Exhaling an audible sigh, he rolled the leotard in a slow glide over her hips, leaving her clad in nothing more than a G-string. His teeth followed in the wake of his hands, nipping a trail of teasing bites along her sensitive flesh.

She should push him away—God knew she wanted to—but could only manage to smother a moan as his tongue outlined the triangle of lace that promised so much more than it concealed. Pleasure erupted when his warm breath streamed over her aching sex. The reflection of his tawny head between her legs seared away any lingering shreds of resistance.

He snatched the control from her as easily as snapping his fingers. She should have fought harder, should resent him at the very least, but anger exploded in a flash of sensation. She writhed her hips, unable to resist the velvet lure of his tongue.

With one quick stroke, Christopher tore away the intrusive scrap of fabric and found her tiny bud. With his strong hands clasped on her buttocks, he drew her closer, edging her thighs apart, assaulting her body until she moaned aloud, desire throbbing in time with the beat of her heart.

His tongue dipped inside her, and she leaned back against the pole, suddenly grateful for its support as the strength drained from her legs and reality spiraled into a burning awareness of him. Of those delicious thrusts that mimicked the most primitive loveplay.

His tongue flicked inside her with precise rhythm, lifting her onto a crest of arousal that made her squirm. She buried her fingers into his hair and pulled him closer, eager... no, desperate to scale the heights of this sensation.

He drew her clit into his mouth, drawing on that tiny nub and making her whimper with the strength of her need. One gentle nip would hurl her over the edge. One tender bite would pitch her into a blaze of ecstasy.

But Christopher had other ideas. His mouth brushed the fine cover of hairs that veiled her sex, then raked a path down the inside of her thigh, leaving her gasping, thrumming with unfulfilled need. He drew the leotard down the sweep of her legs, raining a hail of little kisses on her toes as he drew the leggings over one foot then the other until she stood before him naked.

Vulnerable.

A flash of reason pierced the delicious fog clouding her brain. Christopher had always been in control. Always the one to call the shots. No matter what she wanted.

Right now she wanted him. For once he was going to listen.

In a liquid glide, she dropped to her knees, straddling him like a lap dancer, her breasts full in his face, body yearning for his touch, soul aching with the need to dominate.

He exhaled in a low whoosh and sank back onto his heels. His hard thighs dug into hers. She wove her fingers into his hair and tilted his face to hers.

"You think we're going to do this your way, do you?" she asked, riding the thick length of erection that swelled beneath his sweats.

Christopher slanted her a curious glance. "I'm open to suggestions."

And suggest she did. With her nipple nudging at those full lips.

His hot mouth enveloped her, his deep chuckle sending a warm gust of air across her skin. His hands reached up to cup her breasts, strong hands kneading her as his tongue began a hot dance.

Her hips never slowed the erotic rhythm she set, lightly caressing his erection, then riding that thick length as though she planned to take him inside her with the next stroke.

The mirrors became their erotic theater as his dark hands traveled the outside of her thighs and cupped the pale roundness of her buttocks. She swayed against him, inspired by the music and spellbound by the play of muscles along his broad back, by the sight of his tawny head as he laved such delicious attention on her breasts. Her nipples darkened to ruby and swelled with desire. The moisture from his tongue flashed against her skin. Rolling her head forward, Paige veiled them beneath the fall of her hair, a frail attempt at privacy against their reflection. Against their audience.

"Sweet Christ, you make me hot." Christopher outlined her legs with a firm grip.

"I know." She ground her hips down, savoring this power over him.

His arousal pulsed against her. He slid a hand between their bodies, and suddenly that erection was filling her, stretching her moist flesh until she melted against him with a sob.

Christopher locked his arm around her waist and withdrew, then slid back inside with one smooth stroke. The expression on his face was of such pure maleness, such pure aggressor, that she wanted to scream. His touch was so much more than she had ever imagined, yet exactly what she had always feared. Surrender.

She fought it. With every ounce of her determination, Paige resisted his power to ravage her will. Even as his palm cupped her mound, rubbing with such sweet pressure, the explosion upon her, imminent, unstoppable. She rode the sensation, rode him, trapped in the midst of an inferno that scorched her pride. She moaned, resisting with every shred of strength she possessed and rocking against him with a passionate demand of her own.

She met his every thrust with a rhythm that stole her breath. A violent shudder rocked his powerful body, a groan slipping from his lips and telling her just how close he was to the edge. Bracing her arms around his neck as leverage, she arched against him, determined to take him with her.

Trailing her mouth along his brow, her tongue grazed his temple, the shell of his ear. "You're coming with me," she whispered, swaying against him to emphasize her words.

Christopher rammed deep inside with enough force to make her gasp. "Is this suffering?" She could see the male triumph smolder in his gaze as she reached the first gasping climax.

To deny the effect of their passion would make her a liar, so she let her body answer. Abandoning herself to sensation, she coaxed his orgasm with her throbbing flesh.

Time fell away as he exploded, the sound of his surrender as sweet as her own. This man was everything she had ever imagined. The reality was so much more than the fantasy. As the blaze faded to embers, Paige knew their sex had set the precedent. She had fought with him for control, had tasted the power of his response and discovered an appetite for Christopher Sharp much larger than their circumstances. Much larger than Lewis Goddard.

Paige had more control than she ever realized and over the next few days, she would have a chance to explore it.

To explore Christopher.

Dragging herself from the glorious haze of contentment, she covered his mouth possessively and whispered against his lips, "I was wrong. I won't be the one suffering after all."

Let the Games Begin.

Suffering? Now here was something Christopher hadn't considered. After years of chasing Paige, he had finally caught her, but instead of indulging in that victory, indulging in her, he had to share her with a pervert. He was not thrilled with the situation and considered the effects on their developing relationship. Not good.

They returned to the living room in silence. Paige headed toward the couch while he made his way to the bar. He needed a drink. Eyeing the Johnny Walker covetously, he chose a bottle of wine from the rack instead. Dinner was in an hour. He would need a clear head to deal with Goddard, and there was nothing clear about his head right now.

Or his body.

Every nerve ending echoed with a heady combination of satisfaction and discontent. Paige was a fever raging in his blood, and having her only made him want more. They should be lying in bed right now, basking in the afterglow without Goddard's prying eyes, yet they were forced to work, to apprehend their very sick, and very dangerous, host.

"Coming down is a real bitch." He held up the bottle for Paige's approval. "Want some?"

"Please."

Decanting the merlot into two crystal glasses, Christopher deposited one on the coffee table next to her. "Well, I don't think chemistry is going to be a problem between us."

Paige cast him a sidelong glance. "Doesn't seem to be." She stretched languorously and sank down onto the leather sofa. A fresh stab of arousal sliced through him. He wanted her again. Here and now.

"You said you'd read the whole script," she commented, and with his confirming nod, asked, "Are you going to have a problem with the next vignette?"

"A problem?" He watched her, glass poised at his lips, curious. The second scenario had Paige playing the part of a Celtic priestess and he a Roman slave. "Why do you ask?"

She spared him a shrug, a gentle motion that lifted the hair from her shoulders and made the auburn tresses spark beneath the light. "I just gathered from our rehearsal that you like to be in control. I thought maybe letting me take charge might not be... comfortable for you."

Control. Was it his imagination or did he detect a hint of resentment in her voice? She stretched her legs out on the coffee table and pointed her toes. She sipped her wine. Every gesture casual at first glance. Too casual.

Now here was a twist he hadn't expected.

⁂

Christopher was still puzzling over Paige's allusion to his need for control when they went to dinner. Despite her offhand demeanor, this was obviously an issue, and he mentally retraced the steps of their relationship, searching for a time he had incurred offense. No specific incident came to mind—if he didn't count chasing her through the years since the Academy.

"Please sit down." Goddard motioned to the exquisitely-laid table with a broad sweep of his hand, inviting them into the dining room. "You are my only guests this evening. I want to know how rehearsal went today."

It appeared he had gone through a great deal of trouble to impress them, and Christopher wondered if that generosity translated into approval with their performance.

"You two seem to be hitting it off very well." Goddard lifted his champagne flute in silent toast. "Like soul mates."

Had their performance been too convincing?

Christopher detected the suspicion in Goddard's voice, and his first impulse was to reassure. But something, perhaps Paige's earlier comment about control, made him hesitate, and she slipped into the void.

"I simply have to tell you, Mr. Goddard," she said. "I had my concerns when you first introduced me to Christopher. But after we began to work, I could see why you cast us together." She affected the right tone of feigned awe and humble embarrassment. "We just sort of . . . clicked."

Goddard bought it, and Christopher couldn't help but wonder how much Paige's lap dance had to do with it.

"Clicked? Tell me about it." His tone conveyed only marginal interest, but those hooded eyes roamed over her with the intensity of a laser.

Paige toyed with the edge of her napkin. "We have chemistry," she said simply. "It made all the difference in our performance."

"Good. Good. Some consider my method of rehearsing unconventional, but I've had great success with it." Goddard leaned back in his chair like a king perched on a throne. "I'm not looking for a crude parody of the sex act. Emotions make my films unique, make each couple unique. Conflict brings my movies to life."

"Unconventional or not, your method works." Paige laughed, a sultry sound, as if amused by the whole world. "I was certainly in for a few surprises—emotional and instinctual." She flipped on that feminine charm like a light switch, and Christopher gritted his teeth when their host took the bait.

"Surprises, Paige? Tell me." Resting his elbows on the table, Goddard leaned toward her, like they were two lovers alone in the candlelit room.

Christopher marveled at how quickly Paige turned around this potentially disastrous situation and wondered what Hoover's objection had been. Female agents certainly had a few more tools in their arsenal than their male counterparts.

She looked like an enchantress in a copper-colored sheath that shimmered around every luscious curve. And when she gifted Goddard with a smile, her pink tongue darted out to moisten her lower lip in a sensual display that made Christopher shift uncomfortably in the chair.

The gesture wasn't lost on Goddard, either. His Adam's apple bobbed the length of his throat. Christopher visualized ramming his fist into it.

"At first I thought Christopher was a bit… mature." Paige shook her head, sending a cascade of wild red waves tumbling over her shoulders. "But I was mistaken, Mr. Goddard, and commend your expertise in these matters."

Ouch! Christopher wanted to kick her under the table. Goddard stroked her hand, and a dagger of fury carved another notch in his composure.

"How could you know?" Goddard asked, that pitiful excuse for a mustache twitching like rabbit whiskers when he smiled. "Even though you have worked in my casino, I've been inattentive. But that's behind us now. We have a movie to make." He turned an inviting gaze on Christopher as if welcoming him into some bizarre kind of club.

Christopher forced a smile to his lips, slightly queasy at the look of almost desperate desire on Goddard's face. A vision of Goddard jerking off behind the dance studio mirror flashed in his mind, and for the first time in fifteen years, Christopher questioned all he had sacrificed for the bureau. Putting his life at risk was one thing, but this case went beyond the norm. Christopher had just been inducted by the secret society of voyeurs.

Spreading his arms in a magnanimous gesture that encompassed them both, Goddard said, "What matters now is your rehearsal. Without a solid foundation for your performance, I can't film. So as long as you are both pleased with each other…."

"The bear turned out to be a lion," Paige said with a suggestive half-smile, and Christopher swore he heard her growl.

Goddard laughed. "And you, Christopher?"

With his pride still stinging from Paige's reference to age, Christopher caught her hand and brought it to his lips. "While I'm grateful

I proved myself worthy, I never questioned the lady's talents. But I am interested in your expectations for the second vignette."

Goddard picked up his knife and sliced into the veal. "Submission, Christopher. Think submission."

⁂

"I wonder if he's still suspicious?" Paige asked in a low whisper as she circled the deserted pool.

Christopher felt a surge of male pride in her abilities. "You did a thorough job of turning him around."

"Hmm," was her only reply.

The moonlight silhouetted her graceful form against the black water, and with her head bowed as if in deep thought, she looked like a siren emerged from the deep. He wondered if she could sing.

The pool brought to mind the indoor spa in the west wing that would double as a mystical spring during their next rehearsal.

"Having second thoughts about tomorrow?"

"No." She glared up at him. Starlight caught her lashes and made them glint like embers. "But I think we should take the 'boss' up on his very generous offer of hospitality tonight."

Christopher knew what she was saying—they needed to get a lock on their position. "We're in Goddard's camp with no reconnainssance. I think we should—"

"—determine the security of the area," Paige informed him in a tone that might have intimidated a less experienced agent.

He was not a less experienced agent. But he did understand the necessity of working together and forced back a sharp reply to keep the peace. Besides, he had been about to suggest the same approach. He had trained Paige, after all.

"We need to decide how to get around the security," he said. "I want to determine the sequence and the timing of the sweeps. I know where the cameras are in the west wing, but we need to be able to move around the mansion."

"Let's just run with the porn star routine." She stopped in mid-stride and turned to face him, her skin fair beneath the starlight. "Everyone expects us to be rehearsing the script, so let's give them what they expect."

He fought the urge to run his fingers along her creamy cheek. "In English, please."

"Goddard wants us to get to know each other, right? So no one will notice if we're so busy getting to know each other that we turn up in places where we shouldn't be," she explained as if he was an imbecile.

Christopher scowled. "You want us to march through the halls groping each other? What the hell is that supposed to accomplish?"

"Not groping. Investigating." She shook her head emphatically. "We only grope if someone catches us." She lay a slender hand on his arm, and his blood quickened. "This'll work, Christopher. Trust me."

She gifted him with a smile that brought to mind her display of mind-boggling femininity at dinner. She had definitely calmed the beast there. "Let's give it a shot then, my dear."

With their arms wrapped around each other like new lovers, they marked every room as they toured the house. Goddard's offices surrounded an impressive foyer while his private rooms comprised the east wing with a magnificent view of the bluff. The security office and guest rooms were located in the rear of the house with the production studio in a separate building entirely, reminiscent of a larger scale lot back on the mainland.

Paige's technique was put to the test when they stumbled across a security guard. "Put your hand under my dress," she hissed as a door cracked open a few feet away.

She fell back against the wall. Christopher didn't have time to ask whether she meant underneath her hem or down the bodice before her lips locked onto his like a vice. His tongue met hers in an excited frenzy while he decided on the hem and a chance to cop a feel of her extraordinary ass.

His hand slid up her leg to discover thigh-high stockings and no panties. His fingers locked on to the satiny curve of her buttock just as a uniformed security guard stepped into the hallway.

"Oh." The guard came to an abrupt halt.

Paige pulled out of Christopher's arms. "Excuse us, officer," she gasped in her best bedroom voice, and the guard's chest puffed visibly at the way Paige stressed the title.

His roving gaze took in her every luscious inch as she smoothed the skimpy dress back into place. He apparently liked what he saw. Christopher could just imagine what was going through his mind, and his fingers itched to turn that leer into a toothless maw.

The guard didn't stand a chance when Paige turned those sultry blue eyes on him. "This is so embarrassing. Is it okay to be here?" She giggled. "Except I don't really know where 'here' is. Do you, Christopher?"

Christopher shook his head, but met the guard's gaze with a glare that clearly said "no trespassing."

"This is Mr. Goddard's shooting range, miss," the guard supplied with an indulgent smile before breezing past.

"He was only carrying a standard-issue," Paige whispered once the guard was out of earshot. "I bet the weapon room is inside."

That was Christopher's guess, too, but he couldn't seem to form the thought into words. His blood pounded. Straight to his crotch. It was no wonder Paige had managed this assignment. Not only did she have a quick mind and steely composure, if she ever got burned out on being an agent, she would make a helluva an actress.

But he didn't see that happening. One thing he had learned about Paige over the past twelve hours—she was a junkie for her work. She wouldn't forget Lewis Goddard until he sat in a cell. Christopher had suffered from the same addiction long enough to recognize the symptoms.

While persistence was one thing, the security office was another entirely. Manned by a single guard, the room boasted enough surveillance equipment to make even a federal agent envious. Nevertheless, it was going to be impossible to find out exactly which areas of the mansion and grounds were under observation without luring the guard out of the room—a guard who looked more like a profes-

sional power lifter than security personnel. Like nothing short of
an explosion would dislodge him from that chair.

Or a bomb named Paige.

She assessed the layout of the corridor with a practiced eye.
Slipping the slingback from her foot, she snapped the heel off with
one easy stroke, then gazed up at him with liquid eyes. "Darn, my
shoe broke."

Christopher frowned. Chalk another one up from her feminine
arsenal. "Think you can lure him out?"

"Can't say. He looks pretty hard core, but stay close just in case."
She leaned up on tiptoes and pressed a soft kiss to his cheek. "I need
evidence for trial. A film starring Shelby Moran."

She disappeared around the corner, leaving him standing there
with his jaw slack and his cheek tingling.

A sharp knock resonated through the corridor, and suddenly he
heard Paige say, "Excuse me, officer. I have a problem and wondered
if you could help."

Her voice faded, and Christopher inhaled deeply, trying to dispel
the effects of Paige's touch. The woman had a way of shooting his
composure straight to hell.

When she re-emerged five minutes later, the power lifter was by
her side with her shoe in his hand.

"We'll have to be fast. I can't be gone long."

"I really appreciate your help, Jerry."

The way she oozed the man's name made Christopher gnash his
teeth, but in seconds they had rounded the opposite corner and were
out of sight. Now was his chance.

A burst of adrenaline saw him sailing toward the room, pausing only to make certain no one watched him enter. The room was
a high-tech paradise. Monitors flashed images of the house on a
dozen screens while recording devices blipped and droned as images changed.

Lewis Goddard was a Peeping Tom of the finest water. But even
cutting-edge surveillance equipment could be avoided by knowing
when the cameras were sweeping and where.

Now Christopher did.

Paige had charged him with locating evidence for trial, and the two rooms adjoining the security office provided a bonanza. Within minutes, Christopher had completed his mission. And confirmed the arsenal was connected to the shooting range. And discovered safe zones in and around the house. Not bad for a few minutes of work.

Just as the muted sound of footsteps sounded around the corner, he slipped out of the room and headed back toward the west wing.

"Christopher, is that you?" Paige chimed out after he pulled the door closed. "I'm in the bedroom."

He found her in the closet. "As long as you're here," she said, "would you mind giving me an opinion on this outfit I'm wearing for rehearsal tomorrow. Is it Celtic priestess enough?"

"Will you model it for me?"

"Maybe."

She greeted him with a delighted smile. She was half-dressed and beaming and obviously no worse for the wear. The tension ebbed from him in a rush. Christopher hadn't realized it, but he had been worried about her.

"How'd it go?"

Unable to drag his gaze from the copper sheath slipping from her shoulders and journeying down every slender curve, he fumbled to free the video cassette from his waistband. "Is this what you're looking for?"

She took the tape, eyes darting from the videocassette back to his face. Satisfaction surged through him when delight wreathed her features.

"This is it! Will he miss it?"

"Not unless we're profoundly unlucky. He keeps the films in a room adjoining security. I left a bogus in its place."

He had recognized the names on the tape. Paige's witness and her murdered co-star. "So what's next?"

"I want to access his computer. But first, I've got to conceal this somewhere secure." She gave a short laugh. "As if there's any safe place on this island."

He was inclined to agree, but could not form the thought into words before she slipped the sheath down from her hips and stood before him clad in only a black bra so sheer he could see the outline of her nipples. And thigh-high stockings. She didn't wear any panties, he knew, and his gaze dropped to the fringe of auburn hair between her legs where he'd spent such a delightful time earlier.

He swallowed hard. Technically, he'd seen her in less, but his blood was already pumping.

"I can't believe you got him to leave his post," Christopher commented in an effort to distract himself. He unbuttoned his shirt and found his fingers stiff and uncooperative.

She slipped off her shoe and winked. "Works every time."

"Yeah, but—"

"Unfortunately—or fortunately in our case—a great deal of men don't take women seriously." She pursed her lips in a flirty pout. "I can usually pass without being seen as much of a threat."

Paige was a threat. Maybe Goddard and his men were too stupid to realize it, but she was certainly wreaking havoc on his peace of mind. She slipped the video cassette into the thigh-high hem of her stocking and pulled a leaf green negligee around her.

"Is this Celtic priestess enough?"

He nodded, fighting an overwhelming urge to drag her down to the floor and make love to her. "Listen, Paige," he said, determined to get the information out before he made a complete ass of himself. "The sequences are rotating every four minutes. The cameras linked to the west wing are turned off, so I figure Goddard is monitoring privately." She had unfastened her bra and slipped it through the sleeves of her negligee. The sight of her breasts swaying beneath the silk even more erotic than if she'd just removed the bra in plain view. He bit back a groan.

"That will give us an edge in finding a way off this island."

Christopher should say something, but no reply came to mind. He shrugged off his shirt instead.

"I'm going to hide this in the bathroom." Her gaze trailed to his bare chest, and a slow smile curved her lips. "Behind the tank, I think."

"Good idea."

"Thank you." She reached up on tiptoes and pressed a kiss to his mouth before brushing past and leaving him alone in the closet. A flush of pleasure stole through his cheeks, and he whispered after her, "No problem."

The Tables Turn

The indoor spa where they would perform the second vignette boasted a pool, a Jacuzzi and a resident priestess named Paige. Christopher found her swimming and paused in the entry to enjoy the view.

Red hair billowed around her like a silken cloud, flowing outward as she glided through the water. His first impulse was to dive in and find out for himself if she was really as naked as she appeared, but he checked the urge, reminded of her concerns about his ability to relinquish control.

The script called for him to submit, and he had every intention of doing so. But the idea of becoming a sex slave to a woman who held a grudge made his gut clench tight as a fist.

Somehow he had misread the warning signs at the Academy. Their battle of wills had been part of his initial attraction to Paige, but the parameters of their relationship had been clearly defined.

He was in charge.

But Paige was a leader, too, and while he had recognized that, he had handled her like all his other students, not like a leader in training.

Now she was a seasoned agent with a grudge. He could tell by the way she emerged from the water, dripping, the glint in her eyes promising retribution.

Hindsight was a bitch.

The bikini she wore barely deserved the name—the sheer triangles were a color remarkably similar to her skin, and he could see right through them to her lush ruby nipples and auburn mons.

Drying herself in long gliding strokes, she lifted one leg then the other, revealing tantalizing glimpses of that dewy juncture between her thighs.

Great. Another show.

Dropping the towel, she slipped into a sheer silk negligee that molded her slender curves like a leafy green veil. He could barely draw a breath.

She motioned him to a lounge chair with a seductive smile. "Care to join me?" She might as well have asked, "Any last words?"

He groaned aloud.

"This control thing is going to be an issue, isn't it?" She looked delighted by the prospect.

He sat down but couldn't seem to bend the steel rod that had taken up residence in his spine. "Not at all. I have a good idea of how to play this from the script." He would behave like a vanquished Roman slave and let the conqueror take his body. It was just a matter of...submission.

Goddard's command echoed in his head and must have been reflected in his face because Paige smiled and said, "Liar."

He shrugged. "I know my job."

"That's good. Slave." She kneeled on the chair beside him and unbuttoned his shirt, starting at the collar and working her way down toward his waist. "Now submit."

As her fingertips trailed along his bare chest, any thoughts of resistance splintered.

"Mr. Goddard has been very specific about how he wants this scene performed," her whisper gusted along that sensitive area between his neck and shoulder.

"I understand what he wants."

Paige pulled the shirt from his arms and tossed it into a heap on the floor. Sliding from the lounge chair, she knelt before him. "Good. Then you know what I want, too."

Vengeance. That's what this was all about.

The top of her head ended at the middle of his chest, and he stared down at the rich sweep of auburn with a mixture of excitement and dread. Her fresh herbal scent assaulted his senses, filled his mind with hot images of what it would feel like to plunge deep inside her, to stop playing these games and just make love to her. Without a script. Without an audience.

Her fingers slid into his waistband. "Stand up," she commanded in a throaty whisper.

Christopher obeyed. She tugged the drawstring pants down his legs, and he stepped out of them. Suddenly the humid air of the spa felt cloying, heavy.

Her gaze locked onto his purposefully, and she ran her hand the length of his semi-erect cock. Christopher shuddered.

"You're so stiff."

He got even stiffer and struggled to stand still as her hands glided upward over his stomach then circled around to his buttocks, her fingers exploring every inch of skin along the way.

"Way too stiff," she admonished, moist lips forming a petulant little moue. "Lie down, and I'll give you a massage."

He sank down into the cushions with a groan. Anything to put some distance between them.

But distance wasn't part of the script, and Christopher barely had time to draw a deep breath before Paige returned with a bottle from a nearby shelf and knelt beside him. After brushing his ponytail aside, she applied a palmful of warm liquid to his shoulders.

She was more skilled than he would have imagined. Working her hands in deep circular sweeps, she isolated each muscle and dissolved the tension that had mounted since awakening this morning. Her fingers probed the corded length of his neck and caressed the line of his jaw.

"How does this feel?" she asked, her question a breathy whisper against his ear.

"Mmm," was all he could manage.

While his mind worked just fine, control of his body seemed to be leaving in a hurry. He had to stay on his guard. Goddard lurked at the other end of a surveillance camera, and Paige herself had a less than trustworthy gleam in her eyes. Yet despite his best efforts, the jets from the spa and the rhythmic bubbling of the pool filter lulled him into a state of quasi-awareness. He closed his eyes and surrendered to the smooth strokes of her hands, to the languor flowing like a hot tide through his body.

Her hands traveled the length of his spine, swirling off in little side trips to massage the muscles of his back. Her touch was deep and even, and he gradually became aware of the subtle difference in the way she moved. Only her hands had been a presence before, but now he could feel the warmth of her body as she swayed close. The negligee whispered against him, and he imagined what tantalizing part of her lay below the diaphanous fabric. Her thighs. Her hips. Her breasts.

"You've got the most wonderful ass," she told him, penetrating the fog that rendered him immobile. "I like to touch you here." Her palms slid over his buttocks, and she massaged the lotion into his skin with strong strokes.

Her throaty murmur made desire spiral through the spell of relaxation she wove over him. Veiled skin brushed against him. Her thigh. "And here." Her finger traced the outline of his cleft, parting that sensitive skin just the barest amount.

His body shuddered in response to the intimacy of her touch, and she dipped low over him, pressing against his buttocks. Breasts definitely.

Continuing her journey down his legs, her fingers sailed along his calves, and he thanked whoever wrote the script when she lavished attention on his feet.

"Turn over."

Easier said than done. His muscles had turned to molten lava and moved about as well. With a supreme effort of will that half dragged him from his stupor, he managed. Only now there was no disguising the effect she had on him. The true extent of his desire displayed itself with all the subtlety of a lighthouse.

Paige noticed. A smile tipped the corners of those luscious lips. "I'm glad you're enjoying my massage."

Her gaze melted along his body, and he felt his nakedness as keenly as her amusement. She was enjoying this game much too much for peace of mind. So was he. Slavery didn't feel quite so repulsive with a beautiful woman paying homage to his body.

She rose above him in a graceful motion and straddled his hips. The breath caught in his throat as her thighs trapped him in a velvet vice while she poured more liquid into her palm and began a slow, swirling assault on his senses.

The filmy drape that covered her taunted him with glimpses of the slim curves below, making him itch to drag her full length against him. He checked the urge. This was her game. Goddard's game. He wouldn't give them the satisfaction of losing control.

He would submit if it killed him.

It just might. Only Paige had the ability to shatter his discipline and splinter any thoughts of restraint. She was a siren luring him into a spell, promising him pleasure only she could provide.

His control slipped a little more.

Her hips began a sinuous glide along the length of his erection. Her own heat radiated through the sheer veil that separated them, spurring the flood inside into a downpour. His hips ground against her in purely instinctual need, and he fought the undertow of desire that threatened to drag him away.

Her mouth branded a trail along his shoulder, the pressure of her hips growing more insistent as she moistened the nubby skin around his nipple with a slow stroke of her tongue. Her lips pursed sensuously, and a puff of warm breath cascaded over him.

"No matter how much you want me, Christopher, you can't lose control. Your only thought is to please me, and it pleases me to watch you surrender."

He should say something to diffuse her power, something to temper the edge of superiority from her voice, but speech was quite beyond him at the moment.

He tried not to thrust against her when she slid down his body, the soft fullness of her breasts surrounding his erection. He exhaled in a sound that was neither gasp nor groan, and his hands slipped around her of their own accord.

"I didn't give you permission to touch me," she warned, teeth locking onto the tender skin of a nipple and stopping him short.

Submission.

His hands dropped to his sides, aching to touch her, not daring.

Paige had been right—giving up control did not come easily. He liked the power of command, and if he hadn't realized it before, he was quickly discovering how that need transcended his job and extended into other areas of his life.

Especially sex.

Where Paige had once been the student and he the teacher, the tables had turned. Today's lesson was about relinquishing control.

And his one transgression cost much. With a wicked glint in her eyes, Paige set out to prove how easily he would fail. With what was left of his will, Christopher vowed to resist. He tucked his hands beneath him as she fitted her long body between his legs until her face was level with his cock.

"You are my slave now, Christopher." Her voice was deceptively gentle, but the hand that cupped his balls was firm, out to prove a point. "You are not permitted to lose control. Not until I say."

When she laughed, a chiming sound that made his blood boil, his heart forged in his chest. She never even glanced up, just kept her gaze locked on his traitorous cock as it swelled and jumped beneath her touch.

"He likes me." Her hand ran the length of his shaft to emphasize the words. "And you know what? I like him too." She pressed a soft kiss to the tip, and his hips bucked sharply in reply.

Christopher closed his eyes, could do nothing else. The sound of her voice, deep with desire, carried him away on the edge of a fantasy as her mouth and fingers played a tantalizing game with his body.

"He is beautiful." Her tongue circled the head in a slow glide, her warm breath pulsing against his sensitive skin in airy bursts. "I never dreamed you had him hidden away. He's so smooth." She traced the outline of a vein with a light brush of her fingertip. "Like hot satin. And so thick." Her hand caressed the full length of him. "And so very long."

Christopher's eyes flew open, and he bit down hard to keep from yelling out.

Paige stroked him until a pearlized drop appeared at the head. She brushed away the moisture with her mouth, and when she finally met his gaze, it was with her long red hair tumbling across his thighs and his come gleaming on those luscious lips.

He was going to die. A maelstrom surged through his body, his blood mounting in a familiar torrent that was going to hurl him over the edge and send him crashing into a thousand pieces.

Until Paige clamped her hand around him, effectively cutting off the sensation and making him arch against her in frustration.

"Come, slave." She slid off the lounge chair and out of reach before he even caught his breath. "Let's get in the pool. Looks like you could use some cooling off."

"Arrgh!" He was going to strangle her. Just as soon as he could move again. He could barely sit up, let alone walk, and it didn't really matter because she was already gone, way out of reach.

Covering the distance to the pool in a few graceful strides, she unfastened the negligee and let it slip from her shoulders. The breath he had fought so hard to draw locked in his throat at the sight. His gaze fixed on her breasts, lush nipples outlined through sheer fabric, beckoning him, making him tingle with the memory of how his cock had felt buried between them. How her long, firm body had felt draped across his.

She was an earthy, natural beauty. A born Celtic queen with her high firm breasts, the slender arch of her waist yielding to a graceful sweep of hips. And her legs. Those incredibly long legs made him yearn to sink between them, feel them lock around his neck and pull him toward her hot wet sex....

This was torture in its purest form. His knees were weak as he tried to stand and his temper justifiably blistering when he thought of Goddard and his video monitor enjoying the sight of her beautiful body, watching their intimate game.

Temper diverted him from his own agony enough to make it to his feet, but the cold hard facts of their situation were nothing short of depressing. This was no way to begin a relationship, and there was no doubt in his mind a relationship was happening between them. What he felt was so much more than work, so much more than sex. Paige must surely feel it, too. And if she didn't, well, there was still enough time to convince her.

If he survived this damned rehearsal. Which was unlikely, he decided, as he watched Paige enter the pool. One lingering step at a time. Gifting him with several breathless moments to appreciate every liquid curve of her body before the water swallowed her up.

She paused at the bottom step, water lapping around her waist, full curves of her breasts showcased as she lifted her arms and shook out that glorious mane of hair.

"Think sacred spring. Very cold spring." She shivered, nipples gathering to erect peaks through the flesh-colored fabric. Christopher found his spirits rising at the thought of her own torture.

"If you can catch me, slave, I'll reward you with a kiss."

The challenge in her voice propelled him over the edge. He dove into the opposite end of the pool, the shock of cold water dousing the flame in his groin to a more tolerable level. With long hard strokes designed to shake off his excitement, he swam across the pool, but when he emerged, lungs bursting and body tight with tension, Paige had already begun her flight. She led him a merry chase through the water, pale glimpses of her legs beckoning just beyond reach as she swam ahead like a mermaid.

"Catch me, slave," she dared, and he could not resist her challenge even though the game only whetted his barely-controlled appetite. The contrast of cold water to the heat of his arousal incited a hunger deeper than anything he had ever known. The desire to catch her, to master her, consumed him until his single thought was no more than the need to feel her wrapped around him, to sink deep inside her and wring one draining climax after another from her body. Hunger fueled his strokes until Paige's quick, darting movements through the water could no longer evade him.

He captured her by the stairs.

"Reward me," he said, body throbbing with unfulfilled need.

She writhed against him in an erotic dance, her laughter ringing in his ears. She almost escaped. But the game was wearing on him, so he pressed her back into the handrail and used his body as anchor.

Instead of resisting, she arched sinuously, letting the buoyancy of the water lift her until she clamped her thighs around his cock. The moist suction coaxed him back to full hardness and cost him whatever advantage the cold swim had gained.

Her hands glided around his waist, upward along his back, sending trails of pleasure in their wake. She smoothed the dripping hairs from his face and gazed at him with a sultry smile. "A kiss. Isn't that what I promised?"

Her mouth latched onto his, devouring him, spiking a need so sharp he could only groan against those luscious lips and hang onto the handrail for balance.

She molded into the curve of his body, breasts swelling against his chest. He thrust his tongue into her mouth, unable to resist no matter what the script said.

"You are a bad slave." She tried to pull away.

"I'm not bad," he ground out against her lips. "I just haven't gotten the hang of this yet." It was suddenly important that she know he could.

"I don't know," she whispered, abandoning resistance as her tongue traced his teeth and her legs slithered along his. She locked them around his waist, poising herself open and ready above his sex. "All you want is control." She ground herself against him, teasing him ruthlessly.

Control was nothing more than an illusion and what she asked was beyond his ability. She wanted submission, and he cursed his job, his own need to be in charge and most of all this damned script that seemed to anticipate just how to push him to the edge.

"Paige... ." His words came out a thready whisper, and his cock surged against her in a blind need for fulfillment.

"What, slave?" She laughed against his mouth, sucking on his lower lip, her arms tightening around him when he tried to back away. "You want more practice?" Her hips rolled against him, driving down another glorious, agonizing inch. "Resist me."

To hell with the script!

A bolt of pleasure impaled him, and all his good intentions fled on a wave of need so strong he could do nothing but submit to instinct. His hand slid from the rail, the water cushioning them as he fell back against the wall, and drove inside her in one thrust.

Paige gasped aloud in a strangled sound that afforded him no small amount of satisfaction. She arched back wildly and grabbed the handrail for purchase. He used her position to his advantage and pounded into her again. And again. His hands slipped down to grasp her buttocks and pull her closer.

But letting go of the handrail had been a mistake. Suddenly she was free, lifting off him, and before her escape even registered in his brain, he was alone again, aching...

"Damn it!" He lunged for her.

Paige realized her miscalculation by the time she reached the lounge chair. Like a dripping giant, Christopher loomed above her, teeth clamped, droplets of water spraying off him as he wrestled her onto her back. She struggled, fighting him in a fashion that wouldn't alert Goddard to her physical training. But without her defense skills, levering him off was impossible. He was far too strong. Far too gone.

"Slave, you could die for this offense," she said, hoping to jolt him back to sanity with a reminder that one of them was scheduled to die in the final scene of the script.

His eyes widened, and sanity returned on the edge of a breath. He paused long enough for her to caress his cheek and promise, "Unless I give you permission." She lifted her lips to his. "Why don't you kiss me now. Touch me."

Suspicion honed his features to a sharp edge, and she seized the moment to spread her legs and prove herself. He drew a sharp breath, and his powerful hips sank between her thighs. His mouth dipped slowly toward hers.

Wrapping her arms around his neck, Paige lifted her lips to his, feeling the trap just as surely as he did. What was this feeling… this turmoil? She had started out wanting to drive him crazy, to shatter his iron control, but now all she could think about was making love. Feeling that magnificent erection pulse deep inside her.

The warm weight of his body pressed her into the cushions, spiking desire into a stab of longing so fierce, she could only surrender. She recognized the feeling, the rush of excitement that drove away reason, good judgment and common sense—everything except what was happening between them. Except the reality that Goddard was watching and there really was no choice.

Giving in to the sensation, she explored every hollow and ridge of Christopher's strong back, his waist, his buttocks, and they kissed slowly, deeply, desire melding them together like two halves of a whole.

She had never wanted like this before. Shouldn't want a man who could dominate her so completely. She lost herself to him, irrevocably, irretrievably. But how could she resist?

She couldn't. Not when Christopher arched above her, tasting her breast with soft nips and bites. She sighed, knowing they were caught up in the performance just as surely as Goddard was, not caring. Nothing mattered but the feel of his wet body and the hand that traveled a fiery path along her waist, rounded the curve of her hip. She arched against him, the moan that slid from her lips involuntary.

Taking his erection in hand, Christopher rubbed the head against her sensitive opening, mimicking the tactics she had used on him in the pool.

"What do you want?"

That he could even ask the question amazed her. Gazing into his face, she was touched by the frown that creased his brow, by the strands of wet hair clinging to his skin, but it was the mixture of resentment and vulnerability in his expression that captured her heart, the effort she saw in those deep chocolate eyes that told her how much he struggled to play this game.

Desire warred inside, confusion eddying like a torrent, eroding her will, yet at the same time strengthening her resolve. He still didn't understand how much she feared his domination. She hadn't understood herself until this instant. She would not be trapped by a man who wielded such power over her—the power to make her lose herself in him.

She needed to run, to regroup, but Goddard's script demanded she give herself to Christopher.

Her body. Not her soul.

Even if they had sex, she would use her professional training to detach, to keep her emotional distance and shield her heart from this man.

"Pleasure me, slave."

As his hands clamped around her hips and pulled her hungrily toward him, Paige realized distance was only an illusion.

"God, I am so hot for you," he ground out, filling her in one endless glide, pressing her into the cushions. She shuddered at the strength of his thrust, body throbbing as he rammed into her, hips rolling, drawing his thick heat even deeper.

"Oooh, yes." She threaded her hands into his hair and dragged his face toward hers as emotional distance crumbled.

Everything but the wine-sweet taste of his mouth faded away. She nibbled his lips in erotic bites, tongue plunging into his mouth while his powerful body melded with hers and proved they were meant to be together.

As equals.

"Roll over," she whispered, hands gliding over his muscled chest, urging him to comply.

He scowled. "I suppose a slave has no choice."

"No choice at all."

He obeyed.

Scooping her against him, he carried her over in one strong motion, never letting their bodies break contact as he settled back into the cushions.

"Mmm. You obey well." His submission excited her. Arching her back, she rose above him, reveling in her new position of power and taking stock of the man who lay spread out beneath her. Inside her.

God, he was gorgeous.

His tanned chest and broad shoulders spanned the width of the chair. Long golden strands of unbound hair wrapped around his neck. His skin gleamed from the water that dripped off her hair as she swayed above him, withdrawing almost full length, then driving down onto his thick shaft in one sleek stroke.

He rocked against her, and a moan slid from his lips. His hands cruised along her waist and cupped her breasts, rolling the nipples until she cried out. The time for control was past.

Throwing back her head, she rode him, urgency spurring long slick glides into frenzied thrusts. The sounds of their passion resonated through the liquid stillness of the spa. Resounded along every nerve ending in her heated body. Christopher was hers.

His hands slid from her breasts, twining into her hair, resisting her movements. "Paige, enough," he gasped. "I'm so hot...I won't last—"

She laughed, a throaty sound that echoed her pleasure. "You do what I say, slave." She drove down on him to accentuate her point. "And I say...now."

Reality came crashing down as his gaze locked onto hers, his eyes glowing with an intensity that pitched her over the edge. She drowned in the need she saw there, the understanding that he wanted her—enough to bend his iron will to please her.

She had asked for control, and he would give it. His shoulders tensed, and the set of his mouth grew determined. And though she knew he wanted to turn the tables and command the moment as his, he would yield to her desire.

She desired him now—and took him with deep eager strokes that melted what was left of restraint.

Nothing mattered beyond the ecstasy that gripped her, pulsing like a molten wave with every heartbeat, and that Christopher came with her, unbridled and unbidden, his low growl of release thundering through the room like a lion's roar.

Submission was not in the same category as defeat, but Paige wouldn't have known it by the way Christopher was acting. "I don't want to make the orgasm sounds," she hissed beneath her breath. "You make them."

Their gazes locked. An ocean breeze tossed stray hairs around his face, making the strands glint like gold in the porch light. "I can't hack into his computer, moan and thrash wildly at the same time."

Halting at the top of the portico, she faced him, not ready to enter the house where they would be picked up on audio. "I still don't understand why you get to hack into his system." She sounded like a sulky child and didn't care.

"I'll get past his security codes quicker." If he could have clamped her head between his jaws and bit it off, he would have. "Now stop arguing and help me figure out how to get past the surveillance camera."

"My, my. Someone's got quite a case of the grumpies," she pointed out, knowing she shouldn't tease him, but unable to resist. "Didn't the sex agree with you?"

The tiny gold flecks in his eyes glowed beneath the lanterns flanking both sides of the door, and she felt that familiar swooping sensation in her belly.

"The sex agreed with me just fine."

Humph! The man didn't do submission very well. No surprise there. "I suppose we could hang onto each other and act as if we're looking for a place to screw," she suggested, yielding the first inch. "The camera only covers the doorway. Once we're inside we'll be out of range."

"As long as you make enough noise to hide the sounds of me clicking away at the keyboard."

"All right." She sighed and grasped the door handle. "I'll make the orgasm sounds."

It was the least she could do after watching him struggle through dinner. Goddard had shot questions at them all during the meal.

Such intimate questions that if she hadn't already known he had been watching, she would have suspected.

But Christopher had born the brunt of Goddard's inquisition by being forced to explain—in graphic detail—just how it felt to be taken. A fact that hadn't sweetened his disposition. She would have mercy on him. This time.

They crossed the foyer in a few quick strides.

"All right, Christopher. All right," she said loudly for the benefit of Jerry the security man on the opposite end of the camera. "I'm horny, too. Come on, it doesn't look like anyone's in here." She cracked open the office door and began unbuttoning her blouse as they passed through the camera's range.

Christopher closed the door behind them and looked around. "This will work, babe. I'll do you right on the desk."

Facing him in sultry invitation, she simpered, "Oh, yes. Do me right here."

Christopher smiled for the first time all night.

After a few minutes, Paige fell into sort of an erotic tempo: breathless gasp, throaty moan, strangled whimper, satisfied sigh. Christopher occasionally piped in with a grunt and groan to add to the authenticity of their performance and cover up the assorted blips and beeps of the computer.

He looked supremely amused, as though her debasement was divine justice for the way she had ordered him around today. Paige only smiled, determined to maintain her dignity, and moaned louder.

"Oh, yes, Christopher. Right there. Mmm, that feels good." She enjoyed a brief moment of triumph as he struggled visibly not to laugh aloud.

But he got his revenge by taking forever to download the files she needed onto a disk. Her throat ached. The sounds of her own moans echoed in her head like some catchy tune stuck in playback.

She could have hacked into Goddard's files faster than this, and Jerry the security guard could have masturbated himself to orgasm two, maybe three times by now.

Suddenly the light below the doorway flickered. She spun toward Christopher and signaled him with a nod. Smashing his palm against the surge board, he shut down the entire system and stuffed the disk in his sock.

The key rattled in the lock. Paige flipped herself over the desk, hoisted her skirt up and pointed her bare bottom at him. "Quick," she whispered. "Pretend you're doing something."

"Your wish, my dear." Christopher rounded the desk and came to stand behind her just as the door cracked open.

Jerry got what he thought was quite an eyeful before backing out of the room. "Would you mind taking it back to the west wing."

"No problem." Christopher tightened his grip on her hips and rubbed what was turning into a prime erection against her bottom. "God, I can't get enough of you."

Paige should be flattered, but somehow he just didn't sound pleased.

Paybacks are...

The final scene of the script. The Medieval chieftain vignette where she or Christopher would die during filming. As far as Paige was concerned, it didn't take a rocket scientist to figure out who. While her character seemed the obvious choice, her money was on the maiden slitting the chieftain's throat in a surprise plot twist.

But this was only a rehearsal, and she had no intention of sticking around for filming. She had the evidence she needed and would have been out of here last night if Goddard hadn't sent his personal powerboat back to the mainland. She wanted to avoid this last rehearsal so much she had been tempted to take another boat. But that would have been pure insanity. Goddard's security had state of the art powerboats that she and Christopher couldn't get near.

If they were going to leave, it would have to be on a boat just as powerful, and that meant Goddard's. Hopefully it would be back on the island by nightfall. But until then there was this barbaric little scene to deal with. And one undercover agent who had been in a very foul mood for the past twenty-four hours—ever since she had taken him against his will during the Celtic priestess vignette.

The door slammed shut with such ominous finality that Paige cringed. She was not looking forward to this. Christopher stalked across their suite like a wild animal, the hard lines etched around his mouth lending him a feral look. Unbound, his hair fell to his shoulders and accentuated his rugged features so that even civilized clothing didn't tame his appearance.

Medieval chieftain, definitely.

Perhaps she had been a bit short-sighted to make jokes last night in the office.

"Lay down, Paige. Supine." His command bolted through the air like a gunshot.

She skittered toward the bed without argument. Not so much in response to the steely threat as to clear out of his oncoming path. But in a move reminiscent of how deftly he had taught her to fight at the Academy, Christopher pounced on her, seized both her wrists in a stranglehold the instant she came down on the mattress.

He ripped the front of her dress in one clean stroke. Buttons flew in all directions, bouncing off his chest and scattering onto the bed, even pelting her on the cheek. The dress parted, hanging by only two thin straps and baring her to his gaze.

"What in hell are you doing?" She stared into the hard lines of his face, recognizing his need to dominate. Her heart throbbed in time with her pulse.

With the advantage of strength on his side, Christopher flipped her easily. She fought back, twisting wildly and trying to break his hold. He just laughed and sat on her thighs, loosening his grip only long enough to free her from the sundress.

"Are you crazy?" she yelled, feet scrambling against the satin comforter for purchase while she tried to buck him off. He jerked her arms over her head so roughly that she cried out.

"No. Horny." Silken ropes threaded her wrists, and Christopher ignored her struggles and imprisoned her to a notch on the headboard. "Didn't your mother ever tell you paybacks are a real bitch?"

Surprise squeezed the air from her lungs. He couldn't restrain her. Not with Goddard watching. It was a terrible risk. If Goddard decided to take advantage of the moment, she would be at his mercy. Was at Christopher's mercy.

She was in deep trouble.

"Christopher, please..." the plea lodged in her throat as he wrapped his hand in her hair and lifted her head until she could see him.

"Now it's your turn to submit, Paige." He loomed above with a hard smile. "I'm the Medieval warlord. You are the captive." He gestured around him with a large hand. "And this is my castle. You are mine. No one will come to your rescue." Despite the almost overwhelming urge to fight him, anxiety, or perhaps anticipation, sent a frisson zipping through her.

Especially when he loosened his hold, brought his knees around her waist and hunched over her. His hair fell across her cheek. His mouth brushed her ear, and he said in a voice as low and thick as cashmere, "Now spread your legs before I tie them, too."

A ripple of erotic excitement shimmered like a hot breath along her skin when his hand slipped between her thighs and urged her compliance.

She wanted to resist but knew by the coiled strength of his movements, the fury radiating off him, that she would be far better off conceding this battle. She hesitated only an instant before letting her legs fall apart.

He laughed, a triumphant sound that made her gnash her teeth. He was going to make her pay. And with her arms bound to this bed, there wasn't a damn thing she could do about it. She had unwittingly helped him, in fact, by dressing to entice, to brandish her sensual power like a sword.

A double edged one, she realized a bit too late.

Had she dressed like a Quaker, she would not be lying here now with a bare bottom and thigh-high stockings, her pretty pink sundress laying forgotten on the floor.

Sliding off her, Christopher came to his feet and stripped, never once taking his eyes from her until he was naked. Bold. Powerful.

Twinges of appreciation trembled deep inside. God, just the sight of him made the blood rush in her ears. That warrior's grace and size made him move with the supple savagery of a cat. Every muscle limber. Every movement predatory. His very fierceness excited her, and she couldn't help but wonder what it would be like to have the freedom of exploring that beautiful body at her leisure. To wake up beside him every morning. To become a part of his life.

There was a whole lot more at stake here than her pride—somehow her heart had gotten caught up in the game. Christopher had all the control—again. And his smile told her he planned to use it.

She twisted away.

"Resistance, Paige." His laughter filled her senses, spurred her will to resist. "There's nowhere to hide."

That was beside the point. She wasn't going down without a fight.

"Damn you," she hissed and scrabbled away when he sat down on the edge of the bed, eyeing her in calm amusement.

"Submission isn't so easy when you're the one submitting, is it?" He arched a tawny brow. "What do you think?"

"Arrgh!" Her toes touched the carpeted floor. Her arms were about to break and her upper body wasn't budging, but she still fought. Fought the control he had over her. Fought the impulse to submit.

"This doesn't have to be difficult, Paige. Just admit you want me—that you've always wanted me—and I'll let you go."

Yeah, right. Leave her heart bleeding on the bedspread. She saw that happening sometime before hell froze over. "Don't hold your breath."

Christopher shook his head in mock sadness. "That was my one and only offer."

He lunged. His hand clamped around her knee and dragged her back onto the bed.

"Get your hands off me, you... animal."

He cast her a roguish grin. "Animal, is it?" His hand seared a path up her thigh, rounding the curve of her bottom and stoking the spark deep inside.

"Fuck you, Christopher."

"No, Paige. I'm going to fuck you."

She gritted her teeth against a moan, refusing to give him the satisfaction of a response.

Those gold-flecked eyes glowed. Her refusal only steeled his determination. "Guess I'll have to move on to alternate plan B."

Premeditated revenge. The man was a maniac. Burying her face in the pillow to hide from the sound of his laughter, she quickly discovered plan B was going to be much harder to resist.

Suddenly his mouth was on her skin, strong hands lifting her hips upward, lips and tongue making her writhe against a bolt of pleasure so strong she could not defend herself long in the face of such an erotic assault.

"Still resisting?" His breath breezed in hot bursts along her bottom, and she emitted the most pathetic whimper when he forced her to submit to the series of love bites that jolted every nerve in her body.

She was drowning in sensation, drowning in him. He knew how to unleash this urgency inside her, to make her need him as surely as she needed air to breath. On some level she had known all along, had run from him, fought him. But he had her now. There was no escape.

His mouth trailed up her hip and along her waist. His powerful body covered hers, cradled her possessively, pressed her shoulders into the mattress and left her bottom bare to his touch.

Her arms were going to break. Her neck was already numb, or so she thought. Until he buried his face in her hair.

"You've been a bitch, Paige." His accusation blasted hot against her ear, sending electric tendrils thundering through her. "And now you're going to pay." His hand dipped between her legs.

The breath locked in her lungs. Submission. He wanted her to lose control like he had. And as his thumb centered on that tiny pebble of desire and massaged it with spiraling strokes, Paige knew she would.

"I'm not nearly as selfish as you," he assured her. "I'm not going to tease you. That was your game. I want to feel you respond to my touch, hear you beg me to take you, convince you that no one can make you want like I do."

Her only response was a low moan as his finger slipped deep inside.

"You like that." His words were a statement because no question existed.

Feeling her own moisture surround him as his finger glided in and out, she resisted the urge to arch into his touch and clamped her lips shut against the plea for him to take her. She knew his game and was powerless to resist. He would not stop until she faced the jagged reality of her desire.

One finger suddenly became two, thrusting deep inside, and Paige writhed beneath him, helpless against the onslaught of sensation. Arousal soared through her, lifting her higher and higher until a shudder of the purest pleasure rocked her very soul, and she gasped aloud.

"Feels good doesn't it?"

She burrowed her head in the pillows, willing to asphyxiate if she could just escape the masculine triumph in his voice.

"Don't bother to deny it. You're body tells me everything I need to know." He dug his fingers in a little deeper to prove the point.

A strangled moan slipped from her lips as another stab of pleasure pierced the fading echoes of her climax. With a laugh, he withdrew. Paige sucked in deep gulps of air when he lifted off her.

Christopher leaned over the edge of the bed, and she heard the rustle of clothing as he rifled through his pockets. "I'm sure a tactical blade would be much more impressive, but the first rule of scouting is to utilize what's at hand."

Paige felt the small blade against her skin before she actually saw it. Craning her neck, she caught a glimpse of a Swiss Army knife.

"I don't suppose an apology would do it," she asked, surprised by the catch in her voice. By her excitement.

"Afraid not, my dear. Had your chance." He cut her bra with precise strokes. The pink silk shredded easily and fell away. "Now I want my pound of flesh. Literally."

His erection fitted between her legs, hard, probing, while his hands circled her, cupping her breasts in his palms. He tugged at her nipples, twisting, pulling, until passion mounted again, and she arced back, unable to resist his insistent pressure against her.

"You're going to... torture me." Of course he would. As far as he was concerned, it would be no less than she deserved.

"Not torture, Paige, pleasure." His throaty voice revealed his own excitement. "I want you to admit what is happening between us."

What was happening between them? It was much more than sex.

Christopher was ruthless enough to throw the truth in her face. He had known all along what she was now only realizing—their power struggle was only the result of feelings between them. Feelings she had denied since the Academy.

Paige couldn't deny any longer.

Even now the tangle of emotion unraveled inside, obliterated protest and reason. She wanted to indulge her feelings, indulge her desires. Control didn't matter when he touched her like this, invaded her senses and make her feel... wanted.

But Christopher would accept nothing less than her complete surrender. Determination steeled his touch, fueled his battle for dominance.

"Christopher... ." His name came out a plea, but Paige no longer cared.

"Tell me what you want, Paige. I want to hear you say it." The smooth head of his erection nudged her, stretched her, urged her to give up the fight.

"I want you... inside me," she rasped, wanting him more than she had ever wanted anything. "Now."

With a low roar that conveyed just how tenuous his own restraint had been, he rammed inside her with one forceful stroke.

Long-denied passion ignited as their bodies came together. Paige had known... had feared her response to him, knowing that the instant Christopher caught her she would be powerless to hold anything back.

She gave herself to him, willingly.

And he proved to her just how much she wanted him. He used his body like a weapon, giving no quarter, no mercy, thrusting deep only to withdraw, making her arch greedily toward him, desperate to be surrounded by his male strength as he cradled her with his body.

His chest grazed her back, his hips rocked against her as he plunged back in. She moaned aloud, submitted to the knowledge that this battle was not for power alone, but to make her acknowledge the truth. He had proven what she had been unwilling to admit all along. She wanted him, had always wanted him.

Paige realized for the first time that she didn't mind. She trusted Christopher, and trust changed everything. The desire she had fought since the beginning did not weaken her, but made her strong. He was her other half, a kindred spirit, a soul mate. Together they blazed—not only as agents, but as lovers. A team.

The flames licked higher inside, flaring, consuming, as he took her with long hot strokes until Goddard's presence vanished in a haze of urgent need. Until the world shattered in the face of ecstasy between them. Until they came together as one.

Christopher dragged himself off her and roused enough from the thick haze of passion to untie her wrists. Rolling onto her side, Paige gifted him with a sleepy smile before her lashes fluttered closed. The warmth of contentment washed through him, and he pulled her into his embrace, arranging the comforter to cover their nakedness. He wanted a momentary respite from Goddard's view, peace from the conflict that raged between them.

Paige purred as her long body unfolded against his, every pliant inch conveying satisfaction, glorious submission. Christopher massaged her arms, abashed he had restrained her—that he had needed to—but pleased she had finally stopped fighting what was happening between them.

Would she be back in force once recovered from the effects of their lovemaking? He had dragged unwilling responses from her sweet body and forced her to admit to a truth she had resisted for so long.

A truth that had become more complicated during the past few days. What had started as a purely physical attraction and grown into an obsession had become something so much more. She felt so good in his arms he did not want to let her go. Ever. With a groan, Christopher buried his face in that cloud of fragrant hair. What did he feel... love?

He had expected the passion and the excitement, but not the

longing. They had enough evidence for a conviction—now all they needed was a boat. And then what? Once debriefed, they would be free to go their separate ways, meeting again only to testify in court. Could Christopher let her go, give her months, maybe even a year to rationalize what had happened between them? Or to forget?

A burst of angry denial made his gut clench tight. He ran a hand along her shapely arm, savoring the softness of her skin, the way her breasts molded against his chest. A deep, abiding hunger for her aroused him again, a slow wave of desire that would take a lifetime to satisfy. Christopher wouldn't let her go. Not just because Paige was too stubborn to admit what was happening between them.

Or too scared.

The thought struck him without warning, but once it formed, he knew he had found the missing link. All the pieces fell into place, her avoidance of him, her resentment when he finally caught her. Suddenly Christopher understood.

Paige was scared to fall in love.

What an idiot! He had been seducing her all wrong. Bold pursuit had only strengthened her resistance. Instead of demanding her surrender, she had to come willingly, had to trust him with her heart.

But Christopher didn't see that happening, not after he had forced her submission so completely, had made her beg for him. Even if she did glow in his arms right now. Even if she did snuggle against him like a woman in love. Paige would wake up. And when she did, revenge would be the uppermost thought in her mind.

A Heart to Heart

"We begin filming tomorrow," Goddard informed them at dinner. "The set is ready. The crew is ready. You are ready."

Paige wondered what would be the best way to respond to this announcement since she wasn't supposed to know he had been watching their rehearsals. Goddard was smiling expectantly, but she just couldn't bring herself to reply.

"We are ready," Christopher agreed, setting the fork down and meeting Goddard's gaze in a steady bit of acting that impressed even her. "We had an exceptional rehearsal today. I don't think we can get much better in the chemistry department, but we should spend some time reviewing our lines tonight." He glanced over at her for reinforcement. "What do you think, Paige?"

"We should." She set the wineglass down, hoping Goddard bought the excuse and didn't make them linger after dinner.

"Well, then," Goddard granted her fondest wish, "let's finish our meal so you can be on your way."

Paige went back to pushing beef tips around on her plate. Was it the impending filming or Christopher's lovemaking that had chased her appetite away? She had no intention of filming—she was leaving this island tonight if she had to swim—so it must be Christopher. The one man on the planet who was everything she shouldn't want. But did. Her stomach churned.

She was ready to sprint back to the west wing by the time the last swirl of cognac disappeared and Goddard released them to practice. But Christopher had another sort of running in mind.

"I missed my daily jog this morning and want to get it in before we go over the lines," he explained while leaving the dining room.

"Come with me."

Paige only nodded. They still needed to find out if the boat had returned, and perhaps the exercise would help her diffuse the over-whelming sense of dread that came along with the understanding that she wouldn't be happy without Christopher in her life.

After a quick change, she found herself keeping the pace he set around the island. The night was moonless, the sky clear. A velvet blanket pinpricked with stars glistened above the endless expanse of black water, gilded the rocky terrain in silver lace. A cool night wind piped along with the rhythm of the pounding surf, filling her nostrils with the sea and driving home just how alone they were on this island.

A familiar sense of isolation gnawed at the edges of her mood. A feeling born of undercover work. A feeling Paige had learned intimately during the past two years. She was cut off from the mainland, her contact and the bureau.

But now she had Christopher.

And all these damn feelings that came with him. Even as she watched him stop beneath a twisted tree, her heart squeezed pain-fully in her chest, as much from the run as from the gloominess of her thoughts. Turning her back on the ocean, she faced the only man who could chase the solitude away.

"It's time for a little heart to heart, Paige," he said, sinking down in the grass and leaning back against the tree. "Why did you accept this assignment?"

His white T-shirt and shorts glowed in the darkness, but she could barely make out his features as he stared at the ocean, silent, back straight as if facing demons similar to her own.

"What does it matter?" Her question was a lost whisper in the night.

"It matters to me."

She glanced at him, surprised. There wasn't a command in his voice, or pride, or anger, just a simple statement of fact that she hadn't expected. Shrugging, she paced beneath the starlight, unsure where he was going with this conversation and not in the mood to play mother confessor.

"What difference does it make, Christopher?" she snapped, unable to level the annoyance in her voice. She had played the whore to catch Goddard. The end justified the means. It was that simple.

He wasn't buying it. "I watched you fight to be treated as an equal at the Academy. You were quite vocal about the 'Hooverish' mentality."

For the first time in their acquaintance, J. Edgar Hoover's name rolled off his tongue like an accusation. "Hey, without Hoover the FBI wouldn't be what it is today," she echoed his often-voiced sentiment.

Christopher smiled, a gesture that had the ability to coil her insides into knots, but he didn't respond to her jibe. "This assignment is one of the most discriminatory I've ever come across." He ran his fingers through his hair and shook his head. "You must have had a reason."

His disapproving tone sparked her anger. She whirled on him, ready for battle. "You accepted this assignment, too. If it's so damn distasteful, why are you here?"

"I had a reason."

Oh, that made all the difference, she supposed. Hands propped on her hips, she demanded, "Which was?"

"You."

Whatever Paige had expected, that wasn't it. "What do I have to do with it?"

"I've been chasing after you for the past eight years." He choked back a laugh. "And you still don't get it."

She could only stare at him, anger snuffed out and a tiny flicker of hope sparking to life at the exasperation she saw in his face.

"I accepted this assignment so I could work with you." He hitched an arm across his knee and met her gaze steadily. "If you haven't noticed, I've been turning up like a bad penny ever since you left the Academy."

"Oh, I've noticed all right," she informed him haughtily, determined to keep him at arm's length. "If you didn't notice, I kept running away."

"Why?" His question was a raspy whisper, betraying just how much he wanted an answer and twisting her resolve into a knot in the process.

Admit to the iron spy that she was scared he would take over her life, interfere with her career and swallow her whole? Not in this lifetime.

"You were a tyrant," she accused, a last ditch effort to resist. "I could never please you. Nothing was good enough. You demanded more from me because I was a woman."

"Not because you were a woman, Paige." His earnestness shimmered through her remaining defenses. "Because I knew you could be the best."

She heard the words, saw the sentiment mirrored in his face, and the icy edge of fear thawed.

Christopher believed in her.

And if he still believed in her after all these years, could she take a chance on him?

The truth suddenly loomed before her, and for the first time, Paige took a hard look. Christopher may be bossy and demanding, but he had never tried to destroy who she was in favor of who he wanted her to be. He had trained her, supported her, helped her realize her potential. There must be some middle ground to this control issue. Could they find it?

"I was right," Christopher announced without the slightest attempt at modesty. "You are the best. Agent and woman."

Starlight played like silver strands on his face, and she couldn't resist the urge to touch him. Her hand followed the arch of his neck to stroke a stubbled cheek. "I lose myself in you."

His fingers snagged her chin. "You're supposed to feel that way when you're in love," he said with an eagerness that humbled her. "I lose myself in you, too."

The tightness in her chest eased. Shadows receded and left a glowing ache in their wake. She leaned into his touch, answering the silent need of their bodies even as she wondered if they could really learn to compromise.

"Love?" she repeated, afraid to believe yet daring to hope.

His lips found hers, and he whispered on the edge of a kiss, "Do you really have to ask?"

A lump swelled in her throat.

"We are good together." His hand threaded through her hair, his belief in her so sincere, so sweet. She had let fear blind her to the love of a wonderful man who thought she was worth fighting for. Worth waiting for. Sure Christopher was a tough act to follow, but with him by her side, she could accomplish anything.

Her mouth parted beneath the gentle pressure of his, and Paige answered him with all the emotion that bubbled inside, willing to risk anything for a chance at tomorrow.

Christopher would settle for nothing less than a lifetime. Paige was his, and he undressed her beneath the brilliance of the stars, bathed in the ocean's sultry breeze. Alone. With no eyes except his.

His mouth never left hers as he lowered her to the ground. Every graze of his lips on her skin, every caress of his hands along the curves and hollows of her body expressed his longing, his love. Every touch was designed to lift her onto a wave of passion as strong as his own, designed to answer her every sigh, to satisfy her every shiver.

She clung to him, willing, trusting as he loved her with a long lush rhythm. He didn't take. She didn't submit. They just loved. Together.

He had never suspected such joy could exist in her response. Never knew that such tiny gasps of pleasure could sound like music. Or how much he wanted to charm those sweet sounds from her lips.

With his every breath, he devoted himself to pleasuring her. He cherished every sensation, every sigh of rapture until he felt the first vibration of her ecstasy. Unable to hold back, he rose with her, overcome by a need so powerful, so consuming, that he would never be sated until they had shared their lives together.

He gazed down into her face, both amazed and touched by the tenderness that softened her features, the tears that welled in her eyes. She started to cry, first small little sounds and then big gulping sobs that rocked her entire body. Christopher held her close and kissed the tears from her cheeks.

"I love you, Paige."

"I know." She smiled through her tears with such happiness that he experienced an inner contentment stronger than anything he had ever known.

Rolling onto his back, he pulled her on top of him and snuggled her against his chest. He would never let go. From the beginning, he had known they were destined to be together. She was finally his.

But first he had to get her off this island. "We have to see if the boat's back."

"I'll swim if it isn't." A shudder rocked her body, and he pulled the T-shirt over her shoulders, covering her against the night air. "I can't perform on film."

"Not with what Goddard has planned for the last scene." He didn't remind her that they had already performed for the surveillance cameras.

"Do you think Goddard plans to kill you or me?"

"Both." He used his lips to soothe away the frown line between her brows. They were out of here. Tonight.

"I know that." She turned a soft smile on him. "I was talking about in the script."

"I think the warlord will get too rough with his beautiful captive."

She cuddled against him, and he held her tighter. "I thought so, too, but then I decided the script needed a plot twist."

"Are you going to pull a knife out from under the pillow?"

"The minute you start to come." Her wicked smile made his pulse pound.

He popped her bare bottom with an open hand and made her jump. "Our days of performing for an audience are over, my dear." Even if he had to make sure Goddard never saw the inside of a courtroom. "I've got a few ideas about getting off this island."

"Me, too." She writhed against him, and he couldn't resist kissing her passion-swollen mouth.

"We're a team. Remember?" The thought sent a rush of excitement through him about the future. Their future.

"Yeah. I remember."

"Come on, then. Let's get dressed." He pulled her to her feet, chuckling at her groan of protest. "I've got something to show you."

"This had better be good," she cautioned, visibly shaking off her languor. "I would have enjoyed a few more minutes basking in the afterglow."

"Just as soon as our job is done." Christopher laughed, refusing to even consider the danger that lay ahead. What he had to show her was good. Useful, at the very least.

Paige agreed. There was no mistaking her whoop of delight when he dug up his tools. He unrolled the chamois binding and peered at the items inside with a mixture of relief and satisfaction. His gun. His knife. His lock pick. His good luck baseball cap.

"This is big enough to store the video tape and the disks." Paige caressed the waterproof leather and gazed up at him with a smile. "Just in case we end up swimming back to the mainland."

He couldn't help the rush of raw pride at her pleasure. "It comes in handy."

"There really is a God." She lifted up on tip toes and pressed a soft kiss to his cheek. "And he sent me you."

Contentment blew though his veins like a power surge, leaving him awed in the face of her love. This singular moment would be etched in his mind forever. The amazement in her eyes. The way that look made him feel as if he could conquer the world.

"Let's go, my dear." Christopher strapped the pack around his waist and concealed it beneath his running shorts. "I'm suddenly eager to put debriefing behind me and request a well-deserved vacation." Tugging on his baseball cap, he led her back toward the house.

"My thoughts exactly." Paige laughed, and the sound rippled through him.

The Moment of Truth

Lewis Goddard had other ideas. The excitement of the boat's return shriveled when they arrived back at the marina and an attendant told them, "The boss wants to see the lady in his office right away."

"I'm on my way," Paige said with a smile, but the instant they were out of earshot, she whispered, "Something's up. Would you stay close?"

"Of course." Christopher didn't ask how she knew. He had learned long ago to trust an agent's instincts.

She took a deep breath when they entered the house, wariness sharpening her sapphire gaze to jewel-like hardness. "I could be worrying needlessly—"

"I'll be right here." He dropped a reassuring kiss on the top of her head and disappeared into the shadows of a leafy ficus.

Christopher watched as she pulled her composure around her like a cloak, becoming the bold actress he had become so intimately acquainted with during the past few days. She sailed into the office with confident strides.

"Out for a run, Paige?" Goddard's eel-slick voice echoed through the confines of the marble foyer. "With Christopher? I have some questions I think you might be able to help me with. Get the door and come sit down."

The door swung closed behind her, but didn't click shut.

Goddard's questions could be nothing more than curiosities about their upcoming performance, but something was lifting the hairs on the back of his neck, sending those little adrenaline alarms firing through him. Freeing the gun from his tool pack, Christopher secured it in his waistband and slipped from the shadows to eavesdrop by the cracked door.

Goddard's voice faded to a low rumble as he settled behind the desk, "…all these cutting edge security features on my computer… imagine my surprise when I discovered… doesn't make sense unless the system was expertly bypassed."

Paige hadn't been worrying needlessly. Christopher had gotten past all of Goddard's securities, but it sounded like he might have triggered something else. His hopes sank.

Paige sat in a chair before the desk, and her voice carried through the door.

"Well, yes, Mr. Goddard," she was saying, "we were in here last night…an unexpected detour." He could hear the blush in her voice and smiled despite himself. "But we didn't touch anything." She paused for a moment and then admitted, "Wait. I did flip the surge board on. I accidentally hit the switch while Christopher and I were otherwise… engaged. But I turned it off as soon as I realized what I'd done."

Damn. He hadn't missed one of the securities, but some innocuous program that logged whenever the computer was shut down improperly and the scan disk erased free space on the hard drive.

Paige's cover was good. He reminded himself to give her a kiss for her cleverness and waited in the throbbing silence to see if Goddard bought it.

"I know you and Christopher have grown close, Paige." Goddard's voice grew clearer, louder, as though he was moving around the desk. "With the rehearsals, that's to be expected. But you've been my employee long enough to know I expect loyalty from my people. Don't let your emotions cloud your judgment. I'm going to ask you only once—did Christopher access my computer?"

Looked like cleverness wasn't going to get it this time. Christopher adjusted the rim of his baseball cap, then reached for his gun. The instant he entered the room, security would be alerted, and they would have visitors. But he wasn't about to play games with Paige's life. They had a future to share—together.

Paige didn't believe Goddard had blown her cover. Yet. He thought she was protecting Christopher, apparently hadn't figured out they were working together.

"Mr. Goddard, I would never dream of betraying your trust," she told him, meeting his gaze with a look of what she hoped was quiet desperation. "Not for anyone. You've done so much—"

"I wish it was that simple." He half sat on the desk, towering above her with his deceptively casual posture. "I'm concerned Christopher may not be who he claims. That he may be misleading us."

He must think she was really stupid, but there was nothing stupid about the wicked .44 Magnum he pulled out of his desk drawer.

"Wh-what are you going to do?" she stammered, affecting a nervousness that wasn't all an act.

Goddard hefted the gun in his palm, turned it over for effect and stared at it thoughtfully. "That depends entirely on you. Are you going to answer—"

The door exploded against the wall, and Paige spun around as Christopher burst into the room. The breath caught in her throat when she saw him, broad shoulders filling the doorway, tawny hair swirling around that strong face, the emotion in his eyes reflecting such a violent blend of love and rage that her heart swelled in her chest.

Hurling herself from the chair, she almost broke away, but Goddard's arm snaked around her neck and cut off her escape. With the revolver aimed at her temple, he dragged her against him like a human shield. She met Christopher's murderous stare with a wry grin.

A hostage. Christ, she'd never live this down.

"All right, James Bond," Goddard warned, pressing the gun barrel into her skin so hard she winced. "One more step and her brains will be painting a fresco on my wall. Now why don't you tell me who you really are."

Compared to Goddard's revolver, Christopher's bureau-issue 9mm looked deceptively small, and an image of blood and guts flashed through her mind. Fury hardened Christopher's features. She could almost feel the determination radiating off him, and a zing of hot assurance sliced through her. They had played out this scenario back at the Academy. They could play it again. She winked and hoped Christopher remembered.

He did. She saw the flicker of acknowledgment in his eyes as he held his gun trained on Goddard's forehead. "I'm Special Agent Christopher Sharp with the Federal Bureau of Investigation." Paige couldn't drag her gaze from the sight of him, so masculine, so powerful. Or quell her surge of pride at his announcement. "You're under arrest."

"FBI?" Goddard laughed, to all appearances amused, but Paige felt his body tense. "Shit, Christopher. I should have known you were too good to be true. Did the FBI train you especially for this job? You were quite a natural."

Fury struck hard. Paige fought the urge to bite a chunk out of Goddard's arm and focused on Christopher instead. His eyes had narrowed to slits. As he read Goddard his rights, the muscle in his jaw flexed wildly. The effort was costing him, too.

"So," Goddard asked conversationally, "what are you arresting me for?"

Christopher never wavered. "Murder one among other things."

"Murder!" Goddard leaned back against the desk, catching Paige hard around the throat and pulling her with him. "Now that's a nasty accusation. Who?"

Goddard wasn't really worried yet, Paige knew, he was more concerned with fishing out whatever information he could. The criminal mind was so predictable.

Christopher led him right down the garden path. "You're a suspect in seven deaths related to your pornography ring."

"Pornography?" Goddard cringed in mock horror. "I like to think of it as art erotica. You should know that—you're starring in my latest film." He sighed dramatically, but Paige felt the first traces of fear roll off him like sweat.

"I suppose this means I'll have to recast your role." He rested his chin on her head and inhaled deeply. "A damn shame. You two were magic together."

Christopher stared down the length of the gun barrel, his voice as steady as the gun he held, his fury exhilarating to watch. "You won't be recasting our roles. I'm closing this production down. Permanently."

"You can prove these charges?" Goddard's arm tightened, and Paige struggled to appear calm, not to distract Christopher even though she couldn't breathe.

The iron spy never wavered. "Look around you. You're not exactly hiding anything here."

"Circumstantial. You can't connect those deaths to me, and anything incriminating will disappear within the hour. So how does any of this translate into murder one?" The gun bit into her skin, but Paige felt his hand tremble. They had his attention now.

"I'd have your lawyer pack more than an overnight bag—"

"It's that goddamn kid, isn't it?" Goddard shouted. His body arched tight as a bowstring, but he eased his grip on her throat just a bit. "You've got her, don't you?"

"He's telling the truth?" Paige choked out, gulping air. Opportunities like this didn't come along often, and she wouldn't have missed it for the world. "You murdered those people?"

"Yes." The defiant hiss echoed in her ear. "And you're about to witness another murder." Goddard jerked to his feet, taking her with him.

Paige knocked the gun from his hand and drove her elbow into his stomach. He had barely managed a gasp before she broke free and spun around, ramming the heel of her palm into his face.

Goddard staggered back, but the desk trapped him, and before the revolver hit the carpeted floor, Christopher held him around the throat, gun pressed against his head. "Don't move."

Goddard didn't.

"Please tell me the audio picked this up." Paige stared up at the video camera pointed uselessly toward the door. An audio tape of Goddard's confession would clinch her case.

"Doesn't matter." Christopher rolled his eyes toward the cap on his head. "I've got it all on video tape."

"A microvideo camera?" she burst out, afraid to hope he had a tiny recording device concealed in the emblem of his baseball cap.

That sensual mouth curled into the most radiant of smiles. "I never leave home without it."

"I love you." She blew him a kiss.

"I know."

"You're making a mistake, Paige," Goddard spat out. A desperate attempt by a man who still didn't grasp the whole picture. A man who was scared. "You agreed to star in my film, knowing what it was. You're an accomplice. What do you think the FBI will do to you?"

"Give me a vacation, I hope." Paige grabbed the revolver and cocked the cylinder to check the chambers. Loaded. She caught his gaze and smiled. "At full pay."

Goddard's face went blank.

"Full pay?" Christopher snorted, poking the gun barrel into Goddard's temple to emphasize the point. "I don't think they'll be that grateful."

Goddard's skin took on a decidedly greenish cast, and she could almost see the light bulb flicker above his head as full impact of their words hit. Paige couldn't stop the laughter that burst from her lips. "Should've checked my references."

Crossing the room, she kicked the door open and aimed the revolver at Jerry the security guard who struggled to keep his balance on the other side.

"Drop the weapon and get down on the floor. Now."

"See if he's got cuffs," Christopher suggested.

He did, and in the space of a heartbeat, he was wearing them.

Paige burst through the doorway and searched the foyer for any of Jerry's friends. "It's clear." She motioned Christopher out.

"You'll never make it off this island." Goddard warned with a show of bravado as Christopher dragged him through the door. "Do you honestly think I don't have this covered? My men know what to do if anything happens to me."

"Thanks for the warning, but I don't think they'll risk your life while I'm holding a gun to your head." Christopher called his bluff, and one turn into the west wing proved he was right.

A trio of Goddard's men waited, guns trained and ready, surprise registering on their faces when they saw their boss's predicament.

"Mr. Goddard, what—"

"Don't even think about it, gentlemen, or he's a dead man,"

Christopher cautioned.

Paige covered him, knowing he covered her, feeling a sweet edge to the rush of danger because Christopher was here. He loved her and would protect her. She'd do the same for him.

They sailed past Goddard's men into their suite. She slammed the door shut behind them and threw the lock.

With one powerful blow, Christopher cold-cocked Goddard. "Ouch. Bet that hurt." But he didn't look the least bit repentant as Goddard crumbled to the floor in a flaccid heap. Aiming his gun at the door, he glanced over his shoulder and said, "Go get the disks and the tape. Bring the handcuffs from the bedroom, too."

"There's no other way to do this except out the back door," Christopher said when she returned. "We have to get to the marina."

"They'll be waiting for us."

"We'll protect each other." His face was radiant, and she felt the warmth of his love flow through her.

A smile touched her lips as he bent to hoist Goddard over his shoulder. The running shorts hugged the sexy curve of his bottom. It would be an absolute tragedy to risk that magnificent ass. "Perhaps they'll think twice before they shoot since we've got him."

They did. No one did more than make threats when they left the west wing and headed down the narrow hallway. Even with all the doorways and turns, when Goddard's men had the home team advantage, they did not interfere. Either Goddard had been quite explicit about procedure in the event he was taken hostage, or the team was a trifle shy without the coach.

Christopher led them into Goddard's private apartment and positioned himself in the doorway, gun poised dramatically at Goddard's temple. "Check out the other rooms."

"They're clear." Paige locked the surrounding doors, securing the room. She didn't need any prompting to locate their own surveillance tapes and ran across an assault rifle in her search.

Tossing the tapes into a knapsack, she slipped it and the rifle over her shoulder.

"Hey, Rambo, got our tapes?"

The laughter in his voice jolted her into a quick smile. She patted the pouch. "Wouldn't want anyone to get a hold of these."

"My thoughts exactly."

She covered the distance between them in a few quick strides. Pointedly ignoring Goddard, she brought her fingers to his hair, gliding through the tawny strands in a lover's caress. "You really don't miss a trick, do you?"

"I hate loose ends." A frown creased his brow. She saw the failure flash in his eyes and knew his pride was all tangled up in that little twist of fate. "But I should have known about the scan disk—"

She shrugged, not wanting him to dwell on one oversight when she could never have caught Goddard without him. "You're pretty great, Christopher, but you're not like... Hoover, or something."

"Oh, I'm not, am I?"

She couldn't resist pressing a kiss to that luscious mouth. "You're the man I love. That's even better."

His deep chuckle gusted against her lips. "Works for me."

Paige resisted the impulse to pull him deeper into her kiss. Love was grand, she decided, but that didn't change the fact that they weren't home free yet. Taking a step back, she ruffled Goddard's hair. "Do you think he was serious about this stuff disappearing before anyone can get back with a warrant?"

"Perhaps. But we have what we need. Anything else is gravy."

He was right. Wouldn't do to get greedy now. Not when they still had to make the marina.

"Here we go." She pulled aside the drapery to reveal a wide angle view of the lighted pool and the marina beyond. "His bedroom connects. Just like you said."

"Let's go." He shifted Goddard's inert form higher onto his shoulder. "He weighs a ton."

"And smells bad, too."

A wall of glass doors opened out onto the pool from Goddard's bedroom, providing both the clearest route to the marina and the show of resistance awaiting them. Even through the shadows of the floodlights, she could make out half a dozen men surrounding the dock, armed with enough hardware to take over a small country.

"I'm going out shooting." Paige shoved the revolver into her waistband and grabbed the rifle. She lifted the weapon to survey the left side of the breech casing and flipped the control selector to burst. "Let's hope they want Goddard alive to sign their paychecks."

Christopher nodded, but she could see the apprehension stiffen his spine as he gazed out the window.

"You ready to wrap this up?" she asked lightly, hoping to reassure him.

The hot gaze he turned on her heated her blood. "Let's go, my dear." Paige yanked back the verticals and threw open the door. "You're aiming those guns at two federal agents," she shouted, "back off. Now!" Firing the first salvo onto the ground close to the bad guys, she sent them scrabbling for cover in all directions.

With Christopher on her heels, she took off toward the pool, firing a new burst each time a head popped up over some makeshift barricade.

Paige snagged keys from the boathouse and headed for Goddard's powerboat. Not only was it light and fast enough to compete with the security vessels, it was equipped with enough radio equipment to put them in touch with the mainland.

She leaped in, covering Christopher's back as he dumped Goddard unceremoniously onto the deck.

"Well done, my dear." His dark eyes sparkled, and Paige recognized the gleam of excitement, the flash of triumph.

"I learned from the best." There was nothing like a good escape to get the blood flowing.

Christopher laughed, but she could see him glow beneath the compliment. She untied the boat from the dock while he shoved Goddard into the cramped storage compartment under the bow, leaving the door open for air. They wouldn't have to worry about his safety, and handcuffed, he wouldn't be able to get out without drawing their notice.

Christopher started the engine and within minutes, the bright lights of Goddard's sanctuary faded into the night as they gained the freedom of the Pacific.

He stood at the wheel, wind whipping the tawny hair away from his face, the spray of salt water glistening on his skin. Paige's heart did a somersault in her chest. She wanted to hug him, to feel those strong arms around her.

"Activate the homing device and give me the videotapes," Christopher said, and she settled for the gaze that caressed her instead.

Paige tossed him the backpack, then set up a signal that would alert the mainland field office to their location. She took stock of her meager weapon store. Within seconds, several boats filled with Goddard's men shot out from the harbor. It wouldn't be long before they were within firing range.

"We'll make new memories," Christopher shouted, his voice carrying over the roar of the engine.

"What?" Paige rested the rifle in her lap and glanced up at him, just as he tossed a videotape overboard.

"The Celtic priestess skit," he explained with a grimace. "I couldn't stand to watch myself suffer the agonies of the damned. It's still too vivid in my mind. But the Medieval scene." He held up another tape. "Wouldn't the boys back in Washington just love this. I know for a fact you are more than one agent's fantasy." His wicked grin made a little trickle of apprehension skitter through her. "What do you think?"

He couldn't be serious, could he?

"Toss it," she said, and to her relief, he did.

"The striptease. My personal favorite." Turning the last tape over in his hand, he glanced at it, his grin softening into a fond smile. "You will dance for me again, won't you?"

No loose ends. Of course he would have to ask, flex those control muscles he was so fond of using. That was just Christopher. The man she loved.

"Anytime." She had never meant anything more in her life.

"How about on our wedding night?"

Wedding night?

"What?" Her jaw went slack, and she could only stare at him. Until the first shot screamed past her head.

Christopher slid onto his knees and hunched low over the steering wheel, while Paige aimed the rifle and fired at the headlights that sliced through the darkness, unable to make out individual figures.

"What are you talking about?"

"Our wedding night," he repeated. "You know, the night of our wedding." He cocked the wheel one-handed and the boat veered starboard so sharply that Goddard's head clunked solidly against the fiberglass door frame. "Marry me, Paige."

"You want to get married?" The idea finally started to sink in, but emotion hadn't pierced her shock yet.

"Yeah, we can work together."

Paige dropped close to the deck and reloaded, shock finally dissolving into a wave of exasperated surprise. "I can't believe you're proposing to me while we're trying to escape." Her voice rode the crest of an explosion as she discharged the final burst. Tossing aside the rifle, Paige rolled toward the bow, grateful for the expert way he handled the boat. "We'll probably never make the mainland alive."

Christopher slapped his 9mm into the palm of her hand with enough force to make her skin tingle. "Incentive. We have to escape, so you can shop for a wedding gown." He dangled the striptease tape in front of her. "Do I have an affirmative?"

"That's blackmail, Sharp."

He nodded gleefully, and happiness swirled inside her. Who would have ever guessed the assignment from hell would lead to the love of her life?

"You have an affirmative." The last tape disappeared in the churning waves, and the smile she gave him echoed all the love in her heart.

He reached for the radio transmitter. "United States Coast Guard. This is Special Agent Christopher Sharp with the FBI requesting assistance." She heard the impatience in his voice and couldn't hold back a chuckle when he said, "And make it snappy, will you? I have a wedding to attend."

Damned control freak. He even bossed the Coast Guard around. Bracing her wrists on the gunwale, Paige pulled the trigger with a satisfied sigh. Life was grand.

About the author:

Jeanie Cesarini is a multi-published author who lives with her very own romance hero and their two beautiful daughters in the South. A transplanted Yankee, she particularly enjoys stretching out beneath moss-draped oaks and indulging in her favorite pastime: reading thrilling crime novels and then soothing her jitters with a wonderful romance. **The Spy Who Loved Me** *combines two worlds, and she hopes* **Secrets'** *readers enjoy reading her story as much as she enjoyed writing it.*

Love Undercover

✳⟆⟅⟆✳

by B. J. McCall

To my reader:

The truly rugged individualist, no matter what his day job, is usually a cowboy at heart.

And what woman doesn't want a cowboy...

Chapter One

"I hate meetings," Detective Wes Cooper muttered to his best friend and partner, Tom Jenkins. Just thinking about sitting through another squad meeting with his sexy new boss reminded Wes of his eighth grade year in Miss Hollister's English literature class. Captivated by the beautiful redhead, he'd experienced several embarrassing classroom moments. At thirty-seven, a public erection wasn't likely, but it was damn hard to concentrate on the Lieutenant's comments when all Wes could think about was giving her a slow, intense strip search.

Tom checked his watch. "The Lieutenant's running late. Maybe she'll cancel."

"I can only hope." Wes shifted his gaze once again to the standard beige colored corridor visible through the glass-fronted conference room. When he spied his boss, dressed in a dark blue suit, threading her way past uniformed officers, lawyers, and assorted police personnel toward the conference room, Wes almost groaned.

On any other woman, a suit did little to compliment the body, but on Lt. Forbes an ordinary straight skirt and a double-breasted jacket took on a whole new dimension. No matter how hard he tried, and he had, Wes couldn't ignore the curves filling out the fine blue wool.

How many times had he chastised himself for looking?

Covertly, he'd watch the graceful, fluid swing of the Lieutenant's rounded backside as she navigated the crowded, narrow precinct corridors. Her long, slender legs captivated him.

At night, in his dreams, she walked naked.

If he had to have a female boss, why did she have to be so damned sexy looking? And a green-eyed, redhead to boot?

Like Wes, Tom's gaze was fixed on the new Lieutenant. "The Captain says the boss has a master's degree. I understand she took a bunch of classes at the FBI school."

"Just my luck," Wes replied, thinking again of the sexy, unobtainable Miss Hollister who'd undoubtedly been responsible for his penchant for redheads. He glanced at Tom. "She'll probably want to teach the burglars to read Milton."

"Who's Milton?"

"Never mind." Wes placed one booted foot on the unoccupied chair next to his as the Lieutenant entered the conference room and brushed past him. For a split second her tush was a mere inch from his face. A hint of flowery perfume lingered in her wake.

Wes could just kill the Captain for hiring a female who put his male senses on full alert every time he saw her.

Amanda sorted out her prepared notes, then began. She was tempted to ask Wes Cooper to remove his booted foot from the chair directly to her immediate left, but as usual he sat there, his unsettling blue gaze fastened on her.

Fearless and cool when it counted, the good looking detective was too provocative for Amanda to ignore.

His startling silver-blue eyes enchanted her. His western style of dress and long-legged swagger had captured Amanda's attention and fueled her imagination. Whenever he was near, her concentration suffered, making her uncomfortably aware of how long it had been since she'd felt the caress of a lover's hands on her bare skin, the lustful brush of lips across her breasts or the heated thrust of an erection between her legs.

Her pulsed raced and her thighs tightened at the sensual and erotic images. Just looking at him, her temperature climbed and her underwear felt hot and tight.

Without taking his eyes off of her, Cooper said something to Jenkins in that low, sexy drawl. Amanda had no idea what he'd said. Her attention was focused on his mouth. Her tongue slid across her lower lip. She wanted to taste him, to feel his firm lips easing the pressure of her taut nipples.

Her hands clenched the podium. Her gaze dropped to the bulge enhanced by his tight jeans. Could he justify that delicious swagger?

Someone asked her a direct question, snapping Amanda's attention back to the meeting. She cleared her throat, glanced at her notes and asked for case updates.

As the reports droned on, Amanda swore silently. She'd never faced this predicament. She'd never fantasized about a co-worker before. A set of tight buns would catch her eye, but never had she experienced such plaguing erotic fantasies. Unfortunately, fantasize was all she could do. After a few costly sexual harassment suits, the department had made it clear any sexual contact between supervisors and subordinates, even consensual contact, was forbidden.

She'd never been tempted by the forbidden before. Until now.

Amanda liked cowboys. Raised on a working Arizona ranch, Cooper was the living manifestation of her cowboy fantasies, and an undeniable temptation.

There was something about tight jeans and leather chaps which drew her to western movies and rodeos. At night, alone in her bed, she read western romances.

Last night Cooper had saved her from a group of desperados. His gaze had been heated as he'd removed her torn dress, lace-trimmed chemise and drawers, and taken the only reward she had to offer so gallant a hero. Amanda's gaze slid from the podium back to Cooper. She could recall the feel of his hands on her body, his mouth on her breasts. They'd made love out in the open, beneath a blazing sun. The dream had been so vivid, Amanda tingled at the memory of their entwined bodies brushed by a hot desert wind.

Cooper's eyes narrowed.

Realizing she'd been thinking about making love to Cooper instead of listening to the detectives' case updates, Amanda forced her errant thoughts back to her main reason for calling the meeting.

She was about to speak when Cooper beat her to the punch.

"What about the strip joint robberies?"

"I was getting to that," Amanda said, meeting his intense blue gaze. "We're going undercover."

A few of the guys whooped. As she suspected this was one as-signment they'd all jump on. Cooper stared right at her. His eyes widened. "We?"

She wanted to lean close to him and answer his question in minute detail, instead Amanda forced her gaze to focus on the rest of the squad. "I've arranged for teams of two to work in six clubs, Thursdays through Saturdays, for the next month. Hope you like overtime, Detective Cooper," she said, cognizant that his gaze had remained firmly on her.

Whenever he was in the room, within the scope of her vision, she felt drawn to him. No matter how many times she forced herself to look away, she was aware of him. At times, when their gazes locked across the room, she'd had to remind herself to breath.

He excited her. He scared the hell out of her. If Cooper ever touched her, she wasn't sure she could resist.

"I do, Lieutenant," he spoke in an affected drawl. "Sitting around watching ladies shake their fannies—"

"You won't be a customer, Detective. You'll have to work this one." Amanda enjoyed the skeptical look Cooper gave her. "You're the new bouncer at the Prickly Cactus. All that country music should make you feel right at home."

Amanda waited as Cooper took some good-natured ribbing from the other detectives. When he looked her straight in the eye and grinned, she remembered he'd grinned in her dream. Right before he pulled her, naked and willing, into his arms.

"I hope you don't expect Tom to dance," Cooper drawled.

The detectives' laughter skittered about the room. "That's my job, Detective. And I'll be doing it at the Prickly Cactus. Tom's as-signed to the Bosom Buddies."

The room went silent. So silent Amanda worried he could hear her thundering heart as she waited for his reaction. Every hair on her body stood on end when she looked into Cooper's silver-blue eyes.

He's imagining me naked.

The thought ricocheted in her brain, the image of herself peel-ing down to a tiny bra and G string in front of Cooper. Her cheeks burned along with another portion of her anatomy.

An odd look crossed Cooper's face. "You're joking."

"The robbers are quick and efficient. They know our response time. Undercover is the only way."

One corner of Cooper's mouth twitched. "And where will you hide your badge and gun?" Cooper asked. His gaze was centered on her chest.

Amanda ignored his teasing remark. The guys in vice had needled her until she'd nailed more johns in a street walker sting than any of her female colleagues. So far she hadn't met one female officer who'd hidden her gun in her bra.

"I believe an undercover sting will solve these robberies. The Captain agrees."

Cooper's gaze slid from her face to travel the length of her body. He remained silent, but his cool expression told her he didn't believe she was up to the task, as a cop or a woman. In fact, he looked annoyed. When he finally raised his eyes, Amanda greeted him with a glare which dared him to object. He did. "Wouldn't Barbara Bates... she's worked vice—"

"Officer Bates is assigned to the Bosom Buddy with Tom," Amanda snapped. She understood why Cooper would prefer to be paired with Bates. The woman must be a 38 double D, and gossip had it the two officers were more than friendly when off-duty.

A couple of the guys slapped Detective Jenkins on the back, but Cooper kept his attention focused on her. "Tom's married. Wouldn't it be better—"

"Detective Jenkins, do you have an objection to your assignment?" As Amanda expected, Tom Jenkins gave her a negative response. She read off the rest of the teams and where they would work. "If there's nothing else," she said, looking at Cooper. To her relief he remained silent. "I'll expect all of you to remember that during this operation you are still on duty and your behavior must be exemplary."

After she dismissed the group, Amanda picked up her notes and walked out of the room. All the way back to her office, she felt

Cooper's cool blue gaze centered on her back. She'd be damned if she'd dream about him tonight.

Without the stage lights and music on, The Prickly Cactus reminded Wes of a big black box. The walls were dark gray and the carpet, a dull black and burgundy pattern, managed to hide the cigarette burns. Except for the neon cactus centered on the wall, even the oak wood bar looked dull to Wes. But when the show began and the near-naked girls gyrated beneath colorful lights to deafening music, no one would give a damn.

As the bouncer, Wes had access to the dressing rooms behind the stage. He wanted to go backstage and say hello, but he was quite sure the Lieutenant wouldn't like it.

Instead he sat at the bar, nursed a diet cola and wondered why the hell she'd chosen him to be her partner. Did she have any idea how much she turned him on? Whenever he looked into her green eyes, he could swear he felt a connection. Wes shook his head and swore. Assignments like this were tough enough, but watching the sexy Lieutenant dance half naked all night, then going home alone would be hell. Working with Bates would have been a cakewalk.

He couldn't remember the last time he'd been tempted to jack-off. Maybe he just liked redheaded, authoritarian females. Wes chuckled. He bet the department psychiatrist would have a field day with that one.

The lights went down around six and Wes took his place by the door. The customers, mostly businessmen working in the financial district, began to fill the place. Guys in three-piece suits usually pulled out a credit card, instead of a gun, when they got out of line. Wes liked suits.

When the lights on the stage began to pulse, Wes, along with every other guy in the room, fastened his gaze on the beaded curtains at the far end of the narrow stage. Wes realized he didn't care about the other dancers. He was waiting for *her.*

Since the Lieutenant had joined the squad, she'd worn her hair up in a tight twist. Wes's fingers had itched to remove every pin, just to see how far that mass of red hair would cascade down her back. Tonight his fantasy would become a reality. His pulse jumped as the beaded curtain separated. A lush blonde in a red sequined cowboy hat, vest, and tight, red shorts pranced onto the stage.

Disappointed, Wes turned his attention to the crowd. He'd bet his weekly paycheck that half the customers were married and their wives had no idea they were here spending five bucks for a beer and leering at girls. Chuckling at his holier-than-thou attitude, Wes walked over to the bar and ordered a cup of coffee.

Backstage, Amanda stood before a full length mirror. She tugged the green spangled demi-cup bra down, but that only forced her breasts higher. How would she ever dance with her knees trembling and her stomach doing flip-flops?

"Come on, honey, giv'em a shake."

Amanda looked over her shoulder at her advisor. Lucy Morals, also-known-as Lucy Morales, was the star act at the Cactus. An exotic mixture of several nationalities, Lucy had to be the best looking woman in the business. Her eyes were big and dark, her thick brown hair so long it grazed her butt when she walked.

"The first night's always the hardest," Lucy said as she adjusted her gold sequined bra over a set of pasties. Her bra in place, Lucy demonstrated. Her shoulders barely moved, but her large breasts bounced, jiggled and shifted side-to-side. "The guys love it. Especially if you put'em right in their faces."

"I don't think I can do that," Amanda croaked. Performing before her closet door mirror in her own bedroom was entirely different from what faced her out front. She heard the hooting, hollering and whistling from the men when Candy Redd stepped on stage. Lucy said it was a good crowd for a Thursday.

"You got a boyfriend, honey?" Lucy asked.

Amanda shook her head and fiddled with the fringe of her extremely short skirt. She shifted her hips trying to get comfortable with the narrow strip of material covering her. She'd never worn a thong bikini before.

"Maybe a guy you got the hots for?"

Without responding, Amanda tried Lucy's move. In comparison she looked pitiful. "Guess it works better if you're larger."

"It works better if you're into it," Lucy remarked. "Just pretend one of those guys is Tom Cruise or whoever. Dance for him and let it go."

The image of Wes Cooper in nothing but a pair of jeans leaped to mind. Amanda tried again. It worked.

"Tom Cruise will do it every time," Lucy said. She cocked her head as the music ended. "You're on, honey."

Amanda ran from the dressing room and up the narrow stairs leading to the beaded curtain. Her stomach lurched. If she barfed on stage, she'd never live it down. Candy bounced through the curtain, and said, "It's all yours, Blaze."

As "Achey, Breaky Heart" began to play, she stepped through the beaded curtain. Thankful for the bright lights, Amanda couldn't see the men, but she could hear their whistles and shouts. An "ohhhhhh, baby", and a "give it to me sweetheart," collided in the babble.

She forced a smile.

Concentrating on the music, she dipped and wiggled, but Amanda knew she wasn't giving the crowd what they wanted. Her arms and legs felt stiff and awkward, and her heart was a thundering lump which her brain couldn't seem to control.

Then suddenly the front door opened and two guys walked in and disappeared into the blackness. In that brief slash of light from the marquee outside, she glimpsed Cooper. Staring in his direction, she forgot the men surrounding the narrow stage. Their shouts no longer registered. Only the music, her body, and Wes Cooper remained.

She imagined a bare-chested Cooper watching her, and suddenly her body discovered a sexy rhythm all its own. Her legs and hips began to move and her forced smile transformed into a sensual pout. In time with the backbeat, Amanda rolled her hips. When she thrust her pelvis forward, shrill whistles nearly drowned out the music. She whipped open her vest, then let it slip down her arms a few inches at a time. Twirling the shiny scrap of fabric like a lasso, she danced to the end of the stage. Resisting the urge to fling the discarded vest in Cooper's direction, she tossed it over her shoulder. When she bent low and jiggled her breasts, the crowd roared. Knowing somewhere in the darkness Cooper's silver-blue gaze was fastened on her sent a fiery rush of heat pulsing through Amanda's veins. She turned around and let go with a slow, raunchy grind which felt so good she repeated the move several times.

Ignoring the whistling audience, Amanda kept her focus above the men's faces. She danced only for her blue-eyed cowboy.

As she whipped off her short skirt, she looked toward the front door and imagined herself popping open the buttons of his tight jeans one-at-a-time.

As each button gave way, her bump-and-grind became slower, deeper, and decidedly more sensual. Keeping her gaze in Cooper's direction, she gave him a wouldn't-you-like-to-touch-them jiggle. The crowd yelled and stomped their feet.

Amanda turned away from the crowd and thrust her near-naked hips from side-to-side. In slow, sensual swings she imagined Cooper running his long calloused fingers along the length of her legs, across her belly and finally cupping her breasts. Heat pulsed throughout her body, her breasts tightened, and she throbbed with a fiery heat between her legs.

Right in your face, Cooper.

The men cheered, but Amanda didn't care. She focused on Cooper's silent challenge of her abilities and went into her finale.

With her back to the crowd, she stood with her legs braced apart and pulled off her white hat. She felt the weight of her hair fall as it tumbled down her back. The men yelled louder. She strutted along the edge of the stage and the yahoos showed their appreciation, slipping bills beneath the garter on her right thigh. She endured the lewd comments and suggestive gestures, and made one more pass across the stage, but Detective Cooper never left his post by the door.

By the end of the night, Amanda's legs ached from dancing in high-heeled cowboy boots. Her knees had almost buckled during the last set. Too tired to change, she pulled off her boots, then flopped down on a narrow cot in the dressing room.

Candy Redd had already left. As Lucy tucked her black tee shirt into her jeans, she said, "Ya done good, Blaze."

"Thanks. At least I didn't throw up on anyone."

"I've known girls who have. Really pisses off the boss." At the door, Lucy hesitated. "Go home and soak in a hot bath. It helps."

Amanda rolled off the cot to her feet. Her knees protested. She hoped she never heard "Achey Breaky Heart" again.

She'd just unclasped her spangled bra when the door swung open. A draft of cold air poured into the heated dressing room and fanned her bare skin. Clasping the loose bra to her chest, Amanda spun around. Cooper leaned against the door jam.

"Is there something you want, Detective?"

That cool blue gaze slowly slid over her. "Good show, Lieutenant. Especially that little finale you do. You had'em comin' in their pants."

"Tips weren't bad either." Holding his gaze, Amanda carefully refastened her bra, then glanced down at the lacy black garter circling her thigh. A wad of bills protruded from it like an open fan. "With six of us dancing, the widows and orphans fund should have a banner month."

Cooper grinned then eased his big male frame away from the door and toward Amanda. For a split second she knew how it felt to have the Duke coming at you. Cooper'd even mastered the easily recognizable shoulder-swing. Resisting the urge to step back, Amanda planted her bare feet.

"Then let me give you some advice," Cooper said, pulling a bill out of his pocket and tucking it right down the front of her G String. His warm fingertips grazed over her curls. "Real strippers give the boys a little thrill."

She grabbed his arm. Although the contact was pure reflex, awareness of the corded strength of his forearm and the power he was capable of unleashing held her spellbound. She wished she could uncurl her fingers and let him know she welcomed his touch. He didn't move his hand. His fingertips remained pressed to her bare flesh as she fought hard for control. In a voice she hardly recognized, she said, "You forget yourself, Cooper."

"That's a fifty," he said, removing his hand. "The guy's name is Harold."

"And?" Amanda asked as Cooper turned and sauntered to the door. She could still feel the warm imprint of his hand.

"He wanted to know if you were available after hours," he said quietly, not looking at her.

Amanda smiled as her flesh cooled. "Looks like I can handle it, doesn't it, Detective? At least he doesn't suspect I'm a cop."

Cooper started to close the dressing room door, but Amanda's curiosity had been piqued. She knew she shouldn't, but she wanted him to stay. "What did you tell Harold?"

Cooper glanced over his shoulder and gave her a level stare. "I told the bastard you were my woman."

His woman. Before Amanda could respond, the door closed and she was left alone with her racing pulse and wilder imagination. Had the detective somehow felt her vibes? Did he suspect she'd danced for him?

Amanda collected the bills from her garter and stuffed them in her bag next to her badge. The shiny metal brought a welcome flash of common sense. His little demonstration had been nothing more than an attempt to provoke her. When she'd worked vice, one of the guys had insisted on trying to adjust her push-up bra on a nightly basis. Instead of getting upset, she'd slapped his hands away and laughed. Eventually she'd been treated as one of the team.

The sexy detective was just yanking her chain.

Her pulse back to normal and her imagination in check, Amanda dressed in a pair of comfortable sweats, grabbed her duffle bag and exited the back door of the Prickly Cactus. She scanned the partially lit parking lot and headed for her car. On the opposite side of the small lot, the driver's door of a Jeep opened and Cooper stepped out. *Now what did he want?* She tossed her duffle bag in the backseat, then leaned against her red Firebird, waiting.

She sensed motion in the luxury sedan parked opposite her car. Dragging her gaze away from Cooper, Amanda glanced at the sedan. In the faint light she made out a bobbing head of blonde hair and a white shirt in the sedan's back seat.

"That's not very ladylike," Cooper whispered. His breath fanned her cheek.

Aware of how close Cooper was, Amanda turned. His big hands firmly clutched her hips. She wanted to press her body to his and feel the hard muscles hinted at beneath his shirt and the strength in his thighs. If he had been a bouncer and not her subordinate, she'd take him home, now, this very minute, and spend the night naked in his arms.

Reluctantly she pushed him away.

"Don't go blowing our cover, Lieutenant," he whispered as his fingers fanned out over her backside and his thumbs fastened onto her waist.

She had imagined so many times how it would feel to be in his arms. Amanda forced herself to relax. At least she could satisfy some of her curiosity. "Then don't call me Lieutenant."

He moved closer. So close she could sense how they'd fit together. "Okay, Mandy."

At his use of her family nickname, an odd sense of familiarity slid up Amanda's spine. She liked the way he said it, low and sexy. "The name's Blaze around here," she reminded him.

Cooper eased her back against the car. His fingers slid beneath the waistband of her sweats. "Why don't we just let Candy finish, then we can talk?"

A sense of foreboding slid along her spine. She should push his hands away, now, but his fingers felt good on her warm flesh. Too good to resist. Staying in Blaze's character, Amanda kept her voice low and a little sultry. "Is she doin' what I think she's doin'?" she asked.

"Uhmmm. And from the looks of it," Cooper whispered, leaning into her to peek over the car roof, "she's almost finished."

"I guess we can't bust her." Amanda tried to block the image of two naked bodies locked in climax. She was much too aware of the warm male body pressing her own against the Firebird's cold metal, the strong hands sliding over the rounded curve of her buttocks and the sensual kneading of fingers into her flesh.

Just this once, she wanted to abandon all the rules, to give into the fire her dancing had ignited. Her skin burned. Her sweats felt hot and confining.

She'd fantasized how his lips would feel, hot, demanding, intoxicating. She wished Cooper would kiss her now, fulfill her dreams or dispel them forever.

"Kiss me," Cooper ordered in a husky whisper.

"What?" Had he read her mind?

"I said kiss me."

I can't. He shouldn't. I'm his boss. Reality dissolved the moment Wes Cooper's mouth covered hers.

Either the detective was the best kisser on earth or it had been too damn long since she'd been kissed. Latching onto the latter as the reasonable explanation, she kissed him back. His lips moved over hers as if he knew exactly what she needed. Vaguely she heard a car door open, a woman's giggle, the rustle of clothes. Then there was only the heated rush of her own blood.

Cooper turned them both and leaned against her car. His hands cupped her backside while his fingertips massaged the cleft of her buttocks, pulling her tightly against his obviously thickening shaft. Reality blinked. This was going too far, beyond duty, beyond the job. His probing tongue filled her mouth. His powerful erection pressed her belly.

Fantasy became hard reality. He shifted and bared her to the thighs and Amanda was powerless to protest. Cool air struck her hot skin and her hotter sex as he dragged her sweats lower. The hard promise of his erection rubbed her sensitive mound. Her sex pulsed in eager anticipation.

Cooper's kiss deepened. Amanda felt herself spiraling down, down into a lush vortex of sensation. She strained to seal her body to his. She wanted him. Wanted him inside her. Nothing else mattered. No one else existed.

She thrust against the bulge in his jeans. So close. Sensation rippled through her.

His hand slid between their bodies, his finger slipped between her slick folds, penetrating her heated sex. The intimate contact sent warning bells, ominous as police sirens, off in her head.

She broke the kiss and pushed his hand away.

Wes's deep chuckle barely registered. Suddenly, she was turned and forced against the vehicle, a suspect under control. Instead of the cold steel of handcuffs binding her wrists, she felt Wes's hands, hot and greedy, sliding beneath her sweatshirt, grasping her breasts.

She gasped for air, wanting, needing to protest this assault, this terrible breach of conduct, but his hands began a fierce massage across her needy breasts, his hard erection pressed into her buttocks, forcing her bared belly against the cold metal car, and her protest transformed into a small, whimpering cry.

His lips closed over her left earlobe, suckling, drawing on the sensitive bit of flesh. His fingers rolled and tugged her turgid nipples until pleasure flamed, deep inside her womb, and drenched her sex with undeniable need.

He eased his hold. His tongue teased the tender flesh beneath her ear, and delicately, tenderly, he brushed his big hands over her swollen breasts. His rough palms skimmed her hardened nipples, tantalized her heated skin, driving her mad with desire.

He dropped to his haunches, and his hands slid down her torso, over her hips to clutch her thighs. Long fingers slid between her legs. Hot and damp, she responded to his skilled probing of her swollen folds.

His tongue flicked over the rounded curve of her hip, teased her buttocks, lingered on the sensitive flesh at the crease of each thigh, then slowly meandered to the spot where her skin parted into the distinct globes of her buttocks.

Moaning, lost in pleasure, Amanda leaned against the car and widened her stance. His long fingers slipped inside her. Hot and demanding. Slow and deep. Her muscles flexed wildly, rhythmically, wanting more. Wanting him.

She arched as his tongue licked the small of her back, then explored the valley between her buttocks, and shuddered at the fiery path descending between her legs. The rush of heated blood drummed out the warning bells ringing furiously in some small neglected corner of her brain.

Desire controlled her. Desire and need and wild sensation. She pumped against his demanding fingers, reaching, wanting, then crying out as suddenly he withdrew his hand. In one swift movement, he turned her around, pushed her legs apart and covered her hot, demanding clit with his tongue. Gently, so gently, sipping her desire.

"Please," she whimpered, thrusting her hips forward, surging against his mouth, then crying out in frustration as he pulled away and pushed himself upright.

She grasped the thick bulge stretching his jeans, daring him. He sucked in his breath, and cupped her face in his huge hands.

She squeezed his erection, gently.

He kissed her hard, not gently at all, plundering her mouth.

She fumbled at his belt, then tore at the buttons of his jeans and tugged at his briefs, desperate to free his swollen shaft and guide it between her legs.

He grasped her hips and broke the kiss, then placed her arms around his neck. "Not inside, not here," he gasped, drawing deep gulps of air. "Just ride it."

Lush and wet, back-and-forth over the hard ridge of his length, she followed his command. He was thick, long, hard. She needed this. She needed this forever. Rivers of naked desire, long-denied, raged through her body.

Desire demanding satisfaction.

She was horribly aware of how tight she held him, of how good his flesh felt, hard against hers. Her whole body burned at the searing contact. Seeking, needing, release; she rode him, used him for her own pleasure.

Lost. She was lost in heat, growing hotter, wetter. Waves of heat, centered between her legs, exploding in cataclysmic release. Rack-ing her body, drawing a strangled cry of satisfaction from between numbed lips.

Her body still trembled when Cooper whispered, "Let's go home, Mandy. I need to be inside you."

The impact of his words registered like a wave of cold water. *Oh God.* What had she done? Her lips felt swollen and raw. Her arms hung loosely about his neck. His hands still rested on her bare hips and his hard length throbbed between her clenched thighs. She ached for more. Ached for him to fill her. She drew in a breath of cool air and all her senses slammed back to earth. To the public parking lot behind the Prickly Cactus. To her employee with his hard cock between her thighs.

She'd lost control. She never, ever lost control. "That's a negative, Detective." She sounded far cooler than she felt.

Without a word, he separated their bodies. A rush of cool air filled the space between them and brushed her tender sex like a lover's caress.

She'd actually climaxed, her pleasure had flowed wet and hot over his hard flesh, over his still erect penis. She pulled up her sweats and turned away.

The luxury sedan was gone.

When had that happened?

How long had she and Cooper kissed? How long....?

She sucked air into her strained lungs and exhaled, struggling to control her racing heartrate. Cooper remained relaxed and seemingly unaffected. If he was going to act like nothing had happened, so could she. Damn him!

"What did you want to talk about?" she managed.

"While you're pretending to be my woman, I'm going to pick you up and drive you home."

At the thought of him driving her home and kissing her goodnight on her doorstep, Amanda's body caught fire. The temptation of Wes so near her bedroom was too much. "That's not necessary, Detective Cooper."

"What if some guy corners you out here and decides to do what

I just did?"

"That's not likely. I don't... kiss strangers."

"The hell it isn't. I don't want our cover blown because you have to pull a badge one night when some clown you've turned on follows you home. It happens. And Candy's side business doesn't discourage it."

"I've handled horny guys before," she snapped.

"How? By kissing them senseless?"

Despite the teasing nature of his words, Cooper's voice had a delicious silky texture. She felt his large hands settle on her shoulders. She waited for him, longed for him to kiss her again. He didn't, but his hands rubbed her upper arms. She was tempted to move his hands to her breasts.

"We're partners." His tone shifted, reminding Amanda of her duty. "If I felt Tom was in danger I'd cover him."

Turning around to face him, Amanda asked, "Do you kiss Tom?"

Cooper lifted his hand and cupped her chin. His thumb slid over her lower lip. "Naw, we usually just settle for a hand shake."

"Don't you think we should?"

"We're supposed to be lovers," he said as he fastened the top button of his jeans. "Besides you needed—."

Cooper's head snapped to the right. Out of the corner of her eye, Amanda noticed the back door of the Prickly Cactus had opened. It was the bartender. He muttered a goodnight and headed for his pickup.

"Get in," Cooper said as he opened her car door. "I'll follow you home."

Seizing the opportunity to end their conversation and her completely unprofessional behavior, Amanda slid into the driver's seat. Without waiting for Cooper to return to his Jeep, she started the Firebird's engine.

As she pulled out of the parking lot, Amanda remembered Cooper's half finished statement. Just what did he think she needed? Him?

What else could he think after what just happened?

Face it, Amanda, you want him. Want him so much. Too much.

The fierce reality of desire scared her. Amanda gripped the wheel and glanced at her rear-view mirror. A pair of headlights greeted her. When she turned right, so did the vehicle following her. Amanda stepped on the accelerator.

All kinds of sirens went off in her head. She drove like a mad-woman. When she turned onto her street, she couldn't remember how she got there, as if the drive home had taken seconds instead of the usual twenty-five minutes.

Approaching her house, she pressed the button on the remote control resting on her dash. When her garage door began to rise, Amanda slowed her Firebird and timed her entrance. Once inside her garage, she punched the remote.

The detective's black Cherokee pulled up just as the door began to descend. Amanda waived her hand in dismissal then rushed up-stairs into the safety of her home. When she heard the Jeep slowly drive away, she groaned. If Cooper had gotten his way, she had little doubt they wouldn't have settled for a handshake.

They'd be stripping off their clothes and screwing their brains out.

And tomorrow, while she'd spend the day regretting her lack of control and worrying about her suitability as a supervisor and lieu-tenant, Cooper would probably be swaggering through the precinct with a grin on his face.

The solution was simple. Cooper would not pick her up and escort her home. She was the boss and she would act like the responsible person she'd been prior to laying eyes on his taut buns and broad shoulders. And there would be no more sensual interludes in dark parking lots.

Tomorrow night she'd dance, but Cooper would never know she danced for him.

Chapter Two

At the sound of knuckles tapping on her office door, Amanda felt the same odd rush she'd identified with a dangerous situation. Not quite as intense, but definitely there. That odd mixture of alarm and exhilaration fueled by adrenaline right before she drew her weapon or entered a strange building in search of a suspect. The muscles of her arms, legs, abdomen and back clenched. When the door opened and Officer Bates's blonde head appeared, Amanda felt relieved, yet disappointed. She leaned back in her chair, feigning a humdrum posture she did not feel.

"Morning, Lieutenant. Do you have a minute?"

"Sure," Amanda responded, willing her heart to downshift. "How did it go last night?"

As the blonde officer closed the door, Amanda felt a tinge of jealousy. With her thread-bare jeans molded to her generous hips and her red knit top clinging to her double D's, Bates reminded Amanda of Dolly Parton.

"I was terrified during my first set," Bates said as she slipped into a guest chair.

If Cooper hadn't been in the audience, Amanda wasn't sure she could have gotten through the evening either. But he had been and Amanda had to admit, if only to herself, she'd loved dancing for him. It was a turn on.

So much of a turn on, they'd practically had sex in a public parking lot.

"Embarrassing for you, too," Bates said. "I'm sure my face got as red as yours is now."

Amanda's cheeks burned. She knew they were a bright pink, but not for the reason Bates thought.

"Guys have stared at me all my life," Bates continued. "I grew breasts in sixth grade. But last night… that was way different."

"Do you wish to be relieved of this assignment?" Amanda asked, glad to latch onto something that had to do with police work and not Wes Cooper.

"No, I can handle it. I volunteered because I'd like to be considered for detective. I'm studying hard and my exam scores are improving. I've helped the guys over in vice, but they…."

Before Amanda could respond, Bates jumped to her feet causing her large breasts to sway. What would Cooper have done last night if he'd spent the evening watching Bates dance?

"I'm sorry, Lieutenant. I'm nervous as a cat. I want to advance. Lt. Marks… he wouldn't take me seriously."

"A few of the men didn't think I had what it takes. Some still don't, but I like proving them wrong."

Officer Bates smiled. "So do I."

"This assignment is important. Do well and I'll make sure to note it in my report."

Bates hurried out of the office. A second later she popped her head back inside the door. "Wes said you were really nice. When he told me how well you did last night, I knew I could tough it out."

Since it was nine in the morning, just when had Wes told Bates about her performance? No matter how tempted, Amanda wasn't about to ask. She stared at the closed door. The unwanted image of Cooper and Bates naked and making love came to mind. Cooper's big hands sprawled all over those double D's.

"Damn him." Amanda grabbed the top five file folders off the stack on her desk. The folders, at least one-inch thick each, were the most difficult cases in her section. With the folders tucked securely in her arms, she marched out of her office, across the corridor and into the vacant squad room. Despite the hefty stack of case files on Cooper's desk, Amanda dropped the five folders dead center. "That should keep you busy," she muttered under her breath.

Wes eyed the stack of file folders on his desk which hadn't been there five minutes ago. He put down the double espresso he'd just purchased, flipped through the files, and grinned.

So he had gotten under her skin last night. Good. After she'd spent the evening turning him on, he'd hoped she'd live up to her hair color. He liked feisty redheads. Going toe-to-toe, then one-on-one and trying not to get burned.

Mandy was feisty plus some. Last night he'd gone home and straight into a cold shower. It had worked until he'd flipped on the radio as he crawled into bed. When Achey Breaky Heart came on, Wes had nearly lost his mind. He'd envisioned Mandy's dance all over again. In dreamlike slow motion, he recalled her hair falling down her back, swaying with the gyration of her hips. He felt achey breaky all right, but it wasn't his heart that was ready to break.

He hadn't slept a wink last night.

Tired and horny, he'd dragged his ass out of bed and into the precinct. Most of the squad hadn't shown yet, but Wes prided himself on the number of cases he solved. His numbers were the best. Rumor had it Amanda Forbes was just as obsessive.

Wes worked hard and he played to win. After watching Mandy climax during mere foreplay, he had no doubt she would be his.

He drained his double espresso and left the squad room.

Wes knocked once, then pushed open her office door. His gaze swept the room and riveted on Mandy's navy clad backside. After last night, watching it swing and wiggle, then holding it in his hands, he'd recognize the Lieutenant anywhere. A smile curled his lips. On hands and knees, with her skirt hiked high on her thighs exposing a generous amount of leg, his boss was more fetching than ever.

Ahhh, how he loved that position.

The thought of Mandy, naked, taking him....

He closed the door. Her head popped up and her mouth dropped open. Despite her conservative hair style and suit, those kissable lips and long legs were far too sexy for a lieutenant. Wes crossed

his arms and leaned against the door as he watched her scramble
to her feet and straighten her skirt.

"You should do that on stage."

"What?"

Her cheeks flushed pink. Maybe she was embarrassed to be
caught crawling around on floor, but maybe she knew he was thinking about the two of them. Both on their knees, his hands holding
her bare backside....

"On your hands and knees," he managed. "Your tips would
double."

Her cheeks went from pink to crimson. So she did know what
he was thinking.

She dropped back into her chair, but her gaze never left his face.
"Is there something you wanted?"

He pushed away from the door and closed the short distance to
her desk in two strides. "You bet," he said, placing his hands on the
papers strewn across her desk, and leaning toward her. "I want to
know why you broke every posted speed limit last night? Are you
trying to kill yourself or just take out any unfortunate motorists who
might have gotten in your way?"

She glared at him, but she didn't speak. He expected her to order
him out of her office. With a stroke of the pen, she could change his
assignment. She'd already given him five new cases, but for some
reason she'd picked him as her undercover partner.

"We're partners," he said, leveling his tone. "We're suppose to
watch each other's back, remember?"

"I doubt you escort your male partners home."

"I would if they'd spent the evening dancing naked."

She pushed herself to her feet. "I wasn't naked."

Toe-to-toe. Wes dropped his voice to a hoarse whisper. "Every
man in that place wanted you naked. Don't you understand what
you do on that stage? Every guy has a fantasy. And once in a while
we get lucky. There it is before our very eyes. Promising everything.
Giving nothing."

"That's ridiculous. I was just dancing."

Wes might have believed her if she wasn't looking at him like she wanted him. Her body was rigid, her voice pushing strident, but her eyes were a lush, brilliant green. Wanting.

"Who are you dancing for, Mandy?"

"No one." Her voice caught. "You have no right to question—"

"You liked it. You liked every minute of it. It's like making love. You know when your partner—"

"What does this have to do with making love?"

"When you're up there, you're doin' it. It may all be in your mind, but I felt it. Every guy in the place felt it."

Matching his position, she put her hands on her desk and leaned forward. "I've always excelled undercover. I'm good at it."

One-on-one. Her face was inches from his. Her sweet lips only a movement away. If they were anywhere else he'd kiss her, then he'd pull her to the floor....

"I'll pick you up at five."

"I don't need a keeper, Detective. You will report at six."

"You may be the boss, but you're my partner. Safety comes first. Don't make me go to the Captain."

"I can remove you from this operation."

"Then do it, but make sure you tell the Captain the truth."

"And what is the truth, Detective?"

"You're worried about last night. What happened. Apparently what you do on that stage affects you as much as me. If you need to blow off a little steam, who better than your partner?"

"You're out of line, Cooper."

That was true. She made him feel wild and reckless. He didn't give a damn she was his boss. He wanted her. He wanted her beautiful bum slapping his belly. He wanted to lick his sweat off her bare skin. "And *you* are the hottest thing I've ever seen on stage. So, I will pick you up and see you safely home 'cause no one messes with my wo... partner."

She opened her mouth to speak, but Wes leaned closer. She stood her ground. "I excel at being a partner. I know more about Tom than his wife will ever know. I'm loyal. As loyal to my partner as I would be to a wife."

Her lips trembled slightly. She pushed out a breath. It felt hot against his skin. She said nothing. Wes had to force himself to move back before he caught her next breath with his own and the fine edge of his control disintegrated. Without waiting for a response, he left her office and closed the door firmly behind him.

Amanda dropped back into her chair and stared at the closed door. She could swear he'd almost said his woman instead of his partner? Wife? Had he actually used the forbidden word? She didn't think guys like Cooper dared lest they be stricken.

And that crack about blowing off steam!

Who are you dancing for? You're the hottest thing… You liked it.

She licked her lips. Cooper had wanted to kiss her. Wanted to push her to the floor and take her. Her whole body had tightened in anticipation. Even now her breasts felt full. She was wet with desire. Thank God he'd come to his senses.

It was as if he could see into her heart and mind. As if he knew exactly how to feed all her hungers. She did like dancing and stripping, but only because of him. She wanted him to lust for her. She wanted to drive him crazy. Tonight she would do it again. And she'd want him again, but there could be no blowing off steam with Cooper.

When she caught herself trying to remember if the batteries in her vibrator were still charged, she swore. "Damn you, Cooper."

Amanda, dressed in sweats with duffle bag in hand, stared at the clock by her front door, then checked her wristwatch. If Cooper was a second late, she was leaving for the club.

The second hand swept toward the hour. The detective's Cherokee appeared.

Once inside the Jeep, he was all business. "Tonight's crowd

should be rowdier. Not as many suits. More hats," he said, pointing to his black Stetson. "More money in the till."

They hashed over the possibility of a Friday night robbery. Satisfied with their plan of action, Amanda relaxed as they pulled into the parking lot behind the Prickly Cactus. He hadn't called her Mandy once.

At the dressing room door, he leaned close. "If some guy grabs at you, don't kick him in the teeth, Lieutenant. That's my job," he said. Then he slapped her on the rear and strolled down the hallway toward the bar.

Right before her last set, Amanda remembered that slap. As she moved down the stage, she focused on the guys wearing hats at the edge of the stage, especially the young ones. She licked her lips and blew kisses while she stripped out of her vest and skirt.

Down to her demi-bra and G string, she jiggled her breasts then wiggled her hips in each of their faces. By teasing them, she'd get to Cooper. Like a wave, they jumped to their feet and hooted and hollered. Amanda danced to the end of the stage and rolled her hips and pelvis, performing the bump and grind. One young cowboy lunged forward, but before the guy joined her on stage, a large hand shot out, clamped him on the shoulder and forced him back.

Cooper stepped forward and planted himself at the edge of the stage. If Amanda thrust her pelvis forward, she could tap him on the nose. Instead she pushed his Stetson back on his forehead and pursed her lips in a kiss. Cooper grinned.

She danced in a tight circle, keeping within an arm's length of her protector. With her back to Cooper, she lowered herself slowly to her hands and knees, then pumped her hips in time with the music. The crowd roared. She peeked over her shoulder. The grin on Cooper's face had disappeared. His eyes narrowed. He looked furious.

Pushing herself to her feet, she performed her finale. As she made her way around the stage to collect her tips, the men closest to the stage shoved bills in her garter. One cowboy reached for her G string. She felt a crisp bill, followed by his calloused fingers slide across her backside and beneath the thong between her cheeks, then quickly retreat as Cooper forced his body between her admirer and the stage.

She felt Cooper's hand cup her bare buttocks. As his warm fingers splayed protectively over her rear, he directed the cowboys to the black garter on her thigh.

Cooper walked along the stage as she moved on to collect her tips. No one else grabbed her G string. No one dared. She could still feel the imprint of his hand as she pushed the beaded curtains aside to leave the stage.

Just as he said he would, he'd protected his partner. It was his job, but it was also sexy, sweet and macho.

✻ᘛ⑈ᘚ✻

Amanda shouldered her duffle bag and joined Cooper at the back door of the Prickly Cactus. "No Harolds tonight," she quipped.

He gave her a sidelong glance as they walked. "After that last show, I think you made more than enough tips."

"You were right," she said as they approached his Jeep. "I doubled them."

"I noticed."

When Cooper unlocked the passenger door and opened it for her, she thought about turning around, grabbing him by the lapels of his leather jacket and kissing him senseless. Instead, she climbed into the Jeep and reached for her seatbelt.

He remained silent and well within the posted speed limits as he navigated the Jeep through the city streets, then onto the freeway. By the time they reached her street, Amanda had made her decision.

Despite the rules, she wanted Cooper. Wanted to know the splendor of his lovemaking. Wanted to feel him inside her.

"Would you like to come in?"

Cooper pulled up at the curb and switched off the engine. "I'd like nothing better, but I've got a lead on those retail heists. One of my informants says he knows where the stuff is warehoused. I'm going to check it out."

"I'll go with you."

"Thanks, boss, but you might spook my informant."

Amanda leaned over and stroked his lean jaw. "Just tell him I'm your *woman*."

He reached up and caught her hand in his. "I'm having a hard enough time concentrating on work as it is."

"You don't seem to have any problem at the club."

"I don't when Candy or Lucy is on stage. But you...."

In the near darkness, she couldn't see his expression. His voice was level, devoid of humor or sarcasm. "What about me?"

He slid his hand slowly up her arm, then placed a fingertip on her lower lip. "Don't tease me, Mandy. You have no idea—"

"I'm not teasing, Cooper."

"What are you saying?"

She turned her head and kissed his palm. "I want you, Wes."

"You would choose tonight."

"The night's not over."

He leaned back in the bucket seat. "You're determined to go with me, aren't you?"

"Uh-huh."

"Then put some clothes on. I can't think business when you're almost naked," he said as he opened his door.

"I'm decent," she protested before the door slammed shut.

He walked around to her door and pulled it open. "Any underwear, Mandy?"

"Well, no."

He took her hand. "Then think layers."

She heard the thunk of the car door as she stepped into his arms. "You have no trouble at the club."

"The hell I don't." His hands drifted down her back, beneath her sweatshirt, and under the waistband of her sweats. He cupped her buttocks. "If the robbers had come in while you were on your knees, I'd have given them the fucking money."

His erection, thick and promising, pressed into her belly. "How much time do we have?"

"Not enough to do you justice," he said, setting her body away and taking her hand. "Let's go inside before we start rolling around on the front lawn."

"Ever done it on a lawn?" she asked as they covered the short distance to her front door.

"Not since college." He took her key and unlocked her front door. "I want you naked, Mandy. And once I'm inside you, I'm gonna stay awhile."

"That a promise, cowboy?" she asked as they stepped inside.

He shut the door, yanked off his hat and pulled her into his arms. Their bodies met breast to thigh. "We'll see whose knees give out first."

Amanda wrapped her arms about his neck and kissed him hard. The phone rang. Reluctantly she broke the kiss. "It's my mother. She always calls when I'm out on late assignments."

He closed his eyes. When the phone rang again, his hands slid down her back to rest on her bottom. "I'll take the call in my bedroom while I dress. Don't disappear, Cooper," she said in her Lieutenant's voice as she stepped out of his light hold.

"I wouldn't think of it, boss," he said, slapping her on the backside as she turned away. "One of us might come to our senses."

Amanda grabbed the receiver from its cradle. "Hi, Mom. I got to make this quick, I'm working another robbery case," she said as she pulled off her athletic shoes without untying the laces.

"Did the package arrive?"

"It arrived a couple of days ago," Amanda said thinking of the unopened package she'd shoved under her bed. Her grandmother's recent death had been difficult. She couldn't bring herself to open the box.

"Her only regret was not seeing you wear it before she...."

"I'm sorry," Amanda said softly. "I wish I could have made her happy... I.... I'm going out for a while. We're working a case."

"It's awfully late. Who's we?"

Knowing her mother worried, she tried to assure her by letting her know she wouldn't be on her own. "Detective Cooper. He works for me."

"How old is he?"

Amanda rolled her eyes. "Don't start matchmaking. Cooper's definitely not husband material."

Her remark did little to dampen her mother's curiosity. It irked Amanda that her mother thought being a bride more important than making Lieutenant. "Is he single?"

With one hand Amanda shucked her sweat pants. "About as single as they come."

"Let me speak to him."

"Not a chance. He's an employee, not a date," she said opening her dresser drawer to retrieve a pair of lacy panties and bra. "We're working an important case. Cooper doesn't have time to talk to you."

"Give me the phone, Mandy."

Amanda started at the voice behind her. She spun around. How long had he been there listening? Cooper stepped closer. She motioned him back into the living room. Grinning like a Cheshire cat, he dropped his gaze to her bare crotch and kept coming. She yanked down the oversized sweatshirt as his hand closed over the receiver. For a moment, they wrestled silently over the slender piece of sand-colored plastic, then he thrust his hand between her legs.

Caught off guard, she forgot the receiver and grabbed at his hand. Then his forefinger slid inside her.

"Mrs. Forbes, this is Detective Wes Cooper. How are you?"

His voice was far too calm for what he was doing with his hand. He turned his head so she couldn't reach the receiver.

"Are you crazy," Amanda cried, lunging forward. His finger plunged deeper. His palm fastened over her mound. Although both her hands gripped his wrist, she couldn't free herself without retreating away from him and the telephone. She hesitated, hoping he'd relax his guard. He moved his finger to-and-fro bringing back the heat which had been simmering since she'd stepped on stage to dance for him.

"Yes, I have to agree. She's very pretty." Cooper turned. His gaze moved over her, then dropped to where his hand cupped her possessively. "Yes, she does have beautiful red hair."

Wrenching her body free of his invasion, Amanda stepped back, then lunged forward. Cooper reached for her again. She jumped back. He winked, then licked his finger.

"Don't worry, Peggy," he said into the receiver. "I'll see that she's safe and sound in her bed as soon as possible."

At the use of her mother's Christian name, Amanda lunged forward. She had to disconnect the call. To her surprise, he thrust the receiver in her hand.

"Say goodnight, Mandy," he whispered.

Although her heart pounded and she was mad as hell at Cooper, she tried to sound calm, "I call you tomorrow, Mom."

He dropped to his knees. She danced away from him. The stretched phone cord pulled the base off the bed stand.

Cooper caught it. "Come over here, Mandy."

She glared at him and shook her head. "I've got to go," she said into the receiver.

"Is Detective Cooper as handsome as he sounds?"

"No, Mom," Amanda replied. "He just thinks he's irresistible."

When Cooper gave her a you-don't-mean-that look, Amanda said a quick goodnight to her mother and tossed the receiver at him. He dodged the missile and fastened his gaze on her exposed crotch. "Come here, Mandy. Let me show how much I like red hair."

"How dare you talk to my mother."

"She just wants you to be happy. I can make you happy."

"I don't think a quickie was what my mother had in mind. Watch out, Cooper. She's not trying to find me a lover."

"I want to kiss you."

"Forget it. Get out and let me get dressed or we'll be late."

"We've got time for a kiss." He took off his leather jacket and tossed it on the bed.

Be careful what you wish for, you just might get it. All of a sudden Amanda's anger dwindled. She had to laugh at the irony. Here was Wes Cooper in her bedroom on his knees wanting her, and she was ordering him out. How many times had she fantasized about this very situation? Far too many to count.

As if attuned to her moment of indecision, he cocked his head to one side and lifted his arms. She moved into them.

But Cooper didn't pull her down into his arms. He kissed her. Right between the legs. His tongue lapped at her hidden entrance, easing aside the delicate folds. She felt his big hands curl about her thighs. Hot and gripping, they held her while his tongue explored with slow, deliberate caresses.

Pushing his knees between her ankles, he urged her legs further apart to give him unrestricted access. Amanda complied. Her hands fell to his shoulders. She needed to touch him. She wanted him naked. She slid her hand to his neck, then under the collar of his western shirt. The top snap popped open. His muscles bunched beneath her fingers.

She gave no thought to forbidding his actions. Nothing existed except Wes and the exquisite pleasure he gave her.

He licked her soft flesh. With each lush stroke she felt herself opening to him. Each stroke pushing him deeper inside her. He delved, once, then once again. Her legs trembled. Her knees slumped, yet his hands held her steady.

His tongue withdrew. Using the tip, he slowly circled her heated entrance. She wanted him inside her. Willed him to please her. "Again," she whispered.

She waited for him to enter her. Instead his tongue skimmed over her bud, back and forth until her whole body burned with wanting him.

He drew back a fraction and blew gently. His warm breath flowed over her heated flesh. Lightly he sucked at the tender flesh of her inner thighs.

She moaned. Wrapping her fingers in his hair, Amanda turned his head, demanded his loving. Again he laved her swollen flesh until she quivered. Then he blew gently. His hot breath teasing her heated sex.

His tongue delved inside. Exploring her recesses, he mapped every soft fold until Amanda felt swollen, ready to burst. His tongue withdrew and rested against her entrance. Amanda felt a trickle, hot and molten, slide from her. A harsh groan tore from his throat, then his mouth covered her fleshy outer lips, caressing them, kissing them, making her wetter still.

When his tongue settled on her bud, Amanda cried out. A tidal wave of pleasure engulfed her. Wet and full, she rolled her hips, enhancing her pleasure and easing the great pressure building inside her.

His hands skimmed the back of her thighs and up to the cleft of her buttocks. His fingertip dipped inside her moist channel from behind. She lifted one leg and settled her naked thigh on his shoulder. Using his body for support, Amanda pressed her swollen flesh to his mouth. Her hips moved, heightening her pleasure, bringing her to the edge.

Gently he drew her bud between his lips and suckled. Her back arched. She thrust her pelvis forward, demanding more. Waves of pleasure, moving from the epicenter of his loving, flowed throughout her body.

The muscles in her legs trembled beneath his hands as her orgasm eased. As if knowing he'd pushed her to the limit of pleasure, Cooper laved the swollen tissue. Stroking her. Easing her tender flesh. Bringing her back to earth.

At that moment everything important centered between her legs. She pulled off her sweatshirt, tossed it aside and looked down at him.

His hot blue gaze concentrated for a heartbeat on one nipple, then the other. He licked his lips and grinned. Damn, but he was sexy when he grinned.

"They're beautiful, Mandy. But if we don't get moving, my snitch is gonna fly."

Chapter Three

Amanda stared at him in disbelief as he eased her bare leg off his shoulder and drew himself to his feet. Was he made of steel? Her knees still felt weak. Her body languid. The last thing she wanted to do was dress and meet a snitch in the warehouse district.

She glanced at the bed as he picked up his jacket. She wanted to toss aside the Southwest patterned comforter and make love until the crisp new sheets were hot and slick with their sweat.

His head cocked to one side. That ever present grin teased his lips. Lips that had given her so much pleasure. "You coming?" he asked.

Before she could mouth an answer, he strode out of her bedroom and her fantasy. Amanda frantically looked about for her clothes. Where did she leave her bra and underpants? If she didn't move quickly, he'd be gone.

She snatched her sweatpants from the floor, then grabbed her shoes. Her sweatshirt had disappeared. She rushed to her closet and grabbed a jacket, then raced out of her bedroom.

Cooper turned as she ran into the living room. His mouth dropped open as she shoved her arms into her sheepskin coat. "Get my duffle bag," she ordered, grabbing her key ring dangling from his right hand. "I'll need my gun and badge."

"You can't—"

"Let's go, Detective," she said, pushing pass him. She opened the door and stepped onto the walkway. Although she wore socks, the flagstone felt like blocks of ice.

Without looking back, Amanda ran to his parked vehicle. The cold night air nipped at her legs and curled up her bare thighs. Cooper climbed in behind the wheel, tossed her duffle bag onto the back seat, then reached over and unlocked the passenger door.

She hopped in as he started the engine. When her bare butt made contact with the cold leather seat, she jumped.

The Jeep lunged forward. She heard him stifle a laugh as he flipped on the heater, then pushed the lever to high.

No wonder he was laughing, she thought as she maneuvered into her sweat pants. She'd run out of the house, naked except for a coat and socks, after letting him....

Twice he'd taken her to climax. Pleased her to distraction. At least this time he'd taken off his jacket.

At this rate it would take her a month to get him down to briefs.

If they had a month.

She was playing with fire. Passion fire. Teasing a flame which could easily go out of control. Deep in her heart, Amanda knew she'd have to give him up. They both had worked too hard to throw it all away for a fast burning passion fire....

Or was it a heartfire?

Could this be the real thing? Amanda glanced at Cooper. Lights from passing vehicles flashed across his lean features. "Warm?"

She pulled the deep pile coat across her naked breasts. "I'm fine," she managed. "Can we make it on time?"

"Yeah, if I concentrate on the road."

"Then drive, Detective," she said, trying to dispel the aura of sensuality between them. Like a thin fog it circled them, pulling them together. At the club it blew like a hot wind. In her bedroom it had changed once again. She'd been the explosive, waiting for his spark.

She wanted the passion. And him. But was she ready for love and commitment?

"We're almost there," he said, breaking into her thoughts. "I'll leave the car keys."

"I'm coming with you," she said, suddenly afraid for him.

"Then I might as well kiss this off," he said, pulling into a deserted alley. He switched off the headlights. Slowly he navigated the vehicle down the narrow strip of asphalt. Twenty feet shy of the street, he braked to a stop. Cooper turned off the ignition and handed her the keys. He reached for the door latch, then his right hand shot up to switch off the interior lamp.

Amanda grabbed his lapels and pulled him toward her.

He wrapped his hands around her wrists. "Don't. I have the scent of you in my nostrils and the taste of you on my lips. I can barely think for wanting you."

For a long moment Amanda stared at him. His face was nothing more than a shadow, but she could feel the warmth of his body, the rhythm of his breathing, the solid strength in his hands. Her heart pounded against her ribs. Partly in fear, wildly in love.

Reluctantly she released her grip. "Be careful, Wes."

"Give me forty-five minutes," he said, then pulled away. She heard the soft click of the door opening and shutting, then watched as he disappeared around the corner.

※₰(ʘ֊ʘ)₰ऊ

Amanda started at the tap on the driver's window. She'd been waiting, chewing her nails to the quick, expecting Wes to return from the direction he'd gone. Instead he'd approached the vehicle from behind, taking her off guard. She reached over and unlocked the door. He slipped inside and she dropped the keys into his outstretched hand.

"How did it go?" she asked as he drove slowly out of the alley and onto the deserted street. Although her voice sounded calm, she'd never been so frightened for anyone in her life. But then she'd never been in love with her partner.

Love. Waiting for him, wondering if he were safe, Amanda realized she'd never experienced such powerful emotions. Such need. Alone in the Jeep's dark interior, all she'd heard was her thundering heart. Now it thundered in relief. He was safe.

"The place is full of stolen merchandise. I'll need a search warrant."

"I'll take care of it first thing in the morning." *After we go back to my place and finish what you started.* She needed to hold him.

"Got to do it now. They're moving the stuff this weekend. I'll drop you off at home, then roust Tom out of bed."

"No way, Cooper. I'm going with you."

"I can handle this, boss," he said, glancing over at her. "You're not exactly dressed for work."

She stiffened and didn't say a word to keep from revealing her disappointment. He'd distanced himself from her. She could feel it.

He reached over and squeezed her hand. "Tom and I have worked this case for months. It's our collar, Lieutenant."

Relief washed over her. He wasn't pushing her away, but doing his job. Too many times she'd seen commanders step in and take credit for cases they'd assigned and forgotten. Until they were solved.

"If you need anything, call me." She watched the play of passing street lights flit across his face. "I'll back you a hundred percent." She was rewarded with that irresistible grin.

Ten minutes later, he parked in front of her house. She turned toward him and unbuttoned his jacket. "Turn off the lights, Wes."

At the flip of a switch, they were plunged into darkness. She leaned toward him. Her hand slid beneath his open jacket to wrap around his solid torso. She drew him close. "I want to know how I taste," she said right before her lips met his.

She kissed him hard. Thrusting her tongue into his mouth, showing him as powerfully as she could how much she wanted him, how much she loved him. His arm slid about her back, he held her tight to his chest for a short heartbeat, then relaxed. Reluctantly she ended the kiss.

"You taste lush and sweet and wonderful," he said as his hand dropped away. "And I gotta go."

At five o'clock, Wes's Jeep pulled up in front of her house. Amanda hadn't heard from him all day. She opened the door as he strolled down the walkway. He looked exhausted. "Did you get any sleep?" she asked.

He shook his head. "Grabbed an hour while waiting for the warrant. The place is staked out. We want to nail them inside. Tom is at the warehouse. Grimes is covering the Bosom Buddy."

She stepped back to let him inside. "But he was on leave till next week."

"Captain got an okay from his doctor. Besides Grimes is a regular at the Buddy. He'll fit right in."

She closed the door. "You didn't need me at all."

"I don't need a Lieutenant telling me how to do my job," he said as he pulled her into his arms. "But I need you, Mandy. If I didn't, I'd be at the stakeout with Tom."

He slanted his head and captured her lips. His hands snaked into her hair. His lips moved over hers as his tongue penetrated her mouth. She wrapped her arms around his lean torso and held him tight.

Her hands slid down to cup his firm buns. When she reached for him, he pulled his mouth from hers and sucked in a breath. "Take it easy, honey. I've had no sleep and I've been wearing this hard-on for most of the last three days. If you touch me, I'll burst. Then I'll never get back on my feet."

Amanda folded her arms across her chest. She'd spent the day worrying and wrestling with her feelings. Being in love was hell. Knowing Wes was facing a potentially dangerous situation frayed her usually calm nerves. This would never work. Her perspective as task force leader was shot. "Let me call someone in to cover the Cactus. Then you can rest."

He reached out and planted a large hand about her waist. His other hand cupped her chin. "If you think I'll let anyone watch you dance—"

"Fifty guys watch me dance."

His whole body tensed. The muscles in his arms bunched beneath his black shirt. His eyes burned into hers. "Fifty strangers watch Blaze. If I'm not there, *you* don't dance."

"Maybe I should remind you this is a job—"

His grip on her chin tightened slightly. "What's happening between us... this isn't casual... at least not for me. This has gone way beyond a job and you know it."

"And it has to end when this job is over," she said. Despite the heartpain, she'd made an executive decision for both of them. She wouldn't be responsible for damaging Cooper's career. Nor was she ready to resign. She loved him, but love could be so fickle. Too many of her friends were divorced for her to believe otherwise. She worked too hard to gamble on love.

His hand slid from her waist as his eyes closed tight. He moved his head slowly, side-to-side in denial. As he opened his eyes, he said, "End?"

She wanted Wes. Maybe it wasn't love at all and this passion would burn itself out, but odds were if they became lovers, they'd be discovered. Whenever she looked at Wes, Amanda felt her temperature rise. Someone was bound to notice. "We can't lose everything just because we've got the hots for each other."

He released her chin and ran his fingers along her jaw. "What is it you want from me, Mandy? Am I just a guy to put out the fire after you dance?"

"Of course not. You've built your life around your job," she said softly. "Both of us have. If the Captain finds out you'll be back in uniform and I... it's—"

"It's not worth a career." His hand dropped to his side. He stepped away from her and opened the front door. "Let's go to work, *boss,*" he said as he marched out.

Amanda started out the door, then remembered her duffle bag. By the time she ran outside, he was sitting in the Jeep with the engine running. His lean facial features looked like stone. Cold and immobile.

All the way to the club he didn't say a word, which suited her just fine. Logic and training told her she was doing the right thing. But all the training in the world couldn't keep her heart from breaking.

Why did she have to fall for a fellow cop? Amanda thought of all the men she'd dated, but not one of them had touched her heart. She'd wanted the perfect combination of hero and hunk. She'd found it in Wes.

Strong, honest, and willing to put his life on the line if necessary, Wes had her complete respect. He made her proud to be his boss, but more than that, he always made her feel. He had the power to make her laugh, to make her forget her rank, and to break her heart.

What on earth had possessed her to use the term "hots"? She didn't have the "hots" for Wes Cooper. She loved him. Too much to get him busted down to a patrol car.

Or so she told herself. Deep in her heart, she knew she was taking the easy route. So many times, she'd challenged the odds and won. She'd received several commendations, some for valor. When she thought about testing the odds of love, Amanda didn't feel the lest bit brave.

⁂

Both Candy and Lucy, eager to enjoy Saturday night, had left the club before Amanda finished her last set. Back in her dressing room, she plucked the bills from her garter. The tips were meager compared to the night before, but Amanda hadn't lived up to her previous performance either. All night she'd felt the pain in her heart much more than the beat of the music. Although Wes was somewhere in the blackness beyond the lights, she hadn't felt his heated gaze. Not once had he approached the stage.

She pulled off her boots, then unclasped her sequin-covered bra. After dropping the bra into her duffle bag, she bent to remove her G string. As she stepped out of the garment, the dressing room door burst open. Wes filled the doorway. His big hands hung at his side and his fingers moved as if his hands itched. The frown marring his handsome face softened into a grin as he stepped forward and shut the door with a decided bang.

He shucked off his jacket, letting it fall to the floor, then reached for his belt buckle. "Okay, Mandy, I'm your guy."

The look in his blue eyes alarmed her. She licked her lips, half in fear, half in excitement. He wanted her. Intended to take her. Right now. Right here. She stepped back. The G string slipped from her fingers. He kept right on coming. She knew she should protest, but her tongue refused to move. It might be the nineties, but something inside her coiled, heated and waited to be taken.

Her gaze dropped to his hands ripping at the buttons of his fly. She sucked in her breath when he freed his erection. Then his hands were in her hair, pulling her head back. His mouth covered hers as his hands slid down her bare back to grasp her buttocks.

In one fluid motion, he lifted her up and pushed her back against the dressing room wall, exactly as he had in her fantasies. Trapped between his hot body and the cold wall with her legs open, she anticipated his passionate invasion. Ached for it.

Holding her buttocks firmly with one hand, he reached for her breast. He cupped, then lifted and molded her flesh to his. Slowly he squeezed, a sweet compression of his palm and fingers. Beneath his powerful hand, her breast swelled and ached. Her nipple thrust against the textured skin of his palm.

His hand slid from her breast, down her torso, strong fingers teasing her excited flesh. Everywhere he touched became heated. He dipped his fingertips between her legs as if testing her readiness, then wet her aching nipple with her moisture.

When his mouth covered her breast, a cry caught in her throat. He suckled. With each deep tug, waves of desire rolled through Amanda. Hot, heavy waves building between her legs until the need for Wes was unbearable. She grasped his erection. Her hand pumped his rigid shaft.

Wet and primed, her muscles pulsed. When she guided him toward her heated center, he grabbed her hand. Amanda moved her head in protest. This time she wanted him inside her. Not his long experienced fingers, not his sensual tongue, but him. All of him.

"Make love to me, Wes. Now."

He lifted his head and looked her right in the eye. "You're much too bossy," he said as he reached into his back pocket and pulled out his cuffs and snapped one on her wrist.

Her lungs sucked in air. "I could charge you with sexual harassment," she said, her voice husky with desire.

"Then do it. But we both know who's been harassed. And honey it hasn't been you."

"Use these often?" Amanda asked, excited all the more by the cuffs.

Wes grinned. "Only with uncooperative Lieutenants," he said as he cuffed her to his wrist.

Amanda reached down and grasped his erection. His shaft flexed beneath her rapidly moving fingers. "This could cost you your detective's badge, Cooper. Put you back in a patrol car until retirement."

He locked the fingers of his cuffed hand with hers. "Put your arm around my neck."

She released him. He lifted her high until his belly pressed her center. As his lips close over her nipple, she whispered. "You must look damn good in uniform."

She arched her back. Her taut breast ached. A delicious heat coiled between her legs.

All Wes had to do was touch her and she was powerless to resist him. How could she work with him, see him daily and not want him? He lifted his head, then slid their clenched, cuffed hands gently beneath her buttocks. Her weight securely anchored, he slipped his free hand between her legs. He dipped his finger in her drenched slit. After a few heartbeats, he withdrew his finger and ran the soft tip along her lower lip. It was slick with desire. Her desire.

She wanted to kiss him. Put her lips on him and taste him. She wanted to feel his full, thick erection in her mouth. She needed to feel his heated blood pumping beneath her lips.

As if understanding her thoughts, Wes's shaft moved against her bottom. Inside, her muscles flexed.

"You're wet, Mandy. Wet and hot. If you don't want me, tell me. If this isn't extraordinary, tell me. If the job's more important, tell me."

Amanda couldn't speak. The lie wouldn't come. To remain a couple one of them would have to sacrifice their choice assignments. If they were discovered, both of them could face serious consequences. In her wildest dreams she'd never believed she'd have to choose between a man and her career. Wrapping her legs tight around his torso, she pressed her wet center against his bare belly. She was going to have the man. She'd have to figure out the rest later.

When she licked her lower lip, he slanted his head and kissed her.

He shifted her bottom and pushed her up higher against the wall. Fishing in his shirt pocket, he retrieved a small foil packet and forced it in her free hand. "I want to feel your hand on me. Then I want you."

The cool steel blue gaze she'd known had shifted. His eyes burned hot. Blue fire. Without breaking eye contact, she tore open the foil packet and positioned the condom between her lips.

His heated gaze shifted to her mouth and he stepped back. She dropped to her knees between his legs. Her fingers enclosed him, and his breathing increased. He raised one eyebrow as she positioned her lips on the tip of his penis, then slowly rolled the latex down his hard length, sheathing him as she took him deeper in her mouth. His eyelids partially closed, then opened. He whispered her name.

His strangled voice warned her he was on the edge. Slowly Amanda removed her lips from his pulsing erection. In one supple movement, he pulled her to her feet, lifted her against the wall, and entered her. A trickle of sweat trailed down his temple.

Once again he locked her fingers in his, binding her to him as surely as the cuffs bound their wrists.

Needing to feel more of his hot flesh, she grasped the top snap of his western shirt and in one quick yank, the snaps gave way popping like firecrackers.

Shockwaves rippled through her body as he filled her. Wide open and wet, she welcomed him. He buried his shaft deeper, plunging again and again into her swollen center. His balls slapped against her sensitive flesh. His broad chest, damp with sweat, imprisoned her against the wall, crushing her breasts. With each thrust of his lean hips, he drove himself into her.

Joining them.

Their bodies made those lush sucking sounds of skin against skin and his heated flesh drove her to cresting madness. Then he went rigid. His shoulders and chest heaved. Her breath caught. Her legs clamped his torso, binding him to her.

Chapter Four

Wes's body convulsed and released in heavy waves of pure ecstasy. Mandy held him tight, both inside and out. Her green eyes glowed. Her lips parted slightly. Her breathing, like his, puffed in uneven gasps. He'd pleased her. Satisfied her.

He slanted his head to cover her mouth. He wanted to kiss her while he was still deep inside her, surrounded by her splendid wetness.

He loved the lush feel of her. All of her. His tongue sucked at the hot recesses of her mouth. Her sex flexed and pulled at him.

She needed more.

Her breasts heaved and her nipples tantalized his skin, sparking his tired, sated body to life. He rocked his hips and deepened his kiss. Despite the ache in his legs, Wes willed himself to stay hard, She was still unbelievably wet. Soft and sweet, and demanding. His woman. His love.

He felt her body shudder, then clamp down on him. He pushed his way past her tight folds. Once. Twice. Buried himself. Her sex rippled along his length. Grasping. Releasing. Finally, she stilled.

Their lips parted as she relaxed. Inhaling deeply, he filled his lungs with air. Her scent lingered in his nostrils. She'd taken everything he had to offer. He closed his eyes and buried his face in her hair.

His legs jerked. His thighs vibrated as the exhaustion hit him. Yet he didn't want to let her go.

He hadn't wanted it this way. He'd wanted to love her in that soft bed of hers. He'd wanted to fall asleep with their still damp bodies entwined and the smell of her hair scenting the air he breathed.

Instead he'd shoved her up against a wall, handcuffed her and taken her.

Wes wasn't sure just when he'd fallen in love. But he had. Still embedded in her sweet warmth, he felt a moment of panic. After having her, he couldn't go back to old his life. He didn't want one-night stands or afternoon romps. Quickly done, easily forgotten.

But Mandy wanted nothing more than that. She wanted his heat. His sex. When the operation ended, she wanted the partnership dissolved.

What the hell was he supposed to do? Go to work each day and pretend she meant nothing? Or worse yet pretend she didn't exist?

When had all the damn rules changed?

For a moment he longed for the old days when he'd been the one with the love-them-and-leave-them attitude.

Her lips touched his neck. Soft, gentle nipping kisses. Sweet, and tender. He loved for her to touch him. He lifted his hand and sank his fingers into her long, red hair. He placed his lips to her temple and felt the pulse of her heartbeat. He wanted to remember this moment: her soft breasts crushed to his chest, his hand in her hair, the descending rhythm of their heartbeats and the sweet aroma of their mating.

What would she do if he told her he loved her?

He wanted to say the words he felt in his heart, but given the present scenario she'd probably laugh. Besides Mandy didn't love him. She wanted him, she liked him, but she wasn't in love with him. He'd rather be shot than have her tell him to get lost.

He opened his eyes. She was so damn beautiful. He stroked her hair, then stepped back a fraction. Her legs uncoiled as he withdrew from her warmth. Despite the harsh glare of the dressing room lights, her skin held the pink flush of sensual heat. She had no idea what she did to him.

Maybe it was better that way.

"Wes—"

He wished she'd call him Cooper and maintain the cool distance of passing lovers. She had no right to say his name as if…. He pushed aside the delicious, completely reckless thought.

He uncurled his fingers and released his tight grip on her hand.

"The key's in my pants pocket."

She bent her knees and sank slowly until her weight was balanced on her toes. Her thighs were spread wide. Her gaze focused on his dwindling erection. Damn but this was embarrassing. Why the hell had he cuffed her? Why the hell did he feel so damn possessive?

She fished the key out of his pocket and stood. With quick efficiency she unlocked the cuffs, then dropped the key in his palm. For a long moment they stared at each other. Wes wanted to kiss her, tell her he'd transfer to another precinct, anything to keep her. As long as there were criminals, he'd find work, but he'd never find another Mandy. His hand closed over the cuffs.

What should have been a loving moment, felt awkward and embarrassing. He hadn't been embarrassed with a woman since high school. But then he'd never cuffed a woman before. And he'd cuffed the woman he loved. He pulled up his jeans and turned away.

"I've got a stakeout in progress," he said. Without looking at her, he grabbed his jacket and slammed out the door.

Amanda paced. She'd been prowling her office like a caged cat all morning. And it had nothing to do with the stack of reports on her desk.

Wes Cooper was driving her mad.

All day yesterday she'd waited for the phone to ring. Ached to hear his voice. Twice she'd entered the garage and opened the door of her Firebird only to slam it closed. She wanted to go to him, to tear off her clothes and demand he make love to her.

But pride had overruled her foolish heart. After a few glasses of wine, driving was out of the question.

She rounded her desk again, aware of the black lace garter belt, smoke-colored nylons and the slight scrap of lace barely restraining her breasts, all hidden beneath a soft, clinging forest-green, knit sweater and matching straight skirt. And she knew exactly what had possessed her to dress so daringly.

The possibility of a tryst with Wes flooded her already alert senses. The mere thought of his hand slipping beneath her skirt and his long fingers inside her made her eyelids flutter and her sex wet. After what had happened Saturday night in the dancer's dressing room, the idea of an unoccupied elevator or a stolen moment in her office was far more exciting then stripping off her clothes on a lit stage.

If nothing else, Wes had taught her that fantasy could become reality. That wild, uninhibited sex with the right man was not only feasible, but more exciting than she'd imagined. And utterly satisfying.

Saturday she'd been sated, but Wes had only given her a taste. She wanted more. And she wanted it now.

Too bad it was noon and the place buzzed with human traffic. If only she could wish humanity away for a short hour.

Forcing herself back to her work, Amanda sank into her high-backed, executive chair. The action only heightened her awareness of her lack of underwear. She pushed up the long sleeves of her sweater and picked up a report. The recent crime statistics danced before her eyes. All she could see was Wes's lightly furred chest and the trail of dark hair leading down his lean torso.

She rubbed her wrist. Her breath caught at the memory of Wes filling her....

A bold knock at her office door brought her back to the present and the stack of Monday morning reports. She smoothed back an errant strand of hair which had worked itself loose from her hair clasp. The image of Wes's hands in her hair....

Quickly Amanda pushed the thought aside and bade her intruder to enter.

When the object of her fantasies stepped into her office, file folder in hand, and quietly closed the door, Amanda sat back and crossed her legs. "I expected your report first thing this morning, Detective."

"I've been busy," he said, dropping the case file on her desk and easing his big frame into a chair.

His eyes had been on her since he'd opened the door. He stared at her now. As she rubbed her wrist, she regretted the rash decision to forego underwear. Wes had the power to make her forget everything except how wonderful it felt to be in his arms. Her pulse quickened. Fire caught in her middle and spread to her lips, her breasts and burned hot between her legs. If he touched her, she'd be lost.

This wildness had to stop. Where was the tight control she'd always kept over her emotions? Her feelings for Wes were so powerful, she felt breathless. Her mother had once told her she'd know true love because it would be like a bullet in the heart. Since her mom had never faced a real bullet, Amanda had scoffed.

Not anymore. Loving Wes scared the hell out of her. And it hurt.

"Keeping you satisfied is hard work."

Amanda felt the air in her lungs go still. She swallowed hard. Resisting the desire to touch him, she clasped her hands before her on the desktop. "I understand you had an interesting Sunday. Twelve arrests. Over a million dollars in merchandise recovered."

"I had a far more interesting Saturday night," he said, leaning forward. His forefinger slid along her wrist. The gesture prompted every synapse to fire. Her skin felt hot. She shifted her weight.

Wes grinned. "Miss me?"

"You could have called," she snapped, thinking of all the waiting she'd done. All the worrying.

"Any time you need me, boss." He smiled. A knowing smile that told her he knew she'd been wanting him.

Amanda hated his taunting tone, but it had been her own words, defensive words, which had set the rules. She couldn't blame Wes. She'd ask for sex, temporary loving without complications, and that's what he'd given her. What he planned to continue giving her.

All she had to do was ask and he'd deliver.

All he had to do was touch her and she'd surrender everything. Everything including her heart. Wes owned her body and soul, except he didn't know it. Amanda couldn't let him know it. Not until she had a little time to get used to being in love and decided how to handle the situation. What if Wes didn't love her? What then? And if he did, was he ready to commit himself to the inevitable changes their relationship would demand? Was she?

He stared at her as if he expected her to speak.

The words of surrender had been on her lips Saturday night. When he separated his body from hers, she'd felt a hollow, empty place in her heart. A place only his love could fill.

If she said them now....

He started to rise. "You haven't told me about yesterday," she said.

"It's all there." He poked his index finger at the case file he'd deposited on her desk. "Besides you can hear the details when we meet with the Captain."

"He's called a meeting?"

Wes nodded and pushed himself to every glorious inch of his six foot, two frame. Her gaze slid from his face, down his chest to rest on the button fly of his well-worn jeans. The soft material clung to his hips, outlined his... left nothing to her imagination. She wanted, needed to see him naked and hard.

He leaned over her desk. A sexy grin played at the corners of his mouth. His blue eyes sparkled. "Something I can help you with, Lieutenant?"

Amanda pushed her chair back and uncrossed her legs. He wanted her. She could see it in his eyes. Blue fire. What would he do if she told him she wasn't wearing underwear? That nothing but the stream of civil servants passing her door prevented his lifting her skirt and taking her.

An odd sense of power, erotic and potent, came over her. Wes wanted her as badly as she wanted him.

He felt the change in her the moment she uncrossed her long, glorious legs. The offer, subtle to any other observer, was blatant to Wes. The wave of desire that hit him was as shocking as the idea of taking her right here, right now in her office.

As she pushed herself out of her chair, he caught the gentle movement of her breasts. His hands itched to cover the twin mounds outlined beneath the clinging material of her sweater. He couldn't will away the erection stretching his jeans. He didn't want to. Just looking into her sultry green eyes as she moved toward him gave him pleasure. He liked the way she made him hard. He liked the way she made him feel. Hot, thick and full of lust. And something else. Something catching in his chest. Just as hot. Just as potent.

Something he'd never felt before.

He couldn't think. He reacted. He pulled her hard against him as he stepped back. Blocking the door with his weight, Wes covered her mouth with his. She tasted of cinnamon and sugar. He licked at her lips. He wanted to strip her naked and taste her from head to toe. Explore every hollow and curve.

He pulled up her sweater. A scrap of black lace barely covered her breasts. Her peaked nipples beckoned him. "Come home with me tonight, Mandy."

Pushing his tongue beneath the black lace, he captured her nipple and suckled. A muffled cry tore from her throat. She arched, pushing her breast against his mouth.

Needing no further encouragement, he caught the soft knit of her skirt and pulled it up over her hips. She was naked. She'd deliberately left herself bare for him. If she wanted it wild and dangerous, he was the man to give it to her.

He locked the office door and carried her to her desk. With a sweep of his arm, he cleared the surface. Files tumbled and pens flew as he lowered her onto a leather-trimmed ink blotter. He reached for his belt buckle, then paused. He wanted her. He wanted to feel her tight sex, but he couldn't make love to her without protection. Neither could he ignore her parted thighs. He brushed her red curls with his fingers, played between the folds of her delicate slit until his hand was wet with her need. Her hips bucked and pushed against his hand.

Her muscles clamped down on his fingers reminding him of how tight and wet she was.

"Please, Wes. Please."

Her hands clutched his shoulders. He heard the strain in her voice, knew she teetered on the precipice of orgasm. He withdrew his fingers and pulled her to the edge of the desk, lifting her buttocks so that she straddled his thigh. Friction mounted with each forward thrust and her breasts bounced provocatively. Wes felt her slick heat through the thick material of his jeans. When she found her release, her body arched and another stack of files balanced on the desk's edge slid to the floor.

She shuddered against him, grasping futilely at the fabric covering his aching shaft. "Don't make me come in my pants, Mandy. Not here," he whispered, wishing they were anywhere but in her office.

To his surprise, Amanda slid from the desk to her knees. She made quick work of his belt. Her fingers tore at the buttons of his jeans and eased his swollen erection free of his briefs. When she guided him into her mouth, he groaned. The erotic combination of her lips and tongue with the rhythmic use of her hand sent him over the edge. He closed his eyes as she drew him deeper into her sweet mouth.

He rocked lightly on his heels, savoring each delicious tug of her lips, every caress of her tongue and the erotic movements of her hands. Even as he came, he wanted, needed to be inside her tight, wet sheath. As his climax eased, the sounds of footsteps, voices and ringing telephones beyond the closed door reminded Wes of where they were.

Reluctantly Wes stepped back as Mandy glanced over her shoulder at the disarray of her desk, then back at his flagging erection. A horrified expression filled her eyes. He reached down and pulled her to her feet. Gently he pushed her skirt over her bare hips. "Have I told you how much I like red hair?"

She shook her head and tucked her reddened nipples beneath that scrap of black lace passing for a brassiere, then quickly yanked her sweater down.

He reached out. He wanted her to look at him. He wanted to kiss her, let her know everything would be all right. She didn't move. He lowered his arms and adjusted his clothes.

"I love red hair, Mandy," he said, trying to ease the situation as he buckled his belt. They'd lost control, both of them. Neither of them had given a damn where they were. Wes couldn't recall ever wanting any woman this badly. "Especially those soft, red curls between your legs."

"What are we doing, Wes?" She stepped away from him. "Have we both gone completely insane? Anyone could have walked in here... caught me on my knees...."

Despite the glow of her flushed skin, her lush mouth was pulled into a decided frown and her green eyes.... She regretted what just happened. Had she regretted Saturday night?

"I locked the door," he said as she moved to the opposite side of her desk. He wanted to hold her, wrap his arms about her and never let her go. "Maybe we should try this at home, in bed for once."

She folded her arms before her and looked at the files scattered on the floor. "Maybe we shouldn't be doing this at all."

"And maybe the sun won't rise tomorrow," he shot back.

"What time are we supposed to meet the Captain?" she asked ignoring his remark.

He looked at his watch. "About five minutes ago," he responded. The last twenty minutes had passed in a heartbeat.

"Why didn't you say something?"

"I was busy." He looked down at the wet stain on his jeans and touched the spot with his fingertip.

"Don't ever come in here and lock the door again," she snapped. He looked at her and her cheeks blushed an adorable pink. Her shoulders squared. "Is that clear, Detective?"

"Very clear, Lieutenant." Turning on his heel, Wes yanked open the door and, leaving it wide open, headed straight for the Captain's office.

Five minutes later, Amanda sat, legs crossed, before Captain Miller's desk. His balding head was bent over the report of yesterday's warehouse raid. Detective Tom Jenkins, sat in the chair next to her while Wes leaned against the wall across the room.

Although her gaze remained on the Captain, out of the corner of her eye, Amanda caught Wes's fingers brushing at the still damp stain on his jeans. Again, she felt her neck and face flush with embarrassment. She'd lost control, and Cooper loved reminding her of it.

"Can this be right?" the Captain asked as he poked a thick finger at a list of merchandise recovered. "Panties?"

Cooper grinned. "A truck load of goods intended for a chain of expensive lingerie shops had been highjacked, but we didn't expect to find it yesterday. This group specializes in electronics."

Inside, Amanda groaned. The last thing she wanted to discuss was lingerie.

The Captain shook his head. "But this amount? Can it be correct?"

"You wouldn't believe what a few inches of satin and lace can cost," Cooper said. Amanda could feel the grin in his voice. He was enjoying this. "Some women have stopped wearing them entirely."

When Tom Jenkins looked at Wes, then at her, Amanda shifted in her seat.

"You'd know," the Captain responded, then gave her a sheepish look. "Sorry, Lieutenant."

Amanda merely acknowledged his remark with a slight nod. She was the last person who should be offended by the sexist statement. After all she was one of Cooper's conquests. She glanced at him and immediately regretted it.

He was sucking on his fingertip.

The same fingertip he'd put inside her. She tried to control the hot blush creeping up her neck to her burning cheeks. She heard him chuckle.

Next time they were alone, she'd kill him.

"Good work," the Captain said looking first at Cooper then at Jenkins.

"It was Wes's snitch that provided the information," Jenkins added.

"But I couldn't have done it alone. And the Lieutenant...she backed me up. Gave me a free hand so to speak. I hope I lived up to her expectations."

All eyes were on her. Amanda forced a smile. She hadn't missed the duplicity of Cooper's declaration. She considered a set down, but his performance had been superb. Every single time.

"You haven't disappointed me yet, Detective."

On the way back to the squad room, Tom pulled Wes aside. His dark eyes looked worried.

"What the hell was all that?"

"What?" Wes asked, hoping Tom hadn't picked up on the emotional darts being tossed back and forth between he and Mandy.

"I know you, partner. Tell me you aren't doing the Lieutenant."

Wes decided not to lie to Tom. They'd been partners too many years. "So far we haven't made it to a bed, but I intend to remedy that real soon."

Tom grimaced. "Are you nuts? You can't screw the boss." Anger swept through Wes. Mandy wasn't a convenient screw. "It's not like that. I'm crazy about her."

"Damn right you're crazy. You'll end up working southside in a patrol car. I don't know about you, but I'm too damn old for that shit."

"I love her, Tom."

Tom looked at him and shook his head. "You're gonna ask for a transfer, aren't you?"

Wes nodded.

"We've got it good, partner. What happens when this blows over?"

"This isn't going to blow over. I intend to marry her."

"Marry? Now hold on, Wes. You're talking about house payments and dirty diapers. Spit-up on your jacket!"

"Yeah, I know." The idea of marriage and kids hadn't been a conscious thought until now, but he wanted them. Deep in his heart, he wanted them. As badly as he wanted her.

"No, you don't. I know. It ain't easy."

"And you wouldn't have it any other way." Wes knew Tom was devoted to his girls, and the only way he'd leave Carol was in a casket.

Tom shook his head in disbelief. "Most cop's marriages don't work. But two cops. It's ridiculous. She's a career woman, Wes. Amanda Forbes has brass written all over her. Is she willing to give that up for babies?"

The thought that Mandy wouldn't want his babies tore at his

guts. She could have her career. She'd probably make Captain, too. But he wanted a family.

"Have you told her you want kids?"

"I haven't asked her to marry me, yet."

Tom's mouth dropped opened.

"Don't worry, partner. When I get around to asking, she'll say yes."

Wes turned to walk away, then glanced over his shoulder at Tom. "Close your mouth, partner. You're catching flies."

Chapter Five

Amanda opened her front door to find Wes leaning casually against the frame, a fancy black Stetson in his right hand. "Why are you here, Cooper?"

He stepped inside, pushed the door closed and turned the lock. Looking her right in the eye, he said, "For you, Mandy."

Amanda strolled into her living room. Wes followed. She bit the inside of her cheek to keep from grinning, then she turned to face him. He'd be furious if he realized how predictable he was. She'd known he couldn't resist the challenge she'd made this afternoon in the Captain's office.

Wes's gaze settled on the lit fireplace, then moved lazily over the chilled champagne resting in a silver ice bucket, to the sheepskin rug she'd spread out on the floor, and finally upon the handful of foil packets she'd scattered on the hearth.

"Expecting someone?" His blue gaze fastened on her. Slowly he perused her oversized black sweater, her bare legs and feet, then back to her face. He rubbed a knuckle against his cheek and grinned. "Expecting me?"

She lifted her chin a fraction. "Maybe."

"You got anything on under that?" he drawled.

She kept her voice as cool and as lazy as his. "Maybe. Maybe not."

He glanced at the shiny foil packets decorating the hearth. "Planning on using those tonight?"

Noticing the erection beginning to strain his well-worn jeans, she gave him a sexy grin. "Maybe."

He moved toward her. His big hands flexed. "How do I get past maybe?"

"Strip," she said, sidling over to the sheepskin rug. His gaze locked onto her bare thighs as she sat down and curled her legs close to her body. "You've stripped for your women before, haven't you?"

He shook his head slowly. "Naw, I usually just let'em tear my clothes off."

Amanda separated her legs just enough to let him know she was bare beneath the sweater. She kept her voice low and seductive. "Shuck your clothes, cowboy."

"That an order?"

"Naw, that's a privilege."

He tossed his Stetson onto her couch, then hooked his thumbs in his leather belt. "No music?"

Amanda smiled as she reached for the remote control she'd left beside the champagne bucket. She punched a button and Achey, Breaky Heart began to play. The skin around Wes's blue eyes crinkled as his face split into a wide grin. He hitched a hip on the padded arm of her couch and slowly pulled off a boot. He dropped it, then took off the other. He reached for a sock.

Amanda laughed as he twirled both his socks in time with the music then tossed them over his shoulder. When he rose to his feet and began to unbutton his shirt, her heart raced. He moved his hips from side-to-side, performing a sexy two-step. Turning around, he pulled the shirt off his shoulders, then let it slide slowly down his arms, leaving his back bare and beautiful for her perusal.

He spun around to face her and his blue eyes locked with hers as he reached for his belt buckle. For the first time Amanda understood how a man might feel while she danced. Her cowboy wasn't Nureyev, but he was seductive. She licked her lips at the expanse of his chest, the defined bulges of his arms, and the long, familiar fingers working the buttons of his jeans.

She shifted her legs, aware of the moisture pooling between her thighs as each button popped open, exposing his taut belly then a thatch of dark hair. Then it struck her, he wasn't wearing underwear.

He'd stolen her act.

Her lips parted as his jeans slid down his rock hard thighs and freed his fully aroused shaft. Deftly, he kicked the jeans aside.

Naked and beautiful, and obviously quite proud of himself, he closed the short distance between them and stood before her. "Enjoy the show?"

Incapable of answering in words, Amanda rose to her knees, removed her sweater and did what she'd planned as a prelude to a long night of lovemaking. She took him in her mouth.

When her lips touched the smooth skin of his erection, her eyes fluttered closed. His big hands molded to her scalp, holding her, urging her to take more of him. Encouraged, she explored his taut flesh; tasting his skin, feeling his need, and surveying the length of him. Smooth as velvet. Hard as steel.

He felt so good. She planned to take her time, all night if necessary. There was a lot of her cowboy to love.

Using the tip of her tongue, she teased the underside of his shaft. Her action brought a strangled moan. His.

She wrapped her fingers around the base of his erection, massaging and stroking, increasing the tempo. She wanted to make him come, give him the earth shattering pleasure he'd given her. She needed to feel the power of her loving course through his body.

She'd always strived to be the best, to meet every challenge. Including giving Wes Cooper the loving of his life.

"I can't hold back," he said in a husky voice laden with passion.

She slid her hand between his legs and cupped his sac. He groaned, an unintelligible moan of pleasure. With slow, sensual strokes, she urged him on. Increasing her tempo until his salty fluid filled her mouth.

Amanda slid her lips from his erection, licked them, then looked up at him. Sweat stained his brow. His eyes glowed with a soft fire she'd never seen before.

"Do you have any idea what you do to me?" he asked as he dropped to his knees.

"Touché, Cooper."

An odd smile curled his lips as his fingertip touched her wet lower lip. She leaned forward and licked his lips. "Like how you taste?"

"As long as I'm on you," he said as he slanted his head to capture her mouth.

His kiss was lush and sexy. Their tongues mingled with his pleasure, and his hands cupped her buttocks pressing her sex tight to his. Big, hot and solid, he made her feel delicate, sensual and soft. He guided her down to the plush sheepskin rug. Instead of covering her body with his, he knelt beside her. For the longest time he just looked at her.

A raw gentleness had replaced the blue fire in his eyes. He touched her hair, then ran his fingertips along her jaw, across her lips. He touched the tip of her nose.

Wes could make the simplest gesture sexy. And loving. For the first time in her life she understood how it felt to love a man. No words were necessary. She felt it in her heart. Like wildfire it spread throughout her body, radiating through her skin in waves of heat.

His hand moved down her neck, drifted over her shoulder to her breast. He cupped her flesh, molding it to his palm. He massaged the mound until it swelled beneath his hand. She rubbed her thighs together, trying to ease the sweet pressure between her legs. She wanted to feel his hot mouth tugging at her breast. Needed him to ease the tender ache in her taut nipples.

Inching his way along in gentle, sensual caresses, he skimmed her curves. She pushed gently against his hand, urging him to quell the fire he'd started hours ago in her office.

As he splayed his hand across her belly, his eyes glowed with blue hot desire, raw and palpable.

Every inch of her skin felt hot, every part, lush. Turned on. His fingers curled and gripped her short curls. A possessive act, reminding her of the night he'd escorted her around the stage with his hand on her backside.

That night he'd let the audience know she belonged to him. To-night he was making the same declaration.

"How can you want this to end?"

Amanda wanted to shout "never," but before she could answer, his fingers dipped inside her. When he leaned over and licked her nipple, then took it deep inside his hot mouth she realized he didn't want a verbal response. He was determined to prove she wasn't strong enough to deny the passion. That neither of them could endure another night without being together.

Desire flared as his fingers slowly stroked her. Using his tongue and lips, he explored each breast as if to reacquaint himself with her body. Then he suckled deeply, drawing a strangled moan from between her parted lips. "Wes, please, Wes. I'm burning for you."

Her ache intensified as he ceased his erotic massage and dipped his hands into the melting ice surrounding the champagne. His cold fingers grasped one hot nipple making it constrict into a hard kernel. As his other hand dipped into her hot center, he covered the contracted nipple with his mouth.

The contrast between hot and cold teased her senses. Again he dipped his fingers in the ice. This time he pinched her nipples until she couldn't wait for his hot mouth to ease her ache.

His ice cold fingers probed her sex, teasing her body in easy, yet provocative strokes. He'd heat her to boiling then cool her down and start all over again. Her sex was drenched, her nipples a bright red. Amanda arched her back and pelvis. She wanted him inside her, filling her. She reached over and plucked a foil packet from the hearth.

Gripping his hair, she eased his head back. "I want you. Now."

His fingers moved deeper. "Forever or just tonight?"

Amanda met his intense gaze. "Love me, Wes."

"I can't just walk away from you, from us."

She was too wet and excited to discuss the difficulties of being in love with him. "I burn for you."

Rolling to his knees, he pulled the packet from her fingers and kneeled between her thighs. Wet and aching for him, she watched as he sheathed his bold erection in the thin latex.

Taking her about the waist, he lifted her up like an offering. His hot breath caressed her breast, then his lips closed about her distended nipple. Every nerve ending quivered as he suckled. The breast he ignored tingled.

As if understanding her need, he released her swollen breast and captured the other. He drew deeply, sending rivers of desire to pool where his engorged shaft touched her sex.

He pulled back, his gaze lingering on her swollen and sensitive nipples. A hungry, sensual gaze, telling her how much he loved pleasing her. Slowly, he lowered his head, his tongue laving first one nipple, than the other. Her sex throbbed as he suckled hard on her breast. Wrapping her arms about his neck, she thrust forward, embedding him inside her.

Unrestricted, except by his hands guiding her buttocks, Amanda rode him with abandon. Setting the pace, she squeezed his flesh as she withdrew, then released as she pulled him deep inside.

She closed her eyes. She wanted to feel his love. His passion. His hard heat. Hot sweat formed between their thighs. The tempo increased. Her belly slapped into his. His fingers kneaded her hips. The musky scent of him filled her nostrils.

Poised at the brink of rapture, she opened her eyes. His intense gaze locked with hers and held as she came in slow, magnificent waves.

She collapsed against his sweat-dampened chest. Heat radiated from their flesh, filling the air with her perfume, his scent, their passion. Her knees gripped his hips. She wanted him inside her, forever.

She clung to him as he withdrew his swollen shaft. Although she'd climaxed, Amanda still pulsed with need. Guiding her gently to her knees, his hands grasped her waist as he knelt behind her. The velvety tip of his penis teased her heated opening, then slowly filled her.

Her breasts bounced in erotic rhythm with each penetrating stroke. His hand slid along her belly to her breast. He rolled her sensitive nipple between his thumb and forefinger until her sex throbbed in response.

His thrusts slowed. She felt an exquisite pleasure as his body vibrated. Amanda knew he was riding the edge. His hands caressed her thighs and hips in measured rhythm.

The sweat between their bodies sealed his thighs to the backs of hers as they moved in unison. His hand slid to her belly, and his finger teased her aching bud.

She lowered her head. Her back arched, driving him deeper. His breathing surged as fast and hard as his thrusts.

Amanda gasped, a strangled sound escaping from her throat, as the tempo of their lovemaking escalated into a wild, primitive coupling. His belly slapped her buttocks and his balls lapped against her clit until an unbearable heat built, then burst into orgasm. He thrust deep and held, then shuddered as her sex contracted about his fully embedded shaft. His breath exploded in hard labored gasps similar to her own. He gripped her wet curls until her contractions ceased, then slid his fingers between her swollen labia and rubbed her clit. She cried out as she came.

Moving his fingers in slow circles, he eased her back to earth.

Remaining inside her, he lowered her to the rug and buried his face in her hair. Lying on their sides, he tenderly stroked her belly, caressed her mound.

"I'll never get enough of you," he said, his voice still husky from their lovemaking.

The words of a lover or a man in love? "Never is a long time."

"Not long enough."

Her heart swelled with love. Amanda knew the love she had for Wes would last a lifetime.

Neither of them spoke for a long time. Content in the warmth of his embrace, Amanda listened to the measured rhythm of his heartbeat as he kissed her hair and neck.

"I'd like to stay the night," he said. "I want to sleep with you. Feel you next to me all night."

She reached down and touched him. "You won't get much sleep."

Laughter rumbled in his chest. "Didn't expect to."

Satisfied and deliciously sore, Amanda rolled onto her side and faced the dying fire. Wes curled his big body around hers. His arm wrapped possessively about her and his hand cupped her tender breast. His relaxed shaft rested against the cleft of her buttocks.

Their loving had begun like the fire, hot and consuming. Now the two of them were like the glow in the embers. Still hot, but out of fuel. She closed her eyes.

On the verge of drifting off, she felt Wes kiss her shoulder. A soft, gentle touch that told her he cared.

"I love you, Amanda." He whispered so low she wasn't sure whether he'd said it or she had dreamed it.

It had to be a dream.

⁂

Amanda awoke as Wes brushed his lips over hers. She was in her bed, but she couldn't remember when they'd changed rooms. The bedroom was still dark, except for a pool of light spilling onto the carpet from her bathroom. He was leaning over her. "What time is it?"

"Around four," he said, moving away from the bed. "I just wanted to say goodbye."

"Four?" She rolled over and turned on the bedside lamp. He was dressed in a western-cut, black suit, white shirt and string tie. He looked more like an oil baron than a cop.

"I have to testify at the Delancy trial, remember? My plane leaves for Dallas in two hours."

"Thanks for telling me goodbye," she said, pleased that he hadn't slipped out of her house like a one-night stand. "You must be exhausted."

"I'll catch up tonight at the hotel." He picked up his fancy Stetson, placed it on his head, then ran his fingertips along the brim. "How do I look, boss?"

"If the jurors are women, they'll be eating out of your hand."

"I'll be back in time to pick you up for Thursday's shift at the Prickly Cactus. See you in my dreams," he said as he walked toward the bedroom door.

"I had a dream about you last night. I dreamed you told me you loved me."

He stopped mid-stride, then turned and faced her. His expression was thoughtful. "And if it wasn't a dream?"

"It changes everything."

He arched a brow. "You want me to say it was a dream?"

She shook her head. "This is serious."

"Yeah, I know."

"Then you better get going. If you miss that plane, your boss will have your cute ass in a sling."

Wes grinned and left the room. He called back to her. "Did I tell you today how much I love red hair?"

A moment later she heard the front door close.

⁂

On Thursday, Amanda left the office early and hurried home. She'd spent two days thinking about Wes. A few nights in his arms was one thing, but being crazy in love with him presented all kinds of problems.

There was no middle ground.

They couldn't sneak around until the fire burned out, because Amanda knew the flame Wes had ignited was as close to eternal as it could get. Which meant their relationship had to be permanent, their commitment lasting or not at all.

Knife in hand, Amanda dropped to her knees and retrieved the package stored beneath her bed. With sentimental tears teasing the corners of her eyes, she carefully cut the tape sealing the box. Remembering her grandmother's stories, Amanda lifted the lid and pushed aside the thick pad of tissue.

She fingered the delicate lace, smoothed the transparent material, then lifted the seed pearl headdress. Her maternal great-great-grandmother had first worn this veil in the late 1800's and for the last hundred years, each mother had passed the veil to their daughter to wear on her wedding day.

Now it was her turn.

Before the mirror, Amanda adjusted the cap of pearls onto her head, then fluffed the long veil over her face and shoulders. The lace trim touched her thighs.

Did Wes love her enough?

Never one to back down from a situation, even if it meant she might lose, Amanda decided her course of action.

"I hope you've done some thinking, Cooper," she said aloud. "Cause if you haven't, you're in for one helluva surprise."

❦

"What would you have done the other night, if I'd tossed you out of my house?" Amanda asked, glancing at Wes. His eyes were fixed on the road ahead. They hadn't said more than two words to each other since he'd arrived and hustled her into the vehicle. He glanced over and winked at her. "I'd have rented a room by the airport, and jacked off while I watched a couple of dirty movies."

Amanda grinned. "When's the last time you masturbated, Cooper?"

"Can't recall. But I'm sure I enjoyed myself."

"I'd like to talk to you after the shift at the club," she began. "That is if you don't have plans."

For a quick second, his gaze connected with hers. "I was hoping you would take me home."

"We've got to talk. I'd rather it be at the club. I've made arrangements with the owner for us to lock up the place."

"Why do I get the feeling I'm not going to like this? If it's over, just say it."

"And stop jumping to conclusions. I want you to be certain about your feelings."

"I know how I feel."

"Then we'll talk later." Her heart pounded. Wes had no idea what she had planned for him later. The truth of his feelings would be tested tonight.

A short time later, Wes escorted her to the dressing room door. He pulled her in his arms and kissed her hard. She loved his lush kisses. His tongue parried and warred with hers. His mouth was hot and demanding. His hands cupped her backside and pulled her against him. He was already hard.

"I'm starved for you." His lips brushed hers again and as he turned to leave, he said, "Stay off your knees, Mandy. That is until we get home."

Lucy, eyelash wand in hand, looked up as Amanda opened the dressing room door. "You been out front?" Lucy asked. Amanda shook her head and dropped her duffle bag. "Better take a look at the stage," Lucy warned.

Curious, Amanda left the dressing room and rushed to peek through the beaded curtain. Her jaw dropped. Up to the front, right in the middle of the stage stood a shiny brass pole. Amanda's eyes widened as Wes strolled to the edge of the stage and ran his fingers up and down the slick metal. The grin on his face was priceless.

Back in the dressing room, Amanda looked at Lucy. "What do I do with it?"

"Hold it, wrap yourself around it," Lucy said in a matter-of-fact voice. "Just pretend its a big cock. They'll get the idea."

"Did you know about it?"

Lucy shook her head. She applied a generous amount of lipstick to her lower lip. "I requested it months ago. That thing will double our tips."

Amanda sat down and untied her athletic shoes. "Double," she said, wondering if that shiny brass pole would help her with Wes. She remembered the grin on his face as he ran his fingers along the metal.

"Men like to look at you in this business, but if you really want them to put down their money, each and every one of them has to feel what it would be like to make it with you. They become the pole, if you know what I mean. Then the money just flies out of their pockets."

"Maybe it's because they need the room in their pants."

Lucy laughed. "You're catching on, Blaze. If you can make yourself wet out there, guys will pay for it."

Amanda performed five times, each dance a prelude to her big finale with only Wes to watch her. She'd chosen an unconventional way of speaking her mind, but then their relationship hadn't been ordinary. When she'd told Lucy her plan, the dancer had readily agreed to help.

She'd just placed the veil on her head when the cellular phone in her duffle bag rang. As she listened, Amanda expelled a sigh of relief. The gods were smiling on her. Quickly she made a few arrangements, then fluffed the veil over her face.

Nervous as a cat, Amanda stood behind the beaded curtain. The main club was empty except for Wes, waiting for her at the bar. According to plan, Lucy started the music and hurried out the back door as Amanda stepped onto the stage.

Dressed all in white, Amanda began to dance. She's chosen her costume of white high heels, white nylons, and matching lacy garter belt and skimpy bra, for Wes. The long wedding veil was for her and all of her female ancestors.

By the time she'd gyrated her way to the brass pole, Wes had planted himself center stage. Her back braced against the pole, Amanda lowered herself slowly. The gauzy veil obscured the view, but with her knees spread wide apart, it was obvious she wore nothing but her red hair. As she pushed herself to her feet, she pumped her hips up and down. Despite the filmy material, Amanda could tell she had Wes's full attention. Dancing around the pole, Amanda lifted the veil to reveal her bare backside. Standing before Wes, she grasped the pole and lowered her upper body until she heard his sharp intake of breath.

Looking through her parted legs, she winked at him. He dropped into the prized center chair for a better view. Ever so slowly, she pulled herself erect. Her hands grasped the pole, then pulled and pushed in prolonged, sensual motions, letting him know exactly how it would feel should she do the same to him. She circled the pole several times, thrusting herself up against its length. Moving directly behind the slender metal rod, she placed her high-heeled feet on either side. She flipped the veil back from her face and over her head. Flush against the brass, she dipped, rubbing herself up and down the shiny metal. Wes grinned and licked his lips.

Looking straight into his blue eyes, she touched her tongue to the slick brass and rose slowly. By the time she stood erect, he'd pulled off his hat and had planted himself at the end of the stage. His big hands flexed.

As the music ended, Amanda felt a sheen of perspiration, fueled by exertion and a liberal dose of pure passion, break out on her flesh. She sauntered to the edge of the stage. She wanted him to feel the heat exuding from her body, to inhale the scent of her desire.

"You proposing, Mandy?"

"I told you it was serious."

"Can't have my wife dancing around a pole," he said running his fingertips along her nylon clad legs.

"I only dance for you, cowboy."

"Let's keep it that way," he said as his fingers touched her bare thighs. "I'm sure we can rustle up a replacement for this job."

"Job's over. Jenkins and Bates made the collar at the Bosom Buddies."

She expected him to be disappointed about missing the action, but his attention was focused between her legs. "If you've got something to wear to cover these," he said, brushing the curls between her legs with the backs of his fingers, "I'm up for a quick trip to Nevada. We can get hitched, and make it back by morning shift."

"The Captain will have a fit."

"Yeah, but at least he'll understand why I requested a transfer."

For several heartbeats, Amanda couldn't speak. All she could think of was that Wes was not only ready to hop in the Jeep and make it official, he was willing to change his assignment for her. Her heart swelled.

"My best suit is already packed. That is, if you're sure how you feel."

"I'm sure. I've cleared our schedules until Sunday."

Wes gave her that sexy grin of his. "It might be fun to make it in a bed for once."

Her cowboy was old enough not to be caught up in the heat of the moment, but did he realize how marriage would change his life. She wanted forever, nothing less. "Sure you're ready for this? Ready for one woman? Ready for—"

"Are you, Lieutenant? I'll want babies," he said, sliding his big hand over her almost bare belly. His fingertips slipped beneath the lace trim of her garter belt. "A couple at least."

Amanda's heart began to pound. "As long as they're your babies."

"I plan to marry once, Mandy. Only once."

"Any other demands?"

"None of this feminist shit about keeping your own name. I like the sound of Captain Amanda Cooper." He gave her a concentrated stare. "But at home, I'm the boss."

"Anything else I should know?"

He dug into his jean pocket. "Just this."

Amanda felt her heart do a flip-flop at the sparkling diamond ring he held up to her. He lifted her hand and slid the engagement ring on her finger.

"I love you, Mandy." He held out his hands and she stepped into them. His lips grazed her belly. "Are you always going to be a step ahead of me?"

Feeling his hot breath caress her curls, she answered, "Always."

About the author:

B. J. McCall lives beneath the redwoods of Northern California with her husband, two dobermans and a loquacious parrot. While working as a 911 dispatcher/desk clerk for a small, coastal town, she met her husband of twenty years. That brief career, and the possibilities explored on the Police Chief's desk, provided the inspiration for her story.

Blood and Kisses

✵✺⊂☾⊃✺✵

by Angela Knight

To my reader:

A good vampire is hard to find.

Sad, but true. It seems most vampire heroes (with a few wonderful exceptions) are either whiners or psychopaths. Which is really too bad, because I just love the idea of a romantic vampire. All that menacing sexuality, superhuman strength and animal hunger...

Besides, you know any guy who's been seducing women for three hundred years just *has* to be good in bed.

On those rare occasions when I do find the perfect vampire, he's always paired with a heroine who has the fixed bubbliness of a Laker Girl combined with the raw intelligence of a Boston Fern. By chapter three I'm chanting, "Bite her, Bite her, bite her..."

Why the hell would a three-hundred-year-old nobleman be attracted to a woman who wants to be reincarnated as a rainbow? Puh-leeeze.

So when Alexandria Kendall graciously allowed me to write another novella for *Secrets III*, I knew just what I wanted to write about—a civilized vampire hero and a heroine who is neither vampire nor particularly civilized. And while I was at it, I explored some of my favorite vamp fantasies.

I hope you enjoy the results. Thanks!

Chapter One

Her neck burned as though venom pumped through her blood. Beryl St. Cloud reached up and gingerly touched the wound, resisting the urge to scratch. It had finally stopped bleeding, but that bastard Tagliar would sink his fangs into her again if she wasn't damn lucky.

And for Beryl, luck meant finding Jim Decker. Now.

She ducked into the open maw of the nearest bar, then stopped to let her eyes adjust to the poor lighting. Like the rest of the Huff-Hamilton Interstellar Station, Hot Shots served a clientele of spacers, merchants and mercenaries, and she knew better than to rush in blind.

Even after Beryl's eyes adapted, the dive's interior was dark enough to make her back itch. The only illumination came from the flourescent bar that shed gaudy pinwheels of light over tables and patrons. Not the best conditions to spot a man she'd never met, but she made a careful scan of the room anyway. She was damned if she'd get in a hurry and miss him.

There. A flash of red back in the corner. Beryl snapped her head around and recognized the crimson shimmer of a vampire's eyes staring back at her. He turned his head and the glow disappeared, winking out as the angle of reflection changed. A chill rippled across the back of Beryl's neck, but she started for his table anyway.

Her right hand automatically twitched toward the laser torch that hung on her belt, but she'd hardly win friends drawing down on a possible savior, so Beryl forced her fingers to curl into a fist just short of the torch's comforting pistol grip. She relaxed only slightly when she got close enough to recognize the vampire from

Bill's description.

She'd found Jim Decker at last.

He'd attracted a crowd. Three men and a woman, all dressed in the matte black skinsuits favored by mercenaries. The woman stood between Decker's long muscled thighs, her breasts taunting inches from his face. He glanced up at her, then turned his head again to watch Beryl walking toward them.

"Come on, vamp, let's play," the woman jeered, obviously frustrated with her target's slipping attention. She shook her long blonde hair back and arched her spine to display her breasts. Her skinsuit was so tight the contours of her areolas were visible.

"Thanks, but I'll pass," the vampire said drily. The intensity of his gaze made Beryl's steps falter.

"Oh c'mon, bloodsucker, I know you want a piece." Waving a viblade under Decker's aristocratic nose, the merc purred, "All you have to do is bleed a little for it."

The vibrating blade of that combat knife could cleave steel like paper, and one slash could sever a human arm. Beryl quickened her pace. Decker, however, didn't look particularly worried.

"How about it, perv? You want me bad enough to bleed?"

"Actually," the vampire said, dismissive, "I don't."

The blonde flushed. To either side, her two companions watched in grinning appraisal, their cold eyes fixed on the anger growing on her pretty face.

Beryl recognized this game. The female merc was green, a rookie trying to prove her steel to both her fellow warriors and herself. Unfortunately, she was also dumb as a deck plate, or she wouldn't have picked a vamp for a target. Decker could rip her throat out before she saw him move.

Yet the vampire just sat there, anger tightening the sensual contour of his lips, high, strong cheekbones throwing shadows on his angular face. His eyes were blue except when the light ignited them into a red glow. A flowing white shirt stretched over his broad shoulders, caressing ridges of muscle before tucking into black pants. "Go away, little girl," Decker said softly, his deep voice gently threatening. "You're beginning to irritate me."

"What's the matter, vamp?" the blonde merc taunted. "Don't you have the guts to try for me?"

"Maybe the perv's just not interested, Clarke," one of the men said lazily. His lip curled into a sneer. "Maybe he only does little boys."

Muscle bunched in Decker's cheek, and he turned his head slowly until his gaze locked on the male merc, burning as steady and hot and red as a laser sight. The man took an instinctive step back. Then, as if realizing he'd look bad in front of the others if he retreated further, he stopped and put an unsteady hand on the butt of his torch.

"Or maybe," Beryl said, shouldering into the group, "the vamp knows Clarke doesn't have what it takes." Swinging a leg over one of Decker's hard thighs, she settled onto it, putting herself between him and the merc's weapon. "Maybe I'm the one he's waiting for."

Beryl ignored the startled look in the vampire's eyes and drew a forefinger hard down the cut running from her chin to her collar bone. The pressure made it bleed again, a fat hot bead that looked black and wet in the dim light as it rolled down the length of her finger.

Until, her heart pounding a combat drumbeat in her ears, her mouth dry as sand, Beryl offered her blood to Decker.

The vampire caught his breath. His eyes flicked to meet hers. Focused, sharpened to arc light intensity. Beryl swallowed, aware of the powerful muscle of his thigh between her legs, remembering all too clearly the moment when Tagliar had grabbed her, the feel of his breath, the burn of his fangs.

God, what was she doing here? You could never count on anybody but yourself. You sure as hell couldn't count on one vamp to protect you from another.

His big hand came up and closed gently around her wrist. Beryl blinked at the masculine heat of his fingers, so different from the undead chill she'd expected.

He bent his head, his gaze still locked on her, and opened that lushly male mouth as he guided her forefinger between his lips. His tongue began a slow, velvet swirl around her fingertip. Paused.

Swirled again. His eyes slid closed as he sucked gently.

Beryl's nipples hardened, ached in time with each slow pull as she stared at the dark, gleaming crown of his head. She'd expected to have to endure him.

"Jesus," said Clarke hoarsely, revulsion and fascination a sickly mix in her eyes, "that's disgusting. Let's get the fuck out of here before I heave my rations."

The mercs, laughing uneasily, beat a hasty retreat from the saloon, but Beryl was aware of nothing except the astonishing carnality of Decker's tongue. Inside her a small voice babbled, *But he's a vampire....*

Finally he lifted his head and lowered her captive hand. "What's your name?"

"St. Cloud," she breathed. "I'm Beryl St. Cloud."

"Jim Decker." He studied her. "So who did you piss off?"

Beryl rocked back, disoriented by the cool tone contrasting so starkly with those molten demon eyes. "I beg your pardon?"

"Somebody must be seriously ticked if they sent Damian Tagliar after you."

Feeling her jaw drop, she made an effort to close her mouth. "How did you know?"

"I can smell him on you." Decker nodded shortly at the cut on her neck. "You fought him. Must have done a damn good job, too, because you're still alive. I'd love to know how you pulled that one off. Tagliar doesn't often miss."

Beryl swallowed, remembering the sick terror of returning to her station hotel room to find the assassin lying on her bed, an erection swelling his trousers. *"Let's get started,"* he'd said. *"I want to make you come at least twice before I kill you."*

"I shot him in the eyes with a laser torch at point blank range."

"And fried his optic nerves like eggs." He nodded, approving. "Blinded him. One of the very few ways to slow a vampire down for any length of time. You bought yourself at least four or five hours while he heals."

"Time which is rapidly running out because I spent most of it looking for you." She rose from his thigh, trying to regain a sense of control.

He sat back in his chair. "How much?"

"Time?"

"Money." Decker's face hardened. "How much money are you offering me to kill Tagliar for you?"

That knocked her off balance, thought Decker. Good. She'd been playing him from the moment she'd slung those incredible legs over his and offered him her blood like Eve giving Adam the apple. She must think she could give him one red taste and he'd be willing to kill for more, but he knew damn well he'd never *get* more. Not without forcing her.

For a moment Decker let himself imagine it. The arch of her slim body against his, deliciously feminine, flooding his head with the musky woman scent he'd already drawn into his lungs under the stench of Tagliar. The slow penetration of his teeth into her throat. Blood pouring over his tongue in hot, liquid copper intoxication as he spread those magnificent thighs and pushed inside until she was triply impaled on his fangs and cock.

"I wasn't planning to offer money," she said, her voice cool now, steady. "I'm afraid I'm maxed out."

He banished the erotic vision and cleared his throat. "St. Cloud, if you expect me to do Tagliar out of the goodness of my heart, expect again. I'm nobody's knight in shining armor."

St. Cloud frowned, her twenty-third century mind not catching the reference.

"I don't work for free," he clarified with a cool mockery he was far from feeling.

"I don't expect you to." Her fine jaw squared. "I plan to pay in blood."

Was she saying what he thought she was saying? No. Forget it. She was trying to play him again.

Decker stood, an attempt to establish his dominance he regretted the minute he was on his feet. She looked entirely too damn tempting. And close enough to grab.

St. Cloud was dressed casually, but somehow she looked sexier than the blonde had in skinsuit and pouting nipples. The baggy white top draped over her round breasts, its short sleeves revealing the graceful female muscle of her long arms, just as tough neonylon shorts hugged her hips and showcased lust-inspiring legs. Yet despite all that luxuriant femininity, something in the alert, easy way she held herself hinted of combat training, and a lot of it. Decker had known enough mercs to bet St. Cloud was a pro, and a damn good one at that.

She didn't have a bimbo's face, either. Her features were strong, intelligent, with softly rounded cheekbones and a stubborn jaw, a pair of dimples punctuating a lushly wide mouth that looked like an engraved invitation to sin. Her eyes were as dark as the richly curling hair that tumbled around her sculpted shoulders. There was no fear at all in that midnight stare. He'd never realized how erotic a steady, level look could be. As though all he had to do was reach out for her, and she wouldn't run.

"Let me get this straight," Decker said, torn between scaring her off and snatching her into his arms, "you're offering me blood for my protection against Tagliar?"

"Yes." She didn't even blink when she said it.

"Why?"

"I am... I *was* a mercenary, Mr. Decker. I know what it would cost to hire a vampire bodyguard, and I know I don't have that kind of money." She hesitated and squared her finely muscled shoulders. "In fact, there's only one thing I have you might be interested in."

Heat spun into his cock, tightened his balls. He fought to ignore it. "St. Cloud, I've got a hemosynther back on my ship. I've been living on synthetic blood for five decades, and I can go on living on it for five centuries. Why would I would I be willing to fight Damian Tagliar just to taste your pretty white throat?"

"That depends on how long it's been since you've had a woman."

"You'd whore for a vampire?"

"To keep from being raped and murdered by another vampire? You bet your ass."

"Am I supposed to be flattered?"

"No." She gave him a smile stripped of amusement. "But then, if you accept, I'll owe my life to the fact that vamps have a hard time getting laid."

Which was no more than the truth. When Decker came into the Life back in 1986, women were not a problem. He'd needed no more than a pint or so a night, and he'd enjoyed the challenge of seduction. He'd lived that way for two hundred and thirty years.

But fifty years ago scientists discovered that vampires really did exist, setting off an orgy of stakings and anti-vamp legislation. A blood test was developed to identify the virus that caused vampirism, and vamps were forced to obtain licenses or face execution. Strict laws dictated, among other things, that vampires were no longer allowed to conceal their condition. And because the social stigma attached to vampirism was so great, Decker now had a hell of a time even buying a woman a drink, much less getting her into bed.

But even if he'd had his pick, he'd still find Beryl St. Cloud a tempting proposition.

"What's to keep you from crying off after I've staked Tagliar?"

"You." Her brown eyes were unblinking. "We both know there's nothing to stop you from taking me. You certainly have the strength. And I'm willing to sign a contract giving you the right."

That seductive idea almost finished his resistance, but he fought it off. There was no way she was serious. "What makes you think I won't kill you as quickly as Tagliar?"

"Bill Anderson."

He frowned. "Bill?" He hadn't seen Anderson in... it must be fifteen years. Which was a shame, because Decker had never met a better man. There was absolutely no bigotry in Bill. He honestly didn't give a damn whether you drank hundred proof or hemoglobin, as long as you treated your mercs well and delivered a good paycheck. That clear-headed intelligence was one factor in the success of Occam's Raiders. It was also the reason Decker had left Anderson in charge of the mercenary company when he'd walked away. "What about him?"

"I succeeded Bill as commander of the Raiders after he retired."

Decker sat back. "You run the Company? Why didn't you say so?"

"Because I don't. Not anymore. I disbanded it."

The Raiders had been dissolved? He hadn't realized he was so out of touch. "Why?"

"That is a very long story. Which ends with a vampire after my ass," St. Cloud said, so shortly he knew there was a lot more to it. "When I found out Tagliar was hunting me, I called Bill. He told me my only hope was to go to you for help, so I hit the Spacer's Computer Net to pinpoint the location of your ship, and here I am." She shrugged.

"I trust he'll vouch for you."

St. Cloud reached into a pocket for a chipcard. "Give him a call."

Decker took the card from her long fingers and stood to find a com unit. He located one in a corner even dimmer than the rest of the bar and slipped in the chipcard, which began beeping out the code for an interstellar call. The card spent fifteen minutes playing connect the dots with various computers before linking him with someone in the Anderson household.

Decker had become adept at recognizing the faces of acquaintances under the mask of age, so it took him only a moment to see his clever, wicked executive officer in the 90-year-old who finally came to the com.

"Decker! Good God, you really don't age, do you?" Bill's mouth stretched into a white smile under a shock of hair the same color. That grin was definitely familiar, but it brought home to Decker just how long it had been.

"Hi, Bill. Enjoying retirement?"

"Hell, no. I'm bored to tears." The old man paused and studied him, his blue eyes sharp and perceptive. "I take it you've met my kid."

That rocked Decker back on his heels. "St. Cloud is your daughter?"

"Nah." Anderson waved a hand that still looked the size of a deck hatch. "It just seems like it. I've known her since she was sixteen.

You gonna help her, Deck?"

"Maybe. What's the story, Bill?"

"She really is a great kid, Deck. Have I mentioned her dad was a member of the Raiders?"

Decker shot him a warning look. "Bill, you're not going to bullshit me into forgetting the question."

The old man grunted in disgust. "Hell, that's no surprise. You're the hardest man to bullshit I ever met." Settling back in his chair, he thought for a moment before he began. "Okay, here's the situation. Beryl's been running the Raiders for ten years now, and she's done a good job. Lost a couple battles, but won a lot more. Good fighter, dead-on shot, even kicks ass hand-to-hand, which is not easy for a woman. She's got guts. Tactically she's a goddamn genius. But romantically her judgement sucks."

"Doesn't everybody's? I remember that little blonde you..."

Bill grinned. "Shut the hell up, would you? My wife's in the next room. Anyway, a couple years ago she fell in love with this pretty prick, his name was Daveed Zahn. I never could stand that sonuvabitch. Found out why when the Raiders were involved in this action on Dyson's World last year, and they were ambushed. Zahn had sold them out to the enemy. A bunch of the Raiders got killed...."

Decker straightened in his chair. "Who?"

"Nobody you know. All of 'em came into the Company after you left, Deck, it's been fifteen years. That's a whole career to a merc."

He sighed. "Good point. Go on."

"Anyway, one of the ones that got fried was Zahn, which was a good thing, or Beryl would have killed him herself. She and the rest of the company were captured, had to ransom themselves by handing over their troopship, which was in orbit at the time. Luckily the opposition was hard up for ships, or they'd have been dead."

"So where does Tagliar come in?"

"Well, back home some ugly accusations got made about whether Beryl was in on Zahn's plot. The survivors of the mercs who were killed threatened to sue, and damned if Beryl didn't sell out and pay off. She pretty well busted herself doing it, too."

Decker frowned. "I hate to say it, buddy, but that doesn't sound all that innocent to me."

The old man's jaw took on a stubborn jut he recognized from a dozen old arguments. "She didn't do it, Deck. I know that kid. She would no sooner have betrayed the Raiders than she'd have hacked off her own arm with a butter knife."

"Okay, okay. Go on."

Mollified, Bill said, "Anyway, the Mercs' Union held an inquest and determined there was no evidence she'd sold out, but apparently somebody wasn't satisfied with the results, because soon afterward she got a tip Tagliar had been hired to do her. She contacted me to ask how to kill a vamp, and I told her the only chance she had was you."

"You're probably right."

"Will you help her?"

"Yeah. Hell, I'd stake Tagliar for the pure joy of it."

Bill grinned. "I told her you would. Good thing too, since she doesn't have any money to pay you anyway."

Decker sat up. "You told her I'd do Tag for free?"

"Uh, yeah." The old man looked suddenly uncomfortable. "Hope you don't mind, Deck. You've always had a soft spot for women, and besides, Beryl's a good kid."

After that there wasn't much Decker could do but say his good-byes and cut the connection. For a long moment he sat frowning in the darkened com booth, then reached into the top of his boot and pulled out the ironwood knife he carried in case he ran into a vamp who needed killing. He stared at the slick black wood, with its wicked point and serrated double edge.

If she knew he'd take Tagliar out for free, why did St. Cloud offer to become his mistress? Trying to set the hook, maybe? Or maybe, having talked to Bill, she'd assumed Decker would gallantly refuse her offer once he heard the story. Which he might have, if not for his lingering doubts about whether she really had been involved in Zahn's betrayal.

And if he found out she had... His hand tightened on the knife's carved wooden hilt. The Raiders were his people, though the ones he'd known were probably long retired. Still, he'd formed the Company, and he felt a responsibility to it. If Beryl St. Cloud had betrayed it, she would pay.

Slipping the blade back into his boot, Decker strode back to the table. She looked up at his approach, her eyes dark, wary.

"All right," he said shortly.

St. Cloud's expression didn't change. She certainly didn't look like a woman who'd just reeled in her sucker.

"But this is not a one night stand, St. Cloud," he told her. "The going rate to stake a vamp is twenty thousand, and nobody's ass is worth that much for one night. You're mine for the next year. Agreed?"

She didn't even blink. "Agreed."

He nodded shortly. "I'll draw up a contract. Where's your kit?"

"Back at my hotel." She shrugged those luscious shoulders. "But then, that's where I left Tagliar. He's probably gone by now, but…"

"Screw it. We'll have somebody deliver it when we settle your bill. Let's go." He turned away without waiting for her agreement.

"Wait." St. Cloud caught at his forearm. "Where, exactly, are we going?"

"My ship." Decker headed for the entrance without waiting to see if she'd follow. He knew she would.

After all, she had no place else to go.

Somehow, this wasn't going quite the way she'd thought. Beryl had expected finding Decker to be tricky, and she'd figured it wouldn't be easy getting him to protect her. Instead, he'd talked to Anderson and simply agreed without another word.

What had taken her off balance was his lack of… enthusiasm.

Oh, right, St. Cloud, she thought, disgusted. *He's supposed to be eager to risk his neck for a chance at yours.*

Still, this cold, matter-of-fact agreement left her puzzled. He seemed almost disinterested, though she could have sworn she'd seen erotic hunger in his eyes before he'd gone to talk to Bill.

Oh, God. Bill. Her stomach sank. Bill had told him about the Raiders.

Beryl reached out and grabbed Decker by one hard shoulder and tried to haul him around. It was like grabbing a cliff, but he stopped and faced her. In the bright light of the station corridor, his eyes were a vivid electric blue.

"If you think I betrayed the Company, why did you agree to protect me?"

"Because I'm not sure whether you did or not." He lifted a dark eyebrow. "Did you sell out your men, St. Cloud?"

"No!" Rage swelled in her like hot oil bubbling through water. She was damn sick of being accused of betraying the people she'd loved most.

"Then why'd you settle? Must have been a good bit of change to pay for something you didn't do."

Her rage cooled as the guilt under it rolled to the surface. She slumped, suddenly drained. "It was my responsibility to protect them, and I didn't."

"I doubt that was the first battle you lost."

"Fuck you, vampire."

Decker made a gesture as though warding off her weary anger. "I'm not accusing you of incompetence, St. Cloud, but you know as well as I do that every commander loses battles. I did. Bill did. And you did. So why'd that one hit you so hard?"

She discovered she could no longer meet his eyes. "Because I should have seen what Daveed was, and I didn't." Since the age of sixteen, she'd been a warrior, and a damn good one. It was all she was, all she was good at. And Daveed Zahn had stripped it all away. Now she'd fallen so far she was forced to whore for a vampire to save her life.

Hell, if they'd sent a proper assassin after her, one who would have ended her life with one clean shot... But they hadn't even allowed her the dignity of an honorable fight, an honorable death.

And she had enough self-respect left not to settle for what they had in mind.

So she had no hope but Decker, the vampire who'd led the Raiders as they should be led. She knew his history, she'd heard the stories since she'd been sixteen. Few had died under his command, and the ones who hadn't had gotten rich from his victories.

Why had he been the only one she could turn to?

"Do you want me or not?" Beryl snapped.

For a long moment Decker looked at her as if weighing her, testing the pain he could read in her face. Suddenly the darkness lifted from his features and relief filled his eyes, followed by compassion. "You really weren't involved with Zahn's plot, were you? This hurts you too damn much."

But before she could answer, his gaze shifted into the distance, and his eyes narrowed, his lips peeling back to reveal his canine teeth lengthening into fangs. Crouching, he snatched something out of the top of his boot, then rose and grabbed her elbow. She looked down and saw he held a serrated black knife almost as long as her arm.

"What are you doing?" Beryl gave her arm a jerk, but it was like pulling against an industrial vise.

Decker started towing her up the corridor at a pace just short of a run. "Tagliar's coming."

"Damn," she murmured. "I'd hoped to have more time... Wait, how do you know that? For that matter, how'd he manage to find me so fast?"

He shrugged. "We can sense each other when conditions are right. As for tracking you, he's following your scent. He doesn't know we're together yet, but he will. If we're lucky, we may have just enough time to get this done."

"Get *what* done?"

Decker ignored the question as he drew her into the main atrium, a huge, vaulting chamber filled with trees and vegetation under the dome of a hologram night sky. An immense ringed planet hung overhead, casting a soft, butter yellow light that illuminated the park. The patter of falling water vied with birdsong in air fragrant with honeysuckle, but the vampire didn't even seem to notice as he plunged down a curving gravel path. She scrambled after him.

"Tagliar's got me at a disadvantage," he explained, his voice grim. "Synthblood is a lousy substitute for the real thing; it provides nourishment, but not the psychic charge that taking a human does. And it's that energy which strengthens us. Tagliar's an assassin, and he feeds well and often. Me, I've been drinking synthblood since the Vamp Legislation passed."

"So because you've been living like a monk while Tagliar's been gorging on other people's lives..."

"...He's going to kick my ass. Unless I take you *now.*"

Beryl's gut twisted at the thought, but she forced herself to consider it calmly. And she calmly thought it was a bad idea. "I can't give you that much blood, Decker."

"Of course not, but blood's only part of it. When a woman climaxes, she produces a hell of a lot of psychic energy. Tagliar likes to take that energy by force before he kills, but mutual passion gives a better charge than rape. That, and given that I'll have taken you more recently than he's fed, could balance the scales."

They'd stepped into a clearing. An elaborate fountain splashed water high into the air. Decker headed for one of the marble benches that surrounded it, Beryl resisting the urge to tug against his grip.

"I hope to hell you're not expecting me to generate burning passion on the spot." She dropped down on the bench next to him. "I hate to say it, but I'm just not in the mood."

He gave her a grin so heart-stoppingly charming she blinked in surprise. "You let me take care of that."

Easing closer, Decker reached for her.

Unwillingly, her mind spat an ugly memory of Tagliar: *"I want to make you come at least twice before I kill you."*

"Shhh," the vampire breathed, his fingers brushing her mouth in a feathering caress. "I won't hurt you."

But another thought occurred to her, and she frowned. "What about the vamp virus?"

"You can't catch it from saliva," he told her patiently. "You'd only become a vampire if you drank my blood while I drank enough of yours to weaken your immune system."

Her last reasonable objection banished, Beryl forced her muscles to relax. It was like going into battle, she told herself. Just plunge in and worry later. If there was a later.

A rueful chuckle rumbled warmly in her ear. His hands came up to cup her face, lifting her head so her eyes met his. "Work with me here, darlin'."

There was such kindness in those eyes, an understanding that seemed to speak directly to something in her she never acknowledged. *I know how lonely you've been. I know how you've feared and hid it, I know how you've wanted to reach out, but there was never anyone there. I know how you've suffered*

Part of Beryl yearned to accept that silent offer of understanding, but the rest was pure soldier, and she had learned to distrust anything she wanted that much.

He's three hundred years old, she thought, as his strong fingers gently explored the rise of her cheekbone, the whirl of her ear. *And he's survived most of that time because he knows how to give women exactly what they want, and give it so well they're willing to sacrifice blood to get it.*

Yet those blue eyes looked into her, called to the vulnerable girl she kept locked within a hard shell of cynicism. And that girl wanted him.

He's a gigolo with fangs.

But the warm glide of his fingers didn't feel like pretense. He leaned closer, brushed his lips against her forehead. She forced herself to let go of her fear, to close her eyes.

And surrender to the vampire.

There was something so disarming about her, Decker thought, as she finally relaxed against him. She looked like sex and sin, she thought like a soldier, but underneath... Dreamily he played his hands over her, tracing the fine muscles of her shoulders and down to the thrust of her round, full breasts, letting the connection between them build.

What was it Anderson had said? She'd been with the Raiders since she was sixteen. What the hell had Bill been thinking of, to let a child fight with that gang of killers?

Despite the ghost of that girl he could sense inside her, she was far from childlike now. Pulling her closer, Decker felt her relax another increment as he slowly seduced her into forgetting Tagliar.

He cupped one pretty breast, filling his hand with silken warmth. The thin shirt she wore was no barrier at all, and her nipple budded tightly. He began to stroke her, taking the little peak between thumb and forefinger and squeezing until she gasped in his ear. His vampire hearing picked up her pulse as it took on the rapid thump of desire, and Decker smiled.

Craving more direct contact, he reached under her loose shirt and found the taut, female globe shuddering with her heartbeat. A shiver of his own rippled through him. God, it had been so long.

Decker slipped his fingers up to the eager point he'd been toying with and gently twisted, using all the skill he'd honed for three centuries. Beryl moaned, her breath hot on his skin as she arched her back. Silently begging for more.

She was no virgin, yet she'd never felt such arousal. Her nipples were hard and desperate, and Decker was giving them exactly what they needed, tugging, crimping them between his fingers, building her flicker of cautious desire into a blaze. Beryl twined her arms around his back and held on. She wanted his mouth, she wanted his fingers, she wanted....

But he's a vampire, said the little voice. Beryl told it to shut up.

His breath gusted warm across her ear, then his tongue tip traced the sensitive whirl. Blindly she turned her head, met his mouth with her own. His lips were seductively smooth against hers as his slick, wicked tongue glided inside. His hand found the tender flesh between her legs through the fabric of her shorts. She moaned against his mouth.

Her questing tongue found the sharp length of a fang, jolting her for a moment. But then his right hand tugged gently at her nipple, and his left pressed urgently against her sex, right *there*, at the spot she most needed him, and Beryl shuddered. Long, clever fingers increased the pressure, and she arched into the muscular warmth of his body, moaning. He felt so good holding her. Not like a predatory vampire looking for blood and sex, but a tender, loving man.

And God, she'd had too few of those.

She felt the gust of his breath on her throat, the careful press of his teeth. His tongue bathed her skin. Something stung her neck, built quickly toward pain, but his hands were working her body with such skill she didn't care. The pain became a deep, drawing ache, but somehow instead of puncturing her pleasure it only spurred it. Beryl whimpered, shocking herself with the helpless passion in her own voice.

Then Decker began to feed.

The first tug of his mouth sent a wave of erotic delight through her so hot and dark she gasped in startled lust. He was holding her locked against him now, one arm around her back, a hand fisted in her hair. Ruthlessly Decker shoved the other down the waistband of her shorts and thrust two fingers into her slickness as his thumb sought her clit. Beryl arched her back and moaned, her voice high and trembling with passion. He growled back, still drawing deeply on her skin. His thumb circled her hard little bud. The dark, exotic pleasure was abruptly unbearable, burning through her in time to the suction of his mouth and the pumping of his hand. His fingers flexed within her, making her wish for his erection. She sought it out, finding his cock wonderfully hard and hot and long behind the frustrating barrier of his pants. Decker sucked harder on her throat and twisted his long fingers deep, and she hungered for that splendid, forbidden vampire cock plunging into her as he drank. It would feel so thick, so merciless...

The ecstacy burned hotter. And hotter. And exploded.

Beryl screamed.

And *felt* him in her mind, taking everything she had and giving it back, savagely bright and strong. Under his delicious spur, something in her burst again, wiping out everything else but that starburst of rapture. Which slowly, slowly faded like a spark dying in the night.

Until at last he drew away.

"Don't stop," she moaned, pulling weakly at him.

"No, darlin'," he murmured. "You can't give me any more, or I'll hurt you."

"Oh." She wasn't sure she cared, but could only muster the strength to hang there in his arms, exhausted.

He began to tongue her slowly, painting wet, warm paths along her neck until Beryl stirred enough to ask, "What are you doing?"

He said something technical about vampire saliva and enzymes promoting healing. She barely listened, floating in lassitude as he licked the small wound he'd left, his tongue moving in long strokes over her throat like a cat bathing a kitten. Too sated for further conversation, Beryl simply lay back in his possessive arms, eyes drifting closed as he tongued her.

She was actually drifting off to sleep when a familiar voice snarled, "You been fucking my prey, Decker?"

Chapter Two

Decker lifted his head as a lightning strike of primitive rage forked through him. He'd found his woman at last, her blood was in his mouth, her hot cunt waited for his first thrust, and now that idiot Tagliar wanted to play games. "Go away, bloodsucker. I'm busy."

"I can see that," Tagliar said, eyeing them from the edge of the clearing. He was a big bastard, taller than Decker by a good three inches, with the muscle to back up that size packed on his long bones. He was handsome enough to have been a successful vampire back before the Legislation, but Decker suspected the chill arrogance in his hazel eyes repelled more women than his pretty face attracted. Tagliar had killed so many humans so easily he'd forgotten anyone could give him a fight.

Right now that cold gaze was crawling over the swelling lower curve of Beryl's breast, revealed by Decker hand still thrust beneath her shirt. He let the hem drop.

"Well, well." Tagliar grinned at Beryl in nasty insinuation. "I never dreamed you'd climb onto another vampire's cock so soon after feeling my fangs. You must have liked it."

"And you know just how much, Tagliar. I could tell by the way you screamed when I pulled the trigger." Beryl really should have had fangs of her own to go in that smile. "How are your eyes, vampire?"

Tagliar lost his grin. "Better off than yours, once I dig them out of your head. Take a walk, Deck. The bitch and I have business."

Decker stood and moved to shield Beryl with his body. "You always were a little stupid, so I'll spell it out for you. She's mine. You don't get her."

Tagliar reached into his belt and pulled out an ironwood knife that looked more like a machete. "The knight in shining armor rides to the rescue. Come on, cock sucker, I want to dent your gleaming ass."

"God, Tag, where do you get your dialogue — the Asshole Channel?" To Beryl, who looked as if she was wondering what a "channel" was, Decker muttered, "You still have your torch?"

She nodded, drawing the weapon from its holster. He noticed from the readouts it held a full charge and wasn't surprised. Beryl was a professional to the soles of her battle boots.

"Remember, that's just a backup." Decker showed her the knife. "Nothing will really put a permanent hole in a vampire but this."

Beryl's eyes widened. "Is that *wood*?"

"Next best thing to a stake." He eyed Tagliar, who was pacing around the area as if choosing a good spot for a fight. "How else would two vampires fight?"

Having found a suitable spot for a brawl, Tagliar turned to watch them with reptilian attention.

"Let me help, Decker." Beryl's eyes were cold as she stared at their enemy.

"Sorry, that's my job. You're safer on the sidelines." She looked so offended he had to smile. "I hate to mention this, darlin', but you're only human."

"Don't rub it in."

From across the fountain, Tagliar called, "Any day now, Decker!"

Beryl shot the big vampire a look of pure loathing. "Gut him."

"I'll certainly try." It was time to start.

Before her eyes, the amusement drained away from Decker's handsome features until nothing was left but chill determination. Without another word, he walked away to meet his enemy. Beryl could only clench her fists and ignore her churning stomach. It went against the grain to watch someone else fight for her while she did nothing. She knew she was no match for a vampire's strength, but failing to try felt cowardly.

The duel started so fast she almost missed it. A flash of color, the muffled thud of big bodies slamming together like enraged bulls, and the two vampires were locked in a writhing clench on the ground.

Decker caught Tagliar's wrist, stopping the wooden blade an inch from his chest. His biceps howled as he fought the strength of his opponent's massive arm. Sweat rolled, stinging, into his eyes. Still the knife pushed closer. Tagliar met his gaze and grinned.

Decker released the vampire's knife wrist, simultaneously sweeping his free hand around in a chop that slammed into Tagliar's forearm and knocked the big blade aside. It thumped into the grassy turf that covered the deck, burying itself halfway to the hilt just as Decker slammed a fist into Tagliar's narrow nose. Blood splattered. He jerked his head back from the hot, red spray and kicked, launching Tagliar into the air with one thrust of his legs. Decker rolled to his feet as Tagliar, cursing, somersaulted to his own.

Decker circled to his right. Something wet and warm rolled toward his mouth, and he knew from the scent it was Tagliar's blood. He fought the temptation to lick it off, knowing one taste of his enemy's blood would plunge him into the territorial madness of vampire combat. He needed all his intelligence and skill if he was going to keep Tagliar from killing him and taking Beryl, and the blood rage could strip it all away.

Tagliar lunged again, setting off a flurry of strikes Beryl couldn't even follow. When the two separated, Decker had a foot-long slash across his torso.

A chill skated Beryl's spine. She'd been in everything from bar brawls to battles between interstellar armadas, but this fight was different. It wasn't just the combatants' vampire strength that seemed so alien, it was the vampire rage that contorted their features into something feral and inhuman.

Then Tagliar confirmed that impression. Looking directly into Decker's eyes, he licked the bloody point of his knife, his smile demonic, his tongue abnormally long, pointed like a snake's.

Decker stiffened, and his jaw thrust forward before he dipped his head and tongued the blood from his own blade. Yet instead of Tagliar's nonhuman relish, there was distaste in his eyes, a repugnance mixed with resignation.

What the hell is that all about? Beryl wondered, and waited for the fight to start again.

For several beats the only movement was Tagliar licking his knife as though savoring an ice cream cone. Both vampires seemed to be waiting for something. Finally Decker coiled into a crouch and Tagliar lifted his head from his blade. A low growl rumbled, she couldn't tell from whom.

They hit each other so hard she could hear the meaty thud from across the park. One knife spun away and the other fell into the grass, but the vampires didn't seem to notice as they ripped at anything they could reach with fangs and clawing hands. Blood sprayed the deck, animal growls sawed the air, and for the first time Beryl realized how far from human they really were.

Her stomach twisted as she remembered she'd just agreed to put herself at Decker's mercy. And she wondered if there was really all that much difference between him and Damian Tagliar....

Rage heated Decker's consciousness into a roiling boil that made thought impossible. Just as he'd feared, the other's vampire blood had triggered a flood of hormones that plunged him into a killing rage, but he'd had no choice once Tagliar had licked that damn knife. The vamp rage doubled strength even as it made strategy more difficult, and he couldn't afford the disadvantage.

The reaction was even stronger because Beryl's blood also ran in his veins. Beryl, his prey, his woman, his mate. *His.* Tagliar dared think he could take her away.

And Decker was going to kill him for it.

Fangs bared, he launched himself at Tagliar, grabbing him by the throat as the force of his dive threw them both into the fountain. Decker howled at the shock of hitting cold water, but forgot his discomfort as Tagliar flailed and clawed at the hands still clamped around his neck. Snarling, Decker dug in, his nails gouging so deep blood curled into the water. The sight spurred his frenzy even higher.

Somewhere, far back inside the red riot Decker's mind had become, a last fragment of human intelligence rejoiced. His gamble had paid off. By taking Beryl as he had, he'd gained the strength to defeat Tagliar. All that remained was the kill.

Decker watched hazel eyes widen as Tagliar realized he was about to die. In a moment his neck would break, and though that wasn't enough to kill a vampire, it would paralyze him long enough for Decker to tear his head off his shoulders.

Snarling into Tagliar's face, Decker curled his fingers deeper, tighter.

"Not this time, bloodsucker!" Tagliar gasped, fumbling at his boot until his fist shot up holding a backup knife. He thrust it right toward Decker's eyes. Instinctively Decker jerked back, avoiding the blade but relaxing his hold.

Tagliar threw him off, rolled to his feet and lunged out of the fountain. Snarling, Decker shot to his feet.

But before he could leap after his enemy, a hot red point appeared on Tagliar's shoulder. The vampire stumbled, roaring in shock at the pain of the laser blast carving into his body. Unfortunately the wound wasn't enough to stop him. He recovered and kept going, running hard.

Decker instinctively turned to look for the ally with the torch. Behind him, Beryl was holstering her weapon. Their gazes locked, and she froze there just beyond the stone lip of the fountain, her eyes going wide.

Water beaded her mahogany curls, and the white top she wore was wet through from the splashing kicked up in the combat. Her nipples were clearly visible, dark and puckered under the fabric that clung to her breasts like a man's hand. The twin globes looked taut and full and tempting.

And she was his.

He'd fought for her and won. He would have killed for her. Instead he'd forced Tagliar to flee for his life.

Now he owned her.

The human intelligence that was slowly struggling back to life knew he should go after Tagliar. But his Beast was in control now, and his Beast wasn't interested in whatever threat Tagliar might be later. Its only focus was the woman who stared at him now, her expression stunned.

It took him a great effort, but at last he managed speech. "Come. Here."

Unconsciously, Beryl took a step back. Decker stood in the middle of the fountain, his shirt ripped off his back, thin runnels of blood rolling down his muscled torso from the countless cuts that marked him. His hair was slicked tight to his head, and water beaded on the taut planes of his face. And there was nothing at all human in his eyes.

"Come," he growled. "Here."

Beryl had made her living facing death, and fear was not a new feeling to her. Yet now she felt a fear both physical and sexual that was alien to her tough merc pragmatism, a fear not only of his strength and his vampire hunger, but a woman's fear of a fully aroused and dominant male who'd won a right to her.

"You'll kill me," Beryl said, and was instantly ashamed of the implied cowardice in the protest.

"Fought for you," Decker rumbled. "Mine."

Damn him. Beryl stared at him, taking in the muscled power of his body, the hard bulge of his arousal. He was right. He had fought for her, and he'd won. And if it had only been sex on his mind, she'd have gone to him at once, because even in her fear she felt the hot tug of his attraction. After all, she'd already given herself to him tonight.

But that had been the sane Decker, not this hungry vampire who'd clawed and bitten at Tagliar like a wolf. If she submitted to him now, there was no telling what he'd do to her.

And yet...

And yet Beryl St. Cloud had never backed down in her life. She'd made this man a vow, and she owed it to him to keep it. If she ran from him now, she might survive, but she'd be broken.

Better to die than break.

He purred in pleasure as his woman came to meet him, her head up and her shoulders back, presenting her breasts to him like a gift. Decker reached for them, found he disliked the clammy feeling of her wet shirt, and impatiently ripped it open with a single pass of his hand. Freed, her breasts trembled, taut and pale and wet. A bead of water clung to the end of one nipple like milk. He wanted to suck it away.

But as he bent toward her, Decker looked up into her face. Beryl looked back, as expressionless as a warrior going into a battle that might kill her.

It was that impassivity which awoke the human in Decker from his bloody vampiric haze. And he realized that if he took her blood now, he wouldn't be able to stop. He'd kill her.

Decker looked down at her breast, at the hard, tight point waiting for him, and shuddered with a wave of lust. He couldn't let her go. He craved her wet heat clamping tight around his aching shaft, craved her long, slender female body, her warmth, her humanity. Her. He growled low in his throat at the tearing frustration.

Beryl looked up and met his gaze as he reached out a long hand and closed it around her forearm, his fingers almost burning her with their hectic heat. She sucked in a breath at the stark conflict in his eyes, the hunger struggling with conscience.

"This way," he rumbled.

Decker pulled her into the fountain's spray. Blindly she sloshed after him, wondering as falling drops hit her face what he had in mind. Then they were through the spray, moving toward the sculpture that stood in the center of the fountain. Constructed of countless sheets of metal polished to a mirror sheen, the structure reached almost to the vaulted ceiling ten meters overhead.

Decker pulled her to it. "Bend over."

She hesitated, frowning, until he caught the back of her head and gently forced it to lower. Automatically she grabbed one of the metal plates for balance, and saw Decker moving behind her in its polished surface. His big hands caught the waistband of her shorts and jerked them down her legs. The motion brought his face close to back, and he froze there, his eyes widening, his nostrils flaring as though catching her scent. Then his eyes drifted closed, and he inhaled again as if deliberately savoring her. Decker's lips parted, revealing the white length of his fangs.

He jerked to his full height. Clenching his eyes shut, Decker threw his head back, visibly fighting for control even as his powerful hands caught her bare, slick hips to keep her from escaping.

Beryl stood motionless, sensing that if she moved she might shatter the delicate balance in the battle Decker obviously fought with himself.

His hands stroked over the curve of her bottom, up her back, brushing her ribs. Watching him in the sculpture's countless mirrors, she realized he was careful to keep his head up and back from her vulnerable body, as if struggling not to bite her.

He'd chosen this position to keep her safe.

Bill was right about Decker, Beryl thought, awed. Here he was, so far gone he could barely speak, yet still he fought to protect her from his own ravenous hunger. That said a lot about the strength of both his principles and his willpower.

For the first time since meeting Decker, Beryl relaxed, knowing that despite his feral, erotic appetite she was safe with him.

Then long masculine fingers slipped into the folds of her core, and all thought vanished from her head. As Beryl's eyes widened, Decker delicately began to strum her, testing her heat, her textures. At the same time, his other hand smoothed over the tight muscle of her thigh. She squirmed and swallowed a moan at the sudden, ferocious pleasure.

Behind her, Decker smiled a tight, lunatic smile. His Beast still clawed for control, but he'd had three hundred years to learn how to ignore his vampiric needs in the name of seduction. Instead he focused on the sight of her heart-shaped ass and the rosy, pouting petals of her sex. And those sweet, taut breasts that seemed to swell as he stared at them, silently pleading for his lips.

Beryl was everything he'd ever wanted, everything he'd ever dreamed about in all these lonely decades. A woman who wouldn't break, a woman who could keep up with his demands and give as good as she got.

Slowly, hungrily, he slipped a finger into her. She was still wet from her earlier climax, and he eased another finger in. Beryl caught her breath. And grew still wetter around him. Decker smiled and licked his fangs.

Beryl bit her dry lips, watching Decker in the mirrored surface of the sculpture. He stood behind her, his broad, powerful body dewed from the fountain spray, the thick tendons of his forearm working as he played with her. The feral expression that had chilled her earlier was fading, leaving only a ravenous sensuality and animal possessiveness.

He reached for his fly, and despite herself, she shivered. Wanting to see him, she twisted her head to gaze at him over a shoulder as he freed himself. Long. His shaft was long and thick. Eager for her. Helplessly Beryl set her feet farther apart in welcome.

Decker's hands closed over her hips, drew her backward until the thick head brushed her bottom, found her wetness. And slid inward endlessly. Beryl ducked her head, biting down on her lower lip at the pleasure.

He growled in satisfaction and slowly began to stroke. She shut her eyes and tightened her grip on the plates in front of her. Cool water foamed around her ankles as Decker's hot cock tunneled and withdrew. She threw her head back, letting the spray from the fountain hit her face and dew on her skin. Each hard thrust pulled and twisted at her creamy flesh, his rigid length delving deep into her, feeding the emptiness of her own steadily sharpening hunger.

Opening her eyes, Beryl watched him take her in the mirrors, his handsome head thrown back so the cords of his neck stood in relief, the powerful muscles of his torso lacing as they worked to drive his length in and out of her.

His blue eyes opened and caught her watching him. Whatever he saw on her face spread a satisfied male smile across his own. Deliberately, possessively, Decker began to thrust harder and harder, driving the breath from her lungs and forcing her onto her toes. Pleasure raked her with needle claws each time his big shaft plunged in. She cried out, a wordless plea for mercy and for more, and he took her still faster, pumping ruthlessly.

Beryl felt her climax coming in driving waves as brutal as he was. Even as she opened her mouth to scream, Decker lifted her, pulling her away from the statue and into his arms. Her back hit his hard chest. He shifted his grip, caught her under her thighs and forced her right down on his straining cock. Strong vampire hands lifted her and dropped her and lifted again in time to the merciless pumping of his hips. She shrieked at the incredible sensation, her head falling back against his shoulder as he plunged even deeper than before, all the way inside. All the way to her heart.

She came then, her body twisting against his hands. He held her easily. Beryl was still quaking when he suddenly stiffened and drove himself to the hilt inside her, roaring out his pleasure as he came.

Long minutes passed as she hung in his arms, the spasms of aftershock gripping her sex. When it was over at last, she could only slump there, listening to the hot throb of his heart as his muscled chest worked behind her head.

"You okay?" His voice sounded hoarse, but otherwise back to normal.

"Yeah." Beryl grimaced at the rough croak her throat had produced.

"Can you stand?"

"I'm willing to try."

Gently he put her down. She gasped as her shaking thighs protested her weight and instinctively caught his wrist to brace herself. When she looked up, she was startled at the wary look in Decker's eyes, as if he expected her to lace into him for his feral sexuality.

Beryl said the first thing she thought of. "Well, that was fun. Where are my shorts?"

A grin of relief rather than humor spread over his handsome face. "Glad you enjoyed it. God knows I did." Spotting the bottoms, he stooped and fished them out for her, giving them a helpful wringing to get rid of the water before handing them back. Beryl struggled into them, swearing at the chilled, wet fabric.

"At least it's the middle of the graveyard shift, so there won't be many people around to wonder what the hell we've been up to," Decker told her, pouncing on the rags of her shirt floating past. "And my ship is docked on this deck, so we don't have far to go." He wrung the torn fabric and helped her slip into it before fastening his own pants. "Are you ready?"

"God, yes." She was shivering in her dripping clothing. "Please tell me you've got a ship suit or something I can put on until I can get my own stuff."

"I'm sure I've got something, though I won't promise it'll fit."

Beryl nodded, relaxing a little herself. Decker was definitely back to normal, an idea that filled her with a curious blend of relief and regret. As erotic as the encounter had been, she wasn't likely to forget the hungry Beast that lay beneath his civilized, intelligent facade.

"Wonder where that bastard Tagliar got to?" he murmured. His eyes caught the light and ignited with a spark of red.

And Beryl realized that Decker's Beast was never buried very deeply.

Chapter Three

The mercenary lifestyle isn't one that affords a lot of physical privacy, so being sopping wet and next to nude didn't bother Beryl all that much when she and Decker walked onto the station's hanger deck. She didn't even blink at the spacer who openly leered as she approached, but when the man went pale and backed up, she turned to see what had spooked him.

Behind her, Decker was baring his fangs.

Realizing she'd caught him threatening the spacer, Decker shut his mouth and looked sheepish. "Sorry." To change the subject, he said, "There's my ship."

Beryl turned, followed his pointing finger. And resisted the urge to gape. Compared to the troopships and fighters she'd crewed, the vessel was huge. Like most merchanters, it was laid out in the standard "Bucky Ball" shape, like two geodesic domes placed lip to lip, but she did spot one unusual feature. A series of bumps on the outer hull. Positron cannons. A lot of them.

"What did you do, raid an armory?" Beryl asked, doing a silent count and raising her brows at the total.

Decker grinned, as proudly wicked as a mischievous boy. "Hey, it's the merc motto, 'you can never have.....'"

"'...too many guns.'" Beryl finished. "Yeah, I know." Watching a passenger airlock open and a ramp slide down from the ship's side, she asked, "By the way, why did you retire from the Raiders? You're immortal, so age obviously wasn't a factor."

"Actually, my immortality is the reason I retired," Decker started up the ramp, his long legs eating the distance into the primary hatch. "When you live damn near forever, you can only do something just so long before you get sick of it. And I got really sick of war."

"But why a merchanter? You don't seem the type to haul cargo."

"It wasn't what I had in mind," Decker admitted as they started down a long, narrow corridor. To either side of the bulkheads lay the cargo holds that took up the vast majority of the ship's considerable volume. If he'd followed the standard layout, both Decker's living quarters and the engines would lie at the vessel's core.

"I'd planned to go back to Earth," Decker continued. "Thing is, I'd been running the Raiders since the Vamp Legislation, and I didn't know how bad things had gotten. Once I'd been on the planet for a couple of months, I realized I didn't have the patience to deal with the laws that limit what vampires are allowed to do for a living, what relationships they can have. Not to mention all the intolerant sons of bitches who rapidly got on my nerves." He shrugged. "It finally dawned on me I could either lose my temper and kill a bigot, or head back to space. I've been here ever since. It's lonely, but nobody gives me any shit."

Beryl nodded. Mercs in general had a low tolerance for bureaucracy and rules, and she wasn't surprised Decker shared that attitude. "Still, those fifteen years must have felt like a prison sentence."

He shrugged his broad shoulders again. "Like anything else, it's what you make out of it. I've found ways to keep life interesting." Decker grinned suddenly. "You, for example. By the way, we'll need to stock up on food supplies for you. Give the ship's computer a list of what you need, and I'll order it."

She nodded as they reached the end of the corridor and stepped into the lift. "Quarters," Decker said, and the lift smoothly moved off at a steep diagonal.

He yawned, one hand lifting to cover his mouth not quite fast enough to hide his fangs. Beryl was reminded of a lazy tiger. "'S'cuse me. You may want to order in dinner, since I don't have anything on hand. Just charge it to the ship."

"What registry?"

Decker grinned. *"Bram Stoker."* He eyed her, then sighed and rattled off the ship's ID code. Beryl had the feeling she'd missed a joke.

The lift doors opened on Decker's living quarters, and he led her on a tour. Spacers of every sort tended to have cluttered living areas, chock full of keepsakes and toys to break up the lonely monotony of space travel, but Beryl had never seen anything as opulent as Decker's shipboard home.

Some kind of early rock played in the background, a haunting blend of sax and drum and guitar. Thick carpet in vivid shades covered the deck, and plants and artwork were everywhere, filling niches in the walls or occupying graceful stands carved from genuine wood.

The bridge, where most solo spacers did their sleeping, was dominated by a circular bed inset in the floor in shallow pit. The mattress was heaped with colorful silk pillows and covered with a vast silky black fur throw, and around the pit clustered enough plants to stock a jungle. Beyond lay the ship's command center with its arching control panels and viewing screens, all of them up-to-date tech.

Beryl cleared her throat and said, "This is... impressive."

Decker laughed. "You mean it's a bit much. True." The bridge door opened, and a ink black cat the size of a lynx glided in. He stooped to pick up the enormous feline, giving it an affectionate stroke. "Basically I've turned the *Stoker* into my own private pleasure palace, pets and all." He gave her a wicked grin. "All I needed was a harem."

"A sadly under-supplied harem," she observed dryly.

"I wouldn't say that." His long fingers scratched under the chin of the big cat, which rewarded him with a rumbling purr. "By the way, this is Lestat, so named because he likes to rub up against you and then take a chunk out of your nearest juicy body part."

Beryl eyed the cat cautiously. "I'll keep that in mind."

"That would definitely be a good idea." He strolled toward one of the bulkheads and tapped a spot. A section of the wall slid back to reveal a well-stocked closet. Putting down the cat, Decker reached into the closet and pulled out a one-piece jumpsuit he handed to her.

"One of my ship suits. It should do until you can have your own gear delivered. It'll be a bit baggy, but it's dry and in one piece."

"Which is more than I can say for my current wardrobe." Eager to get out of her dripping clothes, she started stripping, then paused. "You don't mind?"

"Who, me?"

Decker watched with acute male interest as she undressed. Beryl felt a flicker of unease mixed with feminine awareness that was foreign to her normal merc practicality. Trying to ignore him, she tugged on the ship suit, which was just as baggy as he'd predicted. Luckily the sleeves and legs were short, so at least she didn't have to roll up the cuffs. She slanted another wary look in his direction.

The vampire broke the rising tension with another jaw-cracking yawn. "Sorry. Look, I'm going to have to hit the bunk. Between the fight and our other... activities, I'm done. Care to join me?"

"Not just yet. I'm not particularly sleepy at the moment."

"Well, feel free to curl up when you're ready. In the meantime, the com is over there; it's pretty standard, but you can ask the ship's comp if you need help with it..."

"I think I can figure it out."

Decker gave her another quicksilver grin. "Yes, I'm sure you can." He headed toward the sleep pit, stripping off his shirt and kicking free of his pants as he went. This time it was Beryl's turn to watch with appreciation.

Decker had a tough, strong body, broad and well-muscled, as beautifully cut as a Greek statue. He stepped down onto the mattress, giving her an appreciative view of his tight, firm butt and long legs before he more or less fell into the fur. Within seconds he was as bonelessly asleep as an exhausted child.

"I guess you're entitled," Beryl muttered, and went to familiarize herself with the ship's control console. It was pretty standard, except for the banks of automatics that controlled all those positron cannons. She'd seen merc cruisers less well-armed.

Content that she knew the layout of everything important, Beryl ordered the comp to download a list of menus from the station's delivery restaurants, made a selection and had the computer call it in. She made a second call to her hotel to arrange to pay her bill and have her bag sent over to the *Stoker.*

Then, stretching, she turned and froze in sheer erotic appreciation. Decker lay in the bed with his muscled arms flung wide, his thick cock hard with a nocturnal erection. His mouth was open in a slight smile that revealed the points of his fangs.

Beryl grinned. "Bet I know what you're dreaming about."

Her gaze slipped to his erection. She could almost feel its width plowing her again as Decker possessed her cunt and drank her blood.

Beryl had never been... taken like that before. For her, sex had always been either a race for pleasure or a slow exchange of comfort. But Decker had swept her into a hurricane of sexual sensation and given her no choice but utter surrender.

Frowning, Beryl headed for the lift to wait for the deliverybot. She wasn't used to being so out of control. One of the things she'd learned early as a merc was that losing your grip could get you killed. A little fear was good, kept you on your toes, got you thinking, but terror was pure, caustic poison, freezing the muscles and the mind, setting you up for whoever wanted you. She suspected the wild lust she'd known with Decker was just as bad.

Besides, her judgement about men in general was badly flawed. God knew Daveed had royally worked her over, appealing to her need for companionship, for closeness, only to set her up for betrayal.

The thought triggered a familiar surge of rage that Beryl automatically fought down to manageable levels. Zahn was dead now, he'd been dead for months. There was no point in indulging in anger now. It was all gone out the airlock.

Just like the rest of her life.

As soon as the thought crossed her mind, she rejected it. Self-pity was one emotion she couldn't tolerate.

The plain fact was that her situation had changed. She was broke and dependant on a vampire for protection against another vampire. As part of the deal, she had to keep her own vamp sexually satisfied.

There was no point in bitching, she just had to play the situation out as best she could and wait for the wheel to turn. It always did.

One way or another.

The lift doors opened. Beryl strode down the corridor, stepping out the main airlock to discover the deliverybot still hadn't arrived. Sighing, she folded her arms and leaned against the *Stoker's* slick, cold hull to wait.

Patience, like controlling her anger, was something Beryl St. Cloud had learned very well.

Brooding, Beryl stared out across the huge deck as cargo bots scurried around loading and unloading the surrounding ships. Her best course was to keep her relationship with Decker on a business footing. She'd made a deal with him to provide sex and blood for his protection. She'd just make damn sure to keep her emotions out of it....

"Well, well, it's the deviant with the vampire boyfriend."

She snapped her head around and found the mercs from the bar standing at the base of the ramp. Two of them anyway, the woman and one of the men, both of them sneering.

Beryl grinned back in lunatic delight. She was suddenly in the mood for a good brawl. And it damn well had nothing to do with Decker. "Well, well, it's the greenie trying to prove her stones," she purred.

"I am not," Clarke hissed, "a greenie."

"Honey, you're so green your hair's grass."

Clarke flushed and pulled her viblade. "Let's see what color your blood is—if there's any left."

"Sorry, darlin', I'm saving it all for my one true love." Beryl fell into a crouch.

"Pervert." Bigotry and bloodlust in her eyes, Clarke charged up the ramp.

Now that the fight had started, Beryl's mind ticked off the tactical situation with the cool of a targeting computer. Clarke was armed, a considerable advantage, but she'd blunted it by pulling the knife too soon and attacking uphill. She'd have done better to hold the weapon back and wait for Beryl's attack.

Instead Clarke tried to impale her on the viblade like a cocktail olive.

Beryl pivoted out of the way, grabbed Clarke's knife hand and used the momentum of the blonde's charge to slam her into the airlock hatch. Pinning her there, Beryl slowly twisted Clarke's blade hand back while applying agonizing pressure to the merc's elbow with her free hand. The combination proved too much, and Clarke dropped the viblade with a curse.

"Computer, open hatch," Beryl called, and stepped back just as the airlock opened. The merc fell in with a yelp. "Close hatch and ignore commands from occupant." The computer obeyed, trapping Clarke between the inner and outer hatches as Beryl pivoted to face the remaining merc.

He still stood at the foot of the ramp as though he hadn't bothered to move, arms folded, an assessing expression in his eyes. "Who are you?"

"Beryl St. Cloud."

He nodded slowly. "Occam's Raiders. Thought I recognized you. Richard Keven of Andrikov's Commandos."

Beryl's brows flew up. "We tussled with you on Jovan a couple of years back. That was a hell of a fight. And how is the Black Russian?"

"Still cusses you when he's sober. When he's drunk, he says you're the best he ever faced." Keven paused. "And he's right. What the hell are you doing with a vampire?"

"It's a long story." A muffled thumping vibrated the hatch. "And I don't think Clarke has the patience to listen."

"Let her stew, the little idiot." He grimaced. "I can't believe she threw away her advantage like that."

"She just needs seasoning. And maybe a little less desire to prove the size of her stones."

"I'm just not sure she'll live long enough to get 'em."

"Hey, we did." As Keven chuckled, Beryl spotted a vehicle gliding toward them on a bed of antigravity. "Unless I'm mistaken, that's the deliverybot with dinner. Care to join me?" Another series of thuds. "I've even got enough for your friend."

"We've already eaten, thanks." He sighed. "I suppose you'd better turn the little greenie loose. I obviously need to give her more combat training before she gets somebody killed. Like me."

Beryl considered the idea, then nodded. "Open outer hatch, computer." She ducked as Clarke came out swinging.

"None of that, you little twit," roared Keven, striding up the ramp. "That's Admiral St. Cloud. She'll eat your ass like a cocktail cracker."

"Admiral St...?" Clarke must have heard of Beryl. She subsided immediately, then rallied enough for a sullen growl. "I want my viblade."

Beryl nodded sweetly and handed it to Keven. "And no, you can't have it back," he told her. "You'll cut your own arm off. Let's go, we've got some remedial hand to hand to go over."

Keven led Clarke off, chewing her out all the way.

Beryl was still grinning when she collected her meal from the delivery bot.

Carrying the hotpack of food, Beryl walked onto the bridge and flopped into the center seat. Decker still lay in glorious nudity in the bed pit, though she noticed his erection had subsided.

Too bad.

Forking moo goo gai pan into her mouth, she eyed him. He certainly made great scenery. She'd gotten out of the habit of noticing male bodies because ogling your subordinates was bad for morale, but in Decker's case it was safe to make an exception. Which was a good thing, Beryl admitted silently, since she'd been ogling him since she'd met him.

Munching, she meditated on the hard, rippling territory. He'd honed his body to perfection, though with his vampire strength, he could have gotten away with flab and still kicked any human's ass. But then Tagliar would probably have kicked his.

Beryl sucked her fork and wondered if Decker had to fight vampire duels on a regular basis. Of course, that build might also fall under the general category of maximizing your advantages, a solid policy for any smart commander. Or it might just be a way to attract girls.

Beryl grimaced and shoveled in another bite, chewing vengefully. Why the hell should it bother her that Decker had spent three hundred years seducing women? His past had nothing to do with her. She'd never cared about Daveed's sexual history.

Then again, maybe she should have.

Beryl jabbed a piece of chicken viciously. Something furry brushed her ankles, and she looked down to see Lestat looking at her in an obvious demand for food. "Sure, cat. Decker's pets have to stick together."

But as she plucked the bit of meat off her fork and gave it to the animal, she realized what she'd just said.

A pet? Her? *Screw that.*

Beryl St Cloud was damn well nobody's pet. She'd won two wars, six space battles, seventeen ground engagements, and more bar brawls than she could shake a bottle of ale at. She had her own power, her own hunger, and it was time her vampire found out she also had teeth.

Beryl put the hot pack down on the deck with a thump, not even noticing when the cat buried its muzzle into it. Slapping the seal of the ship suit open, she shucked it off and tossed the bundle across the bridge without looking to see where it landed. She stalked down into the pit and crouched, naked, to stare at all that sprawled muscular male nudity, at the sharply cut features that looked almost innocent in sleep.

All hers.

She expected him to wake the moment she touched him, since every merc she'd ever known was a light sleeper. But Decker was also a vampire, and vampires slept like deck plates, as Beryl discovered while delicately stroking the powerful arch of his ribs. His skin felt wonderfully smooth and warm under her fingertips, but he didn't so much as twitch an eyebrow. She grinned, wickedly intrigued. *Let's see how long he can sleep through this.*

A lovely ruff of chest hair spread over his pecs and down over his belly tempting her fingers to comb through it, savor its silky texture.

Beryl sighed, enjoying the sensuous contrast between the soft hair and the hard, warm flesh that lay beneath it. She couldn't remember the last time she'd touched a man just for the pure tactile pleasure of it. Exploring Decker made her realize she'd been cheating herself.

So Beryl set about savoring her vampire, discovering the way muscle wove around bone in each of his massive shoulders, the thick bundles of biceps and triceps, the hard beauty of forearms cabled with tendon. His long, agile fingers caught her attention, with their intriguing white ridges that must date back to his human life, back before medical science could instantly eliminate scars. Delighted, Beryl went on to the arch of his ribs, broad ripples curving toward the rock hard plates of the abdominals that lay over his belly like armor.

His cock was in full, glorious erection, its flushed head hovering over his navel.

Her gaze flew to his face, but his eyes were still closed, though she could glimpse the tips of his fangs in his slight smile.

Beryl's answering smile was predatory. She wanted him *now,* without even waiting for him to wake up. She wanted to take him as mercilessly as he'd taken her after his fight with Tagliar. Take him and own him.

She didn't pause to reconsider. She just swung one leg over his hips, grabbed his stiff length in one hand, and impaled herself in one delicious swoop. She'd grown so wet inside that his cock slid in like a knife into clotted cream. Biting her lip to stifle a moan, she looked down at him.

"Beryl!" Decker's blue eyes were wide and startled, his handsome features dazed. Beryl gave him a triumphant smirk and rose, then sank down on him again. He reached for her, but she grabbed his hands and pushed them back down to the fur spread.

"Forget it, vampire," she growled. "This time you're mine."

He blinked. She glared back. Both of them knew he could break her grip like an infant's. Instead Beryl felt his big body go slack under hers, surrendering. She hummed in satisfaction and pushed off for her next stroke.

Her deliciously wet heat stroked Decker's shaft, her full breasts bouncing as she ground down on him. For once he was utterly stunned. In three hundred years no woman who'd known he was a vampire had ever tried to seduce him.

Seduce hell, Decker thought, staring up into her fierce, beautiful dark eyes. *She's practically raping me.*

He licked his fangs and fought the desire to grab her, roll her under him, and plunge deep. Clamping his hands into the fur spread under him, Decker gritted his teeth and held on. He could sense how much she needed to be in control, and he was damn well going to give it to her.

But God, that long, lithe body, those gorgeous breasts... He eyed her bouncing nipples hungrily and promised himself a taste later.

Beryl leaned back to grab her ankles with both hands, seeking a deeper penetration as she rolled her hips hard. Her slick, hot walls slid up and down his long shaft, and the taut arch of her spine pointed her breasts at the ceiling, the erect stems of her nipples in tempting relief.

His Hunger boiled up, carnivorous and savage. He fought it back.

Sweat rolled down Beryl's ribs as she pumped up and down, her body arching until her hair brushed his ankles. His glistening shaft slid in and out between her thighs with a speed that made his head swim. The lush eroticism of that sight was almost more than he could stand, and he had to fight his body's leap toward pleasure. If he came too soon... But then she writhed over him with a low moan that quickly built to a sustained primal scream, her core clamping and releasing his shaft.

His control exploded. Decker's hands shot up, closed hard over her slim shoulders, pulled her down and under him in one powerful sweep without even breaking the connection between them. His Hunger roared through his defenses, stoked by the purely masculine lust she'd built so relentlessly.

Beryl's dark eyes flared wide for just a moment in surprise before his head swooped for the delicate white length of her throat. The smell of her skin filled his skull with female musk and the rich copper of her blood. Quivering with the force of his need, he sank his fangs into her until the burning red liquor flooded his mouth, and his cock, sunk deep in her wet depths, hardened even more.

Beryl gasped in shock at the warm velvet of his lips and the sharp edge of his fangs. For a moment there was pain, but the burn of pleasure followed, pumping with each pull of his mouth as he drank. Her fading orgasm hammered back into life. She shrieked.

LINK.

A psychic vampire bond snapped into place between them like a door banging open in Decker's mind. Suddenly he *was* Beryl, feeling himself, the width of his own cock, the edge of his own fangs. He could feel what she felt as she came, the pulsing beat deep in her sex, the fire in her nipples, the ache in her throat. The echo of her pleasure drove his own even higher, and he fed it back to her, showing her how her own wet silk walls clasped his cock as her smooth throat arched against his mouth.

She felt him. He was there with her, in her mind, raw and male, strong and dark, vampire lover taking everything she had and funneling it back to her in pounding, glorious waves. There was no separation between them, no way to tell who was Beryl and who was Decker. She, who'd always been alone, at last knew what it was like to touch another, feel another, be another.

And it was too much. *Get out of my mind!*

"Shit!" Decker shot away from her as though something had picked him up and blown him back.

Still pulsing hot from the pleasure, Beryl groggily lifted her head. He crouched at the other side of the sleeping pit, a wary expression on his angular, handsome face. One big hand rubbed his jaw as though he'd taken a punch. "You know, for somebody with no psi," he grumbled, "you have a hell of a psychic force field."

Beryl licked her lips, feeling dazed. "What are you talking about? What happened?"

"We linked. Mentally. Vamps do that, when the emotional connection is strong." He shrugged his wide shoulders. "Then you tossed me the hell out of your head."

"Oh." There didn't seem to be anything else to say. She sat up and curled her arms around herself, feeling suddenly cold.

Decker studied her intently, then gave her a small sympathetic smile. "Mind if I hold you? I promise not to do whatever it was that pissed you off." He paused. "Ever again."

She considered it. "Okay."

Moving back to her side, Decker pulled her gently into his arms. Beryl sighed, feeling his warmth and strength enfold her again. Gradually, she began to relax.

"You know," he said, after a long pause, "Linking really isn't so bad. I think if you gave it a chance, you'd like it."

"Oh, I liked it." Beryl said, remembering the pure, bright core that was Decker. It had felt so seductive, so delicious. So warm. "I think maybe that's the problem."

"What do you mean?"

His heart was thudding under her ear. She relaxed against his chest, feeling the hard muscle under her cheek. This she knew how to deal with, bodies, flesh. Sex. This was safe. Allowing him into her mind was not.

Beryl went lax against Decker as she sank quickly into sleep without answering his question. No surprise, really. She was exhausted.

He frowned, knowing he probably shouldn't have fed from her so soon after the last time. He'd better make sure she had a session in the ship's regeneration capsule to build up her blood again.

Thoughtfully, Decker combed his fingers through the tangled silk of her hair and listened to her heartbeat slowing into the languid rhythms of sleep. He'd never linked with a woman so completely after such a short time. Hell, he rarely managed to link with his partners at all, since the act required a special kind of kinship he'd encountered only a few times in his long life.

Yet Beryl had pushed him away. He couldn't help but wonder why.

The next day, Beryl, Decker and several cargo bots pitched in to load a shipment into the *Bram Stoker's* holds.

"Hey, boss," the *Stoker's* computer said, its feminine voice echoing in the huge space.

Decker put down a crate with a grunt. "What?"

"I just got a call from a Zalman Wirth. Asks if we can run some emergency medical supplies to Dyson's World. Want to talk to him?"

"Sure." Decker walked toward the intercom pickup, leaving Beryl standing frozen with a crate in her hands.

Dyson's World. The scene of her worst defeat, and the last planet she'd ever wanted to set foot on again.

But she wasn't calling the shots this time; Decker was. Besides, the load was medical supplies, and she damn well wasn't going to say a word about it.

Jaw set, Beryl put the crate away and picked up another from the pallet.

His conversation finished, Decker returned a few minutes later. Whatever he read on her face must have given her away. "What's wrong?" His eyes widened. "Shit. Dyson's World. Wasn't that where...."

"Yeah. Don't worry about it." She hefted a box at random and stashed it. "War's over, I'm not a merc anymore. It's done."

Decker studied her with eyes that seemed to see right to her core. "Wirth said they've been hit by Red Plague, and the death toll is climbing fast. They have to have the meds to save the dying and innoculate the rest, or I'd call him back and tell him to kiss off."

Beryl looked up in surprise. "Why would you do something like that?"

"It bothers you."

"I'm a big girl now, Deck." She shrugged. "Besides, this is your business. You can't blow off a commission because your resident piece of ass has bad memories of a business partner."

"I don't see you as a piece of ass, Beryl."

To her surprise, she realized he was serious. "Why not?"

Decker turned and hefted a huge crate that should have taken three men to lift. "A lot of reasons. Including that link we had last night."

She forced herself not to stiffen as he went on, "I learned a hell of a lot about you in those few seconds. Some of it I already knew, like your courage, integrity and sense of honor. I'd found out about those when you came to me after the fight with Tagliar, though most women would have taken one look at me and run like hell." He set the box down, adjusted its position. "But during the link I also discovered that you're hurting over that bastard Zahn more than you let on." He looked up, locking her in an intent blue stare. "I can help you with that."

Beryl set her teeth. "Look, Decker, I appreciate your protection from Tagliar, but that's all I need from you. Any other problems I have I'm more than capable of solving myself." Pivoting, she grabbed a crate. "Where do you want this?"

Decker gave her a narrow glance, then gestured. She stalked off to put the box down where he'd instructed.

Brooding, Decker watched Beryl stack crates, and knew there was something growing between them he'd never felt before.

I'm just horny.

Unfortunately he'd known himself too long to pull off that particular lie. True, he was lonely, and he'd probably be attracted to any receptive female after his long celibacy. But Beryl was something more. Her toughness, decency and strength demanded his respect just as her body demanded his desire. What he felt might not be love, not yet, but it was recognition.

She was not only his mate, she was his match. And after three hundred years, Jim Decker knew just how rare it was to see your heart mirrored in another.

The trouble was, Beryl didn't recognize their rare spiritual connection, and she certainly didn't realize how precious it was.

He was going to have his hands full getting her to see what was happening between them. And as stubborn as she was, she wouldn't make it easy.

But no matter how long it took, he damn well wasn't going to give up.

Chapter Four

Decker brought the ship out of SuperC, punched in the realspace coordinates for Dyson's World, and faced Beryl. She sprawled in the navigator's seat, Lestat draped across her lap as her long, clever fingers scratched behind his furry black ears. *Beryl and that cat have a lot in common,* he thought. *No matter how they purr when you stroke them, it doesn't mean love.*

He grimaced, suspecting he'd just crossed the line into being a prick. For God's sake, the woman had given him a month of hot blood and hotter sex. What more could a vampire want?

Everything, whispered a little voice he'd been trying to ignore without much success.

"I've got a feeling I should apologize about last night," he said, partly to silence that damn little voice.

Beryl slanted him an amused look. "And well you should. All those screaming orgasms gave me a sore throat." Letting her head fall against the back of her seat, she shut her eyes with a cream-licking smile. "Inconsiderate bastard."

He cleared his throat. "I meant the psilink. I know you don't like 'linking, but honest to God, it's not intentional."

Beryl's gaze slid away from his. "I never said I didn't like it."

The question was out before he could censor it. "So why do you always toss me out on my ass?"

The cat leaped from Beryl's lap, leaving her fingers to beat a quick tatoo on her thigh. "Decker, it's not intentional."

"Yeah, there seems to be a lot of that going around," he muttered, and winced as he heard the edge in his own voice.

Beryl snapped him a look. "Are you trying to pick a fight, Deck?"

"No, but I'm losing interest in avoiding one."

"Well, don't." Evidently deciding to take the vampire by the fangs, she leaned forward and braced her elbows on her thighs, fixing him with an earnest stare. "Decker, I get the impression you're trying to make our deal into something it's not. And I'm telling you, you're going to screw it up."

That did it. "The only one screwing things up is you, because you refuse to admit this is becoming a lot more than a business deal."

"Look, I need your protection, and you need my blood. It's a very simple arrangement and it's mutually satisfying, but it ain't love. If you start calling it something else, it's going to blow up all over us." Her fingers were beating that tatoo on her thigh again.

"Daveed really worked you over, didn't he?"

"Jesus." The muscles in her jaw rippled. "He's got nothing to do with this, Decker."

"Oh, yes he does, and it's a good thing the son of a bitch is dead, or I'd kill him." Figuring he'd better get out before he said something he couldn't take back, Decker rose and stalked toward the lift.

"Where are you going?"

"To check those damn medical supplies we're supposed to be delivering."

"We start our approach to the docking station in fifteen minutes," Beryl reminded him. "You'll have to pilot us in."

Decker didn't look back. "You do it. You're the one who's always got to be in control."

Beryl growled a few choice mercenary phrases toward the hatch he'd closed behind him.

Men. They had to make everything so damn complicated.

She spun her chair to face the control panel. On the three view screens above it, Dyson's World hung in space, a perfect glowing sapphire of a planet. Her irritation gave way before a thrust of pain.

This was where it had started. Daveed's betrayal, the deaths of her people, and her destruction.

She'd fought with Daveed that day too, when her merc troopship first fell into orbit. *"You never let me get close,"* he'd said, his full mouth sulky under the long fringe of his bangs. *"The only thing you really want from me is cock, because the only thing you really care about is your goddamned Occam's Raiders."*

Beryl watched the lovely blue globe swell in the view screen. "Was that why you let them buy you and destroy us all, Daveed? Because I couldn't give you enough?"

But that was one question she'd never get an answer for. Daveed was dead, along with far too many of the Raiders who'd depended on her to lead them to safety. Leaving Beryl to grieve and wonder.

If she'd been willing to give Daveed more, would they all be alive?

Docking the *Stoker* was a bitch. The merchant was so damn big piloting it into even a space station's cavernous maw took a skilled hand on the stick. Beryl managed it, though not without a few choice words for Decker and his attitude.

No sooner had the ship settled on its struts than a call came in from the hospital representative who'd ordered the shipment, a surprisingly burly man who looked more like a star marine than a paper pusher. They exchanged pleasantries and arranged to meet at the *Stoker's* primary airlock.

Beryl shut down everything and went to the hold to give Decker a hand, but when she got there, he hefted the crate onto one broad shoulder and told her with chilling courtesy that he didn't need help.

Simmering, she trailed him to the main hatch. While they waited for the airlock to cycle, she eyed his rigid profile. "So Decker, how long are you going to freeze me out?"

He rewarded her impudence with a glacial stare. "Until I get hungry enough to want a fucking snack."

Beryl refused to let the sting show on her face, but he apparently sensed it anyway. "Hey, that's all we are to each other, right? I'm the bodyguard, you're the ass. Who could want anything more?"

"Don't be a prick."

"Oh, why not? I'm so good at it." He banged a big fist into the airlock control button.

Beryl's mouth was open to retort when the hatch opened.

Tagliar stood on the other side, big, blond and grinning, an ironwood knife in one fist. "Hiya, Deck." He lunged while Beryl was still blinking in shock.

"Decker!" She instinctively grabbed him to pull him back from Tagliar's attack, but she was too late. His big body lurched and stiffened, and the crate hit the ground with a crash. Decker toppled, sheer dead weight pulling him out of her arms.

"Deck..." Beryl whispered in horror.

Hard vampire hands yanked her forward to hit Tagliar's massive body with a jaw-snapping jar. "Ah," he purred, "alone at last."

Her grief turned to instant rage. "You cowardly son of...."

Tagliar's mouth mashed off the end of the insult with a vicious faux kiss. Gagging, Beryl managed to jerk back just enough to lift one leg and fumble at the top of her boot. The bastard had hurt Decker. He was damn well going to pay.

Tagliar pulled back at last, his grin was white and reptilian on his handsome face. "Nice. Very nice. I'm going to enjoy this." His big hand came up, stroked the side of her face. "I just love the taste of a woman's blood when I rape her. It's got that certain zing...."

At that moment, Beryl's fingers found the wooden hilt protruding from her boot top. She snatched the knife free. "Which is why I started carrying ironwood, you son of a bitch."

And she drove the blade into the vampire's side, the whole of her body behind the thrust.

Tagliar grunted and staggered. Grimly triumphant, she waited for him to fall.

Instead the vampire caught himself, his lips pulling back from his fangs in a snarl. "You'll pay for that, bitch." Tagliar's head started to lower toward hers.

"When hell freezes over," Decker said, rising behind him like Banquo's ghost. His blood-slicked hand caught Beryl's around the knife hilt.

Tagliar tried to turn, but the blade dug deeper with Decker's strength behind it. He froze. "Goddamn it, haven't you died *yet?*"

"Nothing counts but the heart, Tag," Decker said. "And you missed. I won't." He drove the knife upward, dragging Beryl's hand along for the ride as he cleaved right through Tagliar's ribs.

The assassin roared and slapped Beryl away like a poker chip. She flew through the air and slammed into the interior airlock doors so high she slid down a meter and a half before she hit the floor.

Everything blacked out.

When she faded back to full awareness, Tagliar lay sprawled on the deck. Decker was bent double, his hands braced on his knees, his handsome face gray, bright crimson slicking him from midchest to knee. Beryl realized not all the blood was Tagliar's when his eyes rolled back and he collapsed across his enemy.

Tagliar might have missed the heart, but he sure as hell hit something.

"Shit." Beryl rolled to her feet and lunged for Decker, ignoring the resultant detonation of pain in her concussed skull. Grabbing a double fistful of Decker's bloody shirt, she ripped it away. No stranger to injuries after fifteen years as a merc, she still blanched at what she saw. Blood was gushing from the wound as though Tag had nicked the aorta.

Cursing, she balled up the shirt and mashed the wadded material against the wound, hoping pressure would slow the bleeding. "Computer," Beryl yelled toward the hull pickup, "Call the station's mediunit. We've got a critical here. And send down the portable so we can stabilize him."

Which was when a female voice demanded, "What does it take to kill you, bitch — a starkiller nuke?"

Startled, Beryl jerked her head around to see six armored soldiers with laser rifles trained on her from the airlock hatch. In the lead stood a tall woman dressed in a dark blue uniform of the Dyson Space Service. Judging from the elaborate braid on her padded shoulders, she must be the station commander.

She was also one of the most beautiful women Beryl had ever

seen. Her features were strong and lovely, and her skin was the color of clover honey, the golden tone a stark contrast to her vivid turquoise eyes and curling red hair.

Beryl's stomach lurched in recognition followed by sick fear. "Nice seeing you again, Lacey," she said, fighting to hide her reaction. "Call a mediunit, would you? This man is dying."

Lacey curled a well-shaped lip. "Don't be an idiot. He's a vampire. He's already healing." Compassion had never been Arith Lacey's forte.

"God, Lace, even a vampire couldn't survive a chest wound like..." Beryl lifted the sopping rag of his shirt. The bleeding had already stopped.

Lacey strolled over on her long, booted legs, turquoise eyes assessing the damage. "That sonofabitch Tagliar *did* miss, didn't he?"

Beryl went numb. "You hired him."

"You bet your ass." Her lush mouth curled into a smile that suggested torture chambers and long screams. "You know, St. Cloud, when Decker wakes up, he'll have to replace all that blood. Which means he'll be one hungry vamp. And I know just who to feed to him...."

Beryl braced her legs and concentrated on staying upright between the two troopers who held each arm. She didn't think they'd broken her ribs, but she wasn't willing to swear to it.

On the other hand, she was dead sure she could feel a painful smorgasbord of bruises blooming all over her body. Lacey and her armored buddies liked to play rough.

After they'd all gotten bored with beating her, the guards had marched Beryl off to the chilly confines of the space station's brig. Then, as if that wasn't severe enough, they headed right through to solitary confinement, an area even less inviting than the rest of the jail.

Racks of horizontal tubes were sunk into the bulkheads, each holding a mattress barely wide enough to accommodate a man's shoulders. If you didn't have claustrophobia when they put you in, you would by the time they pulled you out. It reminded Beryl of a morgue, which, under the circumstances, wasn't exactly comforting.

"What I want to know," she said to Lacey around a cut and stinging lip, "is how the hell you got in Occam's Raiders to begin with."

The redhead was watching a trooper load Decker into one of the tube bunks. He was still out cold. "Our boy here has a weakness for a pretty face." Lacey laughed. Beryl had never liked Lacey's laugh, and now she realized why; the woman sounded like she spent her off hours burning puppies with a laser torch. "Do you know, he once reprimanded me for being too bloodthirsty? Imagine, a vampire calling *me* bloodthirsty."

"Did it ever occur to you that should tell you something?"

Beryl tried to duck the backhand she got for that comment, but the troopers held her still.

"You've got a very annoying holier-than-thou streak, St. Cloud," Lacey said. "You really ought to muzzle it. Particularly considering I haven't forgotten the way you drummed me out of the company."

Beryl snorted. "You were lucky I didn't torch your ass. And don't think I wasn't tempted. The Raiders don't beat prisoners, but you just couldn't keep your hands off that kid. He was, what? Fourteen?"

"Fifteen." Lacey leaned too close, vivid eyes narrowing. "And by the time I get done with you, you're going to know just how he felt."

"Yeah, well." Beryl spat blood onto the deck, aiming for a polished boot. "And next time I'm going to torch you until you burst into flame."

Lacey came around the tube after her. The gut punch buckled her knees, but Beryl stiffened them. "Now that we've established we both hate each other's guts," she wheezed, when the redhead had stepped back and the urge to vomit had faded, "why are you still holding a grudge? God knows you must have been sacked before, what with your charming personality."

"This isn't about your firing me, you idiot." Lacey's pretty turquoise eyes narrowed to evil slits. "This is about you *failing* me."

"The only one I failed is that kid by not shooting you."

"Don't play stupid, St. Cloud, you know what you did. The one thing, the only thing, I've ever counted on you for, *and you fucked it up.*" There was a chilling glitter in Lacy's fixed stare that was a long way from sane.

"I have no idea what you're talking about."

"You know exactly what I'm talking about." She reached out a long arm and snagged Beryl by the collar, jerking her onto her toes. "You let Daveed Zahn die, you stupid little cunt."

Beryl, astonished, hung in the big woman's fist. "Daveed died in an ambush."

"I know that. Who the hell do you think set it up?"

Her heels thumped into the deck as Lacey dropped her and turned to pace too quickly. Beryl blinked, wondering if the ringing in her ears was interfering with her hearing. "You arranged the ambush?"

"Of course. And it worked like a charm, didn't it? You and your Raiders waltzed right in."

Beryl suddenly remembered laughing dark eyes and a strong arm curling around Lacey's waist. "Jamin died in that attack. Lacey. He was your lover for six years. Doesn't that mean anything to you?"

Lacey looked startled, as if she could see no reason why it should. "But Daveed was the one I really wanted," she said, in a chillingly reasonable voice. "You know that. He told you so, and then you kicked me out of the Raiders."

"You were having an affair with Daveed?" Beryl was more stunned than she'd been when she'd discovered he'd sold out the Raiders. She could imagine her gentle lover doing something stupid out of hurt and anger, but he'd never sleep with this borderline psychotic.

"Drop the astonished act, St. Cloud. I know damn well he went running to you, because you sacked me a week later."

"I sacked you because I caught you beating that kid."

"Bullshit. We both know the little bastard deserved it. Not that it matters, I wasn't out of work long. They were throwing this lovely little war right here." She folded her arms and rocked back on her heels, smug. "High Command recognized my talent."

Everything began making an ugly kind of sense. "And then the Loyalists hired us."

"It was perfect," Lacey agreed, her face lighting up. "Because I knew the Raiders so well, High Command sent me into Loyalist territory to spy on you. And that's where I found Daveed in a dancebar."

She just might throw up on Lacey's polished black boots. "Oh, God."

"He was drunk, and he wanted to talk. In retrospect, I really don't think he was tracking well enough to wonder what I was doing there. He must have assumed I was working for the Loyalists."

"He told you our plans." And suddenly Beryl could see his face, in the moment before the guerillas had closed in, in the moments before he'd died. Stark white, shocked. *"My God, I've killed us. This is all because of me..."* Once the battle was over, Beryl had remembered what he'd said and thought he'd sold them out. So had the other Raiders who'd overheard. It was a logical assumption, because Daveed had been the only one other than Beryl herself who had known the route she'd planned.

"You'd just had a fight, which evidently wasn't all that unusual to hear him tell it," Lacey continued, her eyes bright with malice. "So I pumped him for your plans, patted his hand, fucked him witless and sent him home. I was worried about him the whole time we planned the attack, but I knew you'd take care of him. You're so very good, you know."

Beryl swallowed bile. Daveed had been stupid, yes, he'd deserved to get his ass kicked for criminal carelessness. But his betrayal hadn't been the intentional treason she'd suspected. "And he died."

"You let him die, you bitch." Lacey's long legs covered the room in two strides. Beryl tried to duck, but the troopers held her still for the punch. "I trusted you to keep him alive, and you failed me!"

"*You* set up the ambush, Lacey," Beryl said over the hard ringing in her head.

"I worked for the Rebels, bitch. That's what I was supposed to do. And you were supposed to keep Daveed safe."

At the corners of her vision, Beryl saw the two troopers exchange a quick glance over her head. *Yeah, boys, your boss is a nutbar.* "So you hired Tagliar."

"Of course. It was the perfect death for you, or would have been if your pet stud here hadn't killed him." She smiled slowly. "But I think this is even more perfect."

With a flourish, she gave the pallet a shove. It rolled neatly back into the insolation tube, carrying Decker's unconscious body. "Put her in with him," Lacey ordered the guards.

Beryl tried to fight, but one too many head blows blunted her struggles, and soon she was stuffed in on top of Decker. A single lightbar let her see the vampire's gray face as she sprawled across his chill chest, and her mouth went dry with worry. He'd lost far too much blood.

Something hit the back wall next to her head and fell to the mattress. As the hatch thumped shut, she saw it was the ironwood knife they'd used to kill Tagliar.

"This is the lovely part," Lacey's voice said over the tube intercom. "When our friend comes to, he'll need all that blood he lost to Tagliar. He's going to be very, very hungry. And you'll be the only lunch in town."

"So what's with the knife?"

"You care about him, you fickle bitch, I saw it in your eyes when Tag stabbed him. So you can live, if you can kill him. Or more likely, he'll kill you." Lacey snickered. "Perfect."

Beryl's stomach rolled. "What if he kills me, Lacey? What will you do to him?"

"Oh, turn him loose, probably. I've got nothing against him. He was a marvelous commander, y'know. For a bloodsucker."

Then the tube fell silent.

Until Decker murmured, his voice sounding as cracked as his chapped lips, "Jesus God, I wonder what she'd do if she had it in for me."

"You're awake?"

He paused to swallow. "Barely."

"You okay?"

"Hell, no." As she stared down at his face, she saw the fine muscle shift in his jaw. "Get off me, darlin'."

Realizing she must be hurting him, she tried to lever herself away, only to come up against the padded ceiling. Attempting to shift to one side, she found there was no room there either. "Damn. There isn't anywhere to go. My head's bumping the ceiling and your shoulders scrape the walls."

He opened too-bright eyes just enough to look at her. "Where'd they put us, a coffin?"

"No, an isolation tube." She stared around at the thick white padding. "They use it for punishment or something."

"Barbarians. We didn't even do shit like this in the Twentieth Century." His face was gray, and dark shadows ringed his eyes.

"You need blood, Deck."

"You're telling me." Decker's eyes drifted closed.

"I can probably spare a liter ...."

His eyes snapped wide. "Don't say that."

She frowned at him, wondering about the veiled panic she could read so easily. "Look, if you take a little from me, you'll have the strength to break the lock on this damn tube. Then you can find a nice juicy guard while I go looking for Lacey and kick her psychotic ass out the nearest airlock."

His face went even more gray. "Good plan. Unfortunately it's got a fatal flaw."

"Yeah?"

"If I took you, I wouldn't be able to stop."

Beryl snorted. "Oh, bullshit. When you first fought Tag, you were so worked up you couldn't even string a sentence together, but you didn't hurt me then."

Decker looked away. "I hadn't lost this much blood. Beryl, if I were human, I'd be dead."

She could believe it. There was a blue tinge to his lips, and the skin was cracked.

He closed his eyes again. "You have to use the knife."

"You mean jimmy the lock? I don't think so. The blade would probably break."

"I'm not talking about the lock, Beryl."

His meaning suddenly penetrated, chilling her until she froze. "You want me to use it? On you?"

"On me."

"Forget it."

"Beryl..."

"I'm not going to stake you, Decker. It's not even an option."

"Then sooner or later I'll kill you."

"Deck, you stopped scaring me the day I met you, so don't even try it."

Decker's head snapped up off the mattress, his lips peeling back from fangs at full extension, his eyes glittering red in the dim light. *"If I didn't love you, you'd already be dead."*

Startled, Beryl jerked back so hard she bumped her head on the roof of the tube. Decker let his head fall again and squeezed his eyes shut as he spoke. "I'm in control now, just barely. I don't know how long I can hold out. You have to stake me before I lose my grip completely."

Beryl's ruthlessly tactical merc mind analyzed the situation, calculated possible solutions and concluded he was right. Everything in her rebelled anyway. She didn't even stop to wonder why. "Forget it. Killing you is not an option. Period."

His blue eyes opened, locked with hers. "Beryl, I'm begging you. Don't do this to me. I can't stand the thought of coming to and finding you dead on top of me."

"There are other alternatives."

"Name one."

"Make me a vampire." The words were out of her mouth so suddenly she blinked in shock.

Beryl St. Cloud, willingly become a vampire? Surrender her human nature to an alien one created by a disease? Give up eating and sunlight to drink blood and become an object of bigotry?

Or remain a human, kill Jim Decker, and grieve for him for the rest of her life?

Put like that, it was no choice at all. She'd rather drink blood for the next three hundred years.

Decker was shaking his head. "I already considered that, but it won't work."

"Why not?"

"To pull it off, you and I would have to link completely. That's what vamp psi is for, so the vampire can guide his mate through the transition. Without linking, you'd die from the blood loss you have to suffer to be successfully infected by the virus."

"So we link."

"You've never let me form the link, Beryl. You've always evicted me from your mind. If you did that when you were teetering on death's door, the transition would fail and you'd die. And I wouldn't be able to save you."

Beryl rested her chin on his chest and slipped her arms around him, instinctively offering comfort in the face of his anguish. "I don't think we've got a hell of a lot of choice, Decker. You don't want to kill me, and I'm sure not going to kill you. Changing me's the only alternative."

"But it's not an alterative, because it still comes down to me draining you, and I'm not going to take that risk."

So frustrated she wanted to scream, she stared into his eyes. And knew he would never give in.

Decker lay under the solid warm torment that was her body. The air was so full of her scent that the roots of his fangs ached, and the fact that she was bleeding from a dozen small cuts made the problem even worse. He knew the least touch, the least movement, would be enough to tip him over into blood madness.

Ironically his very weakness had saved her so far. Had he been even a little more healthy, he could never have controlled the Hunger, but he was so weak, the raw inertia of his body helped him control his vampire instincts.

But if Beryl kept pushing him....

Decker knew what ecstacy awaited him under the smooth surface of her throat, the warmth, the heat, the pure female essence that would give him back his life. But he could also imagine all too well recovering from that sensual delirium to find her lying limp and cold across him. Beryl, all her wit, all her intelligence, all her courage gone, destroyed by his mindless need to live.

Killing her would destroy him far more effectively than an ironwood knife driven into his heart.

He loved her. He could see it so clearly now, in the moment he was so close to losing her. Nothing else mattered, not even the knowledge that he didn't mean anything to her . She was just too scarred by Daveed Zahn to let another man in that close.

But scarred or not, loving him or not, she was going to get through this alive. Even if he had to die himself.

So Decker slid his hand up and found the ironwood knife where Lacey had tossed it. "You're going to have to use this, Beryl. You and I both know that."

She looked at him. "Yeah. I guess you're right."

And she took the knife out of his hand.

For just a moment something in Decker gave a kick of shocked protest that Beryl would give in so readily. But he dug his hands into the padding of the tube and braced himself.

Which is why he didn't react fast enough when she sliced a thin, shallow cut across her own throat. It wasn't deep enough to be fatal, but blood welled and ran in a narrow scarlet ribbon down her white skin. She met his eyes calmly. "Live or die, Decker, we do it together."

Her blood scent hit him in a hammer stroke, and the Hunger surged in Decker like a demon rising out of hell. And he knew he was lost.

"Damn you, Beryl." He snatched the blade away and nicked his own wrist with a pass of the knife. Pushing the wound to her mouth, he fastened his lips against the cut in her neck and began to drink.

At the first taste, the Hunger stripped his sanity away.

Decker's blood seared through her mouth and down her throat like some sweet, impossibly potent liquor. At the same time his mouth worked against her skin, the sensation making her nipples pull into heated, longing points. One strong hand came up, closed hard over her rump and began to knead with demanding strength.

Gasping at the overwhelming combination of his blood and his mouth and his hands, Beryl tried to pull away. Yet the taste of him was so seductive, she had to drink again.

So she drank, dimly aware that Decker was taking from her more greedily then he ever had before as his fingers stroked and probed. Her sense of time stretched out as starbursts detonated behind her closed eyelids. Her lips were growing numb.

Drunk, Beryl thought. *I'm getting drunk...*

Whirls of color spun out behind her lids, comets, stars accelerating away into the dark, shifting toward the red. She was beginning to feel cold, so cold, warmth running out of her until the only source of heat was Decker's lips against her throat. They'd felt so chill at first, but now she could see them glowing against the curtain of her closed lids like crimson stars.

Desperately, instinctively ravenous, Beryl drank Decker's blood as he drained her. And never quite realized when she died.

Chapter Five

Decker listened to her pulse going thready and fought his instinctive panic. He ached to link with her, knowing if he waited too long she'd vanish so deeply into death he'd never win her back. But he also knew if he tried to form the link when she was still capable of shielding herself, she'd eject him from her mind. And then she'd die anyway.

So he counted her stuttering heartbeats and waited for his moment. And prayed to the God of his childhood that he wouldn't misjudge it.

Now.

LINK.

The connection snapped into place, he felt it lock in, but still he didn't sense her. Worried, he opened his eyes to find himself standing on a bare, sandy plane, as completely flat as if it had been smoothed by a giant's hand. Above him an aurora painted dancing red and orange light over the night sky. There was absolutely nothing else around.

Decker frowned. This place was a dream they were having, he and Beryl between them, a symbol of their shared mental reality. Which was why her absence worried him. Had he let her fade too long, go too far into death?

Then he saw the statue.

It stood there on the horizon, a biped figure silhouetted against the glowing darkness. He concentrated....

And was right in front of the statue between one blink and the next. In this place, logic took a holiday, and reality was whatever he made it. Or more accurately, reality was whatever it *was*, deep under the surface of the real world.

Which was why Decker wasn't surprised to find that the statue was actually a suit of medieval armor, pitted and locked in rust. And when he saw the breastplate was molded to accommodate the lush curves of a woman's torso, he knew something else.

Beryl was in there.

Decker leaned down to peer into the helmet's eye slits, but there was nothing inside but utter blackness. His heart jumped in his chest as he realized he had to get her out of that cocoon of rust *now,* because if he didn't connect with her soon and guide her through the vampire transition, she would die.

Taking a deep breath to calm himself, Decker dug his fingers into the rotting steel of the gauntlet covering her right arm. The plate crumbled in his ruthless grip until he could touch Beryl's skin.

Cold. God, she was cold as a corpse.

But as he touched her, light flared from his fingers and lit the gray flesh with a faint, soft glow.

Tossing the mangled chunk of metal away, Decker grabbed another piece. As he peeled it back, he glimpsed the barest flash of a vision: a very young child, a woman, and a man. The adults were dressed in the mesh merc skinsuits popular twenty-five years before. The child was crying, but her mother crouched and held her close. *"We love you, baby. We'll make sure you're always safe."*

Decker knew the vision was a fragment of Beryl memory, but he had no time to puzzle over it. He grabbed the next section of armor and peeled the rusted plate away.

There was the male merc's face now, ravaged with grief. *"She never saw it coming, Beryl. She didn't feel any pain."*

Decker shuddered at the agonizing grief that flashed through him with that memory, but he didn't stop. Grab and pull.

The merc sat at a dingy table, his thick shoulders hunched. Beryl, twelve now, caught him by one beefy arm. *"You've got to get work, Dad. We need money."*

Another section of armor fell apart between Decker's impatient fingers. Now he recognized a younger Bill Anderson, shaking his head at the fifteen-year old Beryl. *"He's always been a good man."*

"Maybe. Fact is, he hasn't given a rat's ass since mother died," Beryl growled. *"I should have let him eat his torch five years ago."*

Crunch.

Beryl's face, screaming. *"Daddy!"*

Decker reached up and jerked the helmet off to look into her dark, grieving eyes. "It wasn't your fault, Beryl."

"Bullshit," she said, her gray lips barely moving. "I was so busy trying to prove to Bill what a badass I was, I didn't see the sniper. So Dad deliberately stepped into the shot that should have burned right through my skull. He loved me, and I killed him."

"No," Decker said softly, "you loved him, and he used you as an excuse to die."

He reached out, touched her face, and the connection snapped to full strength.

Decker was Beryl was Decker was Beryl, fusing into a mental mobius strip of awareness until it was impossible to tell where one left off and the other began. He could feel her strength, her intelligence, the wary love for him that had grown so stealthily even she hadn't known it. Just as she could feel his own solid love, sense how precious she was to him, precious as only something could be after three centuries of searching for it.

And each feeling the other, they flowed together.

Beryl's chestplate cracked like an eggshell giving way. Armor fell around her in flakes of rust as she straightened, shaking out her wings, extending them wide until they stretched twelve feet across.

Blinking her glowing red eyes, Beryl stared over her shoulder at the huge delicate membranes, taking in their iridescent rainbow sheen. Her soft lips parted, revealing fangs. "What the hell are those things?" she gasped.

"Bat wings." A weary grin spread across Decker's face. "Don't worry, they're not real, just a symbol that you sucessfully made the transition. You're a vampire, Beryl. You're going to live."

Beryl awoke sprawled across Decker's warm, hard chest. A wave of chill skated on icy feet over her skin, and she shuddered, remembering with brutal clarity the moment when her father had taken the torch blast for her. "I'd forgotten. How the hell could I have forgotten that much guilt?"

"I don't think you did," Decker said, lifting a hand to stroke her hair, his voice rumbling through his chest. "I think that's why you'd never let me into your mind. Why even Daveed, the poor son of a bitch, could never really touch you."

"Where are we?" Beryl tried to lift her head, but her skull felt like solid lead. She let it fall with a whimper.

"In the tube." He stretched under her, his powerful body rippling. "We never left."

"God," she moaned, cracked lips burning, "I'm so weak..." Something that felt like pebbles shifted in her mouth. Unable to move, Beryl pushed out her tongue and watched in dull horror as two teeth rolled out onto the bunk's gray padding. Exploring with her tongue, she felt a pair of sharp points where those canines used to be. Fangs.

It was true. She was a vampire. Panic and nausea twisted her stomach. "Oh, God, Decker," Beryl groaned, and swallowed bile. "I feel like hell."

"It'll get better once you feed."

Feed. Jesus, she was a *vampire* now. She was going to have to bite someone, drink blood...

Merc that she was, Beryl cut the thought off. You did what you had to do to survive. She'd chosen this, and now she damn well wasn't going to whine about it.

"Get ready, kid. It's time to go." Decker slipped a muscled arm around her waist and braced the other hand against the tube ceiling. He gathered under her, then slammed his booted foot against the tube hatch in a hard, solid kick. The latch broke with a scream of metal, and the door slammed open so hard it crashed into the outside wall. A shove of Decker's hand sent the bunk rolling out of the tube. He flipped off of it the instant it rolled to a stop, the arm around her waist keeping her tight against him as he moved. She squeezed her eyes shut and fought the roll of her stomach.

"What the hell...?" a male voice shouted.

Decker was gone. Deprived of his support, Beryl fell against the bunk and concentrated on breathing, dimly aware of the sound of a struggle that ended almost before it began.

"Beryl, darlin'...." Decker's voice sounded velvety and coaxing over a muffled squealing.

Beryl didn't see how she could stay on her feet, much less walk. "Jesus, Decker, I don't think I can...."

Then she smelled it.

It was wonderful, seductive, musk and copper, raw sex and heat. The very scent strengthened her. Beryl's eyes snapped open. She rolled erect and almost fell, slapping a hand to the bunk to steady herself.

Decker was holding a guard, one hand buried in the man's collar, the other clamped over his captive's mouth to hold his neck in a tempting arch.

The guard. He was the source of that wonderful smell.

Beryl ran into Decker's muscled shoulder as he snatched the man away from her instinctive lunge. "Control, sweetheart. You don't want to kill him."

Good God. *She wanted to drink his blood.*

Even as her old human nature recoiled in horror, Beryl, driven by her new Hunger, babbled an incoherent promise. Decker let her ease close enough to look into the guard's face. His eyes were round and white with terror.

That fear dug through her vampire instincts to touch off compassion. "I won't hurt you," Beryl said, and hoped she could keep her promise as she bent for his neck. The guard yelped behind Decker's hand, his voice muffled. She ignored him and put her mouth against his throat. The vein was there, running hot and strong under the skin. Beryl hesitated. What if she accidently killed this man? "Decker..."

"Your body knows what to do, darlin'," he said, his voice soothing. "Just go with it."

She bit down carefully. Hot liquid spun into her mouth.

It didn't taste anything like blood. It was crimson and burning and sweet, though not as lush to her senses as Decker's blood. Pleasure flooded her, and Beryl hummed against the guard's warm throat. He stiffened, his strong male body forming an involuntary arch, and she crooned reassurance to him while she drank.

As his blood rolled down her throat, lust curled in her belly until she found herself slowly dragging her nipples across his chest. He moaned, the sound husky with arousal as he lost his fear.

Until, too soon, Decker said in her ear, "That's enough, darlin'. You're giving the poor bastard a hardon, and you're making me jealous."

Beryl lifted her head and licked the blood from her fangs. "More. Please, Decker..."

"There's a whole hemosynther on the *Stoker.* You can have as much as you want when we get back. Come on, be a good girl..."

Reluctantly, she let go. The guard promptly collapsed.

Beryl frowned, looking down at the limp body sprawled on the deck. A few hours ago she'd have shot him if she'd had a torch, but what she'd just done seemed different. She was aware of him as a man now, not just an enemy. And she didn't want to be responsible for his death. "Did I hurt him?"

Decker smiled drily. "No, you just showed him a really good time. As soon as the meditechs give him a pint or three, he'll be pistol whipping the prisoners again." He took her arm, his grip firm but gentle as he began to lead her toward the nearest door. "Let's go, sweetheart. We have to get to the ship..."

"I feel...better." She felt better than better. She felt high, soaring. Invulnerable. Immortal.

Decker was studying her anxiously. Beryl wondered why she'd never noticed the love in those blue eyes before. "Yeah, well, be careful. It's a great buzz, but it's deceptive. You haven't really had enough blood to sustain you, and I'm afraid you're going to collapse before we get you home."

The brig hatch opened and bloodscent flooded Beryl's senses. "Ever heard of security cameras?" Lacey purred.

Beryl spun, falling into an instinctive combat crouch. The redhead stood with a laser torch pointed at Decker's broad chest, a gang of nervous troopers at her back.

Lacey sneered at him, ignoring Beryl for the moment. "Watch it, vampire. No matter how fast you are, you're not faster than light."

Beryl saw her chance and didn't stop to think about it. She leapt.

The explosion of powerful vampire muscle took even Beryl by surprise as it drove her into Lacey and halfway through the gang of guards. They all went down in a tangle, but Beryl twisted around until she ended up on top of Lacey with the bitch's torch hand clamped in one fist and her fingers wrapped around the redhead's throat. "I don't have to be faster than light, I ace," she gritted. "I just have to be faster than you."

Lacey stared at Beryl in terror, taking in the fangs, the glint of red in her eyes. "You let him *infect* you?"

"You sound surprised. Didn't you watch the whole show on your precious security cameras?" She caught a movement out of the corner of her eye and added, "By the way, my compliments on your guards. They're like potato chips, I just can't keep my fangs out of them.,," The soldier lying under them stopped trying to work her weapon free, her eyes going wide.

"*I hate to interrupt the fun, darlin',*" Decker whispered. It took her a moment to realize he was speaking directly into her mind through the link that had formed between them during her transition. "*But we really need to get out of here before one of these people grows a spine.*"

"*Good point,*" she thought back. "*Want to take the bitch hostage?*"

"*Sounds like a plan to me.*"

Decker took three running steps forward and cleared the pileup on the floor in one bounce. Before anybody could react, he strode back and hauled Beryl upright, though she still held Lacey locked in her ruthless grip. While he was at it, Decker snatched a couple of torches away from their erstwhile owners.

"All right, people, this is how it goes down," he said, covering the stunned group. "Commander Lacey here is going to provide us with an escort away from your dubious hospitality. If anybody screws with us, I'm going to feed her to my hungry partner. Does everybody read clear on that?"

"No!" Lacey growled, jerking against Beryl's hold as her eyes went wild, "Don't let them take me! That's an order!"

"Shut up, Lacey." Beryl's lip curled as she inhaled the redhead''s scent. Unlike the guard's, there was something about it that made the hair stand on the back of her neck, something bitter and acrid. Even the bloodscent that underlay the bitterness smelled like food, not sex.

"She's female, Beryl," Decker pointed out, his mental voice amused. *"As for the nasty underlay, that's just pure viciousness."* Beryl got the sense of a frown. *"She didn't smell like that when I knew her."*

They headed for the brig exit, Lacey's bootheels scrapping on the deck as Beryl hauled her along. Decker brought up the rear, pointing his torches back toward the guards who followed at a respectful distance. They were obviously torn between making the ordered rescue attempt and a reluctance to take on two pissed-off vampires.

"They don't look too eager to risk their necks for you, Lace," Beryl observed, aiming a malicious grin at her enemy. "I wonder why?"

"Fucking cowards," Lacey snarled at her troopers.

"They're not cowards, Lace, it's just that you're such a charming bitch they can't stand the thought of dying for you. Don't try it, pal," Decker added to one of the guards who was attempting to work his way in closer.

Looking sullen, the man fell back.

The remainder of the trip to the hanger deck where the ship was docked was nerve-wracking. Lacey struggled the whole way, apparently deciding she didn't want to wait for rescue. Beryl controlled the bigger woman easily at first, but soon she began to tire.

Decker was right, the guard's blood hadn't been enough. Her

newly changed body had to have more. Beryl fought keep her grip hard and her step confident, knowing that if Lacey sensed weakness, all hell would break loose.

Somehow the two vampires remained in control all the way back to the hanger, though Decker was forced to fire a few warning shots as they got close to the ship. Beryl barely flinched at the high-pitched whine of his shots, concentrating on putting one foot in front of the other and keeping one hand clamped around Lacey's wrist.

"All right, boys and girls, here's the way it goes," Decker called to the guards, who'd hastily taken cover. "We take off, and your commander goes with us. We drop her off at Freeboot Station, where you pick her up. If nobody gives us any crap, and if she's a good girl, you'll get her back with no tooth marks. Otherwise, all bets are off."

As he covered the guards, Beryl hauled Lacey past him toward the *Stoker's* airlock. If she could just make it inside, she could collapse in peace. "Open hatch," she husked. The ship's computer, recognizing her voice, obeyed.

Suddenly Lacey yanked hard, and Beryl stumbled as her numb, chilled fingers lost their grip. Stooping, the redhead pulled out a length of sharpened wood from her boot top and pivoted to drive the weapon right for Beryl's chest.

It figures the bitch would have a stake, Beryl thought, and met her rush with a single, sharp punch that slammed right into Lacey's face with a wet crack. Blood sprayed up her arm.

Blinking in surprise, Beryl realized she'd just killed Arith Lacey.

"Jesus, Beryl!" Decker dove for her and scooped her up before Lacey's body even hit the ground. Gathering Beryl against his chest, he swept her inside the airlock amid the high whine of powering torches. "Close hatch, computer! Activate antigravs and ready weapons. And get the mediunit up to..."

Beryl watched his mouth keep moving, but a loud, mechanical buzz drowned out whatever he might be saying. Darkness flooded in.

Decker carried Beryl onto the bridge, where the cargobots had already set up the mediunit. Laying her down on the unit's bed, he left her to its automated care. Though every instinct demanded that he see to her himself, Decker knew that if he didn't get them away from the station, she'd die anyway.

Without bothering to wait for clearance, he lifted off and piloted the *Bram Stoker* toward the hanger's primary airlock hatch, which obediently opened for the huge craft. Decker knew the station defense force didn't dare risk a fight inside the landing deck because the *Stoker* could crack the space base open with just a few shots. Which is why they didn't have anti-ship weapons mounted in the deck either, since their own fire could be just as deadly to them.

For a moment Decker considered opening fire anyway, then instantly dismissed the idea. There were too many civilians aboard, and he liked to keep the body count down when he could.

Decker tensed in his command chair as he waited for the huge airlock to cycle. The minute the *Stoker* was out in space at a safe distance, the station would try its damndest to blow them to hell. The key to survival was to fly an evasive course at maximum speed, avoiding enemy fire until they were far enough out to pop to Super-C, where no weapon could touch them.

The massive doors began, slowly, to open. He threw a quick look over his shoulder where the mediunit was giving Beryl a transfusion and allowed himself to commit her lovely profile to memory.

Then he turned back to his monitors, saw the doors were opened just enough, and punched the *Stoker* to full throttle.

And prayed.

Chapter Six

Beryl crouched on top of a massive crate and waited for her opponent, scanning her surroundings with a predator's patience. She could read every label on every crate, though it was so dark in the hold she shouldn't have been able to see a damn thing. Since she was a vampire, it might as well be day.

More than two weeks had passed since the *Bram Stoker* had blasted its way out of Dyson's space. Thankfully Decker had avoided any major loss of life, and the planet's officials decided to let the whole thing drop. Particularly once he'd threatened to sue for false imprisonment over Lacey's actions.

Still, the *Stoker* wouldn't be accepting any more shipments to Dyson's for at least a couple of decades.

Meanwhile Beryl had finally completed the transition, becoming, Decker put it, an honest-to-Anne-Rice vampire. Whoever the hell Anne Rice was.

She was surprised at how easy she'd found the adjustment. It was probably because she was a spacer, and vampires did better in space, where there was easy access to hemosynthers, no dangerously unfiltered sunlight, and no bigots. Oh, she'd have to deal with those things eventually, but there was something about sharing the Life with Decker that made the negatives of vampirism seem like a small price to pay.

Still, Beryl needed to learn how to control her vampirism, from the great strength it had given her to the fantastically acute senses.

Which was what she was doing down in the cargo hold, waiting for Decker to subject her to another one of his "training exercises."

She knew from painful experience that she'd suffer cuts, lacerations and general blood loss in the process, but she didn't much care. She and Decker always ended up naked at the end of the session, which made for a hell of an incentive.

But first she had to find him.

Beryl could tell he was nearby, because she could smell that deliciously tempting Decker scent that never failed to make her nipples harden. Still, though she scanned her surroundings like a hungry cat, she couldn't quite pinpoint where he was.

Beryl curled her lip in frustration. She might be a vampire now, but he still held the advantage of experience, size and strength. And he used it ruthlessly.

But this time she'd take him.

If she could find him.

There was a higher crate twenty feet away that looked promising. Ignoring the small voice that insisted that she couldn't possibly make it, Beryl gathered herself and sprang. For a single, gorgeous instant she was flying. Then she hit, bending her knees to absorb the jolting shock of landing.

Warily, Beryl straightened and was relieved to discover she hadn't broken every bone in her legs this time. Earlier this week she'd misjudged a jump, and though she'd healed with amazing speed, she was in no hurry to repeat the experience.

With a sigh of satisfaction, Beryl folded herself into a crouch and scanned her surroundings again.

There. Something moved off to the left, half-hidden behind a short crate.

She could clear the distance in one bounce, but Beryl's mercenary's instincts told her she should approach more cautiously. Yet the Hunger was thrumming high and eager, and she wanted Decker *now*. Her grin revealing lengthening fangs, Beryl jumped, her body stretching into the air like a pouncing tiger.

Until she saw the glint of metal at the height of her arc and realized she'd made a serious mistake.

A cargobot. He'd suckered her with a cargobot.

Beryl twisted in midair just enough to avoid crashing into the low-slung, tentacled robot as it trundled along. She hit rolling, instinctively trying to put herself as far from Decker's target area as she could.

Taunting male laughter told her she'd failed as strong hands grabbed her. "You've got to learn to manage the Hunger better than that, darlin'."

Beryl only snarled and fought to flip clear, knowing that if Decker got a good grip, she'd never get free.

Decker fought to hold her, laughing and wincing as a small, hard fist connected with his chin. She knew good and damn well she couldn't possibly win, but she was too stubborn to quit. It was one of the things Decker loved about her, but it was a pain in the ass as times like this.

Decker ducked a second punch and grabbed her fist before she could cock it again. She slammed a knee into his gut, and he whoofed out a breath, managing narrowly to hang on to the hand he'd captured. Jerking back, he flipped her onto her stomach and dragged her arm up between her shoulder blades. A half nelson was painful even to a vampire, but Beryl went right on struggling.

"I don't suppose," he asked, midway between gasping and chuckling, "you'd consider a graceful surrender so I can nibble your throat and screw you senseless?"

"I have a better idea," she panted back. "*You* give up so I can nibble your throat and screw *you* senseless."

"Uh, no, that wasn't the agreement." He whipped the length of thin magnetic cable out of his pocket and lashed it around her captive wrist. "The winner bangs the loser, remember?"

"Hey! What do you think you're doing?" She fought to escape as he went after her free hand.

"I just want to devote all my attention to nibbling, kissing and playing with your lush and — cut that out — lovely body." He finally managed to snag her flailing fist and lash it to the one he'd already captured. "Without having to worry about you trying to get away, knee me somewhere painful, or sink your needle fangs into my anatomy."

"I just don't want you to get bored, Deck." She gave him a feral grin. "Don't you get tired of winning all the time?"

"Nope." He pounced on her ankles with a second length of cable. He had to duck several kicks before he could get them tied. Satisfied he had her neatly lashed, he rocked back on his heels and flipped her over onto her back.

Then Decker reached for the neck of her coveralls.

"Don't you dare..."

Rrrriiiiiiippp!

"You dared," she observed drily, watching him strip her with a couple of ruthless swipes.

"I dared," he agreed. "What are you going to do about it?"

Beryl smirked. "Plot my revenge."

"The mind boggles." Actually, she did look rather intimidating. Though her bare, white breasts arched upward temptingly and her lush little cunt smelled of desire between her long legs, her eyes glowed red in the darkness and her fangs peeked from her parted lips.

Decker displayed his own long teeth. He loved a challenge.

Bouncing to his feet, he bent, scooped her into his arms, and deposited her, naked and squirming, head down over his shoulder.

"Oh, look," she purred from somewhere below the small of his back, "Decker haunch."

"Bite me and I'll paddle your little ass," he growled, and started toward the bridge. He had a sudden urge to take her in a bed this time.

"First bondage, now spanking," Beryl mused. "Decker, you're getting kinky. I think I like it."

"Slut."

"Guilty. But you can't say immortality will be boring with me along."

"Truer words were never spoken." He carried her into the lift, where he spent the ride trying to avoid her playfully snapping teeth.

It scared him, being this happy. It had been too damn long.

At last he strode onto the bridge with her and dumped her into the sleeping pit, then pounced with a growl of delighted lust.

It was past time to play.

Decker's hot mouth closed over her nipple with astonishing delicacy after the roughness of their game. Beryl watched him, the fan of his lashes against his hard cheeks, the way he drank her scent with flaring nostrils as his tongue flicked out to tease her hard pink point. His scent flooded her senses, male and vampire and blood and sex, a heady blend potent as straight whiskey, hot and sharp. She writhed, instinctively pulling at the cable that bound her, wanting to touch, wanting to hold him and taste him and pull him deep.

He growled at her as she moved, the sound blending hunger and humor. One big hand came up to pluck the nipple deliciously, warm fingers indenting the soft, white skin of her breast.

"Let me go, Deck," Beryl pleaded, her voice husky. "Let me touch you."

"No way, kid. I won, and I'm keeping you just the way I like you. Naked and helpless." His teeth nipped her as his clever hands worked her body, spanning her waist and gliding over her tight, quivering belly.

"Bastard," she moaned, wet heat flooding between her thighs.

"You bet." He reared away from her suddenly, his eyes striking red sparks, and grabbed his shirt in both hands. Old-fashioned buttons popped and bounced across the room as he ripped it open, the motion arching his spine. She watched hungrily, taking in the broad, lovely torso with its fluid roping of muscle. Catching his eyes, Beryl licked her fangs and grinned.

Decker grinned back, springing to his feet to peel off his boots and strip the tight black trousers down his muscled thighs. His erection sprang free, thick as her wrist and hard enough to jut upward at an angle, his testicles nestling full and taut to its underside. She growled in appreciation.

Decker stood over her, his cock and his fangs aching in full erection, both eager to be buried in her. And Beryl looked up at him, fearless and feral in her bonds, her nipples long rose stems. She treated him to a deliberate wriggle that made her lovely breasts bounce and the muscles work in her lush thighs. A blood vessel pulsed in his temple.

She was his. His woman, his mate, his match, his equal. Even his willing prisoner when it suited her. Here, after three hundred years of searching, was a woman he didn't have to protect from himself. Because Beryl didn't need protecting. She could take his strength and give it back to him.

And for the first time in far too long, he deliberately set his Hunger free.

Beryl saw his powerful body coil, the flame leap high in his eyes as his fine features drew taut. "Mine," Decker growled, as he had that first night he'd taken her.

And it was back, visible there in his eyes for the first time since she'd met him — his Hunger, his Beast, the part of him he worked so hard to control. Had she still been human, it would have terrified her, the naked animal lust in his eyes, the power that radiated from him as he bent toward her.

Instead she freed her own Beast to match his.

Decker didn't like her ankles tied together, so he broke the grip of the magnetic cable and lashed each of them to the opposite wrist. She submitted with a deep, throaty purr that built to a rumbling growl as he shifted to bury his face between her thighs.

Her scent flooded his brain, salt and musk and vampire and female, so eager for him, predator to his predator, pussy to his cock. He growled deep in his throat and feasted on her slick red flesh, opening her with his fingers and licking in long strokes. He sucked and tongued and bit until her wetness covered his face, intoxicating and goading him. Instinctively, helplessly, Decker worked his hips, grinding his cock into the bedding.

To give himself a moment to regain control, Decker lifted his head and watched as Beryl tossed her head in her dark hair, gasping and pulling against her bonds, as lost to the Hunger as he. Growling triumphantly, he buried his face between her legs again, both hands simultaneously reaching up to seize her lush breasts.

Beryl whimpered, mindless in the face of Decker's ruthless skill and the Hunger he'd unleashed. He was everywhere, big body and slick hard muscle and talented hands and wicked mouth. Everywhere but where she wanted him: inside. *Now.*

Then he reared over her, and Beryl's mind lit with a ferocious, animal joy as Decker came down on top of her, spearing her on an endless rush of broad, rigid cock. Then his face was against her throat, and she felt the hot/cold prick of his fangs. Instinctively she bent her head to seek out a thick vein throbbing in the muscle of his shoulder. And bit deep, savoring the burning brandy flood of his blood over her tongue.

Decker promptly let go and pulled away. "Bad girl," he rumbled. "I won, so I get to bite *you.* Those are the rules."

Before Beryl could frame a protest, he flipped her onto her belly and propped her shoulders on the rim of the sleeping pit. Then he speared her again. Beryl gasped at the molten sensation of his length sliding deep. Without so much as a pause, he pumped his powerful hips, sliding in and out even as his strong fingers tightened on her waist, dragging her closer so he could reach up even further. Beryl shuddered helplessly, hissing at the raw, brutal pleasure.

And then his mouth was on her neck again, his fangs slowly penetrating her throat, driving a spike of pleasure right into her skull. She screamed at the deep pulsations of orgasm as his pumping hips rammed his cock in and out.

But Decker didn't slow down. Instead he suddenly pulled his fangs away so he could mercilessly pound her rump. The sensation of his massive erection pistoning inside her was maddening, and Beryl gasped incoherent pleas. He ignored them, wrapping a fist in her hair to hold her writhing body still while he fucked her even harder.

Another orgasm shuddered through her, ripping her voice into a spiraling howl of pleasure. Decker stiffened against her, then suddenly dove for her throat. His fangs entered her again even as her climax hit its brutal peak.

Link!

She felt him, *was* him, felt her own hot, slick walls gripping his cock, felt the smooth muscle of her ass pressing into his groin. Felt her blood rolling sweet and burning down his throat until it was impossible to tell where Decker left off and where she began. They were one.

And she felt his love, shining even through the animal heat of his Hunger, bright and pure, just as she could see her love through his eyes.

As the urgency of the Hunger burned away, extinguished by the power of their pleasure, the love remained, until they were left sated and tangled together on the huge mattress, surrounded by its warm glow.

"Decker?"

"Mmmm."

"If you don't untie me right now, I'm gonna be stuck in this position for the rest of my life."

Without opening his eyes, Decker grinned. "What a lovely thought."

"Decker, I know where you sleep."

"Oh, all right." He dragged himself upright and untied her, then gathered her limp body against his.

"When I get my strength back in a day or two," Beryl said, her voice pleasantly blurred by exhaustion, "I'm going to demand a rematch."

"I'm counting on it." Contented, Decker smiled and curled around her. "You know," he added into her hair, "for a pair of vampires, it really can be happily ever after."

"God, Decker," she murmured, "you can be so corny sometimes."

He bit her.

About the author:

Angela Knight lives in the wilds of upstate South Carolina with her son and her handsome cop husband (who really ought to have fangs to go with the look he gets in his eyes on certain dark nights).

She loves handcuffs and politically incorrect romances, and likes to mix the two whenever possible—and she's secretly relieved whenever anybody else admits to doing the same.

The Barbarian

by Ann Jacobs

To my reader:

"The Barbarian" brings home lusty appetites honed in harems of the East. When he discovers to his pleasure that the bride the king has provided him along with rich estates in England appreciates and shares his enthusiasm for varied bed sports, he is a happy man. Little does he know that from healthy lust will grow a love of a lifetime.

I hope you enjoy the fantasy as well as the gritty reality of this tale of sex and love set in the harsh and unforgiving medieval times. Erotic though this story may be, it is romance as well—the story of one man and one woman, searching for happily ever after.

Chapter One

Giles deVere's promised bride was apparently intent on denying him entry to Harrow Castle. This day, not even the cool rain could cool his impatience to end a useless siege and take this castle he had earned with his sword and lance.

As he sweated within the confines of his chain mail he came to a decision. His coffers brimmed with gold captured from the infidel. He would spend some to repair the damages he was about to inflict upon his own property. "Rolfe, ready the catapults, and set men-at-arms to preparing a ram. We take Harrow on the morrow," he told his brother, who sat his destrier but a few yards away.

"This is your castle now, Giles. Would you cause it such grievous damage?"

"I would have Harrow Castle and my reluctant bride in my power without further delay. Those within the walls who defy me will learn how I earned the name Barbarian."

At first the name, earned by merciless killing of infidels on battlefields in the Holy Lands, had disturbed Giles. Later, after many victories, he came to relish his image as a fierce warrior obsessed with victory no matter what the costs. Such, he told himself, was the lot of a third son—and now, through his bloody service to King Henry, he had gained the prize of land and title his birth had denied him.

His prize had belonged to a robber baron he had chased down and delivered to his fate at Henry's court. The old earl and his followers had purportedly wreaked havoc on the midlands since the time of Stephen with their raping, killing, and debauched acts. No doubt they had earned the punishment Henry had meted out.

All Henry had required in return for granting him Harrow, and all its lesser fiefs, was that Giles wed with the old earl's only remaining child, a lady of the somewhat advanced age of sixteen, for whom her father had neglected to choose a husband. Smiling, Giles fantasized that bedding the Lady Brianna would bring him pleasures equal to those he remembered from his stint as master of the harem in a villa captured from an infidel prince.

Together he and the eunuch Arnaud, who would be his wife's protector, would tutor her in the sensual arts. Giles would conquer the lady Brianna with his body as surely as he would quell her master-at-arms's foolish resistance tomorrow with his weapons of war. Be she fair or ugly, the lady would soon be his love slave.

❧⟨ᵔᴥᵔ⟩❧

"The Barbarian shall never possess Harrow Castle. Never possess me!" Even as she said it Brianna of Harrow feared she spoke a lie. The castle might have survived a siege. It was falling quickly, however, to the Barbarian's mighty army. The gate was giving way to a battering ram even now while boulders hurled from catapults rent the curtain wall. The battle-hardened retainers of Giles deVere outnumbered her protectors by close to a hundred men.

If only, Brianna thought angrily, her true brother had not perished in battle! She would not be standing here with her illegitimate half-brother Eudo, the odious monk her sire had retrieved from his cloister in the hope of having him named heir to Harrow. The very one who had read her the king's letter which ordered her to wed the brutal warlord who had quelled her father's army and delivered him to Henry to be tortured and executed just two months past.

She wanted not to become the instrument of the Barbarian's vengeance, no more than she wished to give herself to the man Eudo described as monstrous in appearance as well as actions. "I would escape him, my brother," she said, meeting the monk's beady gaze as he approached.

"If you would flee, the time must be now," Eudo observed, pausing at her side, his coarse brown robe flapping in the breeze.

"I like not the idea of a religious life." Brianna's body had heated at the sight of maids and men-at-arms coupling in the great hall, at the sounds of soft moans and whimpers they made. She had dreamed of finding the rapture her maids whispered about, of possibly even sharing affection with a handsome lord who would sire her children—the heady joy her lady mother had found in the arms of a virile young lover ere she died.

"Like you better the notion of coupling with deVere? From all accounts, he is more demon than the devil himself. If you make haste, you may escape his ravishment."

Eudo was right. Celibacy held more appeal than coupling with a monster whose very name made strong men speak in hushed tones. Turning from the shattered window, Brianna took boys' clothing from a trunk. "Fetch me a pot of the oil and tar the defenders use to try to quell his invasion," she told Eudo. "And hurry. They batter now at the hall entry."

Her nose wrinkling with distaste at the stench of the peasant garments, Brianna removed her gown. She had donned the filthy rags and was tying baggy chausses when Eudo returned.

"What do you with this?" he asked, setting down the pot of hot tar and kitchen grease.

She sat before the polished metal, staring at her reflection as she grasped the long braid of her hair. "Give me your dagger. I shall be shorn soon enough when I reach the protection of the convent. For now I would improve my disguise."

Hacking mercilessly, she had soon reduced what had been waist-length hair to a series of uneven clumps that stood out like a haystack from her head. "Rub the tar into it. 'Twill change the color." Since childhood, all had commented on the beauty of her pale, silky hair. None would recognize her now, with hair as short as any boy serf's and as black as tar. Even Brianna would not have recognized the pathetic reflection that stared back at her.

Sounds of clanking metal and anguished cries of the wounded and dying came ever closer. At a great crashing noise, Brianna whirled to find the solar door blocked by a huge warrior, bloody sword in one mail-covered fist. Trembling, she assumed the diffident posture of a peasant caught above stairs in the master's solar.

Lifting off his helm as if to improve his vision, he glanced about the solar before settling his gaze upon Eudo. "You, man of God. Get you with my men outside. Your tonsure will protect you from harm." He watched Eudo slink through the door before turning his attention to Brianna. "You are no serf boy, *madam*. You would have done well to take the time to bind those thrusting breasts."

Heat came to Brianna's oil-caked cheeks. Conqueror he might be, but this warrior seduced her senses with his hot, dark gaze. Pity she could not wed with him instead of the Barbarian he must call lord. Her nipples swelled against the rough cloth of her disguise, as she boldly imagined the hard muscle and tough sinew this beautiful man must be hiding beneath the accouterments of war.

"Your name, madam," he demanded, his voice deep and compelling, his Norman French too perfect for him to be any but a nobleman.

"Brianna of Harrow, my lord. I would that you help me escape your master. I would take refuge in a convent before I'd wed with him." This warrior's stance, his demeanor, and his hot, needy gaze made Brianna fantasize that he would give her a taste of the sexual pleasure the convent would deny her for eternity. "I would make it worth your while, sir knight."

The warrior frowned. "What you offer is for your lord husband alone, my lady. And he is as dear to me as mine own self."

Fie! The fates had no mercy, that such a knight would be so loyal to the monster she would now be forced to wed! "You will hand me over to the Barbarian?"

He nodded, his lips parting to reveal a row of straight, healthy-looking teeth. Brianna fancied that the hot look in the warrior's eyes was lust, though she knew not how she could inspire lust, filthy as a swineherd and as ragged as the poorest of villeins. Would that he had come upon her ere she had hacked off her hair!

"I cannot allow you..."

"You have no choice."

Before she could catch her breath to cajole him further, the mail-clad knight was upon her, lifting her over his shoulder and striding purposefully downstairs into the great hall.

"Set me down, you great oaf!" Brianna shuddered at the sight of carnage left in her hall by the Barbarian's army. Olaf. Geoff. That old man-at-arms who used to pat her on the head as she walked by him at his post. Dead. Their lives forfeited as they tried to protect her from this man's master. "What have you done with my brother? Does he lie somewhere, as dead as these men who only did my bidding?" she asked as she searched the hall for Eudo.

"The monk I sent from the solar? I expect he rests now in Harrow's dungeon, milady, along with all we found still living when we took the castle. Fear not. My men would not harm a man of the cloth, not unless he took up a sword against them."

Brianna considered that unlikely. Ungodly Eudo might be, but his sins ran more toward dipping his wick into the honey pots of castle wenches than to defending them with sword or lance. Not even holy orders could cool men's lust, but at least Eudo hadn't looked upon her that way since she had reminded him rather forcefully that she was his sister, and a lady whose virginity must be saved for her husband.

Her husband. Not the white knight of her dreams, a gentle warrior who would woo her with tender care and make her burn for the touch of his hands. Not the dream lover for whom she would be more than the vessel for him to spill his seed. Not the beautiful but fearsome warrior who held her now and made her burn. No, from the tales she had heard, she feared that the man King Henry had ordered her to marry would make her vicious, scheming father appear a mere caricature of wickedness.

She imagined her fate as bride of the Barbarian Giles deVere, shuddering at the thought that he must wield the sword between his legs more brutally than most.

"I beg you, let me escape!" Desperate, she beat his back with her fists, causing him to swing her off his shoulder and against his mail-clad chest.

He smiled in the way Brianna fancied a stalking predator might, his dark gaze riddling her as if with fire. For a moment she thought he might set her free, if only to watch her scurry like a trapped rat for freedom that was not in the cards. Then she knew. *His reference to his men. The aura of leadership about him. This man, as gorgeous as he was to look upon, had to be none other than Giles deVere, the king's Barbarian and her betrothed husband.*

Brianna's heart clenched with fear—or was it with a primal need for the heat this man stirred within her breast? "What say you, sir?" she murmured, her gaze steady as she looked into his laughing eyes.

"I think not, wench. I rather fancy the taming of you, once we wed and I have you to myself. I am Giles deVere, Earl of Harrow. Your husband ere the sun sets this day."

Chapter Two

"By God, Giles, Henry did you no great favor!" Rolfe looked as if they were facing the might of the king's army, not one small, filthy damsel who strained against Giles's restraining arms.

Giles laughed, earning himself another furious pounding from his virago's tiny fists. "She will tame soon enough, brother, once I've taken her to my bed."

"Barbarian! Think you to ravage me as your battering ram sundered the gates of my castle? Never, as long as I draw breath." She pounded Giles's chest until he tightened his grip on her wrists and held her at arms' length.

"Protest will get you naught, Lady Brianna. Rolfe, summon the priest." Weary from fighting to gain what was already his, and angered by having had to search for his bride once he had breached the castle defenses, Giles yearned for peace— and the gentle touch of a woman.

Somehow he doubted he would find either this night with Lady Brianna, although he had no doubt he would find fire. If she brought a tenth of the passion to their marriage bed that she had demonstrated in her attempt to escape him, they would both flame and burn. None too gently he handed his reluctant bride over to two of his knights, instructing them to bring her to the chapel when the time came to say their vows.

Giles would follow his sovereign's orders with dispatch. The hurried ceremony would hardly befit the joining of an earl of the realm with a niece of the dowager queen. But he would not wait. The deed must be done and sealed, ere he venture out to take possession of Harrow's lesser holdings.

An hour later Giles stood before the chapel still in armor, the stench of battle filling his nostrils. Although he thought himself immured against the softer emotions, he shuddered when his young brother booted aside a body as he strode across the bailey.

Two men at arms struggled to drag his bride through the bloody maze. Like him, she came to be wed in the garments she had been wearing when he found her: filthy chausses and a torn tunic that would befit a serf boy. Her hair, hacked off unevenly and smeared with mud and tar she must have taken from one of the vats her men poured on his as they scaled the castle walls, made Giles shudder with revulsion until he envisioned how he would use this sign of her rebellion to conquer and tame her.

Briefly he pictured Brianna in the silk and velvet garments that filled several of his trunks. She would be a beauty, with those indigo eyes staring at him from a perfect oval face scrubbed clean of filth. Those long legs indecently displayed in boys' clothing would clasp him to her when he spilled his seed, and her full, ripe breasts would make delightful pillows for his weary head. Blood rushed to his groin as she approached.

"I will not wed with you," she hissed as Giles's men shoved her to his side.

Giles grasped her hand. "Neither of us has a choice, my lady."

"I will refuse the vows."

Nodding toward his men, Giles grabbed Brianna's chin and forced her to meet his gaze. "You will wed with me or you and the rest of your people will die. Think you I might hesitate? Look about you. Your foolish attempt to hold this castle has cost many lives. Will you make the toll go higher?"

"Nay. I will say the marriage vows. Be wary, Barbarian, for I make another vow this moment. Someday, somehow, I will make you pay for all you take from me this day."

"Defy me and you will be the one who pays, *wife*."

Giles had no taste for raping a reluctant virago, but he didn't think rape would be necessary. Brianna hated him with a passion— but he would soon turn that blood lust to passion for every sexual pleasure he would introduce. Looking to the back of the chapel, he nodded to Arnaud. Then he clasped Brianna's hand and turned back to the priest.

"Strip her, bathe her, and tie her to my bed."

With that terse order Giles shoved Brianna into the arms of a giant, scowling minion who had ordered her cringing chambermaid Elise to leave, the moment he strode into her father's solar. Never brave, the maid had wasted no time scurrying away as if since Brianna had wed, hers was no longer the voice the servant must obey.

Furious, she struggled with her new captor as she imagined her barbarous husband hurrying belowstairs to supervise disposing of the bloody remains of her people who had died trying to defend her home. How, she wondered, could God have bestowed such physical beauty on the beast she had been forced to marry? Why had the brief touch of his lips on hers made her body ache for more? And why had he left her in the care of this fearsome giant?

She glared at the giant as others from the Barbarian's army emptied buckets of steaming water into a tub they had placed before the fire. "Out!" she commanded after the men at arms completed their chore. "Think you I will bathe whilst you gape?"

"What charms you may possess hold no interest for me, my lady. Disrobe and bathe as your lord husband Giles directed." Only the giant's lips moved. The rest of him remained as still as a tree in a peaceful forest.

"Nay. I am no camp follower to flaunt myself before a man. Remove yourself!"

"I remain."

Brianna stomped a foot, wishing the Barbarian's head were beneath it. "Then I shall leave." Before she had taken two steps toward the door the giant had her in his grasp, his hands like a vise around her waist. "Unhand me!" she screamed, kicking out blindly in the hope of inflicting some pain on this implacable brute.

She might as well have saved her energy. Before she realized what was happening he had her naked and immersed to the neck in the steaming tub. His arms resting on his massive chest, the giant stared down at her. Humiliated, for no man but her husband should see her thus, she tried to cover her breasts with her hands.

"Bathe, or I will bathe you," he ordered, and from his implacable expression Brianna surmised that he meant what he said. Squelching her embarrassment and uncovering her breasts, she took up a bar of soap and tried in vain to scour the filth from her hair.

Finally giving up, she scrubbed her body free from dirt and grime as the giant watched, his bland expression unchanging. Did seeing her naked not make him burn with lust? Brianna stole a surreptitious glance at the giant's crotch. Nothing. No jutting bulge beneath his chausses, the sure sign of a man's readiness to mate.

Was there something wrong with her that she did not inspire this man's lust? Brianna gazed over at the bed where tonight the Barbarian would consummate their farce of a marriage. Perhaps like his servant, her husband would not desire her. Why did that thought not make her smile?

Chilly winds passed into the great hall, through gaping holes made by boulders hurled from his own siege engines. Giles shivered as he sat in a tub set before the hearth, soaking away the evidence of battle from his aching body. His cock twitched,reminding him his bride awaited her deflowering in what was now his private chamber.

Rolfe, he noted when he glanced about the hall, had found a cooperative wench to ease his lust. Giles grinned. His brother, despite the time he had spent subduing Turkish harem girls, had much to learn of the subtleties of sex, lessons Giles himself had applied himself to with enthusiasm in the harem of an infidel prince whose castle he conquered while on Crusade.

His harem here would house just one reluctant bride. Giles hardened as he contemplated the tricks he would teach her. The sensual toys. Arnaud. As he had conquered her land, so he would conquer her, enslave her until she would beg to do his bidding.

Giles wondered what the lady Brianna might know of the sensual arts. Nothing, he decided as he watched the castle wenches servicing his men in the plain sight of all in the hall. While he imagined his bride, having lived in this place all her life, knew what coupling entailed, he was certain he would be the first to teach her the art of making love.

Ducking his head under the water, Giles rid himself of the last of the soap and grime. He rose and stepped from the tub, moving to the fire as he rubbed a rough linen towel over his body. After years of fighting he welcomed the luxurious earldom Henry had given him along with the intriguing vixen he could hardly wait to tame.

"You are clean. Get out ere the water cools." The giant grasped Brianna under the arms and heaved her out of the tub. "Dry yourself. My lord dislikes wet bed linens."

Shivering, Brianna stepped closer to the fire and rubbed the linen briskly over her body and hair. She risked another glance down her captor's still-placid body, but that did little to allay the terror she felt at being here with him, alone. Naked.

"Lie down," he ordered, taking the damp cloths from her hands and nudging her toward what had once been her sire's huge bed.

The bed linens smelled fresh, sweeter than any she had known existed. And softer. Weary of fighting a fate she knew was as inevitable as the Barbarian's victory over her sire's depleted army she protested not when the giant rolled her onto her back. The touch of meaty but strangely soft hands against the still-damp skin on her belly startled her from her lassitude.

"Do not touch me!" Perhaps she had been wrong. Maybe this strange giant of a man lusted for her after all. She must not let him take what Henry and the Church had decreed belonged to the Barbarian.

"Be silent."

"I shall scream for my lord husband. He will kill you." *More likely he will slay me, as will be his right if I come to his bed not a virgin.*

"I but follow my lord's orders." The giant shrugged, then drew out four silken cords from his tunic and secured them to Brianna's wrists and ankles. Her struggles were for naught except to make her pant, more from fear than from exertion. "Lift your hips," he told her, his tone matter of fact as he gazed at her naked body.

His tone suggested she would be wise to comply. Big, imposing and not hard upon the eyes, yet somehow different from the men she had known, the giant intrigued Brianna as much as he intimidated her.

Although it wasn't easy to do, the way he had bound her limbs to the four stout posts at the corners of the bed. Brianna arched her back and lifted her hips. A soft cloth, even softer than the bed linens, brushed her buttocks as the giant slid it beneath her body.

Helpless. In all her sixteen summers she had never felt so impotent. She watched her captor rummage through a carved chest he had placed close to the bed. Half expecting him to bring out some instrument of torture, Brianna gasped when he produced a pot, curiously shaped, of colors that reminded Brianna of her mother's precious stained glass window, the one the Barbarian's missiles had shattered during the first hour of his attack.

Opened, the pot produced an aroma that stung Brianna's nostrils. Unfamiliar, exotic, pungent, yet not altogether unpleasant, she thought as she watched the giant dip a finger into the pot and bring forth a slick, pink paste. When he smeared the paste over her mons and between her legs she gasped, shocked that he would touch her there. Whatever this substance was caused her to squirm from its heat. "What do you do?"

The giant grunted a reply she couldn't understand, but the warmth and tingling, and an unfamiliar ache deep inside her body, terrified her more than her huge, implacable captor. Was he about to rape her? Gathering her courage Brianna raised her head and blatantly stared at the still-unthreatening juncture of his thighs.

"I told you, my lady, your woman's body interests me not." Brianna thought he sounded somehow sad, yet she very nearly believed his words.

She looked for the first time at the giant's round, placid face. Light gray, ringed in blue, his eyes bespoke a softness she'd not expected. His cheeks were smooth, as if he grew no beard, but from the stubble on his scalp she guessed he had recently shorn the hair from his head. "Tell me what you do," she implored.

"I ready you for my lord Giles." With hands gentle despite their size he rubbed the paste into her skin, then wiped it away with a soft cloth.

Chilled air swirled against her body. Brianna hadn't thought it possible to feel more naked than she had, spread open and helpless, tethered hand and foot to the bed posts. But she did. Unbelievably she wanted to move—to feel something—to feel a caress between her legs where the giant had just removed that strange warm substance. What was happening to her?

He rummaged through the chest again, bringing out a filigreed silver vial. Uncapping it he held it over her tingling mound. Brianna practically screamed with frustration at the sensation of slick, slithering warmth sliding slowly, tantalizingly downward until it anointed her most secret places with a sensation the likes of which she had never imagined.

"Please," she implored. She wanted more, but of what she did not know.

When he spread the oil, massaging it into her denuded skin with practiced skill, every nerve in her body screamed in need. Then he stopped and set the containers on top of another chest, and she burned.

What was he doing? She watched him bring items from the first chest and arrange them one by one atop the chest that now held the pot and vial. First, a string of large, translucent pearls. Two silvery spheres engraved with exotic symbols, and a hood made of sheer black silk. A glittering blue-green feather and another, stiffer one she thought might have come from a peregrine falcon. An oval-shaped blood-red cylinder of glass, rounded on one end and stoppered with an ornately carved ivory handle on the other. Finally he brought forth a small dagger with a golden hilt and a thin blade honed to a razor edge.

"What…"

"Be silent." With large, smooth-muscled arms the giant pulled one last item from the chest, an exquisite bed cover of sable furs, and tossed it over her tethered body. "Lord Giles comes," he said as he stepped back, apparently inspecting his handiwork.

Moving to the bed again, this strange man took up the black cloth he had laid out on the chest and wrapped it about her hair. Suddenly she pictured herself as she must look with her chopped-off hair, still clumped up with the tar she hadn't been able to wash completely away.

"Thank you," she said, and she watched the giant nod as he stepped away again.

Chapter Three

Her husband took her breath away. The Barbarian in armor had intimidated Brianna more than she would ever admit. Still damp from his bath, his glistening blue-black hair cut short in the Norman fashion and his lean cheeks scraped free of the stubble she had noticed earlier, Giles appeared even more deadly than he had when he burst in upon her as she prepared to flee. His masculine beauty both terrified and entranced her.

She trembled as she recalled the sudden heat that had flowed through her body when he brushed his lips across hers to seal their marriage vows. It was as though, now, every cell of her scrubbed and denuded skin came alive in the presence of his potent male sexuality. When she strained against her bonds, each motion caused the fur coverlet to caress her as if it were some living thing.

This butcher who had slaughtered so many of her people, and most likely conspired to cause her sire's execution at the king's hand, had the look of a dark angel. An angel sent to release the tension that now sizzled throughout her body. This could not be the demon who had stolen all she held dear. If he was, she didn't care. Her bound fingers itched to feel him and her treacherous body urged her to surrender to her conqueror.

"My lady," he murmured, his devastating smile seducing her as he sat on the edge of the bed. The bed robe he wore, deep blue velvet that matched his sparkling eyes, gaped to reveal a light dusting of dark hair against his heavily muscled chest. Brianna squirmed at the growing heat deep within her belly, and the tickling sensation of the fur as it settled between her legs.

She wanted to feel his chest hair tickling her naked breasts. God help her, she needed this man to take her. Anything to soothe the restless, tingling need his simple presence evoked in her.

She watched him turn to the giant, who stood before the fireplace, arms crossed, as if observing a scene in which he played no part. "Is all in readiness?" Giles asked, his voice low and husky as he returned his gaze to Brianna's naked breasts.

"Yes, my lord. Your bride awaits your pleasure."

Giles smiled, showing those gleaming white teeth Brianna had noticed earlier. She felt rather than saw him reach out and touch the silk that covered her mangled hair. "You may seek your bed, Arnaud," he said, and only then did the servant move, inclining his head toward his master before striding from the solar.

Brianna gasped as Giles shrugged out of his robe, lifted the sable throw that covered her, and tossed both to the floor. She didn't need to look to his manhood to sense that he wanted her. The predatory gleam in his eyes, and the way his tongue darted out to wet his lips as his gaze raked her heated body, made his intention clear.

Still she had to look. She strained to raise her head, but from her vantage point she could see only his flat, ridged belly and the ruby tip of his penis that obscured his navel. Her mouth watered as she braced herself for his possession.

She expected him to fall upon her like the beast he was, but he did not. Instead he picked up a feather from the array of objects the giant had set out earlier and sat cross-legged in the space between her legs. Leaning over her he used the tip of the feather to trace a line from her lips to her quivering center, sending chills all the way to her toes.

His muscles rippled with every motion, calling her attention to the breadth of his shoulders and depth of his massive chest. Only a few scars marred golden skin Brianna longed to touch. She needed to see him fully, feast her eyes on the masculine perfection of his sculpted body. "Please," she whimpered as she strained against her bonds.

"Christ's bones, but you're lovely," he muttered, re-tracing the feather's path with a callused finger. "Soft. As pale and precious as these." He lifted the strand of pearls and trailed them over the same path the feather had taken, then let them swing slowly between her wide-spread thighs. Each jewel, cool and smooth, sent a shock wave deep inside her belly as it gently bounced against her naked, open core. His avid gaze set her on fire. "Dare I release your bonds?"

Moisture gushed from her body and trickled slowly downward as he watched, touching her only with his gaze and the pearls, which she felt swinging faster, bombarding her with sensation.

"I would touch you, husband." She had an overwhelming need to touch this stranger she had just wed, entice him to end this torture and fill the emptiness that burned deep within her. Writhing, she tried to pull free of her bonds.

"Be still, Brianna." Harsh words, yet softly spoken in a deep melodious tone very different from the way she had heard him speak to his followers, and her, ere he had shed the accouterments of battle.

"Free me, my lord." By now Brianna was unsure if she wanted freedom or continued enslavement. His heat scorched her when he raised up on his knees and covered the bonds on her wrists with long callused fingers. Hovering hardly a hair's breadth above her naked body, he pulled away when she strained desperately upward to brush against his massive chest.

"Nay. This night I would have you know you are mine, to do with as I will. I would have you know you cannot escape me." His breath blew warm and sweet against her cheek as he toyed with the knot at one wrist, giving Brianna the feeling that he regretted his decision to have her bound.

His heart beat a steady cadence she could feel, so close was he—yet still apart. "Had you not sworn vengeance on me, Brianna, I would loosen this tiny hand that you might feel the luscious softness of yourself, and the strength of my sword that will pierce you and make you a woman."

"Please. Upon my honor I would do you no harm this night." Her fingers itched to touch him, to explore sun-kissed skin that looked like satin pulled taut over muscles of iron. Had she lost her mind?

She must have, to want this man after all he had done to her and her people. But she ached for him. Desperately and mindlessly, in spite of all that had gone before.

'Twas as though this mating had been predestined. As if God had fashioned this man only for her, and sent him here to unleash the fierce animal need in her to become one with him and only him. She had to touch him. "Please."

He smiled and shook his head. Trailing the pearls over her mons and up her body he let them settle in the hollow between her breasts. They seared her tender skin, but his moist, sweet breath burned nearly as hot before he covered her mouth and plunged his tongue deep inside.

Against her belly she felt the sword he would wield to pierce her maidenhead. Fearsome though it was, huge and rigid yet pulsing with life, it made her tremble more with mindless passion than with terror. Her body already wept with need for her lord— her enemy— to take her, to fill the pulsating void that before this night she had never realized was there.

The closely shaved stubble of his beard rasped her skin as he moved down her body, pausing to nip and tongue her nipples before burying his face against her hot, tingling mons. His tongue laved every newly sensitized inch of her there before he moved lower still and lapped at the throbbing knot of nerves he had awakened with the touch of the feather.

When he raised his head, she saw the heat of his passion in eyes so dark they seemed almost black in the dim glow from the candles. "Behold me," he said, rising on his knees and sliding forward until the glistening rosy tip of his throbbing cock nearly touched her lips. "Taste the sword that will pierce you, Brianna. Do not hurt me, or I will take your maidenhead without a lover's care."

Why would she hurt him? Every fiber of her being wanted his full possession. She ached to learn him by feel and touch as well as with her eyes. With both battle-hardened hands he cradled her head, lifting her until she could lick away the salty pearl of moisture she watched emerge from the slit from whence would flow his seed.

Long and thick and gently curving upward toward his flat, muscled belly, his sex enthralled her. Unable to free her hands she sampled him again with her tongue, not knowing why except that she would do anything to fill the emptiness inside her.

Savoring the musky scent and slightly salty taste of him, she clasped her lips around the ruby knob of his penis and sucked him in, swallowing and caressing him with her tongue until she could feel the coarse bush from which his manhood sprung tickling her lips.

'Tis strange, she thought, *that feeling him throb in my mouth makes the emptiness in my belly more intense.* Still she continued until he shuddered and jerked away.

"No more, my lady, lest you unman me," he said, his voice hoarse as he slid back down her body and positioned himself between her widespread legs. "I will go easily. I do not wish to cause you unnecessary pain."

More than anything she had ever wanted, Brianna wanted him to make them one. He felt so smooth, so hot and hard as he rubbed himself along her wet, slick slit. She couldn't move, couldn't wrap her arms and legs about his hard male body and draw him home. But she could watch.

She raised her head. His huge hot cock slid slowly into her body, and she relaxed her inner muscles to ease his way. He stretched her almost unbearably, yet she welcomed his fullness, and the sharp pain and tearing sensation that made her cry out when he breached the last defense of her maidenhead. Thrusting gently, he sank fully into her until she could not see where she ended and he began.

"Tis done. You are mine." The soft, wet kisses he placed on her lips gave sweet punctuation to his harshly spoken words. As if he found her gift precious, he withdrew ever so slowly and slid back home, over and over, faster with each careful stroke, until she felt the pain recede and sensed her body accepting that this man— her enemy and yet her husband— had made her part and parcel of himself. Sensation robbed her of reason and she gave herself over to it.

Brianna had never felt so full. It was as if she were perfectly attuned to the sight and smell and taste of Giles. The way the muscles in his arms bulged as he braced himself above her, almost in concert with the throbbing of his cock within her woman's place and the soft rasp of his chest hair against her puckered, aching nipples, drove her wild.

A hot, urgent feeling began deep in her belly and radiated outward. Her inner muscles clamped down on him when he withdrew, only to relax when he plunged harder and deeper with each measured thrust of his hard, lean hips.

Straining at her bonds she cried out, needing to draw him closer, clasp her limbs about his warrior's body and swallow him up. The heat bubbled through her veins, and she screamed at the kaleidoscope of sensations. His mouth came down on hers, muting the sound. His tongue plunged deep, in time with the cadence of his thrusts. Suddenly a dam burst inside her, sending shards of pleasure-pain to every cell in her body and consuming her as his hot seed shot deep into her womb.

When he rolled to his side, she missed his strength and heat.

❧⟨✿⟩❧

"You are mine." Raising himself off the mattress and staring down at her sweat-glistened skin, Giles bent to sip at a rosy nipple. "Methinks Henry did me no great disservice when he gave you to me," he murmured as he rolled to his side. "You may speak."

Sated, Giles was of a mind to loosen her bonds. He fancied having her learn his body with her hands and mouth, the way he had just learned hers. That must come later, he told himself, thinking of the lesson he had yet to teach his bride.

"If I am yours, why did you bid your manservant to touch me?"

Giles met Brianna's solemn gaze. That had not been the response he expected. "Arnaud?"

She nodded, staring down toward her denuded mons as if to remind him what he had allowed Arnaud to do. "He touched me there."

"He didn't violate you, though." Giles pulled his trophy, the soft white linen stained with her virgin's blood, from beneath her hips and held it up for her to see. "He could not, even should that have been his intent. Arnaud is not a man."

"Not a man?"

"He is a eunuch."

Her eyes widened. "I do not understand."

"Look on me, Brianna." Rising, he knelt beside her shoulder, his sex plainly within her line of vision. "What do you see?"

"Your manhood. 'Tis not so big now." Still her tongue darted out and moistened lips that had recently clenched his cock so sweetly. He felt himself becoming hard again under her questioning gaze.

"That's because you just wrung the life from it, sweeting. Watch. It recovers even as we speak. I am a man. A whole man. When I look upon a woman I swell and harden."

"And a eunuch does not?"

"No. Eunuchs have no seed sac." Lifting his half-hard penis he bared his scrotum to her gaze.

"How sad. I knew not that some men lacked…"

"They are not born that way. Rather, eunuchs are made. The seed sac is taken, in much the same manner that stallions are gelded. Sometimes the rod is removed as well, as it was in Arnaud's case."

"But why? To create keepers for reluctant brides? You are even more of a beast than I first imagined." Brianna turned her head away, as if repulsed by the sight of him.

"I am not the one who took Arnaud's manhood." Giles gently stroked her cheek. "He fell victim to a Saracen's blade two years past. Rolfe and I came upon him in the desert, near death, and nursed him back to health."

"He was your servant?"

"Nay. He was lord of a great estate in the south of France. Not wishing to return no longer a man, he bade us inform his family of his death and asked me to take him as my servant… one of the gifts I would make to my bride."

"Gift?"

"A protector and defender, Brianna. One in whom I—and you—may place complete faith and trust. One who can pleasure you without risk when I am gone to battle."

"You would allow this?"

"From the infidel I learned the benefit of ensuring a woman's sexual satisfaction. Arnaud can ease your lust, yet hone it to a fever pitch for me. I need never fear needing the horns of a cuckold as long as he draws life, for he will guard your life and virtue with his own."

"Why would he do this, Giles? Does it not make him regret his state?"

"His state, pitiable though it is, gave him immense value in the East by making him acceptable to guard and protect the highest born women of the harem. By giving him that value here, in a Christian land where otherwise he would be useless, I give him purpose for having survived and returned."

Brianna met Giles's gaze before looking again at his pulsing rod. Her small pink tongue darted out and licked her upper lip. "If he is as you say, how can he...? Is this the purpose..." She glanced at the articles Arnaud had arranged on the chest by the bed.

Her avid gaze suggested hunger as well as sexual curiosity. Brianna, he thought with satisfaction, would take eagerly to all the sensual arts. Her plump rose nipples beaded up as if begging for the touch of his tongue, and he bent to oblige them before reaching for the pair of silver spheres. Gently he rolled them against her cheek so she could feel the movement of the drops of mercury inside and hear the tinkling of the balls as they bounced together in his hand.

"Arnaud can use them to bring you release. They can also enhance the pleasures we share together. That is why he assembled them here this night. Feel the spheres. They can intensify your wanting," he told her, shifting his hand to her satiny mound and lower. With his fingers he spread her outer lips and inserted the balls, one at the time, deep into her vagina. "Milk them, as you milked me so sweetly," he ordered, pausing to cajole her nipples into rock-hard little peaks with his thumbs and forefingers.

"They feel cold. Not warm and alive. I would know more of my bride-gift. How he came to be unmanned."

"He killed a Saracen whose brothers set upon him and staked him out naked in the desert sun. As Arnaud tells it they slit open his seed sac, took his testicles, and forced them down his throat."

Brianna squirmed, apparently unnerved by Giles's graphic description. "But I thought... you said they took his rod as well," she murmured, beads of sweat forming on her brow.

Apparently her slight movement had set the mercury in motion. Wondering how long it would take for the spheres to drive her into a sexual frenzy Giles continued his story. "They did not. A Saracen physician we captured finished what the infidel warriors had begun. By the time my men and I came upon Arnaud his wound had festered into a mass of dried blood and pus. The physician cut away the rotted flesh that had been his seed sac and rod, and fashioned an opening for him to pass water through, that he might live. Thus Arnaud became a complete eunuch, the kind the infidel princes pay dearly for to guard their harems."

When she began to writhe in earnest Giles reached inside her and retrieved the silver spheres. Never had he seen a woman respond so quickly and completely to the slightest stimulation. That this wanton was his wife made him want to thank Henry again for his unexpected gift.

"After he realized he would not die, Arnaud pledged his life to me, and asked to serve me as the harem eunuchs serve the infidel. While he recuperated Arnaud befriended the physician's wives and concubines, and learned the sensual arts they practice. Soon afterward I conquered an infidel prince's palace, and placed Arnaud in charge of what had become my harem. There I learned of sexual pleasure I had never dreamed existed, erotic delights far more devastating than I had ever known. Skills Arnaud will help me teach to you."

Hot and needing her husband's mighty sword to ease her, Brianna raised her head again. "Release my bonds," she whispered, not certain she wished him to comply. There was something exciting, forbidden, about being bound and helpless to the desires of this mighty conqueror.

"Soon."

With trepidation she watched as he lazily looked over the remaining items on the chest. "What is that?" she asked when she saw him grasp the strange red glass cylinder.

His other hand settled on the hood that covered her ruined hair. "A dildo. Puny as it is, it should soothe you while I rid you of this." With that terse reply Giles took the cylinder and inserted it where he had removed the spheres. Turning back to the chest he picked up the dagger. Brianna gasped, terrified that now her bridegroom intended to kill her.

"Fear not, sweeting. You pleasure me too much for me to wish you dead. Since you chose to hack away your hair in your effort to escape me, I intend to finish the job. I am going to cut away the unsightly mess you left behind." Lifting her head he loosened and removed the wimple.

"You are going to shave my head, as if I had taken holy orders?"

"Yes. The feel of your bare scalp in my hands will pleasure me more than running my fingers through this tar-caked stubble." He loosened but did not release the cords that bound her hands, and she felt his warm breath on her cheek as he raised her to a sitting position, placing pillows at her back. With one hand he pulled the short fringe at her brow taut. She shuddered when he made the first pass of cold steel across her scalp.

"Why did you not order Arnaud to do this?" In one way Brianna thought she would have preferred the eunuch's impersonal touch to Giles's sensual application of the blade to her skull.

"Because I wished to claim your body before taking your hair." The rasp of the dagger and the weightless feeling as locks of her hair fell away gave her a perception of freedom despite her bonds.

Her internal muscles constricted about the cool, smooth dildo, and she felt a scalding drop of moisture drip down theslit between her legs. The fact that Giles wanted to perform this act himself made

Brianna feel in it a purely sexual excitement that overshadowed the shame of being punished, she supposed for the sin of having tried to defy her lord and master's will.

How can the touch of cold Toledo steel make me feel so hot? she wondered as she focused her gaze on her husband's dark, impassioned face. The small jagged scar that marred one otherwise perfect cheek stood out in the dim light, a white and stark reminder that Giles was the Barbarian— warrior without equal, thief of all she held dear.

He rose above her, moving the slow, sensual drag of the dagger across her scalp. His warm, firm cock nestled in the hollow between her breasts, gently abrading her skin with the bush of coal black pubic hair that surrounded it.

She had to touch him. When he shifted positions again she tried to take him into her mouth.

"Cease!"

His terse order lacked conviction. She rested her chin on her chest and tickled the tip of his penis with her tongue. He shifted forward and she took him deep into her throat. When he let out a tortured-sounding moan, she curved her lips around him.

Her head felt naked, yet he kept stroking it with callused fingers, as though searching for tufts of hair his knife had missed. Within her mouth he pulsed with life, and when he pulled away he shuddered.

Suddenly she felt bereft. The dildo didn't fill her the way he did—the way she needed him to fill her now!

"You've too pretty a head to hurt," he said, and the familiar pungent smell of the paste Arnaud had used to denude her body made her realize what he intended.

"No!" *Do not destroy the illusion that you have left me with a short, pale pelt to hide beneath the wimple I must wear to cover my shame.*

"Yes." He set the jar beside her head, where she could see its mottled colors out of the corner of her eye, and straddled her belly. Reaching behind him he removed the dildo.

"Open to me."

He slid down her body until his cock nestled between her wide-spread legs, then thrust upward to impale her.

He filled her completely, and she willed him to move. He did not, except to lean forward. With one hand he steadied her head, while he reached with the other hand into the jar and withdrew a handful of the pink paste.

"I do this to rid you of the stench of oil and tar. I would not have reminders of battle in my bed. Weep not. You cannot feel me pulse within you and yet not know I desire you shorn as much as I could want you if you had kept your flowing locks. Besides, the hair here will grow back. Until it does, you will like feeling my hands and tongue caress the naked skin no one has ever touched before."

At the same time he smoothed a layer of the paste over her scalp, he began slowly to slide in and out of her. Soon she was climaxing again, the way she had before when he had primed her with ever faster and harder rhythmic thrusts of his mighty sword.

The sensations kept building within her, making her oblivious to all but his thrusting cock, his hard male body, and his warm hands massaging her naked scalp. When he anointed her there with fragrant oil, her skin prickled, sending sensual messages pounding through her body.

She thought she could take no more, but when he lowered his head and plunged his tongue into her mouth as he increased the rhythm of his hips, she convulsed around him again just before he bathed her with his seed. The stark pleasure was too much, and she lost consciousness.

※⳻(�´)⳺⁕

When morning came Giles took the black silk from the chest and positioned it over Brianna's naked scalp. His rod grew hard and ready as he watched her, totally naked but for the headcovering someone had decreed that married women must wear. His hands trembled with the need to caress her as he tied thin laces that secured the sheer silk covering and made it conform to the contour of her perfectly oval skull.

As he tugged on his chausses and pulled a short black tunic over his head, his gaze kept wandering back to his bride. Brianna had proven herself a sexual wanton, for which Giles uttered a silent prayer of thanksgiving. He looked at her and marveled at her stubborn spirit that must have prevented her from begging him to free her. Finally he had loosened her bonds, unwilling to wait longer to feel her tiny hands upon his manhood, her legs entwined with his as they slept.

Unchecked, Giles surmised, Brianna's strength would be his undoing unless he proved himself to be her master in every way. Tossing the fur coverlet over her, Giles turned to the smaller of the two carved chests and drew out a small velvet bag.

Chapter Four

"Arnaud!"

The solar door opened and the eunuch appeared. "My lord?"

"The deed is done," Giles muttered, as he tucked the square of bloodied linen which proclaimed he had consummated the marriage into the waistband of his chausses. "I go below stairs to break my fast. Summon my lady's attendants and set them to fashioning braids from the locks she hacked off yesterday. I fancy such a favor to hang from my lance. When the lady Brianna awakens, summon me. I would present her with these gifts ere I ride out." After handing over the bag he had brought from the chest, he strode from the room, intent upon discharging duties less pleasant but no less necessary than the taming of his reluctant bride.

"You!" While she slept, Brianna thought furiously, her husband had left her with the strange giant he had assured her was not a man at all. Her muscles ached from her deflowering and the delicious ravishments that had followed.

"Lord Giles bade me watch you sleep and summon him ere you awakened. Wish you to break your fast?" Arnaud shifted in his chair, making Brianna wonder if he still felt pain from the ordeal that had taken his manhood.

"I wish to go below. The servants will expect their instructions."

"As my lady wishes." The giant rose and called out to someone beyond the closed door.

Suddenly she remembered Giles had shaved her head. Her scalp didn't feel especially cold, though, the way her hands and feet did where the sable failed to cover her. Curious, she raised a hand to her head.

Her fingers skimmed over thin silk when she touched her fore-head... her scalp... even her cheeks and chin. A wimple. Not the starched, white linen one Elsa had set out the night before, but one so sheer and clinging, so revealing that her husband's blatant mark of possession would be evident to all. The very covering the giant had placed on her yestereve.

Brianna hated the way she ached even now to feel Giles's hard, warrior's body join again with hers. Hated her own weakness for taking such pleasure in the way his hands and mouth caressed her as they stole her independence—her very self. Loathed that she had lusted for him even as she felt him run his blade against her scalp, knowing he was shaving off her hair.

Her cheeks heated with embarrassment as she recalled how she had taken his huge cock in her mouth and suckled him even as he completed this subjugation of her person.

She smiled. While Giles had marked her his in a way she could not conceal, he had revealed his weakness for female flesh. Her flesh. She would bring him down with his own sensual arsenal. She would order her giant, unmanned wedding present to teach her how.

"Arnaud, will you teach me how to pleasure my lord Giles?"

"As my lady commands."

"I would learn at once. You will begin my lessons as I put on my clothes." Brianna rose, no longer shy at having Arnaud look upon her naked form, but anxious to don the clothing Elise had set out for her ere she scurried away the night before. "What did you with the clothing my maid laid out yestereve?" she asked when she noted the bare top of the chest where she had last seen the garments.

"I put those rags away. Lord Giles has provided you garments fit for a great lord's bride." She watched Arnaud remove garments from her husband's larger chest and lay them on the bed. "My lord assumed you would be mourning your lord father when he had these garments made for your bride-gifts. There are others in the chest, ones you may wish to wear when the mourning time is done."

A black silk shift, so sheer she could see through it and so slippery it nearly slid through her fingers, would surely caress the sensitized skin on her body just as the wimple, fashioned of the same transparent stuff, was already fondling her scalp. Brianna felt her nipples tighten and her belly cramp when she set the shift down and looked at the outer garments.

The Barbarian had apparently spared no expense. The heavy black silk bliaut and sleeveless hooded cotte of loosely woven black wool shot through with silver threads must have cost him much gold. She was about to pick up the girdle of silver links, obsidian, and garnets when the giant eunuch stilled her hand.

"Come. My lord Giles will be here presently. He wishes to present you with your bride-gifts ere you don your clothing." When Brianna turned about she saw that Arnaud had moved a chair near the solar's large glass window and that he was placing some coals from the fireplace into a small metal brazier. "Stand here," he ordered when she approached, confused.

"What do you do?"

"I fire the needle to pierce your skin for the jewels he will give you."

Brianna reached to brush back her hair but encountered only the feel of silk against her fingers. "No one will be able to see them," she murmured regretfully as she tried in vain to uncover her earlobes

"Lord Giles will see. Stop. You will tear the silk. I will show you how to unlace that later. Stand here in the light. I will ready you for the insertion of your other adornments."

"What?" From a small cloth bag, the likes of which Brianna had never seen, Arnaud poured a handful of sparkling mounted stones onto the table.

"You please me, Brianna. I would adorn you with rubies, set in pure gold from the land of the infidel. Stand still, that Arnaud may numb your skin for the piercing." Giles appeared beside her, his entry as silent as a stalking cat's. When he spoke his hot gaze raked over her naked, burning skin.

The ointment the eunuch was smearing onto her belly and around her upthrust nipples burned, then left the skin it touched feeling as if it were not there. "What do you do?" she asked, alarmed at the lack of sensation when Giles pulled a nipple taut between his callused fingers.

"Insert the wire, Arnaud," he said, and when the hot, sharp prick of the needle passed through her flesh she knew. As Brianna looked down to see rounded, heavy gold wire protruding from behind either side of the nipple Giles still held taut, he grasped her other nipple and tugged it just before another hot, tingling sensation passed through her body. Before she could do more than register that the eunuch had pierced her body twice with red-hot gold, he did it again, this time into her navel.

"Do not move," he ordered, raising up from his task and reaching onto the table. "The jewel, my lord."

Giles let loose her nipples to quiver against the cooling gold, and he went to his knees before her. Whatever he placed into her navel felt cold and hard, so foreign that she barely noticed the pain when Arnaud passed the thick gold wire through the other side of her navel.

Giles put his lips where the needle had pierced her skin. Touched, Brianna reached down to tangle her fingers in his glistening short black curls.

"Behold, Lady Brianna," he said after a moment, positioning the mirror Arnaud had handed him so she could see the huge, glittering ruby that winked from within her navel. "This is for my pleasure. These," he said, reaching up to touch her nipples with a gentleness that surprised her, "will be for yours."

"I wish to see them." When he moved the glass higher she saw how four small rubies formed caps for the gold wires Arnaud had threaded behind each nipple and through narrow gold circlets. Her flesh stung, yet the little peaks quivered proudly, forming a rose-red puckered center for each of the jeweled rings.

"Oh," she murmured, imagining the delicious feeling of slippery silk—or the velvety moisture of the Barbarian's tongue—abrading the upthrust, sensitive tips. That thought made her instantly hot and wet.

"Care you to look upon your face now?"

Arnaud had removed the wimple, and Brianna's earlobes throbbed when he pierced them and inserted earrings that felt nearly as heavy as her knee-length hair had been before she cut it. Suddenly Brianna feared to look, aware that the girl she had been yesterday was no more.

"I would feel them first." Tentatively she raised her hands to touch the hard, cold jewels in her earlobes. Then, bolder, she skimmed her fingers over her scalp as if learning by touch alone the satiny texture and shape of a self no longer defined by the pale, wavy hair that now rested... where? "Arnaud, where is my hair?"

"My lord Giles ordered your ladies to weave the long strands you hacked away into braids."

Giles met her questioning gaze. "I fancy hanging one from my lance at the tourney three weeks hence. Want you to see yourself now?" he asked again.

She inhaled deeply. "Yes." Slowly she raised the mirror and met her own wide-eyed gaze.

A bald woman with sparkling rubies in the lobes of delicate shell-like ears stared back at her. Her eyes looked huge. She did not look repulsive, as she had feared, but she wasn't Brianna, either.

Myself? Nay! I fear I have become some otherworldly sexual creature of my lord's creation.

She raised a hand and touched the satiny smooth surface of her scalp, amazed at how soft it felt. The Barbarian had done this with his own hands, and he had made what should have been a humiliating ordeal into a sensual, almost sexual experience.

She needed him to fill the suddenly throbbing core of her with his thick, pulsating manhood. Squirming now with lust she did not understand and could not control, Brianna set down the mirror and reached out to him.

This creature is me. A sensual, sexual fantasy made real by this man. Giles. My enemy...my lord.

Brianna craved Giles's touch. "Lie with me," she begged as she imagined his dark, battle-hardened hands binding her head to his velvet-smooth, iron-hard cock, his fingers digging into her scalp to hold her steady for the voracious invasion of his tongue.

She yearned for him to cradle and massage her scalp while his talented tongue tortured nipples raised and puckered by his sensual gifts of gold and rubies. When she remembered how he had licked and suckled her as they lay sated after a mighty climax the night before, she burned.

"You need time to recover from your deflowering, Brianna," Giles told her as he cupped her mound in one callused hand. "Arnaud will see to your needs and teach you how best to satisfy mine. I go now to secure the lesser properties of Harrow. My brother Rolfe will see to repairing the castle defenses here. Arnaud, while I am gone, do as your lady bids."

With that Giles dropped a casual kiss on the top of Brianna's head and strode from the chamber.

"If you require relief, lady, I am here to oblige you." Arnaud moved to the chest by the bed and picked up the dildo.

"Nay." She needed not to be reminded how Giles had soothed her lust with that poor excuse for his mighty sword while he ravished her yestereve.

The giant eunuch shrugged. "Perhaps the spheres?"

Brianna hesitated. She hurt with wanting, so much she hardly noticed the soreness from the piercings or the dull aches from newly-used muscles in her belly and thighs. When she had lain motionless last night, the gentle motion of the silver balls in her vagina had soothed the urgent need until Giles had replaced them with his mighty rod and given her relief.

"Perhaps," she said, conceding that her lust overwhelmed her modesty. "I will lie down that you may insert them."

"That is not necessary. Bend forward."

Desperate for relief, Brianna obeyed. The cold metal of first one sphere and then the other slid past the cheeks of her bottom, over smooth skin slick with her own juices and into the aching, empty spot that had lain dormant until the Barbarian awakened it.

"It is done."

Brianna straightened, her legs trembling slightly as the motion caused the spheres to shift within her body. "I would dress and go below stairs now," she told Arnaud.

"As you wish, my lady."

Silently he slid the silk shift over her head, letting it settle on her shoulders. The scooped-out neckline caught on her protruding nipples, making her wriggle in response to needle-like sensation that caused her inner muscles to clench and set the spheres in motion within her body.

She closed her eyes, then forced them open. Glancing down she saw the ruby-studded rings that defined her nipples — reddened, puckered nipples that jutted proudly against the transparent material. Automatically she reached to touch them, wincing slightly at the pleasure-pain the slight pressure caused. Brianna felt her inner muscles begin to twitch again, and the spheres rocked harder against the sensitive lining of her vagina

She could hardly stand still while Arnaud tightened the laces of the heavy silk bliaut. The feel of smooth silk pulled taut against the skin of her jeweled belly nearly drove her over the edge toward insanity.

Realizing that the bliaut left her breasts bare save for the gossamer fabric of her shift, she gently rubbed her nipples again, then pinched and rolled them between her fingers. They tingled and stung, and swelled proudly against the ruby-studded rings.

Brianna was beyond caring what, if anything, her eunuch protector might think. Instead of gaining release, though, she only intensified the fire inside her.

"Sit, my lady." She did, and the spheres rocked together. Her gaze went to the juncture of Arnaud's legs. Nothing. Not even the slightest evidence of a sleeping sword. Giles apparently had spoken the truth when he said the giant possessed neither cock nor balls.

"Summon Lord Giles!"

"He has ridden out, my lady."

"I die. Do something!" Brianna's insides were on fire, and the eunuch's gentle touch as he smoothed the black silk over her skull and around her neck was stoking the flame. She barely felt him tighten the material under her chin or secure it with lacing that began at the crown of her head and continued down her neck. Desperate now she rotated her hips as she reached between her legs to seek the knot of nerves Giles had awakened yestereve.

"Help me." Layers of fabric kept her from her goal.

"Move to the edge of the chair." Arnaud sank to his knees and raised her skirts. Spreading her legs wide she watched as he bent his head and took her in his mouth. Impassively he suckled her until she shuddered. Then he pulled out the silver balls and, with a warm damp cloth, he wiped between her legs.

"That gave you no pleasure, did it?" she asked, relieved in body but inexplicably still yearning for what the eunuch could not give.

"Nay. I but do my duty to my lord Giles. He saved my miserable life, encouraged me to learn the ways of the Turkish harems. When he expressed the wish to bring some of the infidel customs home, I offered myself to him. The Saracen devil who stole my lust along with my manhood made me good for naught but to serve a master in some man's harem. I preferred to do it for Lord Giles than live out the balance of my existence there in the land of the infidel."

"Tell me of these harems."

Arnaud's laugh seemed devoid of mirth. "Every Saracen's home boasts a harem. And every harem has its eunuchs, most of whom were sold into slavery and gelded as small boys. Eunuchs like me, the Saracen physician who healed me said, are rare and costly because most who are made as I am die from the operation that removes the rod as well as the seed sac. All but the wealthiest of the infidels must satisfy themselves with guards who have merely been castrated in much the same way that your hostler might geld a stallion."

"You truly have no..."

"Naught but a tube of blown glass through which to pass my water. Were I in a sultan's harem I would wear this as an ornament in my turban." He reached inside his tunic and pulled out a clear, hollow tube that flared at one end. "Would you that I prove I pose no threat to you or my lord Giles?" Arnaud's hand went to the tie on his chausses.

Brianna shook her head. "Nay. Pray tell me if it pains you, though, for I know something of the healing arts. I would try toease your suffering."

"What is not there cannot cause pain once the wound heals, Lady Brianna. Come, I will accompany you as you see to my lord's household." Arnaud picked up the intricate girdle from the bed and fastened it about Brianna's still-trembling hips.

Reaching beneath the weblike veil Arnaud had secured to her head with a beaten silver circlet, Brianna touched the sheer black wimple beneath it. All would he able to see that beneath the sheer fabric her head was shaven smoother than a nun's.

She would not cower in her solar, or hide beneath her long-dead mother's starched linen wimples. Suddenly, as she saw Giles's men supervising repairs within the hall, Brianna wanted them to know she had bowed her head in obeisance to the power of their lord, Giles deVere, now Earl of Harrow.

From his jovial young brother Rolfe to the crustiest man-at-arms, her lord husband's men treated her with respect. None, however, would tell her more of her fallen warriors than that those who lived languished in the castle's dungeons, their fates to be decided at Lord Giles's convenience.

Brianna had to see for herself. With her giant protector at her side she hurried to the dungeon, trying hard to ignore the dank, musty smell as they descended narrow stone steps. Her sire had not allowed her here, where it was whispered that he subjected his prisoners to the vilest forms of torture. "Hold the light, Arnaud," she said, expecting at any moment to hear the screams of those who had survived the Barbarian's attack the day before.

She heard no screams. Were they all dead? Her sire, she had heard, had tortured his prisoners for weeks ere finally sending them to their deaths in the outer bailey. Could her husband, so fierce yet so gentle as he initiated her to the pleasures of the flesh the night

before, have put her men through such an ordeal that they had suc-
cumbed in less than a day?

"This way, my lady." The torch in Arnaud's hand lit the way into
a large room ringed with iron-barred cells. "On your feet, Norwen,
and bid your new countess welcome," he ordered the young man-
at-arms who stood guard within the chamber.

"My lady," he murmured as Brianna looked past him to the score
of her father's men who lounged within their cells. "Wish you to
speak with one of the prisoners?"

"Nay." 'Twas enough that she saw Eudo, glaring at her as he
gnawed on a joint of roasted meat. Apparently he and the others,
a motley crew of men-at-arms Brianna knew not by their names,
waited here under guard for her husband to decide their fate.

"What will be done to them?" she asked, not at all certainshe
truly wished to know.

Arnaud shrugged. "When Lord Giles returns, he will offer them
the opportunity to serve him as they served your sire, if they are
willing to swear fealty to him. Except for the monk. He will be
escorted to his cloister, with an account of the evil he has perpe-
trated here, unless Lord Giles chooses to deal with his punishment
himself, monk or no."

Was the Barbarian so confident that he would allow those who
fought against him in his midst? Brianna did not understand. Her
sire had dispatched his enemies with ruthless abandon, sparing no
mercy to those defeated in battle. "What evil?" she asked, glancing at Eudo again as the eunuch's prediction of his fate registered
in her mind.

"Your armorer accuses him of having raped his eight-year-
old daughter, causing her to bleed to death, milady. There are
witnesses."

"No! I did not know." Brianna shuddered with distaste.

"Lord Giles tolerates no rape, and no violation of children. Your
brother, if you have forgotten, violated another vow, the promise
of chastity he made to the Church. I doubt that his abbot will take
this kindly."

"What will happen to Eudo?"

"You love your brother well?"

"Nay. He is an odious man. And not my true brother, but my sire's get on a peasant wench. Upon my true brother's death my sire brought him back from his cloister in the hope of making Eudo his heir."

Arnaud glanced at the tonsured creature chewing on his meat. "He should have known that could never be. A bastard and a man consecrated to the church. Perhaps the one, but not the both."

"My sire was a determined man."

Curious, Brianna met the eunuch's gaze. "What will his punishment be if he is sent back to the abbey?"

"Castration. Possibly torture and death. I know not the customs here in England, but in France no abbot would allow a brother who committed such a sin to live. You churchman might be wise to beg Lord Giles to mete out his punishment."

"Perhaps you are right."

Arnaud nodded. "Lord Giles will not go easy on any man, let alone a supposed man of God, who has raped and caused the death of an innocent child."

"I may not hold him dear, but Eudo is the last of my blood relatives, Arnaud. Surely my husband would not have him put to death?"

"Nay. 'Tis a sin to kill a priest or monk. Cease your fretting. The worst that will happen to him at Harrow is to lose his manhood, and in a much more humane manner than if his gelding takes place by one not versed in the Infidel's methods. Rolfe, Giles's young brother, may indeed have already ordered the monk be made a eunuch." Arnaud gestured toward the fire at the center of the dungeon, where a burly man-at-arms was heating a small, open iron ring in a pincer-like device.

"Nay!" Brianna could not imagine the agony that white-hot ring could inflict upon a man's private parts.

"'Tis kinder than hacking them away with a knife, Lady Brianna. He will feel pain when the ring is clamped tightly about his seed sac, then naught but numbness, or so those who have been gelded in that manner say. In a few days his balls will rot and fall off."

"Oh." This travesty might well have been ordered by her husband's young brother, but Brianna had no illusions that Giles would not have done the same, or worse. "My lord husband is indeed the monster he was painted to me before we met," she muttered, angry with herself because she lusted for him even now.

"Do not tell me you do not relish his attentions. According to the houris in the harem, Lord Giles is a most skillful lover. Come, I will instruct you in how to please him if you have satisfied yourself that your people fare none too badly here."

✳♾(ᴄ❣ᴄ)✦❈

When she sought her room that night and for the seven more lonely nights that followed, Brianna immersed herself in the pleasures of her eunuch's impersonal but thorough ministrations.

Each night Arnaud bathed and oiled her, using his hands and mouth to relieve her when her lust became too much to bear. As he did, he instructed her in the ancient arts the houris mastered to please their infidel masters. Brianna ached to put her new knowledge to the test with her own absent lord.

On the eighth night as Arnaud applied the pink paste liberally from her neck down to her toes, she ran her hands over her thighs and upward. Idly she twisted the gold balls on each end of the wire that held the ruby snugly within her navel. The piercings pained her no more, but rather reminded her of how Giles had placed his marks of possession on her body. God, but she yearned for his return.

"Lord Rolfe has had a message. Lord Giles returns on the morrow," Arnaud said, shifting his gaze from his task to look her in the eye.

"Think you I can entice him?"

"My lady, you could make a eunuch's useless cock stand up and swell for want of you."

She smiled. "I could? Surely not. Do not tell me I exciteyou,

Arnaud." Twirling the wires behind each nipple Brianna tugged lightly, still amazed that the delicious tingling shot from her breasts straight to her womb.

"Nay. But had I my rod, I would be forced to bind it tightly between my legs while in your presence, lest your lord note its enthusiasm and decide I needed it no more. Never fear, Lady Brianna, you will enslave Lord Giles." After wiping the paste away he rubbed heated, fragrant oil into her satiny skin. After he had completed her toilette, Arnaud offered her relief. Brianna declined, secure in the knowledge that by this time on the morrow, she would be learning the Barbarian's hard, fit body as intimately as he had learned hers. She promised herself that she would be well upon the way toward enslaving him, the way he already had subjugated her to his iron will.

Chapter Five

God's teeth! Giles thought, his gaze raking the prize that might well be worth more than the pile of stone and wood she had defended. *Brianna.* Garbed head to toe in his colors of black and silver, the small replica of his shield set proudly over her silken mons, his bride brought a smile to his lips and an instant hardening to his groin.

"My lady," he murmured as he dismounted and brushed his lips across her cheek. "I trust you are recovered."

Ruby lips curving upward into a smile, eyes sparkling, Brianna sank into a curtsy. The rubies twinkling in her ears beneath sheer silk made him want to see other jewels meant for his eyes only. "I am well, my lord," she murmured softly as she knelt, her perfectly oval head modestly covered yet not concealed, bowed before him as if in an act of obeisance. Or was it an act of seduction?

Blood pooled between her legs. "Rise, my lady," he growled, using one hand to pull her to her feet. Now was not the time, and here was not the place for his cock to swell in anticipation of her sweet mouth's beckoning warmth. "My other possessions came into my hands without a fight. Come, I would that you show me my castle." *And ease my aching within your tight, wet woman's place if God grants us a moment's privacy among the casks of wheat and wine.*

"I will show you the storerooms." Her smile made his cock twitch with anticipation as they descended narrow stairs to the castle storerooms.

Tightening his grip on her hand, Giles pulled Brianna to him and pinned her between his body and the stone corridor wall. He felt her heartbeat quicken when their bodies made contact through layers of clothing that somehow heightened passions they were intended to cool.

"I would have you now."

"Shall we seek our chamber?"

"Nay." Jerking at the string of his chausses, he loosened them and let them fall about his knees. "Lift your skirts and lean across yon wine cask."

When she complied he rubbed himself along her hot, wet slit. Finding his way easily, he thrust home hard and deep until his sac rested firmly against the knot of nerves he had learned was key to a woman's pleasure. His hands found puckered nipples upthrust proudly against the pressure of the jewels.

Wanting to hear his new bride scream with pleasure he set to fucking her in earnest, pulling her nipples rhythmically with each inward thrust that brought him ever closer to release.

Her inner muscles contracted fiercely around his cock, milking him dry. With a feral growl he gave up his seed. It took him a moment to recover and draw up his chausses.

That fast, hard coupling had hardly taken the edge off his lust. Giles barely managed to beat down the need to claim his bride again until after the evening meal. In the lord's chamber now, his own clothing discarded, his blood burned hotter as he watched Brianna disrobe.

Naked now, she stood before him, her gaze raking his already fierce arousal. "I would place my mark upon you as you did me. Behold the man in this picture," she told him, and his gaze followed hers to the opened page of a pillow book he had brought back from the East. "I would watch Arnaud make you thus."

He bent and ran his tongue over the incredibly satiny skin of her scalp, pausing to trace the rubies that adorned earlobes as soft as velvet.

So she wanted Arnaud to shave his cock and balls. The idea of anyone wielding a blade so near his genitals alarmed him, yet the idea of her running her tongue over newly bared skin had him instantly rock hard and ready.

"As you wish, Lady Brianna." Bellowing for Arnaud to enter, he positioned her on her knees above him, her silken sex within easy reach of his tongue. "I would take my pleasure whilst you take yours, however."

On the bed, his legs as wide-spread as hers had been on their wedding night, Giles lapped Brianna's honey as Arnaud wielded his dagger. Slowly, stopping ever so often to scrape the hair from the blade, the eunuch began at the crack of his arse, scraping the blade against his skin and testing each inch by rubbing a finger over it. Giles struggled to hold his seed, nearly failing when the dagger reached his nearly-bursting seed sac.

He suckled her harder, swirling his tongue around her sex as Arnaud grasped his cock and scraped away the thick bush at its base. He barely felt the eunuch's touch when he spread the paste between his legs. The chilly air swirled about him as warm, musky oil scented the chamber.

"So satin smooth. I like you thus," Brianna said, her breath beating a soft cadence against the sensitized skin of his crotch as she leaned forward and touched him. Then she took his rigid cock in her mouth and drew it deep into her throat while she rolled his balls between her tiny palms.

Christ's bones, if he wasn't going to come again. "Enough!" Pulling her off him he flipped her onto her back, coming over her and driving home in one hard thrust. The sensation of silk against silk, her satiny slit wet and hot against his own denuded skin, sent fresh desire to every nerve in his body.

Each thrust and parry, every movement felt magnified a thousand times. When it was over Giles realized he had submitted to Brianna's lust as certainly as she had fallen prey to his.

Twice in the night he awoke to the feel of her hands and mouth on him, and twice he rose to the occasion, pouring himself into her as he cradled her silken scalp between his own roughened hands.

Brianna slept until midday, waking to find Giles gone but Arnaud on hand to help her dress. Embarrassed when she recalled all she had done with Giles the night before, she managed to contain her sexual excitement as the giant tended her piercings and creamed away her body hair. As gently as if she were a child he dressed her, this time in a white gown and sheer white wimple beneath the same black bliaut, cotte and veil she had worn the day before.

"You may seek your own pleasures, Arnaud," she murmured when he finished lacing the wimple and adjusting the circlet that held her veil in place. "I would see to the needs of my people."

The giant shook his head. "My lord wishes me to accompany you, my lady," he told her. "He would that you attend his court this day."

"Court?" Giles wished *her* to witness his passing sentence upon her people?

"He tries and punishes those who defy his rule. He would have you at his side."

Brianna saw no way to defy the Barbarian, not as long as his giant eunuch was there to enforce his orders. After the pleasure he had given her last night she wasn't sure she even wanted to defy her lusty husband. "Very well. I would break my fast, ere I join my lord Giles."

❦❦❦

"Damn! I've not the stomach for much more of this," Rolfe muttered, shifting in his chair next to Giles as they listened to the tearful accusation by the chief armorer that one of Giles's bowmen had raped the man's twelve-year-old daughter.

Giles tried to ignore the swelling in his groin that had begun the moment he saw Brianna enter the hall. "What say you to this?" he asked his man.

"She enticed me, milord."

"Then you may have the privilege of bedding the wench nightly. You will wed with her as soon as can be arranged." Giles cast his gaze upon the miller and his comely young daughter. "See that the banns are called," he told them before waving his hand in dismissal.

Rising, Giles strode to Brianna's side and stroked her cheek.

"Come with me," he ordered, his rough warrior's fingers tracing rosy lips as soft as satin.

"Giles! There are yet men in the dungeons to be tried," Rolfe called out.

The prisoners could wait. Giles would not. "Let them languish a bit longer, brother. You may hear and decide the minor cases yet before the court. We shall return." Lifting his wife into his arms he strode up the winding staircase, intent upon easing the lust that grew every time he dipped into her honeyed heat.

Each time it was the same, yet different. Today she disrobed him with the skill of a infidel courtesan, her tiny hands making feathery patterns on his cock and balls. She used her tongue to dip into his navel, her hot breath to tickle the skin of his belly.

His fingers trembled as he unlaced her wimple. Naked now, she knelt before him, suckling his seed sac as her hands grasped his cock. Giles shuddered. Her greedy attentions were certain to drive him mad.

"Cease, my lady. I would spill my seed where it may take root."

Her pink tongue darting out to moisten her lips, Brianna looked up and met his gaze. "I would that you take my other maidenhead," she said. "Arnaud tells me that can give you greater pleasure than..."

"He is wrong." Giles had never particularly relished the act she offered. Still, his blood pumped faster when he imagined that tight, rose hole clutching at his sex. After all, this was his wife, not some nameless wench left over from a dead infidel's harem. "If this is what you want, I shall be happy to oblige you."

"It is." Rising, she positioned herself upon the bed on hands and knees, as though she expected him to mount her and take his pleasure. Amused at his wife's innocent eagerness, Giles turned to the chests by the bed and drew out a vial of oil.

"Arnaud must not have prepared you for this, my lady," he murmured as he oiled a finger and very gently worked it around her puckered rear entry. "I would not hurt you. And I would have you do what I do to you, to me, as well." When Brianna turned to meet his gaze he offered her the vial of oil, anticipating her gentle touch on a part of him none had ever breached.

She dipped her index finger into the vial as he turned on the bed. Her first touch felt as gentle as a soft breeze, as tantalizing as a melody coaxed from a lute. When she invaded him he tensed at the unfamiliar yet not unpleasant sensation. "Oil the dildo and place it where your finger is," he told her, needing to know whether what she asked of him would cause her pain.

Slowly, as if she too feared hurting him, she inserted the dildo. Discomfort gave way to a full, stretched sensation as she seated it fully, its handle resting within the cradle of his buttocks. He moved carefully, surprised to find his sex tightening further from this new, forbidden invasion.

Brianna sweetly caressed his throbbing cock before turning back to him. "It is my turn to learn new pleasures, my lord," she murmured, presenting him another dildo as she twisted around to give him access to her lush, rounded buttocks.

Gingerly he entered her again with one finger, then two. When her moans told him she was ready for more he inserted the dildo, inch by painstaking inch, until its rounded head rested flush against her puckered, pink ass. Positioning himself behind her, he buried his cock within her hot, wet woman's place and began to move.

⚜

Almost immediately lust overcame Brianna. Sensation upon sensation, silk against satin, white hot and so intense each movement stole her breath away, washed over her as Giles pumped rhythmically into her from behind. His battle-roughened hands chafed her breasts, the fingers plucking at her nipples and tugging gently at the jeweled rings… his hot, hard rod piercing her over and over… the ivory, jostled into a matching rhythm as his balls pounded into its protruding head.

Her climax came quickly, too quickly, and only when she had rested did she realize Giles had withdrawn both dildos. His cock, still rock-hard and pulsing moments after she had felt his seed flood her womb, prodded against the opening to her rear passage.

"Brianna?" She loved the husky timbre of his voice. Answering his unspoken question by moving to take the tip of him within her, she braced herself for this second deflowering Arnaud had described.

Later, as she lay in his arms, Brianna considered this man who was her husband, the man all called Barbarian. He was a paradox—a man who killed in battle without remorse, but who forced marriage on his own man for having deflowered a servant girl, and tempered his passion with gentle care that he not hurt her as they slaked their mutual lust.

She certainly hadn't conquered the Barbarian. She wasn't certain that she had even begun to tame him, but she felt sure she had pleasured him at least as much as he had pleasured her.

On the morrow she would sit at her lord husband's side as he finished meting out judgment on those of her people who still remained in her father's dungeons. Rubbing a hand experimentally over her hair that now felt like the down on a newborn babe's head, Brianna lay her head on Giles's shoulder and went to sleep.

※؞ᘜ℔ᘓᗔ؞℁

Court began after the mass and a morning meal. After listening to Giles's merciful decisions regarding her people who had defied him, Brianna felt almost happy that King Henry had sent this man to rule in her debauched father's place. Lulled into a sense of contentment, she leaned back in her chair and imagined running her hands and tongue over every inch of her husband's lean, muscular body. Especially the silken skin of his magnificent sex.

When she glanced up and saw her half-brother Eudo being dragged into the hall by two burly men-at-arms, she shuddered at the memory of that molten ring and its grisly purpose. She loved Eudo not, yet he was the last of her flesh and blood. Would Giles punish him further, or return him to his cloister relieved only of his manhood?

"What is your complaint, my man?" she heard Giles ask a freedman she recognized as the castle's armorer.

Her gaze shifted from the armorer to Eudo as the man brought forth a tale that made Brianna's blood run cold. Despite the grisly evidence, she wished she could doubt that her brother, a monk who had long since taken final vows, could have brutally raped the armorer's eight-year-old daughter and left her to bleed to death upon the cold stone floor. "No!" she cried. "This cannot be."

"Hush, my lady. Let the witnesses speak." As if he cared that the accusation caused her anguish, Giles patted her knee beneath the table.

The witnesses' accounts convinced Brianna of her brother's guilt. The sly, unrepentant look on Eudo's face confirmed it. Brianna found herself gawking at his neat, recently-trimmed tonsure and wondering if it would save him from her husband's justice.

"What think you?" Giles asked, his voice low enough that only she and his brother Rolfe could hear.

"There is no doubt of his guilt. I ordered him gelded with the iron ring a sennight past. Were he not supposedly a man of God, I would have seen him suffer a painful death instead," Rolfe replied, his expression fierce.

"You cannot kill one who belongs to the church." Brianna could not bear for Giles to have a monk's death on his soul.

Giles appeared to be pondering his decision. Finally he spoke. "Brother Eudo. You richly deserve to die. I shall leave your fate to your abbot, however. I return you to the cloister under escort, with a letter describing the crime for which you have already lost your balls."

Eudo clasped his crotch through the coarse brown cloth of his monk's robe, his face paling further and his gaze meeting Brianna's. "Have you not done enough?" he croaked, and Brianna touched Giles's hand to gain his attention.

"Cease, my lady. Were this loathsome creature not of the church, I would personally see him not only castrated but disemboweled, drawn, and quartered." Turning toward the people of Harrow who attended the court, he spoke again, his voice deep and clear. "Those who take unwilling wenches in my demesne will be dealt with harshly. The sentence will be carried out immediately." Giles rose and pulled Brianna from her chair. "Come, I would write to the abbot of Brother Eudo's sin."

"What will happen to him?"

Giles shrugged. "If his abbot is a godly man, he will see to the evil monk's demise." His hand at Brianna's waist, he steadied her as they climbed the stairs to the solar.

"Mercifully?" Shuddering at the memory of her father's enemies screaming in agony as the horses rent them limb from limb, Brianna wished a less grisly death for her half-brother.

"I know not. Certainly you would not have the man live after what he did to that child?" Settling into a chair and selecting a piece of parchment, Giles began to pen a letter. "What is the monk to you?"

"He is my father's bastard. When my brother was born, Father dowered him into the cloister, where he remained until my true brother perished in battle. Then Father brought him home, in the hope that the king would allow Eudo to stand as his heir."

Giles met Brianna's gaze, his expression thoughtful. "And you hold this man dear?"

"Nay. He is of my flesh and blood, however. I would wish him a quick and easy death."

Setting the quill aside, Giles took Brianna's hand and pulled her onto his lap. "I would not displease you, my lady. Want you that I..."

"No! I could not rest should you have a churchman's blood ony-our hands, no matter how richly he may deserve it. I beg you, my lord, to return Eudo to the monastery, but to beg the abbot for his mercy." Unable to resist, Brianna caressed the raspy stubble of her husband's beard.

His manhood thickened, prodding at her thigh. "For you, there is little I would not do. Would you have me ask the abbot to let him live?"

"Nay. For what he did to that poor child Eudo deserves to die. Because he is of my blood, I would save him the suffering of torture."

"Then I shall request it. Better yet, I shall send Rolfe with his escort, to voice my wishes directly. One can never be certain some-one at the abbey has the knowledge of written words." Calling out for his brother, Giles crumpled the parchment and tossed it into the fire. "Would you wish your brother farewell?"

"Nay." Reaching down to caress his swollen cock, Brianna wanted it inside her. More than lust, although he certainly inspired that, this man filled a space in her heart that had lain fallow since her lady mother's death. "I would love you," she whispered. "Speak to your brother. I will await you in our chamber."

Giles was so hard, he hurt, and he relayed his message for the abbot to Rolfe with haste. Handing over a pouch of coin to be donated to the abbey in return for the favor he would ask, he bid his brother farewell, cautioning him to complete his journey quickly, that he not miss the tourney scheduled to honor Giles as the new earl of Harrow.

Brianna trusted him to honor his word, he realized as he strode to the bedchamber they shared. He liked that. In bed she was everything a man could want. That had been his hope ere they wed, but now he yearned that they might become friends as well as lovers. Impatient, he stripped off his tunic before he opened the chamber door.

For a moment he wanted to commit murder, until he reminded himself that the man sitting on the edge of his bed rubbing oil into his wife's luscious body was not a man, but Arnaud, and that he had charged the eunuch with Brianna's care.

"Join me, my lord husband." Naked, her body tingling from the fragrant oil Arnaud was rubbing into her skin, Brianna watched as Giles quickly divested himself of his clothes. Like a pagan god, he stood before her, magnificently naked and aroused, scowling at the eunuch as he smoothed the oil gently over her breasts.

"Arnaud. You may leave!" Giles's voice was tight, as if it were all he could do to restrain himself from grabbing the eunuch and tossing him from the chamber. "Now!"

"As you will." A bland expression on his face, Arnaud ceased his ministrations and hurried away.

Giles sat where the eunuch had been, and traced a feathery pattern with his fingers over Brianna's breasts. "Like you the eunuch's touch?"

He is jealous. "Well enough. I find it soothing," she replied, her heart beating faster at the thought that Giles might be coming to care for her.

"Does my touch soothe you, too?"

Brianna smiled. "Nay. You enflame me. Come, ease the ache that begins each time I look upon your warrior's body."

"You no longer think me a barbarian?"

Shifting so she could feast her eyes upon his pulsating erection, he bent his head and took her nipple in his mouth. With his tongue he rotated the jeweled ring, sending a burst of heat through her. Instinctively she reached out to cradle his satin-smooth scrotum, rolling his testicles gently between her fingers.

"I think you a good man, my lord. Much more merciful than my late sire. I would offer you my thanks for treating my brother more gently than he deserved." Her breasts tingled as he suckled first one and then the other, the slight tug of the rings enhancing the delicious sensation. "I would taste you," she murmured, her tongue tingling at the prospect of laving his clean-shaven manhood.

"Love me because you desire it, not as thanks."

"I do love you." The man called Barbarian because of his legendary fierceness in battle had taken Brianna's heart, as surely as he made her body go up in flames.

"Then say my name. I yearn to hear it from your tender lips." Straddling her, yet holding himself just outside her reach, he seared her with a heated gaze.

"Giles."

He moved closer, close enough for her to breathe in the musky, clean scent of his arousal yet not near enough that she could feast upon his flesh. "You please me, Brianna," he murmured, "more than I ever dreamed a woman could. I know not of courtly love, yet you have found a place within my heart." Suddenly he rolled onto his back, legs and arms spread wide. "Do as you will with me, sweeting."

He tasted of salt and sweat and sex. His skin had the feel of velvet to her questing tongue, and his heart beat ever faster as Brianna caressed him with her hands and mouth. Pointing her tongue she lapped up the bead of moisture from the very tip of his engorged cock.

She wanted his mouth on her. She wanted his cock inside her, stretching and filling her. She wanted to feel his seed bathe her womb, that she might give him the heir all men wanted more than any other gift. Rising, she straddled him, positioning herself before taking him slowly within her body.

His callused hands chafed at her tender breasts as he rose to her, driving deeper with each upward stroke of his powerful body. The tension rose, breaking into a glorious climax. When her senses returned she felt him still hot and hard within her body.

"Giles?"

"Hold on." Deftly he rolled over, taking most of his weight on his massive shoulders. Slowly, he began to move above her, stoking her flame again until this time her climax came on the heels of his own.

"I pray to bear you a son come next spring," Brianna murmured as she lay quietly in the glow of a late afternoon sun that sent shadows over their entwined bodies.

Giles pulled her a little closer and rubbed one hand lazily down her back. "I would be as happy with a daughter, sweeting. Although the thought of losing you to childbirth is more than I can bear," he added after hesitating for a minute, and Brianna thought those words sounded as if they were being torn from his very soul.

He had said not the words she longed to hear, but Brianna sensed she had gained his love. "God willing, I shall bear you healthy babes for years to come, my love. I would not leave you, not for all the rewards of heaven."

Epilogue

Giles proved his strength in the tourney the following month, winning the fealty of those who remained of the old earl's followers. His talisman, he said, was the braid of Brianna's pale golden hair that she hung from the tip of his lance ere the ceremonies began. That night she told him she was carrying his child.

On the first day of the following spring, Giles paced with his brother and the eunuch Arnaud while Brianna brought forth their firstborn son. Mother and babe thrived, as their doting father would tell all who chanced to visit Harrow Castle. Peace abounded in the land in the coming years as the earl and his countess loved and made love. Giles deVere, the Barbarian of minstrels' lore, confined his warfare to the tiltyard, and the wielding of his legendary sword to the chamber he shared withBrianna, his wife and his only love.

About the author:

Ann Jacobs, multi-published in contemporary single-title romance under another pseudonym, sought out Red Sage Publishing when a sensual medieval warlord home from Crusade kept urging her to write his story. She hopes "The Barbarian" and the hot-blooded daughter of the rogue Earl he brought to justice will titillate readers' senses as they evolve from enmity in their forced marriage, through mutual hot and steamy lust, to an earthy, adventurous love.

Dear Reader,

We appreciate you taking the time out of your full and busy schedule to answer this questionnaire.

1. Rate the stories in *Secrets Volume 3* (1-10 Scale: 1=Worst, 10=Best)

Rating	The Spy Who Loved Me	Love Undercover	Blood and Kisses	The Barbarian
Story Overall	_____	_____	_____	_____
Sexual Intensity	_____	_____	_____	_____
Sensuality	_____	_____	_____	_____
Characters	_____	_____	_____	_____
Setting	_____	_____	_____	_____
Writing Skill	_____	_____	_____	_____

2. What did you like *best* about *Secrets*? What did you like *least* about *Secrets*?

3. Would you buy other volumes?

4. In future *Secrets*, tell us how you would like your *heroine* and your *hero* to be. One or two words each are okay.

5. What is your idea of the *perfect sensual romantic story*? Use more paper if you wish to add more than this space allows.

Thank you for taking the time to answer this questionnaire. We want to bring you the sensual stories you desire.

Sincerely,
Alexandria Kendall
Publisher

Mail to: Red Sage Publishing, Inc.
P.O. Box 4844
Seminole, FL 33775

If you enjoyed *Secrets Volume 3* but haven't read other volumes, you should see what you're missing!

Secrets Volume 1:

In *A Lady's Quest*, author Bonnie Hamre brings you a London historical where Lady Antonia Blair-Sutworth searches for a lover in a most shocking and pleasing way.

Alice Gaines' *The Spinner's Dream* weaves a seductive fantasy that will leave every woman wishing for her own private love slave, desperate and running for his life.

Ivy Landon takes you for a wild ride. *The Proposal* will taunt you, tease you, even shock you. A contemporary erotica for the adventurous woman's ultimate fantasy.

With *The Gift* by Jeanie LeGendre, you're immersed in the historic tale of exotic seduction and bondage. Read about a concubine's delicious surrender to her Sultan.

Secrets Volume 2:

Surrogate Lover, by Doreen DeSalvo, is a contemporary tale of lust and love in the 90's. A surrogate sex therapist thought he had all the answers until he met Sarah.

Bonnie Hamre's regency tale *Snowbound* delights as the Earl of Howden is teased and tortured by his own desires—finally a woman who equals his overpowering sensuality.

In *Roarke's Prisoner*, by Angela Knight, starship captain Elise remembers the eager animal submission she'd known before at her captor's hands and refuses to be his toy again.

Susan Paul's *Savage Garden* tells the story of Raine's capture by a mysterious revolutionary in Mexico. She quickly finds lush erotic nights in her captor's arms.

Secrets Volume 4:

An Act of Love is Jeanie Cesarini's sequel. Shelby's terrified of sex. Film star Jason Gage must coach her in the ways of love. He wants her to feel true passion in his arms.

The Love Slave, by Emma Holly, is a woman's ultimate fantasy. For one year, Princess Lily will be attended to by three delicious men. She delights in playing with the first two, but it's the reluctant Grae that stirs her desires.

Lady Crystal is in turmoil in *Enslaved*, by Desirée Lindsey. Lord Nicholas' dark passions and irresistible charm have brought her long-hidden desires to the surface.

Betsy Morgan and Susan Paul bring you Kaki York's story in *The Bodyguard*. Watching the wild, erotic romps of her client's sexual conquests on the security cameras is getting to her—and her partner, the ruggedly handsome James Kulick.

Secrets Volume 5:

B.J. McCall is back with *Alias Smith and Jones*. Meredith Collins is stranded overnight at the airport. A handsome stranger named Smith offers her sanctuary for the evening—how can she resist those mesmerizing green-flecked eyes?

Strictly Business, by Shannon Hollis, tells of Elizabeth Forrester's desire to climb the corporate ladder on her merits, not her looks. But the gorgeous Garrett Hill has come along and stirred her wildest fantasies.

Chevon Gael's *Insatiable* is the tale of a man's obsession. After corporate exec Ashlyn Fraser's glamour shot session, photographer Marcus Remington can't get her off his mind. Forget the beautiful models, he must have her —but where did she go?

Sandy Fraser's *Beneath Two Moons* is a futuristic wild ride. Conor is rough and tough like frontiermen of old, and he's on the prowl for a new conquest. Dr. Eva Kelsey got away once before, but this time he'll make sure she begs for more.

Secrets Volume 6:

Sandy Fraser is back with *Flint's Fuse*. Dana Madison's father has her "kidnapped" for her own safety. Flint, the tall, dark and dangerousmercenary, is hired for the job. But just which one is the prisoner—Dana will try *anything* to get away.

In *Love's Prisoner*, by MaryJanice Davidson, Jeannie Lawrence experienced unwilling rapture at Michael Windham's hands. She never expected the devilishly handsome man to show back up in her life—or turn out to be a werewolf!

Alice Gaines' *The Education of Miss Felicity Wells* finds a pupil needing to learn how to satisfy her soon-to-be husband. Dr. Marcus Slade, an experienced lover, agrees to take her on as a student, but can he stop short of taking her completely?

Angela Knight tells another spicy tale. On the trail of a story, reporter Dana Ivory stumbles onto a secret—a sexy, secret agent who happens to be a vampire.She wants her story but Gabriel Archer believes she's *A Candidate for the Kiss*.

Secrets Volume 7:

In *Amelia's Innocence* by Julia Welles, Amelia didn't know her father bet her in a card game with Captain Quentin Hawke, so honor demands a compromise—three days of erotic foreplay, leaving her virginity and future intact.

Jade Lawless brings *The Woman of His Dreams* to life. Artist Gray Avonaco moved in next door to Joanna Morgan and now is plagued by provocative dreams. Is it unrequited lust or Gray's chance to be with the woman he loves?

Surrender by Kathryn Anne Dubois tells of Lady Johanna. She wants no part of the binding strictures of marriage to the powerful Duke. But she doesn't realize he wants sensual adventure, and sexual satisfaction.

Angela Knight's *Kissing the Hunter* finds Navy Seal Logan McLean hunting the vampires who murdered his wife. Virginia Hart is a sexy vampire searching for her lost soul-mate only to find him in a man determined to kill her.

Secrets Volume 8:

In Jeanie Cesarini's latest tale, we meet Kathryn Roman as she inherits a legal brothel. She refuses to trade her Manhattan high-powered career for a life in the wild west. But the town of Love, Nevada has recruited Trey Holliday, one very dominant cowboy, with *Taming Kate*.

In *Jared's Wolf* by MaryJanice Davidson, Jared Rocke will do anything to avenge his sister's death, but he wasn't expecting to fall for Moira Wolfbauer, the she-wolf sworn to protect her werewolf pack. The two enemies must stop a killer while learning that love defies all boundaries.

My Champion, My Love, by Alice Gaines, tells the tale of Celeste Broder, a woman committed for a sexy appetite that is tolerated in men, but not women. Mayor Robert Albright may be her salvation—*if* she can convince him her freedom will mean a chance to indulge their appetites together.

Liz Maverick takes you to a post-apocalyptic world in **Kiss or Kill**. Camille Kazinsky's military career rides on her decision—whether the robo called Meat should live or die. Meat's future depends on proving he's human enough to live, *man* enough, to make her feel like a woman.

Secrets Volume 9:

Kimberly Dean brings you *Wanted*. FBI Special Agent Jeff Reno wants Danielle Carver. There's her body, brains—and that charge of treason on her head. Unable to clear her name, Dani goes on the run, but the sexy Fed is hot on her trail. What will he do once he catches her? And why is the idea so tempting?

In *Wild for You.* by Kathryn Anne Dubois, college intern Georgie gets lost and captured by a wildman of the Congo. She soon discovers this terrifying specimen of male virility has never seen a woman. The research possibilities are endless! Until he shows her he has research ideas of his own.

Bonnie Hamre is back with *Flights of Fantasy*. Chloe has taught others to see the realities of life but she's never shared the intimate world of her sensual yearnings. Given the chance, will she be woman enough to fulfill her most secret erotic fantasy? Join her as she ventures into her Flights of Fantasy.

Lisa Marie Rice's story, *Secluded*, is a wild one. Nicholas Lee had to claw his way to the top. His wealth and power come with a price—his enemies will kill anyone he loves. When Isabelle Summerby steals his heart, Nicholas secludes her in his underground palace to live a lifetime of desire in only a few days.

Men you've been dreaming about!

Secrets

Satisfy your desire for more.

eel the wild adventure, fierce passion and the power of love in every *Secrets* Collection story. Red Sage Publishing's romance authors create richly crafted, sexy, sensual, novella-length stories. Each one is just the right length for reading after a long and hectic day.

Each volume in the **Secrets** Collection has four diverse, ultra-sexy, romantic novellas brimming with adventure, passion and love. More adventurous tales for the adventurous reader. The **Secrets** Collection are a glorious mix of romance genre; numerous historical settings, contemporary, paranormal, science fiction and suspense. We are always looking for new adventures.

Reader response to the **Secrets** volumes has been great! Here's just a small sample:

"I loved the variety of settings. Four completely wonderful time periods, give you four completely wonderful reads."

"Each story was a page-turning tale I hated to put down."

*"I love **Secrets**! When is the next volume coming out? This one was Hot! Loved the heroes!"*

Secrets have won raves and awards. We could go on, but why don't you find out for yourself—order your set of **Secrets** today! See the back for details.

Secrets, Volume 1

Listen to what reviewers say:

"These stories take you beyond romance into
the realm of erotica. I found *Secrets* absolutely delicious."

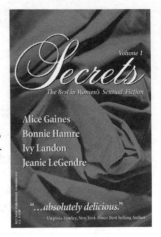

> —Virginia Henley,
> *New York Times* Best Selling Author

"*Secrets* is a collection of novellas for the
daring, adventurous woman who's not afraid
to give her fantasies free reign."
  —Kathe Robin, *Romantic Times* Magazine

"...In fact, the men featured in all the stories are terrific, they all want
to please and pleasure their women. If you like erotic romance you will
love *Secrets*."

> —*Romantic Readers* Review

In *Secrets, Volume 1* you'll find:

A Lady's Quest by Bonnie Hamre

Widowed Lady Antonia Blair-Sutworth searches for a lover to save her
from the handsome Duke of Sutherland. The "auditions" may be shocking but utterly tantalizing.

The Spinner's Dream by Alice Gaines

A seductive fantasy that leaves every woman wishing for her own private
love slave, desperate and running for his life.

The Proposal by Ivy Landon

This tale is a walk on the wild side of love. *The Proposal* will taunt you,
tease you, and shock you. A contemporary erotica for the adventurous
woman.

The Gift by Jeanie LeGendre

Immerse yourself in this historic tale of exotic seduction, bondage and a
concubine's surrender to the Sultan's desire. Can Alessandra live the life
and give the gift the Sultan demands of her?

Secrets, Volume 2

Listen to what reviewers say:

"*Secrets* offers four novellas of sensual delight; each beautifully written with intense feeling and dedication to character development. For those seeking stories with heightened intimacy, look no further."

—Kathee Card, *Romancing the Web*

"Such a welcome diversity in styles and genres. Rich characterization in sensual tales. An exciting read that's sure to titillate the senses."

—Cheryl Ann Porter

"*Secrets 2* left me breathless. Sensual satisfaction guaranteed…times four!"

—Virginia Henley, *New York Times* Best Selling Author

In *Secrets, Volume 2* you'll find:

Surrogate Lover by Doreen DeSalvo

Adrian Ross is a surrogate sex therapist who has all the answers and control. He thought he'd seen and done it all, but he'd never met Sarah.

Snowbound by Bonnie Hamre

A delicious, sensuous regency tale. The marriage-shy Earl of Howden is teased and tortured by his own desires and finds there is a woman who can equal his overpowering sensuality.

Roarke's Prisoner by Angela Knight

Elise, a starship captain, remembers the eager animal submission she'd known before at her captor's hands and refuses to become his toy again. However, she has no idea of the delights he's planned for her this time.

Savage Garden by Susan Paul

Raine's been captured by a mysterious and dangerous revolutionary leader in Mexico. At first her only concern is survival, but she quickly finds lush erotic nights in her captor's arms.

Winner of the Fallot Literary Award for Fiction!

Secrets, Volume 3

Listen to what reviewers say:

"*Secrets, Volume 3*, leaves the reader breathless. A delicious confection of sensuous treats awaits the reader on each turn of the page!"

—Kathee Card, *Romancing the Web*

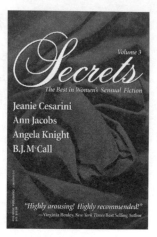

"From the FBI to Police Dectective to Vampires to a Medieval Warlord home from the Crusade—*Secrets 3* is simply the best!"

—Susan Paul, award winning author

"An unabashed celebration of sex. Highly arousing! Highly recommended!"

—Virginia Henley, *New York Times* Best Selling Author

In *Secrets, Volume 3* you'll find:

The Spy Who Loved Me by Jeanie Cesarini

Undercover FBI agent Paige Ellison's sexual appetites rise to new levels when she works with leading man Christopher Sharp, the cunning agent who uses all his training to capture her body and heart.

The Barbarian by Ann Jacobs

Lady Brianna vows not to surrender to the barbaric Giles, Earl of Harrow. He must use sexual arts learned in the infidels' harem to conquer his bride. A word of caution—this is not for the faint of heart.

Blood and Kisses by Angela Knight

A vampire assassin is after Beryl St. Cloud. Her only hope lies with Decker, another vampire and ex-mercenary. Broke, she offers herself as payment for his services. Will his seductive powers take her very soul?

Love Undercover by B.J. McCall

Amanda Forbes is the bait in a strip joint sting operation. While she performs, fellow detective "Cowboy" Cooper gets to watch. Though he excites her, she must fight the temptation to surrender to the passion.

**Winner of the 1997 Under the Covers
Readers Favorite Award**

Secrets, Volume 4

Listen to what reviewers say:

"Provocative…seductive…a must read!"

—*Romantic Times* Magazine

"These are the kind of stories that romance readers that 'want a little more' have been looking for all their lives…."

—*Affaire de Coeur* Magazine

"*Secrets, Volume 4*, has something to satisfy every erotic fantasy… simply sexational!"

—Virginia Henley, *New York Times* Best Selling Author

Volume 4

Secrets

The Best in Women's Sensual Fiction

Jeanie Cesarini
Emma Holly
Desirée Lindsey
Betsy Morgan & Susan Paul

Provocative…seductive…a must read!
—*Romantic Times* Magazine ★★★★

In *Secrets, Volume 4* you'll find:

An Act of Love by Jeanie Cesarini

Shelby Moran's past left her terrified of sex. International film star Jason Gage must gently coach the young starlet in the ways of love. He wants more than an act—he wants Shelby to feel true passion in his arms.

Enslaved by Desirée Lindsey

Lord Nicholas Summer's air of danger, dark passions, and irresistible charm have brought Lady Crystal's long-hidden desires to the surface. Will he be able to give her the one thing she desires before it's too late?

The Bodyguard by Betsy Morgan and Susan Paul

Kaki York is a bodyguard, but watching the wild, erotic romps of her client's sexual conquests on the security cameras is getting to her—and her partner, the ruggedly handsome James Kulick. Can she resist his insistent desire to have her?

The Love Slave by Emma Holly

A woman's ultimate fantasy. For one year, Princess Lily will be attended to by three delicious men of her choice. While she delights in playing with the first two, it's the reluctant Grae, with his powerful chest, black eyes and hair, that stirs her desires.

Secrets, Volume 5

Listen to what reviewers say:

"Hot, hot, hot! Not for the faint-hearted!"

—*Romantic Times* Magazine

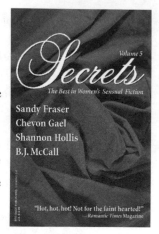

"As you make your way through the stories, you will find yourself becoming hotter and hotter. *Secrets* just keeps getting better and better."

—*Affaire de Coeur* Magazine

"*Secrets 5* is a collage of lucious sensuality. Any woman who reads *Secrets* is in for an awakening!"

—Virginia Henley, *New York Times* Best Selling Author

In *Secrets, Volume 5* you'll find:

Beneath Two Moons by Sandy Fraser

Ready for a very wild romp? Step into the future and find Conor, rough and masculine like frontiermen of old, on the prowl for a new conquest. In his sights, Dr. Eva Kelsey. She got away once before, but this time Conor makes sure she begs for more.

Insatiable by Chevon Gael

Marcus Remington photographs beautiful models for a living, but it's Ashlyn Fraser, a young corporate exec having some glamour shots done, who has stolen his heart. It's up to Marcus to help her discover her inner sexual self.

Strictly Business by Shannon Hollis

Elizabeth Forrester knows it's tough enough for a woman to make it to the top in the corporate world. Garrett Hill, the most beautiful man in Silicon Valley, has to come along to stir up her wildest fantasies. Dare she give in to both their desires?

Alias Smith and Jones by B.J. McCall

Meredith Collins finds herself stranded overnight at the airport. A handsome stranger by the name of Smith offers her sanctuaty for the evening and she finds those mesmerizing, green-flecked eyes hard to resist. Are they to be just two ships passing in the night?

Secrets, Volume 6

Listen to what reviewers say:

"Red Sage was the first and remains the leader of Women's Erotic Romance Fiction Collections!"

—*Romantic Times* Magazine

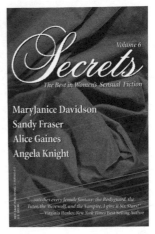

"*Secrets, Volume 6*, is the best of *Secrets* yet. ...four of the most erotic stories in one volume than this reader has yet to see anywhere else. ...These stories are full of erotica at its best and you'll definitely want to keep it handy for lots of re-reading!"

—*Affaire de Coeur* Magazine

"*Secrets 6* satisfies every female fantasy: the Bodyguard, the Tutor, the Werewolf, and the Vampire. I give it Six Stars!"

—Virginia Henley, *New York Times* Best Selling Author

In *Secrets, Volume 6* you'll find:

Flint's Fuse by Sandy Fraser

Dana Madison's father has her "kidnapped" for her own safety. Flint, the tall, dark and dangerous mercenary, is hired for the job. But just which one is the prisoner—Dana will try *anything* to get away.

Love's Prisoner by MaryJanice Davidson

Trapped in an elevator, Jeannie Lawrence experienced unwilling rapture at Michael Windham's hands. She never expected the devilishly handsome man to show back up in her life—or turn out to be a werewolf!

The Education of Miss Felicity Wells by Alice Gaines

Felicity Wells wants to be sure she'll satisfy her soon-to-be husband but she needs a teacher. Dr. Marcus Slade, an experienced lover, agrees to take her on as a student, but can he stop short of taking her completely?

A Candidate for the Kiss by Angela Knight

Working on a story, reporter Dana Ivory stumbles onto a more amazing one—a sexy, secret agent who happens to be a vampire.She wants her story but Gabriel Archer wants more from her than just sex and blood.

Secrets, Volume 7

Listen to what reviewers say:

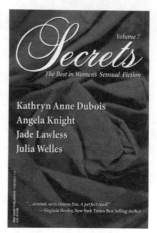

"Get out your asbestos gloves — *Secrets Volume 7* is...extremely hot, true erotic romance...passionate and titillating. There's nothing quite like baring your secrets!"

—*Romantic Times* Magazine

"...sensual, sexy, steamy fun. A perfect read!"

—Virginia Henley,
New York Times Best Selling Author

"Intensely provocative and disarmingly romantic, *Secrets, Volume 7*, is a romance reader's paradise that will take you beyond your wildest dreams!"

—Ballston Book House Review

In *Secrets, Volume 7* you'll find:

Amelia's Innocence by Julia Welles

Amelia didn't know her father bet her in a card game with Captain Quentin Hawke, so honor demands a compromise—three days of erotic foreplay, leaving her virginity and future intact.

The Woman of His Dreams by Jade Lawless

From the day artist Gray Avonaco moves in next door, Joanna Morgan is plagued by provocative dreams. But what she believes is unrequited lust, Gray sees as another chance to be with the woman he loves. He must persuade her that even death can't stop true love.

Surrender by Kathryn Anne Dubois

Free-spirited Lady Johanna wants no part of the binding strictures society imposes with her marriage to the powerful Duke. She doesn't know the dark Duke wants sensual adventure, and sexual satisfaction.

Kissing the Hunter by Angela Knight

Navy Seal Logan McLean hunts the vampires who murdered his wife. Virginia Hart is a sexy vampire searching for her lost soul-mate only to find him in a man determined to kill her. She must convince him all vampires aren't created equally.

**Winner of the Venus Book Club
Best Book of the Year**

Secrets, Volume 8

Listen to what reviewers say:

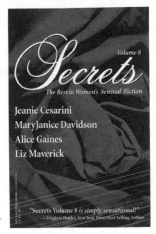

"*Secrets, Volume 8*, is an amazing compilation of sexy stories covering a wide range of subjects, all designed to titillate the senses. ...you'll find something for everybody in this latest version of *Secrets*."

—*Affaire de Coeur* Magazine

"*Secrets Volume 8*, is simply sensational!"
—Virginia Henley, *New York Times* Best Selling Author

"These delectable stories will have you turning the pages long into the night. Passionate, provocative and perfect for setting the mood...."
—*Escape to Romance* Reviews

In *Secrets, Volume 8* you'll find:

Taming Kate by Jeanie Cesarini
Kathryn Roman inherits a legal brothel. Little does this city girl know the town of Love, Nevada wants her to be their new madam so they've charged Trey Holliday, one very dominant cowboy, with taming her.

Jared's Wolf by MaryJanice Davidson
Jared Rocke will do anything to avenge his sister's death, but ends up attracted to Moira Wolfbauer, the she-wolf sworn to protect her pack. Joining forces to stop a killer, they learn love defies all boundaries.

My Champion, My Lover by Alice Gaines
Celeste Broder is a woman committed for having a sexy appetite. Mayor Robert Albright may be her champion—if she can convince him her freedom will mean a chance to indulge their appetites together.

Kiss or Kill by Liz Maverick
In this post-apocalyptic world, Camille Kazinsky's military career rides on her ability to make a choice—whether the robo called Meat should live or die. Meat's future depends on proving he's human enough to live, man enough...to makes her feel like a woman.

Winner of the Venus Book Club
Best Book of the Year

Secrets, Volume 9

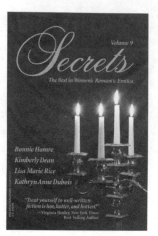

Listen to what reviewers say:

"Everyone should expect only the most erotic stories in a *Secrets* book. ...if you like your stories full of hot sexual scenes, then this is for you!"

> —Donna Doyle Romance Reviews

"SECRETS 9...is sinfully delicious, highly arousing, and hotter than hot as the pages practically burn up as you turn them."

> —Suzanne Coleburn, Reader To Reader Reviews/Belles & Beaux of Romance

"Treat yourself to well-written fictionthat's hot, hotter, and hottest!"

> —Virginia Henley, *New York Times* Best Selling Author

In *Secrets, Volume 9* you'll find:

Wild For You by Kathryn Anne Dubois

When college intern, Georgie, gets captured by a Congo wildman, she discovers this specimen of male virility has never seen a woman. The research possibilities are endless!

Wanted by Kimberly Dean

FBI Special Agent Jeff Reno wants Danielle Carver. There's her body, brains—and that charge of treason on her head. Dani goes on the run, but the sexy Fed is hot on her trail.

Secluded by Lisa Marie Rice

Nicholas Lee's wealth and power came with a price—his enemies will kill anyone he loves. When Isabelle steals his heart, Nicholas secludes her in his palace for a lifetime of desire in only a few days.

Flights of Fantasy by Bonnie Hamre

Chloe taught others to see the realities of life but she's never shared the intimate world of her sensual yearnings. Given the chance, will she be woman enough to fulfill her most secret erotic fantasy?

Coming July 2004...

Secrets, Volume 10

Private Eyes by Dominique Sinclair

When a mystery man captivates P.I. Nicolla Black during a stakeout, she discovers her no-seduction rule bending under the pressure of long denied passion. She agrees to the seduction, but he demands her total surrender.

The Ruination of Lady Jane by Bonnie Hamre

To avoid her upcoming marriage, Lady Jane Ponsonby-Maitland flees into the arms of Havyn Attercliffe. She begs him to ruin her rather than turn her over to her odious fiancé.

Code Name: Kiss by Jeanie Cesarini

Agent Lily Justiss is on a mission to defend her country against terrorists that requires giving up her virginity as a sex slave. As her master takes her body, desire for her commanding officer Seth Blackthorn fuels her mind.

The Sacrifice by Kathryn Anne Dubois

Lady Anastasia Bedovier is days from taking her vows as a Nun. Before she denies her sensuality forever, she wants to experience pleasure. Count Maxwell, known for his mastery of dark, sexual secrets, is the perfect man to initiate her into erotic delight.

The Forever Kiss by Angela Knight

For years, Valerie Chase has been haunted by dreams of a Texas Ranger she knows only as "Cowboy." As a child, he rescued her from the nightmare vampires who murdered her parents. As an adult, she still dreams of him—but now he's her seductive lover in nights of erotic pleasure.

Yet "Cowboy" is more than a dream—he's the real Cade McKinnon—and a vampire! For years, he's protected Valerie from Edward Ridgemont, the sadistic vampire who turned him. Now, Ridgmont wants Valerie for his own and Cade is the only one who can protect her.

When Val finds herself abducted by her handsome dream man, she's appalled to discover he's one of the vampires she fears. Now, caught in a web of fear and passion, she and Cade must learn to trust each other, even as an immortal monster stalks their every move.

Their only hope of survival is...*The Forever Kiss*.

It's not just reviewers raving about *Secrets*. See what readers have to say:

"When are you coming out with a new Volume? I want a new one next month!" via email from a reader.

"I loved the hot, wet sex without vulgar words being used to make it exciting." after *Volume 1*

"I loved the blend of sensuality and sexual intensity—HOT!" after *Volume 2*

"The best thing about *Secrets* is they're hot and brief! The least thing is you do not have enough of them!" after *Volume 3*

"I have been extreamly satisfied with *Secrets*, keep up the good writing." after *Volume 4*

"I love the sensuality and sex that is not normally written about or explored in a really romantic context" after *Volume 4*

"Loved it all!!!" after *Volume 5*

"I love the tastful, hot way that *Secrets* pushes the edge. The genre mix is cool, too." after *Volume 5*

"Stories have plot and characters to support the erotica. They would be good strong stories without the heat." after *Volume 5*

"*Secrets* really knows how to push the envelop better than anyone else." after *Volume 6*

"*Secrets*, there is nothing not to like. This is the top banana, so to speak." after *Volume 6*

"'Would you buy *Volume 7*?' YES!!! Inform me ASAP and I am so there!!" after *Volume 6*

"Can I please, please, please pre-order *Volume 7*? I want to be the first to get it of my friends. They don't have email so they can't write you! I can!" after *Volume 6*

Finally, the men you've been dreaming about!

Give the Gift of Spicy Romantic Fiction

Don't want to wait? You can place a retail price ($12.99) order for any of the *Secrets* volumes from the following:

① **Waldenbooks Stores**

② **Amazon.com** or **BarnesandNoble.com**

③ **Book Clearinghouse (800-431-1579)**

④ **Romantic Times Magazine**
Books by Mail (718-237-1097)

⑤ Special order at other bookstores.
Bookstores: Please contact Baker & Taylor Distributors or Red Sage Publishing for bookstore sales.

Order by title or ISBN #:

Vol. 1: 0-9648942-0-3	**Vol. 6:** 0-9648942-6-2
Vol. 2: 0-9648942-1-1	**Vol. 7:** 0-9648942-7-0
Vol. 3: 0-9648942-2-X	**Vol. 8:** 0-9648942-8-9
Vol. 4: 0-9648942-4-6	**Vol. 9:** 0-9648942-9-7
Vol. 5: 0-9648942-5-4	**Vol. 10:** 0-9754516-0-X

The Forever Kiss: 0-9648942-3-8

Red Sage Publishing Mail Order Form:

(Orders shipped in two to three days of receipt.)

	Quantity	Mail Order Price	Total
Secrets **Volume 1** *(Retail $12.99)*	_____	$ 9.99	_____
Secrets **Volume 2** *(Retail $12.99)*	_____	$ 9.99	_____
Secrets **Volume 3** *(Retail $12.99)*	_____	$ 9.99	_____
Secrets **Volume 4** *(Retail $12.99)*	_____	$ 9.99	_____
Secrets **Volume 5** *(Retail $12.99)*	_____	$ 9.99	_____
Secrets **Volume 6** *(Retail $12.99)*	_____	$ 9.99	_____
Secrets **Volume 7** *(Retail $12.99)*	_____	$ 9.99	_____
Secrets **Volume 8** *(Retail $12.99)*	_____	$ 9.99	_____
Secrets **Volume 9** *(Retail $12.99)*	_____	$ 9.99	_____
Secrets **Volume 10** *(Retail $12.99)* [July 2004]	_____	$ 9.99	_____
The Forever Kiss *(Retail $14.00)* [July 2004]	_____	$11.00	_____

Shipping & handling (in the U.S.)

US Priority Mail:	UPS insured:
1–2 books .... $ 5.50	1–4 books $16.00
3–5 books $11.50	5–9 books $25.00
6–9 books $14.50	10–11 books $29.00
10–11 books $19.00	

_____

SUBTOTAL _____

Florida 6% sales tax (if delivered in FL) _____

TOTAL AMOUNT ENCLOSED _____

Your personal information is kept private and not shared with anyone.

Name: (please print) _____

Address: (no P.O. Boxes) _____

City/State/Zip: _____

Phone or email: (only regarding order if necessary) _____

Please make check payable to **Red Sage Publishing**. Check must be drawn on a U.S. bank in U.S. dollars. Mail your check and order form to:

Red Sage Publishing, Inc.   Department S3   P.O. Box 4844   Seminole, FL 33775

Or use the order form on our website: **www.redsagepub.com**

Red Sage Publishing Mail Order Form:

(Orders shipped in two to three days of receipt.)

	Quantity	Mail Order Price	Total
Secrets Volume 1 *(Retail $12.99)*	_____	$ 9.99	_____
Secrets Volume 2 *(Retail $12.99)*	_____	$ 9.99	_____
Secrets Volume 3 *(Retail $12.99)*	_____	$ 9.99	_____
Secrets Volume 4 *(Retail $12.99)*	_____	$ 9.99	_____
Secrets Volume 5 *(Retail $12.99)*	_____	$ 9.99	_____
Secrets Volume 6 *(Retail $12.99)*	_____	$ 9.99	_____
Secrets Volume 7 *(Retail $12.99)*	_____	$ 9.99	_____
Secrets Volume 8 *(Retail $12.99)*	_____	$ 9.99	_____
Secrets Volume 9 *(Retail $12.99)*	_____	$ 9.99	_____
Secrets Volume 10 *(Retail $12.99)* [July 2004]	_____	$ 9.99	_____
The Forever Kiss *(Retail $14.00)* [July 2004]	_____	$11.00	_____

Shipping & handling (in the U.S.)

US Priority Mail:	UPS insured:
1–2 books .... $ 5.50	1–4 books $16.00
3–5 books $11.50	5–9 books $25.00
6–9 books $14.50	10–11 books $29.00
10–11 books $19.00	

_____

SUBTOTAL _____

Florida 6% sales tax (if delivered in FL) _____

TOTAL AMOUNT ENCLOSED _____

Your personal information is kept private and not shared with anyone.

Name: (please print) _____

Address: (no P.O. Boxes) _____

City/State/Zip: _____

Phone or email: (only regarding order if necessary) _____

Please make check payable to **Red Sage Publishing**. Check must be drawn on a U.S. bank in U.S. dollars. Mail your check and order form to:

Red Sage Publishing, Inc.   Department S3   P.O. Box 4844   Seminole, FL 33775

Or use the order form on our website: **www.redsagepub.com**